THE CARRADICE CHAIN

'Come, Jacintha,' she said firmly, 'we have a long way to travel and it will soon be dark.'

A crowd of neighbours with their children stood on the pavement outside our front door, their attention centred on the long black motor car at the kerb and the tall man in uniform who was shooing the children away from it. They had never seen such a car, and they stood in silence as I walked forward clutching my mother's hand. The tall man with the peaked cap picked me up bodily in his arms and placed me on the seat inside the car opposite the woman in black. The door closed, but through the window I could see my mother watching, white and shaken, as the car moved away. I wept long and bitterly during that drive in the dark, watched by my companion, who betrayed neither compassion nor dismay. I never saw my mother again.

Sara Hylton

THE CARRADICE CHAIN

THE SHERIDAN
BOOK COMPANY

This edition published in 1994 by
The Sheridan Book Company

First published by Hutchinson 1981
Random House, 20 Vauxhall Bridge Road, London SW1V 2SA
Arrow edition 1982

Printed and bound in Great Britain by
Cox & Wyman Ltd, Reading, Berkshire

ISBN 1–85501–645–1

1

My earliest memory is of a room rosy with firelight and the glow from a brass oil-lamp standing under the window across which wine-coloured plush curtains are drawn. In the centre of the room there is a large round table covered by a plush tablecloth edged with deep tasselled fringe. I am sitting on the rug in front of the fire playing with a floppy rag-doll.

A man sits at the table poring over a thick ledger and there is a pile of ledgers besides him on a chair. The light from the lamp burnishes his silver-fair hair and a woman comes to stand beside him, placing her arm around his shoulders, bending her head so that her cheek rests against the top of his head. She laughs, first at him then at me, before she comes to lift me in her arms. I can smell the perfume of her hair.

The man starts to cough – hard racking coughs which cause him great pain. Concerned, she puts me back on the rug and hurries to his side. There is such anxiety and love in her face that I remember it though other memories escape me, and I can still see the medicine being poured into a large spoon, blood-red and thick as honey. His coughing becomes less severe and much of the pain has gone from his face, but as the woman turns to go from the room the petals from a large bowl of roses in the centre of the table flutter onto the cloth. When their eyes meet, she smiles.

My next memory is of a smaller, more squalid, room. It is cold and the fire burns low in the grate. I recognize the plush cloth, although the table is square now and not nearly so big since the tassels seem almost to touch the floor. Beside the wall stands a treadle sewing machine and over the fireplace a single sickly gaslamp is lit. The curtains at the window are not drawn, however, and outside it looks grey and dismal.

There is a pile of sewing on the table and my mother – for I know now that this was my mother – sits at the table, an open workbasket besides her, stitching silently at some thick grey material. She appears to be listening for something. Every now and again, she lifts her head, inclining her ear to the street outside; then, reassured, she carries on with her work. Now and again she looks across the room at me and smiles gently. I cannot understand why there should be tears in her eyes.

After all these years, I can still remember the prickly sensation in my legs from the horse-hair chair I sat upon, seeing my short plump legs encased in black ribbed stockings and ending in laced leather boots – stumpy and unattractive sticking out straight in front of me. I am wearing outdoor clothes, a blue woollen coat and bonnet and there are warm woollen gloves on my hands.

I know now that it was my mother in the earlier remembered scene, but in the second picture she is different. The shine has gone from her thick golden hair, and the rounded serene face has been replaced by pallor and the pinched look of poverty. She pulls the woollen shawl closer around her thin shoulders.

There is a sound outside the room and she looks up sharply; then, jumping to her feet, she looks out of the window. Her face is flushed and quickly she smooths her hands over her hair before taking off her apron. Something of her nervousness conveys itself to me. I can still feel my fingers clutching at the doll in my lap for reassurance, and after all these years I remember that her name was Annabel.

It is the sound of wheels we can hear along the cobbled street and another sound also, like the growling of a large dog, causing me to look up startled, suddenly afraid. It seems like an eternity before the expected knock is heard. My mother starts back anxiously, then with a visible effort she squares her shoulders and moves forward to open the door. I do not know whom or what I expected to see, but I was unprepared for the tall aristocratic figure of an older woman dressed in a dark travelling cloak and wearing a hat adorned with osprey feathers which fascinated me.

She had a cold severe face and offered no greeting to my nervous little mother, although she accepted the chair which was pulled forward for her. Her fine dark eyes moved round the room without expression and she sat bolt upright, both hands resting on the ivory top of her umbrella. Me she ignored totally.

They spoke quietly together and I could not understand their words. Periodically my mother glanced towards me; I became sure they were speaking about me and I felt my heart tremble with fear. I wanted to jump down from my chair and run to my mother for reassurance, but there was something in the hawk-like profile of the older woman which stopped me. I felt that she would look at me sternly, quelling my need for affection with an attitude of contempt.

My mother mentioned refreshment but our visitor shook her head impatiently. From her large black handbag she took out a package which she placed upon the table. My mother rose from her chair and came over to me. She knelt on the floor beside my chair, holding me closely against her. She was crying and I could taste the hot salty tears as they rolled down her cheeks. The older woman had risen to her feet, standing proud and stern just within the doorway in an attitude show- ing quite plainly that she wished to leave without further delay.

'Come, Jacintha,' she said firmly, 'we have a long way to travel and it will soon be dark.'

A crowd of neighbours with their children stood on the pavement outside our front door, their attention centred on the long black motor car at the kerb and the tall man in uniform who was busy shooing the children away from it. When he saw us, he came forward and the crowd parted silently to allow our guest to walk to her car. The children gathered round again, staring open-mouthed. They had never seen such a car, not even when the mayor came to visit our school, and they stood in silence as I walked forward clutching my mother's hand. The tall man with the peaked cap knelt in front of us; and, although his smile was kind, he firmly disengaged my fingers before he picked me up bodily in his arms and placed me on the seat inside the car opposite the woman in black. The door closed, but through the window I could see my mother watching, white and shaken, as the car moved away. I wept long and bitterly during that drive in the dark, watched by my companion, who betrayed neither compassion or dismay. I never saw my mother again.

The woman made no effort to comfort me – indeed, now that we were embarked upon our journey, she appeared to have lost all interest in me. Once or twice the lights from the village street lamps illuminated the gloom of the interior but we passed swiftly out of their range, each twist and bend in the road seeming to put a thousand miles between me and the one person I loved. At first I was afraid of the noise of the engine but I sobbed until I slept. When I awoke, my limbs were stiff and cold and at first I was unable to comprehend fully where I was. The car had stopped and there was light streaming through the windows from outside.

The car door was opened by the man in uniform and he stood stiffly to attention waiting for the woman to climb down onto the roadway. I remember wondering at the time why he did not help her, but I learned since that she disliked help from anybody, preferring always to do things her way or not at all. He lifted me from the car, putting me down at the entrance through which the light streamed. It was very cold after the warm interior of the car and it had started to rain.

In spite of my private misery, my interest was aroused and I peered with wide eyes through the open door into the hall beyond. A tall thin man dressed entirely in black was speaking to the woman, but all I was interested in was the wide shallow staircase carpeted in rich ruby and the highly polished floor on which luxurious rugs were laid. There were weird figures set in alcoves round the hall. They were merely suits of ancient armour, but on that night when I was a child of seven the sight of those stiff steely shapes with their dreadful faces filled me with terror.

The staircase led up from the centre of the hall in a majestic curve. At its foot and halfway up to the first landing there were marble statues of Grecian goddesses holding torches lit by gaslight. Faced with such wonders I allowed the tears to dry on my cheeks and briefly forgot why they had been shed.

The woman who had brought me there appeared to have forgotten my existence. She was deep in conversation with the tall thin man in black as they moved down the hall towards one of the doors at the back. After a further few whispered words from them, the man walked back towards me and she called after him, 'Ask Miss Hanson to come to my sitting room and bring the child with her.'

'I believe Miss Hanson is ill, Mrs Carradice. A bad head-ache, I am told.'

'In that case, find Mrs Parry; no doubt she has been attending to a room somewhere in the house. Tell her to hurry; we have travelled a long way and I for one am very weary.'

The man hurried up the stairs and I suddenly remembered that I was in that house with that cold uncompromising woman and I wanted my mother. I screamed for my mother so loudly that the butler peered down at me in consternation from the realms above. The next moment he ran down the stairs accompanied by a stout panting woman dressed in black, over which she wore a large snowy apron. She knelt beside me with her arms round me saying, 'The poor lamb; she's as cold as ice and missing her mother. You'll soon be in your bed, my pretty, with a nice glass of warm milk.' Her attempt to comfort me was interrupted by the haughty voice of my travelling companion saying, 'Bring Jacintha in here, Mrs Parry. I cannot have her rousing the rest of the household by her display of temper.'

I was dragged protesting loudly across the hall, with chattering teeth and woebegone face down which great tears rolled. Since that night, I have seen that particular sitting room many time and I know every piece of furniture, every picture on the walls, every ornament – but I noticed nothing of it then. All my mind was focused on the haughty elegant woman, now shorn of her outdoor clothing, sitting in the depths of a blue velvet chair before the fire. She was eyeing me with the utmost distaste, and in turn I looked back at her with all the dislike I was capable of registering on my child's face.

She was the first human being I had ever wholly and completely hated. I hated her then and, God help me, I hate her still.

One day, perhaps, when I too am old and my memories for past evils and shabby little cruelties are forgotten, then and only then will I find it in my heart to forgive Elaina Carradice, my grandmother.

Between the butler and the housekeeper I was pushed and pulled up the wide shallow staircase towards the dark regions above, along corridors and across landings dimly lit by gaslight, but I was in no position to look around me as Mrs Parry's talon-like fingers bit into my shoulder through the material of my coat.

The bedroom I was finally pushed into was small, lofty and

chilly, as though it had not been used for many years. The butler made his grateful exit and I was made to wash in lukewarm water while I stood on the linoleum which surrounded the carpet. My feet were icy cold and I was glad of the long flannelette nightdress which was pulled over my shoulders. The sheets, too, were cold, but, just when I felt all the world had deserted me, a young maidservant entered the room with a glass of warm milk. She and Mrs Parry stood over me while I drank it, but I was totally unprepared for what happened next. I had been accustomed to a nightlight left burning in my room and the thick darkness when the gas jet was turned off terrified me. I curled myself into a ball underneath the bedclothes and cried myself to sleep.

I don't know how much later it was when I awoke to the sound of rain beating against the window and all the fury of a storm. The branches of the trees lashed across the panes like the hands of a skeleton trying to get in, and then I heard a low insistent whooshing noise ending in such an almighty roar I cowered under the bedclothes in fear of my life.

Daylight crept fitfully into my room, so grey and dreary that it failed to chase the shadows from the corners, and still I crouched beneath the bedclothes, peeping out for brief moments so that I might listen to the sounds of the morning.

At least I was still alive. The whooshing sounds had stopped and I told myself that maybe the monster was at his most ferocious during the night hours and the first feeble light of day saw him slinking back into his cave. The wind, too, had died but I could hear the rain monotonously pattering against the panes.

It was during one of my adventurous peeps that the door opened and Mrs Parry came bustling in, pulling back the bedclothes unceremoniously, commanding me to rise.

'Come, missy,' she said briskly, 'there's much to do today. You must wash and eat your breakfast; then I'm to take you to see Mrs Carradice in the sitting room. You heard what she said last night.'

Once more I stood on the cold linoleum while she sponged me down from head to foot, then I was dressed in the clothes I had worn yesterday apart from my coat and bonnet. My hair was brushed and tied at the back with a satin ribbon and

10

while all this was taking place I had the opportunity to look round the room.

It was a singularly bare little room. I hated linoleum and this linoleum was faded in places from too much scrubbing. The tapestry carpet square was also worn in places and of such a miserably dark hue I could not name the colour. The walls were papered in an indeterminate shade of fawn in a floral pattern and the bedcovers too were fawn – a colour I shall hate until my dying day. Apart from the single bed, there was a chest of drawers across one corner, a narrow wardrobe and a bedside table. As I looked round, I could feel my eyes pricking with unshed tears, remembering my tiny bedroom at home. It had been neither grand or expensively furnished, but it had been cheerful, with pretty pink wallpaper and chintzy curtains and bedcovers.

'Stay here, missy, until one of the girls comes with your breakfast,' the housekeeper admonished me, and I replied pertly, 'My name is Jacintha, not missy.'

'I'll have no cheek from you, young lady. If I choose to call you missy, missy you'll be.'

She left me alone and I moved over to the window. It was that sort of fine rain which appears like mist and all I could see of the garden beneath my room were huge boulders with gorse bushes and clumps of thrift. I half expected to see a cave and perhaps two red eyes glaring at me from within, but all I heard was a long, low, plaintive sound coming at regular intervals, and quickly I ran back to crouch upon my bed, believing that the sound came from the creature who was either in pain or tied up and anxious to be free.

Time passes slowly for a child, and it seemed to me that I waited an eternity before the door opened again – this time to admit a young country girl with a white cap on her tousled black curls and a dark overall covering her dress.

'Hello,' she said cheerfully. 'You're awake then. Mrs Parry said I was to see if you were ready for your breakfast.'

I didn't answer her. My childish thoughts were bitter about this household, I wanted neither their food nor their hospitality and I pressed my lips together tightly, refusing to speak.

'Cat got your tongue then?' she said. 'You'd better eat something; you don't get asked twice in this establishment. What's your name?'

'Jacintha,' I said in little more than a whisper.

'Well, that's a pretty name and no mistake. Can't rightly say I've heard it before. How about breakfast, Jacintha. What do you usually have, porridge?'

'No, I hate porridge. Jam and bread,' I volunteered hopefully, realizing for the first time that I was very hungry. Apart from the glass of hot milk the previous evening I had eaten nothing since my last meal with my mother and that had been in the morning.

'I suppose we can manage that,' the maid said. 'You'll get milk and biscuits in the schoolroom later this morning.'

'The schoolroom?'

'Yes. I don't suppose you'll be let off school. Can you read?'

'Of course. I can read and write. I can do sums too and draw pictures.'

'My aren't you clever, who taught you to do all that?'

'My mother.'

'Well, isn't that nice then? Now stay there while I bring your breakfast.'

Again I was left alone. Perhaps I should have asked her about the moans of the monster when she came back, but I was afraid to put my fears into words and have them confirmed. Although I believed there was a monster beneath my window, I did not want to know for sure that he was there, breathing fire and ready to devour little children.

She came back quickly with my breakfast, thin slices of bread and home-made damson jam. There was also a mug of strong dark tea which I screwed up my face at and refused to drink.

'Gracious, but it's cold in here,' she complained. 'I suppose the fire should be lit but I've had no instructions. Have you nothing warmer to wear than that little dress?'

I pointed to my belongings, still in their valise on the floor beside my bed. The maid rummaged through my things and finally found a pale-blue hand-knitted cardigan, holding it up to examine it before she helped me into it.

'This is a pretty little thing and will go nicely with that dress. I suppose your mother made it for you?'

I nodded wordlessly, my voice too choked with tears to reply with any degree of confidence. She put her arm round my shoulders and gave me a tight squeeze.

12

'Never mind, Jacintha, your mother would want you to wear it, I'm sure. Now finish your breakfast and then Mrs Parry'll come to take you to the mistress.'

'Is that the lady who brought me here?'

'That's right. She's Mrs Carradice but, since you're her granddaughter, I'm sure I don't know what she'll ask you to call her. You'll no doubt meet the other children in the school-room later on.'

'Who are they?'

'Well, there's Miss Isobel and Miss Lavinia and Master Teddy. There should be Miss Ruthie but she's in bed with a bad chill and won't be back at her lessons for a while.'

I was still staring open-mouthed at the door long after she had closed it.

I knew about grandmothers. I had a friend called Mary Saunders and she had had a grandmother who came to stay with them for long periods during the summer months. She came armed with fruit and sweets, home-made jams and cakes, as well as garments she had knitted in the winter time. She was a wonderful grandmother, who petted Mary and cared for her as much as my mother did me, but I could not visualize Mrs Carradice being a grandmother like this. All the same, I brightened up considerably, thinking that, if Mrs Carradice really was my grandmother, then surely we must visit my mother and she must visit us.

The door opened again, and, although I had been led to expect Mrs Parry, it was the young maid who entered.

'Mrs Parry's cut her finger with the bread knife and it's bleeding something awful. I'm to take you down to the sitting room. Are you ready?'

I nodded my head.

'You can call me Lucy if you like. I don't know if I'm supposed to call you Miss Jacintha or not. We'll know after this morning. You can leave the doll here,' she said, noticing for the first time that I clutched Annabel by the hand.

'I would rather take her if you don't mind,' I answered. 'She doesn't like this house and would be afraid to be left here alone.'

'Oh well, have it your own way, but hurry, I've got work to do.'

The sitting room looked much larger to me than it had the

13

evening before and I was bidden to sit in the chair across from Mrs Carradice, who was reading her morning mail. There was a bright coal fire blazing in the fireplace and the flames instantly seemed to dispel the cold misery of the morning.

She was attired in pale grey, some soft woollen material which fell in graceful folds to the floor. Around her long neck were several ropes of pearls and on her long thin fingers rings flashed. Many of the letters were laid aside disdainfully, and long experience has since taught me that this was the way she greeted all tradesmen's bills and other commonplace correspondence. Some of the letters she scanned with impatience, others with interest, but only one in particular appeared to give her pleasure.

She frowned as I wriggled impatiently in my chair, and looked up irritably when the door opened to admit a tall slim man who started at once to speak to her.

'I am waiting for the car to be brought round, mother, but I must speak to you before I leave.'

She held up her hand imperiously for silence and I held down my head as the man looked at me in some surprise. She made him wait several minutes until she had read her letter through, and in some impatience he went to stand at the window looking out across the gardens. I, too, would have liked to leave my chair to look out with him but I was too afraid.

At last she spoke to the man standing at the window.

'The letter is from Adrian, Robert. He has finished at Winchester and hopes to spend a few days here before he joins his parents in France.'

'I don't know about here, mother. He could do with spending some time with me at the mills if he's going to take charge there one day.'

'That is all in the future, Robert. He is going up to Oxford in the autumn to read history. The mills will be there waiting for him when he's ready.'

'I fail to see what a history degree can do for a man who is destined to become a woollen manufacturer. He should walk the factory floor – learn about cloth and how to manage people.'

'Your son is supposed to be doing that, but all I seem to hear about Roger are the scrapes he gets into, his mismanagement of people and his over-indulgence with the factory girls. I

14

have had to speak to him here about his familiarity with the maids. I have never had this trouble with Adrian.'

'Roger is high-spirited, mother; he will mature.'

'I very much doubt it. You wanted to speak to me, Robert?'

He looked at me quickly, and she said, 'You can speak in front of the child, Robert. This is Jacintha, Allan's daughter. I have brought her to live here so that she can be educated with my other grandchildren. I regard it as my duty.'

'I would have thought her mother more capable of educating the girl than the governess the children have at present.'

'Her mother needs to earn a living and would have little time to spend with her daughter. I have given her a small sum of money which will stand her in good stead until she finds employment, and I have undertaken to give Jacintha a home. I have no responsibility towards Catherine Lester.'

'She was Allan's wife.'

'Regrettably. They did not have my permission to marry and Allan had no money apart from what I gave him. She took him away from my home and from the mills, the only thing he knew anything about, and what was she trying to put in their place? He was a clerk in an accountant's office struggling to pass exams he had no aptitude for. If she had not taken him away from here he would in all probability be alive today.'

'He did have consumption, mother. You can't blame his wife for that.'

'I do blame her; I blame her for everything. I brought up my children to be mindful that they had a duty to the business your grandfather and your father worked themselves into early graves to establish. I educated them in such a fashion that they could look for their partners in life amongst the aristocracy and the gentry – men and women with similar backgrounds to their own – and I was not having some impecunious little governess coming into my house and ensnaring one of my sons. If she thought Allan had money she was sadly mistaken, but they defied me in the hope that I would relent and allow him to take his share. I grieved for my son. I grieved that he had not been born with more sense; but this child is my granddaughter – I have a duty to her.'

'Is she to be allowed to see her mother?'

'I think not. It would be bad for the child.'

There was silence in the room for what seemed an age and

15

the man stood looking down at the woman with the strangest smile upon his face.

'Why do you look at me like that, Robert? I was not aware that I had said anything amusing.'

'I was just wondering how you managed to salve your conscience about Allan.'

'What do you mean?'

'Well, to my mind, he did nothing worse than your eldest son. Roland left the family business to marry a French woman and has made his home there. He has shown absolutely no interest in the running of the mills but has not been ashamed to take his full share of the dividends. Allan, on the other hand, was your youngest son and because he fell in love with a governess and left the firm you cut him off without a penny.'

'Roland had the good sense to marry into the French aristocracy, a woman with a fortune as large as his own, and the circumstances were different. When Marguerite's father became too old and infirm to manage his business, he looked to his daughter's husband to assist him. I think that is only natural. He was well aware that I had three other sons and I am fully expecting Adrian to take his father's place on the board.'

'But you're not sure, mother; it could be that Adrian too will be more interested in growing grapes than weaving cloth.'

'Adrian knows where his duties lie – I have made it quite plain to him over the years, but you can be assured I will reaffirm it when he arrives in the morning. Now, what is it you wish to see me about? This child is missing her lessons.'

'A message from Celia, actually. She was wondering if you would be able to join us over the weekend. You know we are having the Edlingtons to stay with us for a few days.'

'I'm afraid it won't be possible, Robert. Adrian will be here and Maud Edlington and I have very little in common. I can't really think I want to spend a weekend in her company.'

'One has to make an effort, mother. Her husband is an important business associate, but then you know all that.'

'I do know it. But I, for one, am too old to be expected to make polite conversation with people who bore me. I am simply not interested in anything that woman has to tell me, but you may tell Celia I hope to see her before long.'

As you can imagine, this conversation had little significance for me then, but the general gist of it has been repeated so many times over the years it has become all too familiar. On that morning when I was seven, one thing only emerged with any clarity, and that was that I had found another person to dislike. Because we had not met, my dislike was unfair and unreasonable, but any person who could bring that doting look of pure affection into my grandmother's haughty face was in my estimation a person to be detested. From that moment, I also hated my cousin Adrian Carradice.

She read his letter through again with evident satisfaction, then she placed it on the table beside her chair and looked at me over the top of the rimless spectacles attached to a long gold chain round her neck. In her hooded and faded blue eyes there was scant affection.

'Did you sleep well, Jacintha?' she inquired.

'Yes, thank you, Mrs Carradice.'

'You know who I am?'

'Yes, Lucy told me.'

'Very well, then I shall expect you to address me as either grandmother or grandmama – I do not mind which.'

'When shall I go back to my mother?'

'You will not. Your mother has her living to earn and she has gone away. I want no tears, Jacintha. Here you will be with other children, your cousins, and you will have an excellent governess, Miss Hanson.'

'My mother was a governess. Why could she not have taught me?'

'I am well aware that your mother was a governess and have no doubt that she could have taught you most adequately. However, although I cannot expect you fully to understand now why I have brought you here, you will come to thank me in time. If you had stayed with your mother, you would have had no money, it is probable that you would have lived in squalor, and because you are my son's daughter I could not sit back and allow that to happen.'

We sat looking at each other for a long time and there was antipathy like a living thing between us. Then in exasperation she said, 'Have you no curiosity about your cousins, Jacintha? I find this sulky silence most unnatural in a child of your age.'

I did not answer and she went on irritably, 'Isobel is the eldest. She is the daughter of my son Robert, the man who was here a little while ago, and she has a brother, Roger, who is.

seventeen, but since he no longer lives here you need not trouble yourself about him. Ruthie is about your age and Lavinia and Teddy slightly older – they are twins, the children of my daughter and her husband. Ruthie is the daughter of my son William. Are there any questions you wish to ask me?'

'No,' I whispered miserably.

'No, grandmother, Jacintha. You will be respectful from the outset. Try to emulate Isobel, who is both pretty and gracious; she is an excellent example for you younger children to copy.'

I was dismissed as she rose to her feet and pulled the bellrope beside the fireplace. In only a few seconds Lucy was there, her large enveloping apron now replaced by a smaller white one edged with needlework and a parlour maid's cap on her curly hair.

The schoolroom proved to be a large chill room at the back of the house. The wind rattled the tall wide windows which overlooked the dark rolling hills and forests of evergreens. The children and their governess sat round a table in the centre of the room and there were bookcases all along the wall. In one corner was a sphere representing a map of the world, and there were four individual desks as well as the large centre table.

The little group looked up as we entered the room and Miss Hanson rose to greet me. She was a tall thin young woman with a pale complexion and prominent teeth, clad in dark clerical grey, relieved only by a silk scarf in primrose yellow which she wore round the neckline of her dress. When I came to know her better, I realized that she always wore a scarf because she felt the cold – not as a means of ornamentation. Poor Miss Hanson came from the south, where the climate was milder. How she must have hated the wild stormy days of winter, when Ravenspoint and the elements seemed to be one.

'This is Jacintha, Miss Hanson,' Lucy explained. 'The mistress said you would know what to do with her.'

Miss Hanson smiled and held out her hand. 'Come to the table, Jacintha, and meet your cousins.'

My eyes were immediately drawn to the older girl sitting at the head of the table. She was lovely – very dark, though surprisingly her complexion had the pink and white bloom of an English rose and her eyes shone light blue with a startling clarity. She eyed me curiously but without much welcome and, because I felt myself to be staring, I lowered my head in some confusion.

'This is your cousin Isobel,' Miss Hanson was saying, and then led me to the other two children. 'And these are your cousins Lavinia and Master Edward – he will want you to call him Teddy as we all do. He and Lavinia are twins.'

Teddy looked at me solemnly through steel-rimmed spectacles, a small nondescript fair-haired little boy of about my own height with an owlish expression. His sister, too, was fair with those light-blue eyes. On Isobel, with her darkness, they were unusually attractive; on Teddy and Lavinia they were ordinary and somehow cold. I judged them to be a little older than myself, possibly around nine years old.

I sat with them at the table and immediately a book was pushed into my hands by Isobel, who haughtily inquired, 'Can you read?'

I nodded, not trusting myself to speak, and she said, 'Why don't we ask her to read something, Miss Hanson, and then we shall know if she can read?'

'I have every intention of asking her to do so, Isobel, but I suggest we let her get accustomed to us and the schoolroom first.'

The book in my hands was *Kenilworth* by Sir Walter Scott and I stared at it in dismay. Until then I had read only children's books, mostly illustrated fairy stories – none like this impressive volume of close print without pictures to aid the story. Miss Hanson must have seen the dismay on my face for she reached over and took the book from my hands.

'Really, Isobel, you surely don't expect Jacintha to read this? You must remember she is only seven.'

Isobel giggled and tossed her head, then Lavinia joined in the merriment. I was given another book, an English exercise book with short sentences, none of which gave me any trouble, and I read clearly and distinctly as my mother had taught me to do.

Halfway through the morning Miss Hanson disappeared for her mid-morning lunch and we went next door into what was once the nursery. Milk and shortcake were served to us and I found myself the butt of the cousins' amusement while Isobel bombarded me with questions.

'You're the governess's daughter, aren't you?' she asked. 'Where is your room?'

'I'm not sure. Somewhere at the side of the house.'

'Is it a big room?'

'No, very small.'

'Mine is a big room at the front of the house. It is beautiful with blue velvet curtains at the windows. Lavinia and Ruthie are at the front of the house, too, but Teddy's room is at the back – it's very small, probably like yours. Are you going to be living here all the time now?'

'I don't know, I suppose so.'

'I don't suppose your mother will be allowed to come here.'

'Why not?' I snapped. 'Why won't she be allowed to come here?'

'She was a governess, wasn't she, and my grandmother never wanted Uncle Allan to marry her. My mother was gentry and so was Ruthie's mother; Lavinia's mother is my father's sister and she married a man my grandmother approved of, not like Uncle Allan.'

I sat there with my small fists clenched in my lap, hating every one of them, even Teddy who had not said a word but sat looking at us solemnly from behind his absurd spectacles. How did they dare talk about my mother as though she was nothing? I felt like rushing at them with my fists flying, but already I was learning it would not be wise to pit my puny strength against other members of this formidable family.

'Will you like living at Ravenspoint?' Isobel asked next.

'I don't know.'

'Have you seen the gardens?'

'No,' I answered her briefly, but something in my voice made her look at me sharply.

'Are you afraid to go out on your own into the gardens?'

'I'm afraid in case he might be there.' At last I had the courage to voice my fears, but I needed to know the measure of my adversary in spite of myself. Isobel would tell me, indeed she would glory in telling me.

'He?' she asked sharply. 'Who do you mean?'

'The monster. I heard him in the night.'

Three pairs of eyes were regarding me as though I had taken leave of my senses, but then Isobel, whose wits were sharper than her cousins', put a hand on Lavinia's arm warning her to keep silent.

'Oh yes, the monster. You heard him then. What was he doing?'

'He was creeping underneath my room, then he roared as he came nearer and I hid under the bedclothes in case he came through my window.'

'That is the Carradice dragon you heard,' she informed me proudly. 'He comes for all the Carradice children.'

'Why didn't he come for you then?'

'He did. He came for me a long time ago and I had to prove that I was stronger than he so that he would go away. You too will have to do so.'

'How can I do that? What will I have to do?'

'Next time it is stormy you will have to go outside the house into the gardens and stand by the steps that lead down onto the rocks. Then you will have to say, "I am Jacintha Carradice and I command you to go back into your cave and bother me no more." '

'Suppose he will not obey me?'

'Then he will eat you – but, don't worry, he nearly always does as he is told.'

'Has he ever eaten anybody?'

'Of course, but not for a long time. He is older now and has got fat and lazy. If it is fine after lunch I'll show you where you will need to stand so that he can hear you, but it has to be during a storm.'

'Why only then?'

'I told you, he's old now and enormously fat. He sleeps all the time when it's calm but the wind and rain make him angry and wake him up. Then he comes looking for the Carradice children.'

'Why should he want to eat me? I haven't made him angry.'

'Perhaps when he was a young dragon some other Carradice children teased him and he has made a vow to destroy us if he can. You will simply have to show him that you are not afraid of him, as I did.'

My three cousins laughed and tittered together, not in the least sympathetic about the perils I must face. After lunch the rain stopped and a pale watery sun encouraged us into the gardens. Isobel made a point of showing me the archway at the bottom of the shrubbery where I must stand to challenge

21

the dragon, but then at her insistence we retraced our steps towards the back of the house. We climbed the long low hill on whose summit a group of Scots pines tossed their feathery heads in the sharp wind and I walked behind with Teddy, trying without much success to make conversation. I think he must have been very fed up with girls and he regarded me as just another sent to torment him.

It was teatime when we returned to the schoolroom, and there we found Ruthie waiting for us. Instantly I liked her. She had a porcelain pink and white prettiness and an air of extreme fragility. I was happy to sit next to her at the schoolroom table and from the start Isobel and Lavinia teamed up against us when they saw that we were friends. Teddy merely plodded on with his lessons, ignoring us all most of the time and only taking sides when his twin sister ordered him to do so. Lavinia was by far the more dominant twin; she was also Isobel's faithful disciple.

'You are to have lunch in the dining room tomorrow, Isobel,' Miss Hanson informed her.

'Why is that?'

'Because your cousin Adrian has arrived and your grandmother thought it would be a good idea.'

'Why Isobel and not the rest of us?' Lavinia wanted to know.

'Because one day I shall marry Adrian,' Isobel informed her. 'I shall go away to Switzerland to finishing school and come back a young lady. Then, when Adrian sees me looking finished and beautiful, he will marry me and together we shall be the heads of the family.'

'He won't marry you; he can't marry you – you're first cousins.'

'What difference does that make? Ruthie's parents are first cousins and grandmother was pleased to have them marry.'

'Who told you you would marry Adrian?'

'Nobody told me. I just know I will. Wait and see.'

'Children, this talk is most unseemly. I wouldn't like your grandmother to hear you,' Miss Hanson said firmly.

'She would laugh,' Isobel said. 'Anyway, I shan't mind marrying Adrian; he's very handsome and we could spend half the year in England looking after the Carradice fortunes and the other half in France at the chateau.'

'Well, at the moment, young lady, I require you to delve a little deeper into English history and let the Carradice future settle itself.'

After lessons Ruthie invited me into her bedroom to play card games. It was a large airy room at the front of the house with a thick carpet on the floor and delicate chintzy curtains at the windows. I was happier than at any time since I had arrived. I believed I had found a friend and even the cold dreariness of my room when I returned to it could not quench the glow I was experiencing in my new-found friendship.

Next day, too, was happier. Isobel was absent from the schoolroom and Lavinia, without her idol, seemed better disposed towards me. Teddy was never any problem, and the early afternoon found us climbing the hill in peaceful companionship. It did not last long. The wind rose, whining desolately through the trees, and overhead dark clouds gathered, menacingly near. We took to our heels and ran as the thunder rolled threateningly over the hills, arriving in the schoolroom just as the storm broke and the first great drops of rain descended in a straight deluge from a leaden sky, interspersed with flashes of fork lightning.

In the schoolroom we found Isobel waiting for us, eager to tell us about the luncheon party, with vivid descriptions of the food they had eaten as well as her conversation with that paragon of all the virtues, Adrian Carradice. My lack of interest must have shown in my face because at the next clap of thunder which shook the windows of the room she caught hold of my arm so tightly that her fingers bruised my flesh.

'Now,' she hissed in my ear. 'Now you should go out into the storm and call upon the dragon to do his worst.'

'But I shall get soaked,' I complained, 'I cannot go out into the rain.'

'If you don't, he will come for you. The storm makes him angry. Don't you hear him raging on the rocks below us? I wouldn't like to be you if you don't go out to challenge him now.'

She watched with unholy glee the expression of fear crossing my face. The others watched, too, – Lavinia with something like malice in her light-blue eyes, Ruthie puzzled, but Teddy interested in spite of himself. With fumbling fingers I took my mackintosh out of the locker and pushed my cold feet into my

23

wellingtons. Then I ran down the stairs and out into the storm.

The rain lashed down mercilessly now, so my feet slipped and slithered through the puddles along the paths, but out here in the garden I could hear the monster plainly, awake and belligerent below the rocks. I could barely stay on my feet in the wind and my voice, when it came, was so thin and terrified that I knew the dragon would not be able to hear it. As I was about to try again I felt my arm seized in such a powerful grip I screamed. I looked up with wide terrified eyes, but it was not the teeth of the dragon which held my arm but the fingers of a tall young man with stormy dark eyes, his black hair soaked with rain and a look of incredulity on his handsome face.

'What the devil are you doing here?' he asked angrily. 'And who are you?'

My teeth were chattering with cold and terror and, without further ceremony, he dragged me struggling towards the house. I was furiously angry. If I did not talk to the dragon in the storm he would never let me be, and if I did not stay to face him now I would never find the courage to come out in the storm again. Now here was this arrogant stranger pulling me away. When we reached the safety of the hall we stood looking at each other – he from his dominant height, I with tears of rage rolling down my cheeks, both of us oblivious to the rain running down our mackintoshes and ending in muddy puddles on the polished floor of the hall.

'Who are you?' he asked again.

'Jacintha Carradice, and I want to talk to the dragon.'

'So you're Jacintha. What is all this nonsense about a dragon?'

I was close to tears and my voice trembled. 'I had to talk to the dragon. Isobel said it had to be stormy, it wouldn't do at any other time.'

'For heaven's sake, child, I wish you'd make some sense. Now tell me what dragon you are talking about and what the storm has to do with it.'

'It's the Carradice dragon who lives in the cave below my bedroom.'

'And have you seen this formidable monster?'

'No, I've only heard him, but Isobel says he comes for all the

24

Carradice children and we have to show him we are not afraid of him.'

'I might have known Isobel had a hand in it,' he said, looking down at me with the utmost exasperation in his dark eyes. 'Come with me, Jacintha, I will show you your dragon.'

He dragged me protesting along the corridors leading from the hall and into a room I had never seen before. It was a beautifully proportioned room with a dark-blue Chinese carpet on the floor and wide small-paned windows looking out into what seemed a misty void. I could plainly hear the roars of the dragon – so close that I expected him to come crashing through the windows at any moment. The man pushed my face up close against the panes.

'There is your dragon, Jacintha. Now take a good look and let us have done with this nonsense.'

I could see nothing but water, mountains of it, and white flying spray as waves came crashing in one after the other. As the water fell upon the rocks below, the roar was deafening in my ears. My eyes were wide open surveying the scene, but the fear had gone. The whooshing noise was made by the waves before they crashed upon the rocks, and then the white spume flew upwards and lay upon the rocks and in the crevices as though snow had fallen.

Wordlessly, I looked up at my companion.

'That is the sea, Jacintha. Have you never seen it before?'

I nodded. Then, in a small subdued voice, I whispered, 'But it was not like that; it was flat and blue and there were little boats bobbing up and down upon it.'

'There are days when it is blue and calm here, Jacintha, but this is a treacherous coast and the storms whip up so suddenly it is not safe for bathing or for taking a boat out unless one is very experienced. You must never bathe from those rocks or allow Isobel to tempt you younger children into a boat. I will speak to her about your dragon. She should not have frightened you.'

I did not answer him but continued to stare at the sea, fascinated by the power of its anger as it seethed and boiled against the rocks. I was no longer afraid and when at last I looked up into his face I found him gazing down at me. There was humour in his glance and I thought again how beautiful he was – quite the most beautiful human being I had ever seen

25

except for my mother.

'Do you live here?' I asked him boldly.

'No, my home is a long way from here, but I visit Ravenspoint whenever I can.'

'To stay with my grandmother?'

'My grandmother, too, Jacintha. I am Adrian Carradice.'

Childishly, unreasonably, I resented him. I resented his handsome face and arrogant charm. I reminded myself that he was my grandmother's favourite, the one she doted upon, the one whose letter had brought that tender curve to her cold uncompromising mouth. Snatching my arm away from his grasp, I took to my heels and ran as fast as my legs would carry me out of the door and up the stairs, never pausing until I reached the sanctuary of my bare little room.

I stood panting at the window, looking out into the storm, flinching at the flashes of lightning, my hands over my ears to shut out the sound of the thunder claps, my eyes straining through the swirling mist for a sight of the boiling sea. The storm was at its zenith now, wild and terrifying and magnificent. I was no longer afraid. From that moment the sea became my friend, my confidant and my comforter, and I accepted that my enemy the dragon was no more. My sleep that night would be calm and peaceful, lulled by the sound of the sea as it swept inland towards the point, but I also knew with childlike certainty that the only dragon I needed to fear at Ravenspoint in the years ahead was my grandmother.

2

I have lived at Ravenspoint for eight years and tomorrow will be my sixteenth birthday. These years have done nothing to erase old resentments. Rather they have made me realize that, although I am a Carradice by birth, I am not a Carradice by persuasion. I am what my grandmother regards as her duty and, perhaps because I resemble my mother, I am a constant reminder of the disappointment my father caused her. I am tall for my age and slender. My hair is like my mother's – heavy fair hair that shines golden in the sunlight but appears dark under the lights from the chandeliers – and my eyes are not light-blue Carradice eyes, but darker, bordering on slate. I have been told that I am pretty, mostly by my cousin Roger, who knows well how to flatter a girl. My grandmother regards him as unreliable and something of a playboy. She is probably right.

I long to be like Isobel, who returns to us for holidays from her finishing school in Switzerland, sophisticated now and elegant, dark and vivacious, her light-blue eyes attractive against her blue-black hair. Or like Ruthie, who is fragile and beautiful, like a piece of delicate porcelain. I tell myself that my mouth is too large for beauty, although my teeth are good, and that my face has an altogether too determined expression. Lavinia, too, longs to be like Isobel, but unfortunately she suffers from adolescent spots and considerable puppy fat. Poor Lavinia, always promising herself that she will slim tomorrow, but undeniably weak about the chocolates and sweets which make her fat. Perhaps unkindly, we tease her about it.

It took Isobel and Lavinia a long time to accept me, but the old antipathy between my grandmother and me is still as intense as ever. I think that, over the years, it has given her considerable satisfaction to make me aware that I am different from my cousins, but I have never forgiven her for separating me from my mother. Fortunately, Ruthie accepted me almost at once, possibly because she had little in common with either of the other two.

I stopped minding about my tiny bedroom at the side of the house because Teddy's was of a similar size and just as spartanly furnished. I didn't even mind that my clothes were hand-me-downs from Isobel or Lavinia, but I did mind those times when they left Ravenspoint to be with their parents and I ate my solitary meals in the schoolroom or under the eagle eye of the housekeeper. Once I ate lunch with my grandmother, but I was so nervous that it seemed the food turned to sawdust in my mouth and all my fingers became thumbs so that I dropped the cutlery and spilled my soup on the tablecloth. After that dismal effort, my grandmother seemed quite relieved to have me go back to the schoolroom.

In the very severe winter two years ago, Teddy caught a chill which kept him indoors for several weeks, and my grandmother came to the conclusion that it was because the bedrooms on that side of the house were particularly cold and damp. As a result, Teddy moved into a more palatial abode next door to his sister and I came to share Ruthie's bedroom – a state of affairs which pleased both of us at the time.

My schooling too took on an unfamiliar pattern. Contrary to all expectations, Miss Hanson left Ravenspoint to marry the curate of a village some ten miles distant. He was brought for our inspection, a pale earnest young man who seemed entirely appreciative of his good fortune and in those few weeks before her marriage Miss Hanson blossomed into something approaching comeliness. My grandmother decided she would not employ another governess. Governesses were unreliable; the first one had usurped the affections of her youngest son and the second had had the temerity to put her private passions before her calling. Consequently, Isobel went to Switzerland earlier than expected and Ruthie and Lavinia were sent to boarding school. I was enrolled at the girl's grammar school in the nearest town, and during the weekends I became dependent upon my own company after Teddy departed for his new public school some fifty miles away. I saw little of my cousins during their holidays because they spent much of their time with their parents either in their own homes or at holiday resorts, only coming to Ravenspoint for odd weekends or longer intervals in the company of their parents.

I met Adrian's parents only once, when they came from France for my grandmother's seventieth birthday. I knew at once where Adrian got his Latin good looks. His mother was beautiful, slender and elegant, with dark hair and large blue-grey eyes, though she seldom smiled. I remember that she was fond of pale grey and mauve, colours which gave her a somewhat melancholy air. His father, Uncle Roland, brought back vividly my earliest memory of the man who pored over his books on the red plush tablecloth, but my father had had a warm and tender smile, whereas Uncle Roland's face was cold, his smile remote and withdrawn, never quite reaching his eyes. Like Uncle Robert he was tall but his hair was silver fair like my father's.

Isobel does not resemble her mother, who is a large garrulous woman. Fond of furs and feathers, she appears to me to float around the house like a ship in full sail, her ample bosom well suited to the ropes of pearls she favours. She has taken little notice of me, being constantly engaged in defending the waywardness of her son against my grandmother's tirades. Ruthie's mother, Aunt Ruth, is very different, slender and fair with a pink and white English rose complexion. Ruthie's father, my Uncle William, is smaller and plumper that either of his elder brothers and has a face that seems always to smile. They have been kind to me and I am fond of them, though I had never expected to be fond of any members of the Carradice family.

Lavinia and Teddy's parents are a horsy pair. Aunt Myra resembles my grandmother, being tall and thin with high cheekbones and fine dark eyes, and Uncle Gwillan seems to spend all his time in riding breeches; indeed, their entire conversation revolves around the breeding and racing of horses, point-to-point meetings, stables, gymkhanas and county shows. They deplore the fact that Lavinia is allergic to horseflesh and Teddy's eyesight precludes him from taking part in equestrian events.

I am fond of my cousin Roger. He is quite outrageous in the things he says and is a constant tease. As fair as Isobel is dark, he has pale laughing blue eyes and a complete disregard for my grandmother's disapproval when he flirts with the maids and pays too much attention to me. I have seen Adrian seldom since the morning he dragged me from the garden and commanded me to look out of the drawing-room window at the stormy sea below. If we meet, I am angry with myself when I find my face blushing furiously under his dark scrutiny. In some strange way I seem to amuse him but, since he is my grandmother's undoubted favourite, my dislike for him continues.

In all these years one thing and one thing alone has sustained me and that is my passionate love for Ravenspoint. Isobel hates it; she hates its loneliness and the sound of the sea which one can never escape from. Ruthie and Lavinia, too, prefer the city with its bright lights and concert halls. At Ravenspoint there are no parks where the bands play, no gentle boating on the placid river, no tea dances in scented hotel rooms, for Isobel and her retinue of young men. There is nothing but the sound of the sea crashing against the rocks and the harsh grass waving on the endless dunes.

They cannot understand how desperately I love the house which stands stark and lonely on its rocky point, surrounded on three sides by the ocean, as much a part of the coastline as the cliffs themselves and the wild sweeping dunes along the shore.

I have come to love the sea in all its moods so that, looking back, it seems incredible that I should ever have thought that it was my enemy. I love it when it crashes and roars below the house during a storm, or when it is gentle and benign, rolling in silver crescents under the moonlight. It excites me when it is angry, and delights me when it is calm, peaceful and blue under a summer sky, with only the gulls swooping and wheeling above it, filling the day with their mournful cries.

At such times, I sit alone on the rocks, my heart sick with resentment that one day I must leave this place because the house will belong to Adrian and Isobel – and unreasonably, perhaps, I suffer at the thought that it should go to Isobel who hates it and to Adrian who is so insufferably remote that he does not seem to have the capacity for loving.

Adrian and Isobel are the beautiful Carradices. I have watched them riding their horses along the sands, sitting them with superb grace, or jumping them recklessly at local point-to-point meetings. When they are all away, I love to wander round the stables, and the groom has taken a liking to me – so much so that he has taught me to ride. I ride Isobel's horse, although as yet she does not know it. His name is Sultan and he is beautiful, half Arab and very gentle, a warm chestnut gelding with no vices but a dashing turn of speed. Beside him, Adrian's hunter Caliph is huge and he terrifies me. He is a black stallion described by the groom as 'that black devil', because for no reason at all he will rear upwards, hooves flashing, eyes rolling and teeth snapping, and Adrian merely laughs when others find him unridable. Somehow Adrian and that great black horse go together.

It seems to me that our grandmother has charted our lives as surely as a captain charts his ship's path across the oceans. My father disobeyed her and did not live long enough to pay the penalty in full, so I am now being punished for his mis-demeanours. Ruthie and Teddy are pliant – they will obey her too when the time comes – but I am not sure about Lavinia. Like Isobel, she is wilful and stubborn, but I believe Isobel is so well satisfied with the future my grandmother has planned for her that she will obey her without question. Roger and I are the rebels, but Adrian, dear Adrian, will do exactly as she asks.

My birthday coincides with the end of my schooldays, and in front of me stretches the prospect of long summer days with nothing much to do but run along the shore or scramble across the rocks. I am not expecting much company. For the last few weeks, all I have heard at Ravenspoint and at school has been talk of war, and the servants go around with long faces or talk in hushed whispers and I cannot make head or tail of it. Mr Godfrey, the groom, says he doesn't see how we can possibly keep out of it, and at school we have been told the story of the assassination of the Archduke Franz Ferdinand and his wife in the Bosnian town of Sarajevo. Now it seems Austria and Serbia are at war and the butler says gloomily that it will spread through Europe like a forest fire, though as cook says, why should such an event have anything to do with England?

I want the summer to go on for ever, for my future life is uncertain. I adore these long golden days when the sun sparkles on the water, rippling in golden crescents over the wet sand and with only the gulls to talk to. I look for old Meg along the shore where she goes to gather driftwood for her fire, then I help her to carry it back to her decrepit cottage on the far side of the bay in an old carpet bag. We have little conversation, but now and again I find her shrewd old eyes watching me, disconcertingly intelligent in comparison with her shabby attire and unkempt appearance. Her wrinkled face is as brown as a horse chestnut under her disreputable felt hat, and the housekeeper has berated me soundly for talking to her.

'She's no fit companion for you, Miss Jacintha,' she scolds testily, and Lucy elaborates by calling her an 'old witch'.

Once Ruthie was with me when we saw her on the beach and I ran along the sand to help her, calling to Ruthie to follow me. She hung back trembling, saying, 'She's an old witch, Jacintha, I'm afraid of her.'

'What nonsense,' I said. 'She's old but she's not a witch. Besides her arthritis is troublesome and she needs the wood for her fire. Do come on, Ruthie, she'll do us no harm.'

Reluctantly, she came with me and I had to agree that Meg looked particularly revolting that morning. Her skirt was torn and greasy and she had tied an old piece of sacking round her waist. She had a black shawl on her head, and the hands and face which peeped out from it were skeleton-thin with the skin stretched tightly over the bones. Her smile, too, was a grimace in her wrinkled face and showed two ageing and yellowing teeth.

'Look for something with pitch on it,' I called to Ruthie. 'It burns better.'

We carried the driftwood back to her cottage and Ruthie wrinkled up her nose in disdain at the grimy walls and threadbare pieces of carpet. Chickens ran inside and out of the patch of garden and a small goat dozed with the dog in front of the fire.

We were handed two mugs of goat's milk and, when Ruthie looked at it askance, I couldn't resist remarking sharply, 'It's very good, Ruthie, and much better for us than cow's milk.'

We sat with our chairs pulled up at the table and Meg sat opposite us, amused, I think, when Ruthie shrank away from her.

'Is it true that you're a gypsy, Meg?' I asked her somewhat impudently.

'No, that it ain't. Who says I'm one?'

'But you can tell fortunes,' I persisted eagerly.

'Aye, when a've a mind to.'

Even Ruthie betrayed some interest at this piece of news, and backed me up enthusiastically when I begged her to tell ours.

'Please, Meg, tell me my fortune and then tell Ruthie hers.' I held out my hand, palm uppermost. She took my hand in her thin claw-like fingers, holding it lightly, her face screwed up into lines of concentration and we watched her with bated breath, entirely fascinated.

'What sort of fortune are ye wantin' to know, child?' she asked.

'The truth, Meg, but only if it's good. I don't want to know any bad fortune. I've had too much of that already.'

She laughed. 'You should take the rough with the smooth, lassie. My, but it's a strange fate I see in your hand.'

'Strange. How strange? I don't want to know about that, I only want to know if I shall marry someone handsome and fall in love.'

'Oh, Jacintha,' Ruthie snapped. 'How can she possibly tell you that?'

Meg laughed. 'I'll tell you one thing, lassie, you two reckon on being friends now, but it won't last.'

I snatched my hand away sharply and Ruthie ran towards the door. 'I want to go home, Jacintha. I told you she was horrid.'

My curiosity was aroused and I turned my dismayed face to find Meg watching me slyly and with a kind of crafty malice. I held out my hand to her with more courage than I felt.

'I want to know, Meg, please, what do you see in my hand?'

'The other lassie has more sense than you, missy. She doesn't want to know about the future. It'll come whether you're ready for it or not. Better to take each day as it comes, that's my advice.'

She was holding my hand again in her gnarled old claw, and curiosity brought Ruthie back to the table.

'There's a long life afore you and a healthy one, but there's hurt and anger and tears too, so many tears afore the peace comes. It's sad it should be such a long time coming.'

'But shall I find somebody who will marry me, Meg? I don't want to know about a long life and peace. I just want to know

33

if I can be taken away from my grandmother?'

'In thirty years from now, my girl, you'll wonder why you ever scoffed at peace and the like. Aye, you'll marry, but before then and more than most you'll suffer. It could be that this lass here will be a part of your suffering.'

I looked at Ruthie in amazement and she was watching us intently now, her face bright with colour. Hoarsely she asked, 'Why do you say I shall hurt Jacintha. I shall never hurt her; she is my best friend.'

'Time alters many things – you'll find that out for yourself one of these days. I'm telling you both, your friendship's not meant to last and in the end it's you who will suffer the most.'

'Me? why shall I suffer?' Ruthie demanded.

Meg laid my hand down upon the bare wooden table and sat back in her chair, regarding us with something akin to sorrow in her rheumy old eyes. Her voice, too, had taken on a new weariness when she dismissed us.

'Go home now. Enjoy what you have. Too soon it is gone.'

We were unusually quiet as we walked back along the shore, kicking the soft sand so that we had to remove our shoes and stockings and walk barefoot across the beach.

'The day's spoiled,' Ruthie complained. 'Really, Jacintha, why did you have to talk to that horrid old woman and listen to her lies?'

I didn't answer her as we plodded onwards, screwing up my eyes against the bright sunlight. The tall cliffs cast purple shadows across the sand and the sea rippled gently warm over our bare feet. Ruthie was right, the day was spoiled. Next day, after breakfast, she returned to her parents' home and I was alone once more.

There were presents beside my breakfast plate next morning and several birthday cards. Notepaper from Ruthie and chocolates from her parents. A dressing gown from Uncle Robert and Aunt Celia and, outrageously, from Roger, a pair of pure silk stockings, the first I had ever owned, bearing a card, 'For Miss Jacintha Carradice, a young lady of fashion.' I was not disappointed that I had received nothing from Isobel. She invariably forgot my birthday and her present usually arrived three or four days after the event. From Adrian, surprisingly, I received a beautifully illustrated book on sea-birds and seashells, and despite all my prejudice I treasured it. There was a box of Swiss handkerchiefs from my grandmother and a French and English dictionary enclosed with a cryptic note written in her large spindly handwriting adjuring me to make good use of her gifts.

I rejoiced in the kindness of my family, but I rejoiced even more that it was my last day in school and the start of the long summer holidays. I could hardly believe my good fortune as I stepped down from the afternoon train carrying my school satchel for the last time, with my diploma advertising the fact that I was an adequate scholar rolled at the bottom under my books. As always, the pony and trap waited for me at the bottom of the station steps, but the boy who met me had an errand to do in the village and rather than wait I decided to set off home across the beach.

The sun was warm on my arms and I took off my school hat, which I quickly thrust inside my satchel together with my shoes and stockings. I leaped and danced across the sand, whooping with joy, and with only the wheeling of the gulls to witness my exultation. It was only when I was within sight of the tall cliffs that I became aware of a man standing at the edge of the sea looking into the distance where the white horses played. He was standing in the dark-purple shadows under the cliffs and I frowned, wondering who the stranger was who dared to trespass on my lovely day and on the beach I had come to think of as exclusively my own. I slowed my steps, waiting for him to turn towards me, but when he did my heart gave a sudden jolt and all the joy I had been feeling suddenly left me. I had no word of greeting for my cousin Adrian as he walked slowly towards me, but I thought he looked like the pictures I had often seen of the devil, darkly handsome, lean and graceful as a cat. The smile on his face mocked my immaturity, making me feel tongue-tied and absurdly young.

'What is it about the sea, Jacintha, that I always know I can find you here?' he asked quietly.

'My grandmother is not at home,' I said, and I knew that my voice was cold.

'I know. I came to see the house and to wish my little cousin a happy birthday. Did you like the book I sent you?'

'Oh yes, thank you, Adrian, thank you very much. It's a

beautiful book.'

'Well, I know your passion for all things connected with the sea. I thought you might find it useful.'

His voice was impersonal as he walked by my side in the direction of the steps which led up from the beach to the house on the top of the cliffs. I couldn't resist asking, 'Why did you want to see the house when my grandmother is away?'

He smiled down at me, a gentle teasing smile which for the moment disarmed me.

'I did not know when or if I would ever see it again. There are things and places I can bear to leave with impunity; Ravenspoint is not one of them.'

'Why, are you going away?' I asked, surprised, but trying hard to keep the unexpected note of hope out of my voice.

'A great many of us will be going away, Jacintha, not all of us will be coming back.'

'Because of the war, you mean? The butler says if there is a war it will all be over by Christmas, he says we'd all be better employed reading about the cricket scores than about some silly Austrians and Serbians fighting over nothing at all.'

'And that is all it means to you, Jacintha?'

My voice was doubtful even in my own ears. 'I don't know. What does it mean to you, Adrian?'

'It means that life may never be quite the same again for any of us.'

He screwed up his eyes against the sunlight and there was the strangest expression on his face – almost as though this golden perfect day mocked him. Something of his bewilderment came to trouble me also. I had the most uncanny feeling that somewhere at some other time we had stood together before a blue sea with the sunlight warm and golden all around us, and that his words then had troubled me with their air of finality. From somewhere across the bay a gull rose shrieking into the sky and the moment was gone.

'Will you have to go?' I asked him quietly.

'If there is a war, yes.'

'And Roger and Teddy?'

'Roger certainly, Teddy perhaps not. His eyesight may keep him out.'

'And then, when it's all over, you'll come back to Ravenspoint to marry Isobel?'

He threw back his head and laughed, but when I looked indignant he sobered up instantly. 'It will depend how well my guardian angel looks after me, but the idea of my marrying Isobel is as much a figment of her imagination as your dragon was all those years ago.'

'You mean you never intended to marry Isobel?'

'We are cousins, Jacintha, and I don't particularly think it is a good thing for cousins to marry. Think of the many vices we should hand down to our children.'

'But my grandmother has said you should marry.'

'Not to me. You will see, Jacintha, that Isobel will romanticize about a great many young men before she meets one of them at the altar.'

'My grandmother will not want you to go to war.'

'Perhaps not, but I'm afraid her wishes will be totally disregarded when the time comes. Do you intend to walk up the cliff path without shoes and stockings on your feet?'

I looked down in some dismay, then hurriedly wiped my feet on the handkerchief in my satchel and pulled on my stockings and shoes. The path was steep, with only a slender handrail for protection, and neither of us spoke again until we reached the top. As if by mutual consent, we turned and looked back the way we had come. Below us the sea made hardly any sound as it swirled amongst the rocks, forming shallow shell pools of sparkling water before the rocks rose sheer and cruel to their summit.

'Your dragon is quiet today, Jacintha. I take it you have long ago made your peace with him.'

I blushed a little, remembering vividly the terrified child I had been and how much on that day I had hated him. I suddenly knew that I no longer hated him as I stole a look at his profile, dark and severe as he looked down at the rocks below us. It was a strangely brooding profile, but his smile when he turned towards me was undeniably sweet.

'Am I on trial still, Jacintha?' he inquired quietly.

'I thought I hated you, but now I don't hate you any more.'

'Why should you ever have done so? I did nothing to deserve it.'

'I hated you because my grandmother loved you. Now I know that it was foolish, but I shall never stop hating her.'

'But why, when she has given you a home and an education?'

'I already had a home and love, which I don't have here. Why have I never been able to see my mother? What terrible thing did she ever do to deserve such treatment?'

'You are very like her, you know.'

'You knew my mother! Oh, Adrian, tell me about her, how did you know her?'

'She was my governess.'

I stared at him in amazement, then my face cleared. Of course. My mother came to Ravenspoint to be a governess to the older Carradice children – that meant Adrian and Roger. My words tumbled over themselves in asking too many questions.

'Please, Adrian, tell me about her and about my father. Were they terribly in love and was my mother very beautiful, and why has my grandmother never been able to forgive her for taking my father away?'

'I remember that she was beautiful and exciting to be with. She tried very hard to make our lessons interesting and at that time your father was the only son still living at home. My grandmother had plans for him to marry the daughter of Colonel Westerman and she was constantly invited to Ravenspoint. It was a bitter blow when he fell in love with the governess she had employed to teach us. They left the house one morning after a stormy scene in the sitting room and I never saw your mother again.'

'Nor my father?'

'Yes – he came here once to ask my grandmother to visit them. He probably hoped that if she saw how happy they were together she would relent and take them back into the fold.'

'But she didn't, did she? Yet she wasn't ashamed to take me away from her. Why couldn't she see how beautiful and kind my mother was? She was every bit as good as Isobel's mother or Ruthie's.'

He smiled, somewhat grimly. 'Perhaps so, Jacintha, but they were the women she wanted for her sons. In my grandmother's eyes, they brought wealth and breeding into the family – infinitely preferable to beauty, I expect she thought. I'm not sure that she has ever really forgiven my father for having married a Frenchwoman and elected to reside in that country, but at least it is an undisputed fact that my mother's family are aristocrats who own large estates and considerable wealth.'

'My grandmother is a snob, a hateful rotten snob,' I stormed.

'I'm afraid so.'

My indignant eyes looked into his amused ones for several moments, before our laughter rang out across the cliffs, echoing back at us, and the louder we heard it the longer we laughed.

That night I did not dine off a tray in the morning room but with Adrian in the splendour of the oak-panelled dining room, and there were many times when our laughter rang out across the hall and through the open windows into the scented dusk.

I had dressed for the occasion in my best dark-blue crêpe de Chine. It had been new for Isobel's twenty-first-birthday party and I knew that it brought out the colour of my dark-blue eyes. The long skirt hung in graceful folds, emphasizing my long slender legs, although my figure was yet unformed and I wished most fervently that I had some sort of shape under the softness of the material which moulded the bodice. I had brushed my hair until it shone, tying it back from my face with a blue bow of watered silk and, though I wore no make-up on my face, it glowed with the freshness of youth.

Adrian was amusing. Not as Roger was amusing, with risky innuendos and vague allusions to his innumerable conquests, but gently teasing, much as an older brother might have been. For the first time since I had come to Ravenspoint, I wanted the evening to go on for ever – I had never enjoyed myself so much.

It was almost midnight when we walked together up the wide shallow staircase, pausing at the head of the stairs, for his room was at the opposite end of the house to mine. A shaft of bright moonlight came through the tall window at the head of the stairs, lighting up the severe planes of his face and silvering his hair so that the contours of his head stood out in sharp relief against the murky darkness beyond. The sensation was suddenly frightening; it was as if some moment of recall had come to taunt me from another life, making me feel that I had stood with Adrian before in some place where the moonlight sent tentative fingers to dispel the shadows around us and that then, as now, those shadows had been potent with menace. I had had this same feeling standing in the sunlight on the cliff top. Now, in the shadows at the top of the stairs, I shivered.

'You are cold,' he said solicitously.

'No. Oh, Adrian, I was wondering when, if ever, I would see you again with the moonlight all around us and no terrible war to take you away.'

He did not speak at once and I could not but wonder if he too was plagued by things he did not understand. He answered me lightly enough, however.

'I lead a charmed life, Jacintha. I ride an unridable horse and climb unclimbable peaks. I cannot think that the Kaiser's soldiers will defeat me where other dangers have failed. You and I will laugh together on the cliffs of Ravenspoint again, never fear.'

'Are you very afraid, Adrian?'

'Only a fool would say he was not afraid to go to war. When I am most afraid, I shall remember how you were prepared to face the dragon in the midst of a storm just to prove how little you feared his glowing eyes and tongue breathing flames.'

'Now you are laughing at me, Adrian Carradice, and I think that perhaps I ought to hate you after all.'

He threw back his head and laughed, then soberly he bent his head and lightly kissed the top of my hair.

At the end of the corridor, I turned to watch him walk away and it seemed to me then that his tall slender figure was surrounded by a great loneliness. I wondered with a new maturity if my visions had belonged to the past or were part of the future.

It was a long time before I slept. I lay quietly looking out of the window, watching the full moon sailing in and out of the clouds, listening to the sighing of the wind through the branches of the trees outside my window and the gentle rhythmical sound of the surf along the shore.

The morning sun was only a promise in the eastern sky when I ran down the stairs the following morning, and my disappointment was so intense it seemed like a physical pain in my breast when I learned that Adrian had already left the house.

3

Looking back, it seems incredible how little the war in Europe altered our lives in those first few months. My grandmother came back to Ravenspoint and called a meeting of the family, from which Roger and Adrian were conspicuously missing. Adrian was with his cavalry regiment and Roger had enlisted only recently in the Royal Engineers. The Carradice mills were working to capacity to weave cloth required for uniforms, and the family had no need to complain that huge sums of government money were not already swelling the profits.

Aunt Celia was in tears for most of the meeting, insisting that Roger should have waited until he was called instead of volunteering for active service, and Isobel raged and fumed because my grandmother was insisting that we were to remain at Ravenspoint for the duration of the war, instead of living in the town, which was liable to suffer from zeppelin attacks.

'It stands to reason,' my grandmother said, 'if the Germans are going to bomb England, it will be where there is industry. Besides, I don't want the girls living in a garrison town which will be overrun with troops. There will be quite enough young women getting into mischief as it is.'

Only Teddy, it seemed, was to return with his parents to Wellsford.

'You can make yourself useful at the mills,' my grandmother admonished him. 'You will not be suitable material for the services since your eyesight is so bad, but there is no reason why you should not assist the war effort in other ways.'

One thing alone cheered me and that was my grandmother's decision to stay in what she called the town house, a large stone house in the centre of Wellsford where she could keep her eye on the Carradice empire of five gigantic mills, each of which contributed to the pall of blue smoke which hung like a permanent umbrella over the city.

The summer lingered on and in those first few months all we were expected to do was amuse ourselves. We walked across the fells and along the country lanes gay with foxgloves and honeysuckle. We ran laughing along the shore, splashing in the shallows, throwing bread to the gulls; then suddenly it was autumn and in Europe the battle of Ypres raged.

The names of those killed and wounded began to appear in the morning papers and before Christmas Lucy brought her young man into the sitting room for our inspection, all scrubbed and shining in his new khaki uniform. Two days later, we gathered along the road to see the new recruits march out of the village on their way to their depot. They represented most of the young men of the tiny lakeland hamlet and they all looked absurdly young in their shapeless khaki, puttees wrapped tight around stalwart country calves, wearing great-coats that had surely never been designed for them. The music and the brave sound of their drums brought hot stinging tears to my eyes and I stood there unashamedly allowing them to roll down my cheeks onto my coat.

To cover her own emotion, Isobel snapped, 'What are you crying for? You don't know any of them, unless it's Sam, Lucy's friend, and you don't really know him.'

'I'm crying for them all,' I wailed. 'They might never come back.'

'Of course, they'll come back. You heard what Sam said, they can't wait to get there. None of those boys was ever likely to leave the village, let alone see the continent; it's a great adventure for them. You'll see, they'll all be treated like little tin gods when they come back and nobody's going to have any time for the ones who didn't go.'

Later that night, I sat on Ruthie's bed and we planned together that we would do something useful like nursing or driving an ambulance in one of the big cities. There was never any conviction in our promises; the ever-present spectre of my grandmother was too insistent and neither of us had the necessary defiance to combat it.

Christmas was upon us almost before we realized it, and to my grandmother's great joy Adrian arrived, as well as the other members of the family. Only Roger was missing, which caused his mother the utmost distress. I was surprised to see how tall Teddy had become, although he still blinked owlishly behind his thick lenses and flushed like a frightened rabbit when my grandmother snapped at him, which she frequently did.

We girls felt bitter about the enforced inactivity but our complaints fell on deaf ears, as did Isobel's tantrums. The house was cold, with coal burning only in the drawing-room firegrate, so, early on Christmas Eve, we sallied forth into the forest to cut pine logs, bringing them back to the house in sleighs or in the pony cart which Isobel drove. After that, fires burned in the library and the dining room and, in spite of the war, a tall young spruce stood grandly in the hall decorated with shining baubles and candles.

Looking along the dining table later that night, it was hard to realize that somewhere in Europe a war raged and that men were lying wounded and dead in rat-infested trenches. At Ravenspoint the chandeliers shed their light over the table shining with silver and polished glass and there was no shortage of food yet. Only Adrian in his officer's uniform struck an incongruous note, but the other men wore black dinner jackets and the women were dressed in their finery, glowing with the warmth of candlelight on silks and satins, sparkling with gems. I wore my one evening dress and the gold locket I had had as a child, but I had brushed my hair until it shone like burnished gold and I hoped my youth was all the adornment I needed.

My grandmother sat at the head of the table, austere in her black dinner gown, her silver hair immaculately dressed, one thin emaciated hand twisting and untwisting the strand of pearls around her throat. It was easy to see her favourites. She sat between Uncle William and Adrian, whose dark head continuously leaned towards her deferentially, while Ruthie, sitting between her parents, seemed more animated than I had seen her for some time. Isobel, on Adrian's right, was a radiant vision in rose chiffon, and she sparkled vivaciously, her witticisms entertaining all those who sat near enough to hear them. Now and again Adrian would throw back his head and laugh at something she had said, while her parents and my grandmother looked on indulgently.

I was placed at the other end of the table next to Teddy and opposite Lavinia and her father. Teddy had little conversation so I was able to watch and listen to all that went on, amused at

Lavinia's sulky face as she endeavoured to peer round her father's portly girth. Teddy sat morosely eating the food set before him, seldom taking his eyes from his plate, and once I saw my grandmother eyeing him with a vexed frown on her face before she snapped, 'Edward, please take your food to your mouth, not your mouth to your food, and Jacintha, stop fidgeting.'

'I wasn't fidgeting, grandmother,' I retorted indignantly.

'And don't answer back.'

'Really,' I muttered under my breath, 'one would think I was still ten years old the way she treats me.'

'She'll never treat you any differently,' Lavinia hissed. 'You'll always be ten years old as far as she's concerned.'

I looked up and my eyes met Adrian's, so filled with amusement that I looked away quickly, blushing furiously. It was all right for him – he never did anything wrong in her eyes. I don't suppose he'd ever been told not to fidget at table or that he was not eating properly. The old animosity washed over me and I found myself disliking him once more. I met Teddy's eyes and grinned at him. At least he was more often than not as much out of favour as I was.

The men sat over their port for a while before they joined us in the large drawing room for coffee. Then Isobel asked the question I had wanted but not dared to ask. 'What are we going to do for the rest of the evening. Surely we're not expected to sit around staring at each other?'

'And why not?' her mother snapped. 'It won't do you any harm to sit quietly for once without this constant craving for excitement. Think about your brother, who's probably in France by this time.'

'I do think about him, mother, but there's nothing I can do about it. As for excitement, when do we ever get any excitement living here?'

'Poor Roger,' was the only reply she received as Aunt Celia dabbed her eyes.

'There's a dance over at Langdale at Colonel Hesketh's,' Isobel went on airily. 'I was invited but said I didn't think I could go because I wouldn't have transport.'

'Who invited you?' Lavinia asked.

'Mary Hesketh, at church last Sunday. There's to be a crowd of young people, her brother Harry's home on leave and he's brought some friends with him. I don't see why I can't go. I'm going to ask grandmother anyway.'

'Ask her if we can't all go,' Lavinia called.

'Of course you can't go. For one thing you're too young, and for another you haven't been invited. Adrian shall take me.'

We were sure it was the weight of Adrian's persuasion that cajoled my grandmother into allowing them to go. In less than half an hour Isobel was back in the drawing room wearing her mother's furs over her gown, long evening gloves, and a look of delighted anticipation on her face. Then she and Adrian departed together.

'You can play my gramophone records if you like,' was her parting shot. 'You'll find them in my room.'

Instead, we sat at the schoolroom table playing the games we had played as children, Lavinia, Teddy and I. Ruthie had elected to stay in the drawing room with the older people, which surprised me although it did not seem to surprise the other two.

'Surely she can't want to stay down there,' I said.

'She must do or she'd be up here with us,' Lavinia answered. 'Don't, for heaven's sake, ask her what we've been missing. I wouldn't like her to think we're interested.'

'She's very close to her parents,' I said, a little wistfully.

'Unnaturally so, if you ask me. It's your move, Teddy, unless you've gone to sleep.'

'Fat chance with you two nattering on,' Teddy retorted.

We played on for another half-hour, then Lavinia abruptly swept her chips to one side saying, 'I'm fed up with this game. I can't concentrate.'

'Are you fed up with it too?' Teddy asked me plaintively.

'I don't think it's very interesting.'

'In that case, I might just as well go to bed,' he said. 'I'm not staying here to listen to you two talking scandal all night.'

'Scandal, here!' his sister retorted.

'Well, you're always on about who's going to marry whom. Trust me to get lumbered with four girls; it was different for Adrian and Roger.'

'Trust us to get lumbered with you,' Lavinia snapped. 'Any other brother would have asked grandmother if he too could take his sister to the dance.'

Lucy came into the room bearing a large jug of cocoa and

45

four cups and saucers. 'What, only the two of you then?' she commented.

'Teddy's gone to bed and Ruthie didn't elect to join us,' Lavinia replied. 'You can leave the jug, Lucy. There'll be twice as much for us.'

'I'll take Master Teddy a cup to his room, Miss Lavinia, and you can share what's left. I don't know about Miss Ruthie; she'll probably have something in the drawing room.'

'Yes, and it won't be cocoa,' Lavinia retorted to Lucy's retreating back.

'You don't like Ruthie, do you Lavinia?' I asked.

'Not a lot.'

'But why?'

'Because she's spoiled. Ruthie's always had to have everything she's wanted. It was just the same when we were small, even before you came to live here. Whatever Isobel or I had, Ruthie had to have it too, or something bigger and better.'

'But I thought it was Isobel who had everything.'

'Isobel gets things from her father, Roger was her mother's favourite, just as I get attention from my father, but Ruthie gets it from both her parents and grandmother.'

'Like Adrian.'

'Well, yes, something like Adrian, but Ruthie's more devious.'

'But why Ruthie?'

'It's obvious, isn't it? Her mother was grandmother's youngest brother's daughter, so she's a niece as well as a daughter-in-law. That must make her a favourite twice over.'

'I'd forgotten her parents were first cousins.'

'You've lived here all these years but you don't know very much, do you, Jacintha?'

'I didn't particularly want any of you to think I was all that interested.'

Lavinia was in an expansive mood and appeared only too anxious to bring me up to date on matters I knew little about. She informed me that my grandmother was not over-fond of her own father – I had suspected this for some time, but now I learned there was little love lost between them.

'My father was old Sir Joshua Hardcastle's nephew,' Lavinia said, 'and he spent a lot of time at the hall when the old man was alive. He was mad keen on horses and so was my mother, and you must admit he is rather good-looking. He's got too fat now, but when he was younger he had all the girls after him, and my mother's never been a raving beauty. He hadn't any money. Old Sir Joshua left him a bit when he died but it didn't take my father long to run through that. He gambles, you know, and he doesn't always win; besides which, he buys horses he can't really afford and he's never been taken into the business.'

'Why is that, do you think?'

'Gracious, he doesn't know anything about wool; he'd be a liability. All he knows is horses. He buys and sells them, sometimes he races them in local point-to-point meetings or at the race tracks in Yorkshire. Sometimes he makes money, but he's just as likely to lose it at the next meeting. Both my parents are dotty about horses. They must be disappointed in Teddy and me.'

'If my grandmother is so opposed to your father, why was he allowed to marry into the Carradice family when my mother was considered unsuitable?'

'Well, it's different, isn't it? I suppose my mother had to have a husband and my father did have good connections, not like your mother. I don't care that she was a governess, Jacintha. It served my grandmother right that she ran off with Uncle Allan from right under her nose. The only thing is she'll never let you forget it, never.'

'It will be different when I'm married. She'll have to treat me differently then.'

'Whom will you marry, for heaven's sake? There's nobody round here, with a war on, so when are you likely to meet anybody?'

'I don't know, but I shall. Then I expect he'll take me away from here and I shall try to find my mother.'

'I hope you do, but you'll have to go an awful long way from here to escape from grandmother. When I marry, I shall put half the world between us. I shan't marry at all if I can't do that.'

'How about your parents?'

'My father would understand; I should think he's entertained those sentiments for most of his married life. I'm not so sure about my mother.'

We sat on in the chilly schoolroom like two old conspirators, and for the first time in my life I felt close to Lavinia. I did not hear Ruthie come into the bedroom we shared, but it must have been very much later because I read for at least half an hour before putting out the light.

Next morning, after church, I found myself walking back along the lane with Adrian beside me. Searching for some topic of conversation, I asked. 'Did you enjoy the dance, Adrian?'

'Very much. What did you do to pass the time?'

'Oh, we went into the old schoolroom to play games.'

'We?'

'Teddy, Lavinia and I. Then we got fed up, so Teddy went to bed and I stayed with Lavinia just chatting.'

'Tearing some unfortunate person's character to shreds, no doubt.'

'We were talking about the family and what we would do when we got married.'

He laughed as though the idea of either of us being married gave him great amusement. 'And what world-shattering notions did you arrive at?'

'That we would live as far away from grandmother as possible so that we could run our lives without interference, and that we didn't care whether we had any money or not.'

He offered no comment, but continued to look amused, so that I found myself snapping, 'You don't seem to think we meant it.'

'Oh, I'm sure you did. I just happen to think that you are both very young, and that time and experience will alter many things.' With the briefest of smiles, he left me and joined Isobel. As I watched them walk off together across the dunes, I bit my lip angrily. He was maddening, so cynical and superior, but one day he'd see that I meant what I said.

Immediately after lunch, Adrian and Isobel saddled their horses and did not return for dinner. The following morning I stood in the background of the group bidding Adrian god-speed as he returned to the front.

As we drifted back into the house, I saw my grandmother's erect, stiff-backed figure disappearing into her sitting room, and heard the door close firmly behind her. She would sit there alone thinking of Adrian and I wondered if Isobel, too, was sad that he had gone so soon. I found Ruthie sitting on the window seat in our bedroom gazing out towards the sea. She did not turn her head when I entered the room so I went over to join her.

'Are you sad that Adrian has gone back?' I asked her curiously.

'Not particularly. I wasn't thinking of Adrian; he's always been the one person I've never thought of as a Carradice.'

'Adrian?'

'Yes, why not? He's half French. Besides, Adrian seldom talks to me and I never know what to say to him.'

'I thought he was very kind the night I had dinner with him.'

'Perhaps he doesn't notice me, or if he does he doesn't like me.'

'Of course he likes you, Ruthie. Don't you like him?'

'No. I think he's sinister, sinister and cold.'

She picked up the book she had been reading from the seat beside her, indicating that she had nothing more to say, and I was left wondering if I would ever be completely sure about the members of the Carradice family.

To everybody's surprise and Aunt Celia's great joy, on the afternoon of Boxing Day Roger arrived at Ravenspoint in the company of a young woman none of us had seen before. We all agreed with Isobel that he had probably been on leave all through Christmas but had only now elected to join the family. The girl's name was Polly and she was charming and beautiful, with an elfin face which seemed always to smile. She was a dancer in a London revue, but because she was recovering from a bout of influenza she was out of the chorus line for several days. I for one adored her. She was cockney-bright and witty, with a fund of stories about the theatre and the stage-door johnnies who hung about nightly waiting for women to leave the theatre. She would dance for us in the old schoolroom to records played on Isobel's gramophone, kicking her incredibly long legs high above her head, smiling her bright showgirl's smile. She taught us how to shimmy and dance the modern dances which were sweeping London. I was indignant when Isobel said, 'She's not Carradice wife material. I suppose Roger knows he won't be allowed to marry her.'

'Why shouldn't he marry her if he loves her?'

'I'm surprised at you asking such a question. If he did marry her, it would be your mother and father all over again. Look what happened to them.'

Even Teddy responded to her warmth and her laughter, permitting her to tease him out of his awkwardness as she struggled with his efforts to master ballroom dancing. She was fascinated by the sea, confiding in me that she had only seen it once before and that was on a half-day visit to Margate with her grandmother when she was a child. She was like a little girl leaping and dancing out of the path of the incoming tide, hunting for shells along the shore, fascinated by the seabirds, and I thought how different her life had been from Isobel's, yet they were exactly the same age.

She exclaimed delightedly over Isobel's wardrobe and there was no envy, only honest admiration. In no time at all she could mimic my grandmother, making us laugh uproariously as she strutted stiff-backed across the room, imitating my grandmother's haughty expression and her cold clipped manner of speaking. I could see that Roger adored her, but when I said as much to Isobel she said, 'Oh, Roger's adored lots of girls. He's never been serious about any of them. I can't think Polly's any different.'

That saddened me, I would have loved Polly to be part of the family. Like a clean fresh wind, she would have swept the cobwebs away.

On the day before New Year's Eve, we accompanied Roger and Polly to the station. He looked tall and handsome in his subaltern's uniform, his cap set at a jaunty angle, his face filled with laughter, while Polly hung onto his arm with a proprietary air. We stood on the station platform waving madly until the train entered the long tunnel through the fell, but we were strangely silent on our walk back to the house along the narrow country lane. The sea in the distance was dark and still, and snow was falling, light and powdery like fine dust. The hedgerows were white with frost and it was so cold that we had to stamp our feet and beat our arms against our sides to keep warm. The house on the cliff loomed darkly as we climbed up to it through the gardens. The curtains had been drawn against the fading light and for the rest of the journey we were silent. It was a sad, empty silence and, unable to rid myself of a feeling of acute misery, I had to brush the tears from my eyes.

I had the strangest premonition that something terrible was going to happen, but angrily I told myself that I was becoming fanciful, that it was the December gloom and nothing more. Once we were inside the house, the feeling passed with the cheerful warmth of the log fire in the hall and the dancing flames of the candles on the tree.

That night we sat on Isobel's bed and talked in whispers until long after the rest of the family were in bed. Poor Isobel – she felt her frustrations more than any of us and I understood her chagrin. That expensive school in Switzerland had promised her so much in the way of balls and theatres, escorted by an endless retinue of dashing young men in glamorous uniforms, and now here we all were isolated as nuns in this great stone house on its windy headland.

The butler's prophecy that the war would be over by Christmas had proved to be a forlorn one, and none of us took much notice of his forecasts until, in May 1915, the Lusitania was torpedoed and he proclaimed adamantly that at last America must come into the war on our side. This was a popular belief in spite of the misery the loss of that gallant ship caused, and suddenly we were happy and full of hope, willing that bright young nation across the Atlantic to join us.

The birthday presents beside my breakfast plate that year were indicative of the times. Warm woollen gloves and stockings, home-made gifts all – because there was little to buy in the shops and even food was becoming a problem. My grandmother's gift was a pair of stout shoes for the days we had to walk down to the village to attend the sewing circle, and even Ruthie's parents sent nothing more imaginative than a thick woollen hat and scarf adorned with giant pom-poms.

There was one package bearing a field regiment stamp and I was quite sure this must have come from Roger. I was wrong, and the sight of Adrian's familiar handwriting, caused my fingers to tremble so that I could hardly unwrap the package. There was silence around the breakfast table and all eyes were upon me as I took out a leather-bound volume of Rupert Brooke's poetry, which I passed round the table, quietly stuffing Adrian's letter into the pocket of my dress to be read later.

'Poetry!' Isobel said. 'I hope he doesn't send me poetry.'

'I'm surprised he's sent me anything at all; there's probably nothing much to buy.'

'They've surely not run out of perfume.'

'Oh, Isobel,' I snapped, 'you're so ridiculous sometimes. How will he be able to get perfume? He's probably miles from any shop.'

'They get leave. Anyway, I just hope he doesn't send *me* poetry, that's all.'

It was late in the afternoon when I could finally escape on my own, and I ran as fast as my legs would carry me through the gardens towards the edge of the cliff. It was a cool day, unlike the time I had stood with Adrian on the sands with the sun warm and golden on our bare heads. Today a chill wind came sweeping in from the sea and there were storm clouds above and white horses on the grey sea.

His letter read:

My dear Jacintha,

I am sorry. I have not been able to find you anything more exciting but there is nothing here for a young girl embarking upon womanhood. I thought you might like to have this book of poems by Rupert Brooke; it is my own, and so many of the poems match our mood at this time.

For my own part, I think the inactivity is the hardest thing to bear, and I find myself wishing I was with the infantry divisions at the front instead of this interminable waiting behind the lines. The desolation is indescribable, but it is the awful silence after the sound of gunfire which I shall remember most if I am spared.

I have had no news of my parents for many months now. The chateau lies behind enemy lines and I can only hope and pray that they are all alive and well. I think of Ravenspoint often and long for its rugged beauty on those formidable cliffs and the glint of sunlight on the sea. Such thoughts keep me sane in the midst of such misery, and always, when I think of Ravenspoint, I think of one afternoon in particular, when I watched an English schoolgirl, carefree and happy, dancing barefoot across the sand, swinging her school satchel above her head. I fear we shall both have changed considerably, little cousin, if we are fated to meet again.

It was signed simply 'Adrian', and after I had read it I put my head down upon my hands and sobbed for all the young men who had marched so bravely into battle – for Roger, who treated the war as a light-hearted adventure, and Teddy, who felt only bitterness that he would not be called, and for all those absurdly young village boys who had swaggered down the country lane in their ill-fitting uniforms, praying that the war would not be over before they got to it. Most of all I wept for Adrian because I had hated him, and now I asked God to take it back and to keep him safe so that I could tell him that I didn't mean it.

In the distance I could see old Meg walking along the shore and hurriedly I scrambled to my feet and ran down the cliff path to meet her. She took one look at my tear-stained face and shook her head sadly.

'There'll be tears a plenty afore it's all over, lassie,' she said quietly.

'But they'll come back. won't they, Meg? They'll come back?'

She did not answer me immediately but went on gathering her driftwood; then, when she could hold no more, I took some of it from her and together we walked slowly back across the sand.

'Those two young men,' she said softly, 'they be not for Ravenspoint, neither of 'em.'

I felt suddenly cold, as though some grim spectre held me by the hand, and I looked at her with wide frightened eyes.

'Oh no, Meg, they can't both be going to die, not Adrian and Roger.'

She shook her head, suddenly confused. Then she said, 'You mustn't come any further, lassie. The tide's coming in fast; you could get caught with it.'

She took the bundle out of my arms and hurried away, stumbling in the soft sand and muttering to herself. It was the last time I was to see her. A few days later one of the villagers walking with his dog along the shore found her lying on the wet sand. She was dead.

I sat with Ruthie on the cliffs watching them take her few pathetic belongings out of the cottage, wheeling them in a wooden handcart along the beach. Another villager took her livestock: the few scrawny chickens, the goat and her dog.

'I would have liked her dog,' I confided to Ruthie. 'He was a nice little dog and he knew me.'

'My grandmother would never have allowed you to keep him. He was only a mongrel,' Ruthie said, and I was glad then that the villager had taken him.

Reading the daily newspapers now was torture – headlines and photographs of 'More of our Stricken Brave' splashed all over the front page, while inside page followed page listing those killed or missing in action. We were fed on Rupert Brooke and Lawrence Binyon and the aggressive patriotism of Rudyard Kipling filled us with pride.

My grandmother came to Ravenspoint on fleeting visits but always at the wrong moment. On one occasion she arrived shortly before midnight and found Isobel, Lavinia and me out on the cliffs in our night attire looking out to sea where flashes of gunfire could plainly be seen.

We were lined up in front of her chair in the sitting room where she admonished us, firstly for being improperly dressed and secondly for being out of the house at such a late hour.

Isobel tried to argue with her. 'But grandmother,' she said, 'there's something out at sea, gunfire, or a ship going down. We couldn't sleep through that. Listen, you can hear the noise from here.'

'You can do nothing to help those poor unfortunates by making exhibitions of yourselves and it will all be fully reported in the press, I have no doubt. Now return to your rooms. I want no more disturbance tonight.'

'It isn't fair,' Isobel stormed as we marched upstairs. 'Girls younger than ourselves are working in hospitals or driving ambulances. If I stay here much longer, I shall die of boredom.'

In the bedroom I shared with Ruthie I found her staring out to sea.

'You can see just as well from here,' she said quietly.

'I suppose you can. It's just that being outside made us feel we were part of it. I suppose you know grandmother's back.'

'Yes, I saw the car. I'm glad I wasn't with you.'

I looked at her sharply. For the first time I began to have thoughts about Ruthie which were not altogether charitable, and long after her quiet, even breathing from the next bed told me she was sound asleep I continued to watch the play of light on the ceiling of the room with my thoughts confused and miserably vexed.

Several days later we read that a merchant ship had been sunk only miles off the coast of Ireland and the gunfire we had seen from the cliff top had been from the warships guarding the convoy.

In September I went with Lavinia to the little churchyard with flowers for the Carradice tomb and the harvest festival. A woman was leaving the church. She wore a heavy black shawl over her head and the tears were running down her cheeks. We both stared at her, although we were becoming accustomed to displays of grief in that tiny community. The vicar walked with her to the gate, his arm around her shoulders, and a little girl ran from where she had been sitting on a tombstone to take hold of her hand. When the vicar returned along the path he was shaking his head sadly and, seeing us standing there, he said, 'Poor Mrs Rushton heard this morning that her husband has been killed.'

I knew Bill Rushton well; he had worked on the milk float for Farmer Singleton and had been a familiar figure throughout my childhood, trundling his float pulled by fat patient Daisy up the country lane. Many times he had lifted us up and sat us on Daisy's broad shining back; now he was dead and I would never hear his deep musical baritone singing along the lane again.

That was not the only tragedy we heard of that morning. Soon after lunch, one of the village women came to tell my grandmother that her son had lost an arm and was coming home soon because for him the war would be over. He had been one of our gardeners in the days before the war, and she had come to ask if there would still be a job for him at Ravenspoint. I remember my grandmother saying that, if he could work competently with one arm, then there would be work for him, but I couldn't help wondering if there had ever been a time when she could say the gracious and kind thing without her voice sounding so cold and uncompromising.

Almost every night now we trudged down to the village hall, where pound after pound of thick khaki wool was knitted into gloves and socks, pullovers and balaclava helmets, and we rolled bandages until our fingers ached and packed mountains of Red Cross boxes with cakes and biscuits as well as the garments we had made. I pitied the poor soldiers who would be expected to wear our offerings, since none of us was adept with the knitting needles and I had no idea how to pick up dropped stitches.

The walk home from these proceedings usually found us listening to Isobel's tirades on what she called useless, pathetic activities which could quite easily have been undertaken by people who were three times our ages. Ruthie and I took little part in these arguments and Lavinia stomped along beside us, her brow furrowed as though she were obsessed with other matters.

We later found that Isobel was enclosing notes in the garments she packed and very soon letters came in answer to these notes. We read them avidly; then we pinned them on the wall in the hall until my grandmother saw them on one of her visits and accused us of spoiling the woodwork. After that, Isobel grew bored with the practice.

4

After the battle of Verdun early in 1916 the authorities urged
my grandmother to make a contribution to the war effort by
turning Ravenspoint into office accommodation for one of the
ministries or a nursing home for wounded soldiers. She
decided upon the latter. She wanted no indolent civil servants
wandering the corridors of Ravenspoint carrying cups of tea,
she said, and very soon the Red Cross moved in to convert the
rooms into some semblance of a nursing home.

The library and the large drawing room were left untouched
but the main bedrooms were turned into dormitories for the
use of three or four men. For those unable to get up the stairs,
several of the downstairs rooms were also made to serve as
bedrooms.

Extra staff were brought in from the village to act as ward-
maids, to wait on table and do the laundry, while professional
nursing staff arrived to care for the wounded. We were told we
should make ourselves useful by reading to the men who
could not see, running errands for those who could not walk,
and writing letters for those who were unable to use their
hands. We should not, my grandmother said, forget that we
were family, as opposed to the paid staff, and under no circumstances were we to countenance any familiarity from the
officers.

We stood at the first-landing window above the main door
watching the fleet of ambulances arrive. Some of the men
walked into the house on crutches assisted by nurses, others
were carried in on stretchers. A handful of them wore
bandages round their eyes and these I thought were the most
pitiful of all.

'It's going to be horrible,' Isobel complained bitterly. 'The
war looks as though it's going on for ever. We shall never have
any fun again, and certainly not with this lot.'

'How selfish you are,' I retorted angrily. 'They've been

wounded defending England and us, we should be glad to care for them. Besides, any one of them could be Roger or Adrian.'

'I thought you didn't like Adrian,' she snapped back.

'That has nothing to do with it. I don't want him to get injured – he is, after all, my cousin.'

'They'll not always be wounded,' Lavinia said. 'They'll get better. Besides, one or two of them are good-looking; it could be fun.'

'How can it be fun when they've lost arms or legs?' Isobel wailed. 'I don't want to stay buried in this mausoleum. I want to dance and have fun before I'm old and ugly. Nothing, absolutely nothing, has happened to me since I left Switzerland.'

I never argued with Isobel. She was spoiled and wilful and accustomed to having her own way. Arguing with her took too much energy and she always had the last word. I disagreed with her in silence, though there were times when I longed to tell her to shut up and stop being ridiculous.

Somehow it wasn't my sea or my shore any more. There were strange young men sitting under the trees in the garden, gazing hungrily out to sea as though they were hoping to see the scarred and desolate battlefields from the safety of the cliff top. We soon found ourselves writing letters to mothers and wives and sweethearts, changing library books, reading aloud and making ourselves useful in a great many ways. I was amused to see how, in those first few months, Isobel enjoyed playing the role of ministering angel, and without exception the men adored her. She charmed them with her beauty, and the clothes which had originally been purchased for her advent into county society were now being worn to dazzle young officers. She was in her element sweeping down the shallow curved staircase in silks and chiffons, pausing to create the right effect, with one slender hand resting lightly on the balustrade and one elegant foot poised for the next step. This behaviour lasted several weeks, until she grew bored with it, and then the young men too lost interest, turning to us younger ones instead. After talking to them, I realized that Isobel had enjoyed fantasizing to them about her handsome fiancé in France, and I thought I recognized Adrian in all this, remote and darkly handsome, the hero of his regiment, counting the days until he could get leave so that he could come home to marry her.

'Why, oh why, doesn't America come into the war?' Lavinia wailed constantly. 'They'll *have* to come in the end. Why can't it be now?' Lavinia was singularly uninterested in Englishmen. She had developed a penchant for all things American and we all knew what to expect if ever they did come in on our side and some of those young men found their way to Ravenspoint. I knew that Lavinia saw it as the only escape she was ever likely to have from the clutching tentacles of the family.

In France the battle of the Somme raged mercilessly and the news was bad. We were suffering appalling casualties and many of the young officers who were well enough to rejoin their regiments left Ravenspoint only to be replaced by others returning from the front.

It was the end of July – long golden days with the sky a vault of cloudless blue and the sea clear and sparkling. I had gone back to the house to look for playing cards and stood for a long moment looking out of the drawing-room windows, which had been flung wide, letting in the sounds of summer – bird song and the steady hum of bees. A small warm breeze rustled the leaves of the giant beech trees and from somewhere on the cliffs a gull cried mournfully.

Quite suddenly, I felt cold, as though an icy hand had reached out to touch me, and I found myself trembling with fear while the hot salty tears rolled slowly down my cheeks. I felt that some terrible thing was going to happen to this household and I turned quickly and ran out of the room and down the stairs. I paused at the curve in the staircase to regain my composure but the illusion of tragedy was not done with me yet. I could see my reflection in the tall mirror over the fireplace in the hall. My face was pale and my dark eyes looked unnaturally large, as though they could not rid themselves of the vision of horror they had just seen. My imagination peopled the staircase with vague shadowy forms, while beside me more shadows, wraithlike and intangible, drifted with me down the stairs.

The sudden opening of the drawing-room door came to me like a clap of thunder, and the next moment Lavinia was beside me where I sat trembling on the bottom stair.

'Good heavens, Jacintha, what's the matter with you? You look as though you've seen a ghost'

I was shaking so much I couldn't answer her and she cried, 'Aren't you well, Jacintha? We're all waiting for you in the drawing room.'

'I'm feeling a little sick, that's all. I'll come with you now,' I managed to answer. I followed her across the hall with trembling legs and a vague sick feeling at the pit of my stomach. At the library door, however, I had the presence of mind to pinch my cheeks to restore a little of their colour, but I thought that Ruthie looked at me rather oddly as we entered the room.

Although I joined in their games, I was still shaken by my experience on the stairs, and in my imagination it gathered momentum until I believed that the house must surely be haunted, or else that I had had a premonition of some terrible happening. Ravenspoint was the sort of house which lent itself to phantoms and other unspeakable evils – but not, surely, on a warm July day when the rooms were filled with sunlight and the scent of clover. I found myself thinking about the dragon of my childhood and the tricks my imagination had played on me then, but I had come to Ravenspoint in winter, when the wind raged and shuddered against the stone walls, rattling the windows, sending the bare branches of the trees against the panes in wild unholy glee while the sea crashed and seethed amongst the rocks.

In the days that followed, my experience on the stairs was seldom out of my mind, but I did not speak of it in case I encountered Isobel's mockery.

One morning, when I had carried a tray down to the kitchen, I found cook enjoying a solitary cup of tea. I sat down opposite her and she at once pushed over a plate piled high with jam tarts, inviting me to take one.

I ate two, then asked, 'Cook, has there ever been anything odd about Ravenspoint, do you know?'

She looked up startled. 'Odd? How do you mean, odd?'

'Could it be haunted, perhaps?'

'Haunted! Good gracious, who's going to haunt it? I never heard anything so silly, and you're not to go frightening Miss Ruthie with such talk. She's always been a nervous one.'

Her plump homely face was wary and for some quite unaccountable reason I felt my question had unnerved her in spite of her staunch denials. Deliberately I selected another jam tart, which I ate slowly and indifferently. I watched her expression alter from wariness to inquisitiveness.

'What makes you say the house is haunted, then? Old houses are full of creaks and rattles.'

I shrugged my shoulders with complete unconcern. After a few minutes, when I knew she was longing to shake me, I said airily, 'Oh, I only wondered.'

'What, what have you been wondering?'

'It's nothing, cook. After all, if the house isn't haunted, it's bound to be nothing, isn't it?'

I forced myself to rise unruffled to my feet and, with a small swift smile in her direction, I sauntered slowly to the door.

'Miss Jacintha,' she called after me sharply, 'you come right back here and tell me what you've been up to. If there's things going on here that I don't know about, I want you to tell me.'

'But you said the house wasn't haunted.'

'No more it is. Have you been talking to Lucy?'

'Lucy! What has Lucy to do with it?'

'The girl's got a loose tongue in her head. She's been told much and more to keep her opinions to herself. Here, drink this milk and tell me what all this is about.'

'But cook, it's nothing, honestly.'

I was on my guard. Obviously cook was not sensitive to atmosphere, but Lucy was and in those few short minutes I determined to say little to cook but to get hold of Lucy as soon as possible.

Cook probed and I prevaricated. She was crafty but I was more intelligent and she was obviously on the defensive. Cook was a local woman; Ravenspoint had been her life and she was intensely loyal to the house and its family. If she knew of anything sinister, I was not to be told, although she was quite determined to find out what I knew.

'Now then, young missy,' she began, 'I want the truth. Are you up to something to frighten Miss Ruthie? Up to now, it's always been Miss Isobel frightening the younger ones with a lot of her nonsense.'

'It's nothing, cook. I was only teasing.'

'But you saw something you shouldn't have seen.'

'A shadow on the stair, nothing more. It was probably my

imagination anyway.'

'What sort of shadow?'

'I've told you, it was nothing.'

'When was this?'

'A few days ago.'

'Did anybody else see it? Who was with you?'

'Really, cook, if this house isn't haunted, why are you asking me all these questions?'

'Because, if I thought it was that Lucy trying to frighten you, she'd get the length of my tongue.'

'Lucy hasn't said a word, honestly. Thanks for the milk and the tarts, cook – they were delicious.'

I ran out of the kitchen and up the stairs. Somewhere in the rooms above, Lucy would be dusting or polishing and I had to find her before she saw cook. That woman would put the fear of death into her if she saw her talking to me, and in spite of cook's urgent denials I had not missed the apprehension in her sharp eyes. I found Lucy on the top landing outside the linen cupboard, and swiftly I pulled her inside, closing the door firmly behind us.

'Lucy, I've got to talk to you,' I hissed, 'and please, please be honest with me.'

'What about? I'm supposed to be finished up here by twelve o'clock. If I'm not, the housekeeper'll be after me.'

I told Lucy of my experience on that warm sunlit afternoon and as I talked I saw her face become pinched and pale and she was trembling.

'Oh, Miss Jacintha, don't ask me to tell you anything. I got drawn over the coals by the housekeeper and later by the mistress herself. I don't ever want to talk about it.'

'But we must talk about it, Lucy. Honestly, whatever you tell me won't be repeated to a living soul, but I have to know for my own peace of mind, otherwise I shall surely think there is something wrong with me.'

'The housekeeper called me a wicked foolish girl. She said I was trying to frighten people and that she's been here nigh on thirty years and seen nothing unusual.'

'Lucy, I don't know what I saw. It was a feeling more than anything, a shadowy thing without substance, but I felt so cold, as though someone or something watched me on the stairs, and I felt so unutterably sad because something dreadful was going to happen.'

'But nothing's happened, Miss Jacintha. P'raps, like me, you imagined it.'

'Lucy, did you ever know of any person who has had some strange experience in this house?'

'Well, there was Mrs Ramsden, the wife of one of the gardeners. She used to come up every Tuesday to do the silver. She won't set foot in the house now, winter or summer.'

'What happened to Mrs Ramsden then?'

'It was just before the old master died, your grandfather. He was poorly at the time and the doctor was coming every day, so there was extra work in the house. She'd been upstairs to collect the tray from outside his room and she said it was the shadows on the stairs. She thought something on the stairs was watching her and she felt cold and her heart was thumping fit to burst. She dropped the tray on the stairs and ran screaming into the kitchen.'

I nodded, 'And you, Lucy, what did you see?'

Still reluctant, she shook her head miserably and I took hold of her arm urging her to tell me.

'I don't know, miss – only, like Mrs Ramsden, I was cold and shivering, and it was like somebody watching me and I felt like crying. Next thing I was in the kitchen screaming my head off and the mistress said I was a stupid hysterical girl and the housekeeper poured some cold water over my head to bring me to my senses.'

'And did somebody die after that, Lucy, and after Mrs Ramsden's experience?'

'Well, your grandfather died about a week after Mrs Ramsden left, and, soon after I 'ad my experience your father, Mr Allan, died.'

'Oh, Lucy, it's a warning, I *knew* it. Something terrible is going to happen again and Roger and Adrian are at the front.'

'Don't say that, miss, and don't ever tell a soul we've talked about it. Your grandfather was an old man when he died and poor Mr Allan had consumption. It was something we imagined. Some people are like that – they see things that aren't there. Nothing is going to happen to Mr Roger or Mr Adrian.'

Although her words carried conviction, her voice did not and neither of us believed what she said.

In the days that followed I seemed to be living in limbo, waiting for I knew not what. When there was laughter in the house it seemed like a mockery and I felt it should not have been there; when we had to leave the house to go down to the village, I was afraid to go back in case the blow had fallen during our absence. Either way there was no escape. Whenever I saw Lucy, she scuttled away like a frightened rabbit and I could only suppose cook had lectured her against talking to me. It was like living with the sword of doom suspended above our heads.

The old schoolroom was still our special domain and in this room we usually ate supper. It was a warm summer night and the windows were wide open, letting in the smell of damp earth and the scent of pine trees after a gentle rain. It was dusk but still we sat round the large schoolroom table, now resplendent under its red plush table cover; we had not bothered to light the lamps or draw the heavy curtains.

We all heard the sound of wheels on the gravel along the drive and wondered who could be arriving so late in the evening, when the lights in the dormitories of those seriously hurt had long since been put out and even the common rooms had few occupants.

'Perhaps it's another ambulance,' Lavinia volunteered.

'It can't possibly be,' said Isobel. 'We're already bursting at the seams; there's just not enough room for another wounded officer.'

'If they want us to make room for one, they'll manage it somehow,' Lavinia answered her.

Isobel jumped to her feet and ran over to the window followed by the rest of us.

'It's not an ambulance,' Ruthie said. 'It's not big enough.'

'Move over, Lavinia,' Isobel said. 'It's a private car. Hang onto my dress while I lean out of the window.'

Her face was pale in the moonlight which filtered into the room fitfully and her voice trembled slightly. 'It's my father's car. I wonder what he's doing here so late in the day.'

I knew. I knew as surely as if I had travelled in that car with him along the quiet roads which edged the lake with the moonlight gleaming in the water and only the lonely sighing of the night wind for company.

We drew the curtains and lit the gas lamps, then we sat in silence round the big table, not speaking, ignoring the plates of biscuits and coffee, afraid to look into each other's eyes in case we should see something we dared not believe.

It was Mrs Parry who came for Isobel. Her face was red and swollen as though she had been weeping and Isobel went with her quietly, her eyes anxious and shadowed with fear.

We sat on round the schoolroom table not speaking, the steady ticking of the clock sounding unnaturally loud in the silence of the room. I couldn't tell how long we remained there, but suddenly Lavinia jumped to her feet, sending her chair crashing backwards against the floor so that Ruthie and I looked at her in shocked surprise.

'I don't care, I'm just not sitting here wondering,' she said heatedly. 'I'm going downstairs to find out what's going on, even if I have to listen outside the sitting room door.'

'You can't do that, Lavinia,' Ruthie cried sharply. 'You know what my grandmother is like about people who listen at doors.'

'I don't care. Besides, how do we know she's here? Perhaps it's only Uncle Robert who's come down.'

She opened the door quietly and bent her head to listen for any sound from down below. All we could hear was a jumble of voices and Lavinia said, 'I'm going down. It can only be Roger or Adrian – probably Roger or they wouldn't have sent for Isobel.'

'They would if Adrian was going to marry her?' I objected.

'Oh, for God's sake, Jacintha, don't be so romantic. Adrian was never to marry Isobel; it was just something she dreamed up. I'm sure he never gave her any encouragement. You should know by now that she lets her imagination run away with her.'

After she had gone Ruthie and I sat in silence again, but it was an uneasy silence fraught with foreboding of tragedy, and I was shocked to see Ruthie's slim white fingers tearing to pieces the delicate lawn handkerchief she held in her hands. Her gentle porcelain face was pale and, when she looked up to find me watching her, she jumped swiftly to her feet and ran across to the window.

'I hate this house,' she wailed passionately, and the tears

65

streamed down her face as she crouched on the cold schoolroom floor with her head buried in the heavy folds of the
curtains.

Helplessly I knelt beside her, endeavouring to comfort her,
but she would have none of me, and all the time her voice
moaned monotonously, 'I hate this house, I hate it.'

I went back to sit at the table alone. Somehow it seemed an
affront to me that Ruthie should hate Ravenspoint when I
loved it so. I had no illusions about my role within the family.
I was the poor relation, dependent upon my grandmother's
charity for every mouthful of food and every article of clothing. One day Ravenspoint would belong to Adrian – which
perhaps was just as well since the others detested it – but what
would become of me? With a cynicism beyond my years, I
wondered if Adrian might tolerate my presence as a companion for his future wife, or perhaps even as some kind of old
retainer if there was no alternative.

My thoughts were interrupted by the arrival of Lavinia,
who let herself into the room quickly, closing the door behind
her with the barest suspicion of a click. Ruthie came back to
the table and Lavinia sat down opposite us. Her face was pale
and she was breathless with running, but she was also trium-
phantly excited that she had news to impart.

'Grandmother's here,' she said. 'She's doing most of the
talking and I could hear Aunt Celia wailing in there as well as
the others.'

'Others! What others?' we wanted to know.

'Isobel, of course, and Uncle Robert, and there's somebody
else in there. I was trying to see who it was through the
keyhole but Mrs Parry came up from the kitchen with a tray
and I had to hide in the shadows until she went away. I'm sure
it was Polly's voice I heard.'

'*Polly!*' Ruthie and I said simultaneously.

'Why not Polly? She came here with Roger, didn't she, and
I'm pretty sure all this has to do with Roger. Polly wouldn't be
here if it was Adrian.'

'What did you hear?' we both asked together.

'Ssssh,' Lavinia whispered, 'there's somebody coming.'

It was Isobel, but a distraught and sorrowful Isobel, who
came to sit at the table with us. Her face was pale and streaked
with tears and before she could speak to us she put her head

down on the table and sobbed while we looked on helplessly.

She told us, in between sobs and longer bouts of weeping, that Roger had been killed in action, but it was Polly who had brought them the news because Polly was Roger's wife. They had been married on his last short leave and Polly was expecting his child.

We sat in stunned silence at this piece of news. I too felt the hot tears pricking my eyes when I thought of Roger with his happy laughing face and his silver-fair hair glinting in the sunlight. He had been like a piece of quicksilver, making us all laugh with his outrageous humour. Now I could not bear to think of him cold and still in death.

Polly was now in the same position my mother had been in, an unwanted Carradice bride, and her child would be, as I was, my grandmother's duty. I wondered how Polly would react to my grandmother's animosity, which I was quite certain she would encounter. This was another age – I had no doubt that Polly would fight my grandmother with weapons my own mother might never have heard of.

The house was plunged into mourning; we wore black armbands round our arms and black clothes if we had any, while my grandmother put on an expression of resigned sorrow which, I thought, did not exactly correspond with the feelings she had had for Roger when he was alive.

On Sunday we attended the morning service in the little village church, a tightly knit band of family in shades of mourning, but we were not alone. The battle of the Somme had taken its toll from the life of that little lakeland village, and many of those young men I had seen marching down the country lane on their way to war would not be coming back. They had been country boys, more used to handling the plough than the weapons of war, and each week more and more of the congregation were attired in blackest mourning.

Whenever I met Lucy on the stairs or in the rooms, she went about her work quickly, avoiding my eyes, refusing to accept that the thing we had talked about had any bearing on Roger's death.

Polly stayed only two nights and I did not see her after church on Sunday. She left in a taxi she had ordered, with a loud slamming of several doors, and we stood huddled together on the first landing overlooking the hall listening to her final words, which were flung back into the hall for all who cared to hear. She said she wanted none of the Carradice money any more than she wanted to be part of the Carradice family. She would have her baby and bring it up in her way, and to hell with the lot of us.

Why couldn't my mother have said that, I wondered sadly. I wouldn't ever have minded being poor – I was poor now. So great was my bitterness that I took to going off on my own across the dunes, sitting for hours morosely looking out to sea.

Roger's death affected Isobel strangely. At times she would be unnaturally gay, then she would suddenly burst into tears. Her gaiety was brittle and feverish, so that when it snapped the tears would flow.

'I can't stand it, Jacintha,' she said one morning, pacing about the schoolroom floor like a young tigress. 'It's going to get worse and I can't stand to look at these boys with their blood-soaked bandages and missing limbs. I can't even stand their courage when it's so false.'

'How do you mean, false?'

'Because it is. How can anybody laugh and joke and talk about the good times when the war is over, when they know they can't grow another arm or leg or might never be able to see again? Fancy not being able to see the sea or the sun or be able to dance with a girl in your arms.'

'Perhaps men are braver than us. Perhaps if they didn't laugh and joke about it, they'd want to die.'

'The woman's a fool who marries a man who goes to war. Who wants to make all those high-sounding vows about a tomorrow that might never come?'

'Then you wouldn't marry Adrian, even if he came back from the war to marry you?'

She looked at me sharply and tossed her dark head. 'Oh, that,' she said. 'That was only something grandmother once said when we were children. She said we looked well to-gether, both so dark and different from the others. I don't suppose she ever meant it seriously. After all, we *are* first cousins – and Adrian would take too much living up to for my liking.'

'How do you mean, living up to?'

'Oh, you know. He would hate to marry a frivolous woman,

somebody like me who doesn't think too deeply and needs entertaining all the time. You're far more suitable for Adrian than I am, but don't go getting ideas about him – he's far too practical to marry his cousin. Where do I even begin to look for a husband while this wretched war continues?'

'Why not stop looking and wait for somebody handsome and nice to come along?'

'I don't care whether he's handsome or not, I don't even care about him being nice as long as he's rich. I want him to have so much money he won't want any of mine; that way, I can tell my grandmother that she can keep her stupid Ravenspoint and her lame ducks.'

Both Isobel and Lavinia were outspoken about their needs and desires; it was only Ruthie who left me wondering. She listened to the other two quietly or read during their tirades, but I had not forgotten her impassioned cries on the night we learned of Roger's death and somehow, because she had given so much away, she became distant with me and all our old camaraderie seemed to have gone. I had believed that the friendship I had shared with Ruthie would go on for ever. Now I was realizing painfully that nothing lasted for ever and more and more I sought my own company.

5

It was September 1916 and on the distant slopes of the lakeland hills the heather bloomed red and purple and the hedgerows glowed with a riot of scarlet berries. Wild geese flew inland in search of their winter nesting grounds and between the sombre forests of firs and spruce the bracken turned brittle and golden.

The last contingent of those leaving Ravenspoint had gone in a flurry of farewells and now we stood at the window of the first landing overlooking the drive, waiting for the replacements to arrive.

'It gets worse,' Isobel complained, frowning at the stretchers being carried into the house. Then came the ambulances bringing the men who were able to walk with the help of sticks and crutches. As they passed into the house beneath us, a young officer looked up and, with the meeting of our eyes, the warm blood flooded my face and he smiled. He walked with the aid of a stick and he wore one arm in a sling. He was tall and slender and the late afternoon sunlight fell upon his hair burnishing and gilding it. He was good-looking, with an English boyishness that I found absurdly appealing, so that I suddenly became impatient with my racing heart, and troubled that a pair of blue eyes looking into mine for the first time should be the cause of it.

'Why are you blushing, Jacintha?' Isobel taunted gaily, missing nothing as usual.

'I'm not blushing,' I denied in confusion.

'Oh yes, you are,' Lavinia said. 'I know which one it is. It's the tall blond one with the stick and his arm in a sling.'

'Why don't you both mind your own business?' I ran away from them, followed by their laughter.

From that afternoon, I found myself looking for excuses to enter the drawing room when I knew the men were resting after luncheon. I walked through the gardens when they took their exercise, and overnight became a more eager runner of errands, a more willing changer of library books. I saw the blond officer and I resented the blushes that came so readily into my cheeks whenever our eyes met, but if he was absent from the room I felt desolate and somehow bereft.

'I've found out who your young lieutenant is,' Isobel said to me one morning when we met halfway up the stairs. 'He's called Martin Vasey. His family are in cotton but they're not nearly so well off these days as they used to be. Besides, he's the youngest son, so you can't expect him to be a good catch.'

'She means he won't have any money,' elaborated Lavinia from just below.

'Well, I only know what my father says,' said Isobel, pleased to be able to be so knowledgeable. 'The cotton mills in Lancashire are holding their own now because there's a war on, but the outlook is grim. We can't grow cotton in this country and soon the cotton producers in the far east will beat us at our own game, at a fraction of the cost, too.'

I listened as Isobel and Lavinia argued the respective merits of wool and cotton, and I suddenly realized how little I knew about Carradice cloth and the workings of those five gigantic mills in the industrial part of Yorkshire. I knew even less about cotton – but I did know I hated the tall mill chimneys which covered the towns of the north with a permanent pall of smoke. To me, they were stark and ugly monoliths on horizons which had once been beautiful.

'Why should cotton be expected to fail after the war, when you are so sure that wool will not?'

'I've told you,' Isobel snapped, 'because we've got sheep, whereas the cotton-growing countries will produce the material for themselves. It doesn't do to be so clever and teach them everything we know.'

I walked thoughtfully down the stairs. From the landing above, Isobel called, 'I shouldn't get too fond of that particular young man, Jacintha. There'll be better fish in the sea.'

'I'm not interested in money,' I retorted indignantly.

'You should be; you have none of your own,' was her parting thrust.

Such conversations only served to remind me more forcibly how dependent I was on my grandmother. I certainly wasn't what one might call a good catch for any young man who expected to do very well for himself and, as my grandmother had constantly asserted in my presence, in the world of north-country manufacturers, money married money.

The morning after this conversation with Isobel, I found Martin Vasey standing at the gate leading out into the road. He was leaning heavily on his stick and trying to open the gate with the other hand and the letters he was carrying fell and scattered on the ground. I hurried forward to pick them up while he watched helplessly, his face flushed with embarrassment.

'I missed the postman this morning because the doctor came in to look at my leg,' he explained. 'I was trying to take them to the box along the road.'

'But the box is almost in the village. It's quite a long way.'

'Perhaps I should wait then. There's nothing urgent except for the letter to my mother.'

'I'll take them for you gladly. You really shouldn't try to walk so far.'

'I don't want to trouble you.'

'Oh, please, you're not troubling me, I'd like to take them. I have nothing else to do.'

'I've seen you about the house, haven't I, but you're not a nurse?'

'No, but we help whenever we can – posting letters, changing library books, things like that. It's all we're qualified for.'

'We?'

'My cousins and I.'

'I say, you're family, aren't you? You really must forgive me, I thought you worked here.'

'Well, I suppose I do in a way. My name is Jacintha Carradice, the others are Isobel, Lavinia and Ruthie.'

'Which is which?'

'Isobel is the tall, dark, beautiful one. Lavinia and Ruthie are fair. Ruthie is the smaller one of the two.'

'The shy one who hides round corners and runs whenever we look at her?'

'Does she? I didn't know.'

'Would you mind if I walked down the road with you for a little way? My name is Martin Vasey.'

'As long as you feel up to it. Isn't your leg paining you?'

'It's not too bad, but I don't want it to get stiff. It's better for me to get some exercise.'

We walked slowly along the country road talking happily together, and it was only when I saw his face becoming pale and pinched that I realized his leg was beginning to trouble him.

'I think you should go back now, don't you? You've come far enough.'

'Is it far to the postbox?'

'Yes, I'm afraid it is, and I have to go on to the vicarage. You wouldn't be able to walk that far. Shall I come back with you?'

'No. I was going to suggest sitting by the roadside until you returned, but that would only make you rush your errand. I'm quite able to go back alone if I take my time. Perhaps we could do this again one day?'

'Yes, why not?' I said, and for some quite unaccountable reason I felt my heart lifting with joy. From the first moment I had watched his shining blond head disappear beneath the window I had been attracted by him; now we were friends and, like me, he wished that friendship to continue. When I returned from my errand later that morning I purposely did not mention our meeting to either Isobel or Lavinia, and for the first time I was secretive with Ruthie though I could not have said why.

After that day, we met often in the gardens and on the road, and we always walked together as though we had met by chance. I knew it wasn't always by chance on my part, and because we saw each other more and more I could not think it was by chance on his part either. Inevitably Isobel noticed and made fun of our friendship. It amused her to taunt me and I wished her taunts didn't make me so angry. After one of my encounters with her, I set off across the dunes, walking swiftly, talking heatedly to the gulls and the sea as I should have talked to Isobel. Meg's cottage was derelict now; the outer walls were standing but the wall which marked the end of her little garden had been swept away in the spring tides. I felt suddenly sad, wondering what Meg had been like when she was young, if she had ever been pretty and if some man had loved her.

As I retraced my steps across the sand, I saw Martin walking towards me, limping from the shrapnel wound in his leg, and I wondered what pain it had cost him to climb down the steep cliff path to the beach. He paused, smiling a little as he waited for me to reach him.

We sat on the rocks and it seemed we talked about all the things under the sun. He told me about his home on the outskirts of an industrial Lancashire town where he was the youngest of three brothers and one sister, and I pictured his boyhood in that large stone house surrounded by other children, and dogs and horses.

'You never talk much about your family,' he said.

'Well, I suppose the Carradices are my family, but I'm not like the others; I have never felt that I really belong.'

'But they're your cousins, aren't they?'

'Yes, but they have parents still alive, whereas my father is dead and I don't know where my mother is.'

He took my hand in his, squeezing my fingers gently. 'I'm sorry, love, I didn't realize there was some sort of tragedy. Were your parents separated?'

I told him the whole sorry story and he listened without interrupting until I had finished, then he put his arm round my shoulders and drew me against him.

'Try not to mind so much, my dear. I expect that, at the time, your grandmother thought she was doing her best for you. You would be a lot happier if you could come to terms with it.'

'I never shall, Martin, and don't think I haven't tried. It grieves me to see my cousins all together as normal families should be, when my own mother isn't here. My grandmother gave me a home. She feeds me and clothes me but she has never given me love and she never will.'

'She may regard what she has given you as a substitute for love; perhaps she is not a very loving person.'

'Oh, I can vouch for that, but it would have been better if she had never bothered about me at all, because one day I shall have to move on and, unlike the others, I may have nowhere to go.'

'Why must you move on?'

'Because Ravenspoint will belong to Adrian. One day when the war is over Adrian will come back to claim what belongs to him. My cousins have said that when my grandmother dies he will get the lion's share and I can't think there will be anything in it for me.'

'But you don't know that, Jacintha.'

74

'I don't know for certain, but I'm pretty sure they're right. Besides, sometimes I've seen Adrian looking at me as though he feels sorry for me, although one can never really tell with Adrian, he can be so maddening.'

'How do you mean, maddening?'

'Well, sometimes he's amused by me; at other times he's merely puzzled. He probably wonders what on earth he is going to do with me when the time comes.'

Martin told me he adored his mother and they were very close, but he was not his father's favourite. His father, he said, was a hard-playing, hard-drinking man who appreciated neither books nor music. He wanted all his sons to take after him and had little time for his youngest son, whom he considered to be an ineffectual dreamer because he liked Brahms and Mozart and preferred the company of intellectuals rather than the hunting and racing crowds his father and elder brothers mingled with. His father had been mollified somewhat when Martin volunteered for active service before he was called, but I could tell that he was not looking forward to the day when the war was over and he would return to the family business and his father's house.

For the first time in my young life, I was in love, and the confession that he loved me in return was like heavenly music in my ears. In peacetime lovers can afford to tease and quarrel, but wartime lovers must learn quickly in case the chance eludes them and their tomorrows do not come.

Martin's stay at Ravenspoint was not expected to be long, and each day I saw an improvement in the way he walked, until the limp had almost gone. He no longer wore his arm in a sling and soon we were riding along the country lanes and across the fells. Isobel was generous with Sultan when she was feeling lazy and needed me to exercise him, and Martin rode Cleo, the mare that had belonged to Roger. Suddenly it felt wonderful to be young and alive and in love, and my obscure future no longer came like a thief in the night to trouble me. Now Martin loved me, it no longer mattered that Adrian would come back to claim Ravenspoint, depriving me of a home. Martin would take me away soon and after the war together we would face both his father and the cotton industry.

There are no summers like lakeland summers, when the

trees vie with one another in colourful splendour until the autumn, when they turn to red and gold along the lanes and the maples flame magnificently along the margins of the lake. It seemed to me that year that the scenery was more splendid than usual, but I know it was because Martin was there to enjoy it with me. We were fortunate enough to find a romantically minded ally in Major Stephenson, who was the proud possessor of a small disreputable two-seater. It proved in the days that followed to be more than a car. It was a magic carpet for transporting us to all the beauty spots within reach. We had our favourite places, of course. Martin loved Ullswater, pointing out to me with pride from the slopes of Kirkstone the three reaches of the lake, whilst I in turn loved Thirlmere, dark and mysterious under the dark shadow of Helvellyn. Even when the winter came, and the countryside was silver-white where it had been glowing and golden, it could not dampen our enthusiasm. Now wildfowl covered the lakes and the wild geese flew inland in search of their winter nesting-place. The leaves of summer had gone and only the sombre evergreens threw their long dark shadows across the snow.

I became afraid, wondering how long Martin could remain at Ravenspoint. His leg was almost well again; he was able to ride with me across the fells, while in the evenings we danced together in the old schoolroom to records played on Isobel's new gramophone. Foolishly, perhaps, I wanted this time to go on for ever.

Martin became persuasive in his attempts to show me my grandmother in a softer light. 'Try to put yourself in her place, darling,' he would say. 'She is a proud, stubborn woman who had laid great plans for all her children. Surely you must see it was natural for her to be disappointed when your father failed to conform. Some grandmothers would have ignored the children of such a marriage; at least she had some thought for you. I doubt if my own grandmother would have behaved as well.'

I looked at him in surprise and he smiled his slow gentle smile. 'She was always a bit of a martinet, old grandma Vasey. I remember Aunt Netta was not welcome in the family circle for years because she had had the temerity to marry a grocer. It was only when his business expanded rather rapidly and he took over several more establishments that she capitulated and allowed her to rejoin the family circle.'

'And she came back, just like that?'

'Of course. For the grocer to have married a Vasey did his business a lot of good and Aunt Netta was sensible enough to want her share of anything my grandmother decided to leave.'

'I think that's horrible. What about your brothers? Haven't they been able to choose their wives?'

'Of course. Girls from their own circle whom they had known for most of their lives. I can't remember the family ever quarrelling with their choices.'

'You mean they married for money?'

He threw back his head and laughed. 'We never say that, darling. There's a difference between marrying for money and marrying where money is.'

'There's no difference at all. I think it's despicable. Martin, I have no money of my own; everything I have in the world comes from my grandmother and I am not a favourite with her. I have no means of knowing what will happen to me when she is dead. I want you to be quite clear about that.'

'Then, my darling, shouldn't you try just a little harder to show her that you are grateful for what she has done for you instead of giving her nothing but resentment?'

'Wouldn't you have resented somebody who took you away from your mother and told your mother that she must never try to see you again? That is what my grandmother did to me and I can never forgive her for it.'

'But your mother allowed you to go. She obviously realized you would have a better life with your father's family. By keeping up this long-standing resentment, don't you feel that you are diminishing her sacrifice?'

'It didn't have to be like that, Martin. Why couldn't they have accepted my mother? My father loved her. She was good and beautiful. She should have been made welcome here, not ostracized as unsuitable to be part of such a family.'

Martin sighed. He was being patient with me, too patient, and because I loved him I sensed that he was finding me more than a little tiresome. He sat with his arm around my shoulders and now and again he stroked my hair. 'I don't want to talk about it any more, Martin,' I said tremulously, but then he pressed home his advantage with sweet and clever blackmail.

'Try to get along with your grandmother, darling,' he

urged. 'When we are married you will see her seldom. Isn't it worth a little effort now? After all, we shall need her consent to our marriage and it will do no good to antagonize her.'

I looked up at his young sensitive face. He was so good-looking and I loved him so desperately I would have promised him the moon. What he did not understand was that my resentment against my grandmother had been with me too long, and her cold nature did not invite my affection.

I loved him utterly – his charm and his laughter, his boyish good looks and his sensitivity. There were times when I found him staring into space thoughtfully, as though there were worries on his mind he could not share with me; then I would try to tease him into laughter but although his lips smiled his eyes did not.

'Is it the war that is worrying you?' I asked him. 'Are you afraid to go back to face those terrible trenches? Adrian once said that a man was a fool who said he was not afraid to go to war.'

'You must care for Adrian an awful lot, Jacintha. You are constantly quoting him.'

'I'm not,' I retorted hotly. 'As a matter of fact, most of the time I don't like him very much; he's so insufferably superior.'

'I'm sorry. I didn't know he was such a sore point with you.' Martin laughed, pulling me close to him. Then, in a voice from which the laughter had gone, he said. 'I'm not so much afraid of the war as the peace.'

'The peace! But you should long for peace to come; you should want to come back to me and your family and all the lovely things there will be to do when peace comes.'

'I suppose so. I just wish I wasn't such an ordinary kind of chap. I wish I was clever and could do something with my life. Honestly, darling, all I know is cotton.'

'Well, that's all right, isn't it. Cotton is what you will come back to. Those mills in Lancashire won't run away.'

He smiled, a sad remote smile, and once again I felt uneasy. There were things I did not understand and I wanted to understand. It was blissful to be in love, but I was finding out that love brought problems I had never dreamed of.

Christmas was barely two weeks away and I was hoping

against hope that Martin would not be recalled before then. My grandmother was anxious that as many of the officers as possible should go home to their families at Christmas because she expected to hold the family gathering at Ravenspoint as always – so I knew he would not be with me, but I wanted him to come back in the New Year, if only for a little while.

It was decided by mutual consent that Ravenspoint should at least have its Christmas tree to stand in the hall, so those who were fit walked up to the spruce forest behind the house to find an appropriate one. We were a cheerful and noisy crowd and Isobel was in her most enchanting mood. I tried my best to persuade Ruthie to come with us but she said she had letters to write and told me not to fuss. Reluctantly, I left her alone. Since Martin had come into my life, my friendship with Ruthie seemed to have weakened, but I felt it was as much her fault as mine – she was so uninterested in anything I needed to tell her.

'Stop worrying whether she comes or not,' Lavinia said. 'She's probably jealous anyway.'

'But why? Not of me, surely?'

'Well, you must admit he's very good-looking, and Ruthie doesn't seem to attract any of them. I can't understand why. She's quite pretty.'

I pondered this as I waited for Martin to join me in the hall. It was true what Lavinia had said. For months now, the house had been filled with young attractive men and not all of them had been helpless invalids. Ruthie had mingled with them like the rest of us, but not one of them had singled her out for special attention. She was beautiful, far more beautiful than I – or so I thought – but Martin loved me, and Isobel and Lavinia had more admirers than they knew what to do with.

I was standing looking thoughtfully into the fire when Martin joined me, slipping his arm around my waist gently.

'Penny for your thoughts, darling,' he said softly.

I looked up startled, then said, 'I was thinking about Ruthie. She's so pretty. Why is it none of you ever notices?'

'But we do.'

'Then why don't you flirt with her as you flirt with Isobel and Lavinia, or love her as you say you love me?'

He laughed, but when he saw I was serious he said,

'Perhaps being pretty isn't enough. On the surface she appears sweet and pliant – too sweet perhaps. There's just something about Ruthie a fellow can't get close to. Isobel is maddening but one can laugh with her, and Lavinia is witty and fun to argue with, but Ruthie I think would always be Ruthie for all her sweetness.'

'And what about me?' I couldn't resist asking.

'Well, what about you?' he laughed. Then he said earnestly, 'You are adorable, as lovely as Isobel, as tantalizing as Lavinia, and I love you.'

I laughed happily, welcoming his embrace, delighting in his love.

'Where are the others?' He looked round at the empty hall.

'They've gone on ahead. We'll have to hurry to catch them up. What did the doctor say about your leg?'

'That it's practically as good as new.'

'Does that mean that you will have to leave sooner than you thought?'

'I don't know, darling. Some of the men have had to go back to the front in far worse shape than I am in. Perhaps we should live one day at a time; that's what most of us are doing anyway.'

I nodded miserably. I had lived with thoughts of his return to France for a long time, but putting such thoughts into words only served to bring the time nearer.

'Cheer up, darling,' he said, laughing down at me. 'I'm not going today.'

The others were well ahead of us as we let ourselves out of the side gate, almost colliding with a woman standing on the grass verge. I thought she looked at me strangely – so strangely that I paused in a puzzled way to look back. She was standing where we had left her looking after us up the lane – an ordinary middle-aged woman in a dark woollen coat with her felt hat pulled firmly down over her hair. For a while her face nagged at me. I felt that in some way she was familiar, although she was not one of the villagers. I thought about her all the way up the hill, but when we caught up with the others and, in the midst of much raillery and good-humoured back-chat, I forgot about her.

The afternoon was gay as we searched for our tree, deciding at last upon a well-shaped spruce richly endowed with dark-green needles. The men decided that the tree should be up-rooted instead of felled, although Isobel insisted it could never be planted again. It was almost dusk before we walked back down the hillside, pulling the tree behind us. There was much good-natured banter; the chill breeze which swept across the fell brought a warm glow to our cheeks and we sang the songs the soldiers sang with happy enthusiasm.

As we took off out outdoor clothing in the hall, Mrs Parry came hurrying up from the kitchens.

'Here you are at last,' she fussed. 'Miss Jacintha, there's a woman waiting for you in my room. You'd better hurry. She's been waiting most of the afternoon and she has a train to catch at six o'clock.'

'A woman for me!' I exclaimed. 'But who is she?'

'Come quickly now. She'll explain why she's here.'

I let myself quietly into the housekeeper's room and found the woman sitting at the table. Beside her was a tray bearing the remains of a light meal. I recognized her instantly as the woman I had seen in the lane.

I smiled at her but before I could speak she said, 'I thought it was you on the road, Jacintha, but you won't remember me after all these years.'

'No, I'm afraid not, and yet your face did seem familiar.'

'It was a long time ago, luv. You were only a little girl at the time. My, but you were a bonny little thing and your mother used to dress you so prettily. Made all your clothes herself, she did.'

'You know my mother?'

'Bless you, that I did. Your father too, till he died, poor thing. You used to live round the corner from my house. Then, when your father died, your mother moved into something smaller and less expensive. I visited her even after she moved, but I don't expect you will remember.'

'Will you tell me about my mother, please? Where is she living and how is she?'

Her face softened and became sad.

'That's why I'm here, luv. She died in hospital in June, but she made me promise faithfully that I'd see you got the few things of value she had. I'd have come sooner but my husband's not been well these last few months and we've left the town and moved into the country. Today was the first chance

I had.'

It had been a great many years since I had seen my mother but suddenly my memories became very real as I thought about the lamplight shining on her golden hair and her tired face watching me with so much pain and anxiety. Now she was dead and I had not known it. It had taken this stranger to tell me of it and I hated the gay afternoon I had just spent when I could have been listening to the news about my mother. It seemed now that there were so many years and so much pain I must know about, and I became aware that the woman was speaking to me as I looked at her face through a blur of tears.

'She didn't leave any money, poor lamb,' she said. 'She had to work so hard, sewing for all those people – dressmaking, you know – and not charging enough to keep a sparrow alive. She made such lovely things, and most people took advantage of her good nature. She'd have earned more sewing in the factories but she wasn't strong enough. I always said she should have stuck to her old job teaching, but she had no references and she'd been out of it for too long.'

'What did she die of?' I asked.

'Pneumonia she had, luv. She was such a fragile little thing she didn't stand a chance. They took her into hospital and I was with her the night before she died. It was then she gave me this box.'

She reached down into the depths of her shopping bag and took out a wicker workbasket. In that brief moment I recognized it as the one in my earliest memory, standing on the plush tablecloth beside the bowl of roses.

She rose to her feet and put her arm around my shoulders.

'Open it quietly when I'm gone. It's better for you to be alone at a time like this.'

I nodded wordlessly. Then, as she stood with one hand resting on the doorknob, I said, 'Please forgive me but I don't remember your name.'

'It's Spenlove, Jacintha, Mary Spenlove. Me and my Harold are living in Grange now and I've put my address in the workbasket. I'd be ever so pleased to see you if you'd care to visit us. It's a nice little cottage, near the sea front.'

I thanked her for her invitation and promised that if I was ever in Grange, I would most certainly pay her a call. I thought that she too was crying as she left the room, but I am ashamed to say I wanted the poor woman gone so that I could wallow in my own private misery.

I didn't want to open the box in the housekeeper's room in case she returned. On the other hand, I didn't want Isobel and Lavinia crowding round. How I wished at that moment that the house wasn't full of young officers, and that somewhere in the dark vastness of Ravenspoint there was a corner I could hide in to feel my mother close to me and hold with loving fingers the things she had left me.

In the downstairs rooms was all the bustle of tables being laid for dinner and the clatter of pots and pans from the kitchen. Upstairs the house loomed dark and quiet and I guessed that officers and family alike would be congregated in their respective rooms awaiting the evening meal and that upstairs I would have the bedroom to myself.

My fingers were trembling as I undid the ribbons fastening the box. It was a pretty thing in itself, lined with rose satin, and there were padded pockets for scissors and thimble. The scissors were pretty, silver and ornate, the thimble too was silver and fitted my middle finger far better than my own. The box was not full. It contained a petit-point manicure set and a delicate gold chain and locket. I opened the locket, not knowing what to expect, and facing me was the photograph of a child I recognized instantly as myself. Opposite the photograph was a lock of bright gold hair, probably my own, and through a blur of tears I put it away to see what else I could find. There were several links of beads and a thin silver chain ending in a pearl drop. Apart from these, there only remained a square jeweller's box marked with the name of a jeweller in York.

I had thought it might be a dress ring and was totally unprepared for the splendour of the diamond which sparkled and glowed against the black velvet inside the box. It was a square-set, a single beautiful stone, and immediately I asked myself how my mother could possible have died in poverty when she had this gem in her possession.

I laid it aside, strangely afraid of its opulence as it lay winking at me in the light of the single lamp. Then I saw the envelope bearing my name. My heart was racing at a frightening pace as my fingers nervously opened it. Inside in the same writing was a single piece of pale-blue notepaper. I knew it was my mother's handwriting and her words reached out to me from the other side of the grave:

My dearest daughter,

There are so many things I want to say to you but it would take too long and you would tire of reading my letter long before the end. I just want you to know that there has never been one single day when I did not think about you with love and remembered joy. My wish is that you will find happiness and contentment in your life and experience the deep joy of two people sharing their life together when the time comes. Besides the ring which your father gave to me as a token of our engagement, I have little of value, but I want you to have these small things which have given me pleasure.

Think kindly of me in the years that lie ahead. Parting with you, my darling, was the hardest thing I ever did, but I did it loving you, believing that a life with your father's family would be a better one than any I could hope to give you.

It was signed simply, 'Your loving mother.'

I sobbed quietly in that lonely empty room, desolate and abandoned until I became aware that below my room there was the sound of voices and the opening and closing of doors. I bathed my face, rubbing it dry fiercely in an endeavour to erase the traces of tears. I thrust the letter into the pocket of my dress and pushed the workbasket onto the top shelf in my wardrobe. I wore the ring on the third finger of my right hand. Later that evening I would show it to Martin, but as I ran down the stairs into the hall it felt heavy on my finger and even in the dark it mocked me with the sparkle of hidden fires.

My hand was on the knob of the drawing-room door when the door to my grandmother's sitting room opened and the housekeeper came out.

'Has your visitor gone, Miss Jacintha?' she asked loudly, and then I heard my grandmother's voice saying, 'Jacintha, please come in here.'

I stood in front of her like a miscreant who had earned her displeasure and she kept me waiting while she pored over the household accounts which the housekeeper had obviously brought for her to see. For the first time in weeks, I was able to look at her closely and I was surprised how much she seemed to have aged. Her thin hawklike profile wore its customary severe expression and I could feel myself becoming nervous, the tension mounting inside me with each embarrassing minute. At last she gathered the accounts together in an elastic band and pushed them into the top drawer of her desk. One of them fluttered onto the carpet at her feet. I bent down to retrieve it, laying it silently on the desk in front of her, and the ring on my finger caught the lamplight and seemed to dance and glow with a life of its own.

She looked up sharply. 'May I inquire where you got that ring, Jacintha?' she asked in a cold voice.

'A lady brought it for me along with some other things.'

'What other things?'

'Things that belonged to my mother.'

'Are you telling me that your mother has made contact with you in spite of her promise to me? Who was your visitor, Jacintha?'

'Her name was Mrs Spenlove. She knew me as a child.'

'Your mother sent her here?'

'Yes.'

'How dared she? I made her promise that she would make no effort to see you or contact you again.'

'My mother is dead.'

We stared at each other and there was anger and resentment in both our faces; but, if I had looked for compassion because of my dead mother, I saw none in her cold aloof expression.

'This woman came to tell you of your mother's death? When did it happen? How long ago?'

'Several months. She died in hospital. Mrs Spenlove brought me her workbasket and the few things she wished me to have.'

'And the ring you are wearing, was that also among your mother's belongings?'

'Yes. My father gave it to her. It was her engagement ring.'

'Your father had no right to give it to her. The ring was mine.'

'Yours!' I cried incredulously, and I looked at it stupidly where it winked and glowed on my finger, too big for my slender hand and strangely obscene.

'Sit down, Jacintha,' she commanded sternly. 'I wish you to know about that ring.'

I sat down weakly in the chair opposite her. I did not want to hear about the ring. I was sure her words would destroy the last pitiful illusions I had about my parents, but I knew she would make me listen however terrible the story.

'When my children were very young I bought four rings. I chose the stones from a diamond merchant from Amsterdam in this very room, then I consulted a jeweller in York, and together your grandfather and I decided upon the settings. Diamonds were a sound investment, you understand, and we knew they would only appreciate in value for when our children became adults. When my daughter came of age I gave her a ring. The others were intended for each of my sons when they chose a suitable wife.'

'One suitable for you, you mean,' I ventured boldly.

'One suitable for each one of my sons and approved of by me. That ring remained in my safe after the others had gone, waiting for my youngest son to choose the girl he would marry. Your father left this house like a thief in the night taking that ring and the children's governess with him. He had no right to it and neither had your mother.'

'But he knew the ring was to be his. You are surely not accusing my father of stealing it?'

'That is exactly what I am doing. He knew that I did not wish him to marry your mother. Under no circumstances would I have parted with that ring so that he could give it to her.'

How coldly implacable was her stern face opposite mine, making me feel the ring burn into my finger, bruising the delicate skin. I looked down to see my fingers twisting it round and round until the bright red blood came. Savagely I tore it from my finger, slamming it down on the desk in front of her.

'Here is your ring,' I cried, 'I never want to see it again.'

She took it up, holding it in the palm of her hand, then almost contemptuously she laid it aside.

'I have my own rings, Jacintha, all of which will go on my death to my sons' wives and their daughters. I will see that a clause is made in my will ensuring that this one comes to you.'

That night I cried myself to sleep while Ruthie slept contentedly in the other bed. I cried for Martin, wanting his arms around me, his calm voice reassuring me that we belonged together – that he cared nothing for my grandmother or her money, that he would take me away from Ravenspoint, and that we would be together even if it meant the whole world was against us. If my father had had the courage to do it, why not Martin?

There was little festivity in the house on Christmas morning. All the officers had departed on Christmas Eve to be with their families; some had been carried out on stretchers, others had walked with the assistance of their nurses, some, like Martin, had stepped out jauntily down the road. I watched him go with desolation in my heart, in spite of his promise to think about me every second he was away and my prayers that he would return for a while in the New Year.

The talk round the dining table on Christmas Day was of the war, the price of wool, the influenza epidemic which was keeping half the Carradice workforce in their beds, and more of the war. I was sad to see the change in Isobel's mother since our last meeting. She had lost a great deal of weight and her hands played nervously with the long strand of pearls around her neck. It seemed that with the death of Roger all her enthusiasm for living had gone.

'Your mother doesn't look well,' I commented to Isobel. 'She must be very unhappy now that Roger has gone.'

'He was always her favourite, but she'll get over it in time. One has to. She's very involved with a lot of good works.'

'Don't you miss him too?' I asked curiously.

'Of course I do, silly, but I'm not one to go around wearing my heart on my sleeve. For one thing, Roger would have hated it, and for another it's not my style.'

'Are your parents going to do anything about Polly?' I asked innocently.

'Like what?'

'Well, her baby will be their grandchild. One would have thought they might show some interest.'

'They'll see she has enough money, but my mother's too old to have a baby on her hands. It was just like Roger to go off and do a stupid thing like getting married without telling anybody.'

'If it's a boy, he could take Roger's place.'

'I've told you before, Polly was never Carradice wife material. Even if the baby becomes acceptable, Polly won't be.'

'I think that's monstrous.'

'Well, you would, wouldn't you? But you've been here long enough to know what the Carradices are like.'

'We're another generation; we shall never be like that.'

'Perhaps not, but whilst grandmother lives the family won't change. You must just keep hoping your young man comes back to rescue you and leave alone what doesn't concern you.'

To my great joy, Martin did come back, on 3 January, with a great many of the others and some new ones besides. He was limping again – his wounded leg had suffered a slight setback from an infection, and I blessed that infection, which would keep him at Ravenspoint for longer than he had thought.

My grandmother returned to the city with the rest of them early in January, and Ruthie caught a very bad cold which kept her confined to her bed for several days. She lost weight and became so lethargic that the housekeeper telephoned her parents and Uncle William came at the weekend and carried her, still wrapped in blankets, to his car. We had no idea when we would see her again – possibly in the spring, he told us.

The days of January were cold and white with frost, but I for one felt exhilarated by the icy winds from the mountains which brought the roses into our cheeks as we walked down to the village to attend either church or the local sewing circle. It was on one of these walks that Isobel said, 'Come to the schoolroom tonight, Jacintha, directly after dinner.'

'Why?' I asked curiously. 'What is happening?'

'You'll find out tonight. Not another word now.'

I fretted and fumed impatiently all through dinner. For days Isobel and Lavinia had been giggling together in corners and I wondered if it was a foretaste of some new form of devilry and some particularly unpleasant form of teasing. I was the last one to arrive in the old schoolroom and was surprised to find Teddy as well as the two girls sitting around the schoolroom table, where Isobel appeared to have adopted the roll of chair-woman. She sat with a notebook in front of her, her pencil poised, while Lavinia asked in a conspiratorial whisper, 'Is anybody about?'

'No, they're all in the kitchen clearing away the dinner things.'

'Let's get started then.' Isobel said. She looked round the little group, well pleased with herself, then consulting her notebook she announced, 'February the second is Lavinia and Teddy's birthday, so we've decided we're going to do something about it. I suppose you're game, Jacintha?'

'It depends. What are you going to do?'

'We're going to have a concert in the large drawing room where the piano is and we want the names of everybody who can do something. We'll turn the whole room into a theatre and put the chairs in rows, the dais where the piano is can serve as the stage. We've found chests full of old clothes in the attics, so tomorrow we can go up there and rummage. Teddy, you can find out from the officers if there's any talent amongst them.'

'You won't get me to sing or dance or do anything stupid,' Teddy stated emphatically. 'I don't mind helping with the furniture but that's all.'

'That'll do for a start,' his sister snapped, 'but it's your birthday as well as mine. Anyway, you'd probably fall over everybody.'

'You could say some poetry,' Isobel said, 'that thing you used to say when you were small.'

'I've forgotten it. Anyway who wants to listen to poetry?'

'I don't know that I can do much either,' I said woefully.

'You can sing, Jacintha. You have a very pretty voice. I've often thought so listening to you in church.'

'But my voice is untrained, and I wouldn't know what to sing.'

'I know for a fact your old music mistress told grandmother your voice should be trained.'

'I didn't know. Who told you?'

'My mother. But grandmother said there was no point in you having your voice trained because it could only be for your own amusement. Carradice women did not sing for entertainment, she said.'

Her imitation of my grandmother's accents amused Lavinia greatly, but I merely repeated that I would not know what to sing.

'We can soon find something for you. You can sing the war

songs and ask everybody to join in. Heaven knows, there's plenty of scope in these days of noble sacrifice and flag waving.'

We pulled our chairs closer together and argued about the form the concert should take, while Isobel scribbled away in an effort to keep pace with all our ideas.

'Why does it have to be music all the time?' complained Teddy. 'Why can't we have some sort of game?'

'Who wants to play games at a concert? We can do that every night,' Lavinia snapped.

'You and your games,' grumbled Isobel. 'It really is time you grew up, Teddy, and found yourself a nice girl. I have a feeling you're going to be one of the world's bachelors unless you do something about it in time.'

Teddy's face blushed bright scarlet as it always did when girls were mentioned, and Isobel never missed an opportunity to taunt him. Where, I wondered, was Teddy likely to find a girl acceptable to his grandmother in the wilds of Cumberland, particularly when it was so necessary to find one that was Carradice wife material?

Immediately after breakfast we went up to the attic, led by Isobel. I was surprised at the number of them, great lofty rooms under the eaves extending for the entire length and breadth of the house, and they were crammed with old unwanted furniture, ornaments, chests filled with books and others filled with discarded clothes. The dust swirled and spun around us as we threw out old shawls and shoes, but there were beautiful hats piled high with chiffon flowers and tulle, or lavishly adorned with ostrich and osprey feathers. There were gowns, too, of another age but ideal for Isobel's purpose. Gowns with deeply cut décolletages and tiny waists, their skirts ending in short trains or bustles. The materials were beautiful and I imagined the fashions had changed long before the dresses wore out. We were in our element, and by lunchtime we had selected more than sufficient to keep us occupied for the rest of the afternoon. It was the day of the doctor's visit and there was nothing for us to do downstairs, so we spent all afternoon in the schoolroom struggling to fasten ourselves into the gowns.

'Gracious, what tiny waists they had!' I cried, trying to pull the fasteners round Isobel's slender figure. 'I doubt you're going to get into this.'

'I shall. You must have seen pictures of women with hour-glass figures. They had enormous busts and hips. What you'll probably have to do is let the waist out and take in the rest of the dress.' Isobel had first choice, of course – a gown in apricot, glowing and lovely against her blue-black hair, with a hat in a slightly deeper shade, large-brimmed and adorned with ostrich feathers the exact shade of the dress. I stitched all afternoon, but I was amply rewarded by the finished result. She looked so beautiful and well pleased with the effect that she began to hunt around for something to suit Lavinia and myself. Lavinia wanted only a black gown with an extremely low neckline, leaving her arms and shoulders bare, and show-ing more of her proportions than we thought decent.

'Oh well, why not?' Isobel laughed. 'That gown is going to do more good for those men than twenty visits from the doctor.'

She rummaged through the rest of the things, intent on finding something for me. 'There's nothing here,' she said finally. 'We shall have to go back to the attic. It's your hair, Jacintha.'

'What's wrong with my hair?' I asked indignantly.

'Nothing, but this dark green will do nothing for it, and I can't see you in puce. You're fair, but it's not Lavinia's fair-ness, and we've got to find something that does you justice.'

So back we went to the attics and this time she produced a watered-silk confection in green.

'I don't know that emerald is Jacintha's colour either,' Lavinia objected.

'This isn't emerald, it's jade, and look at this hat, it's perfect.'

It was indeed a beautiful hat, with a great sweeping brim in jade-green watered silk under which bloomed a cluster of pink chiffon roses. I tried it on and stood back to receive their comments.

'You'll have to do something with your hair,' Isobel said, 'but the hat suits you. I'd swop with you, but you'd look positively frightful in that apricot thing of mine. Besides, it's been altered to fit me now.'

The dress didn't need much altering for me and, after Isobel had brushed my hair into strands she could pile on top of my head, I was both surprised and flattered with the results.

'You look beautiful,' Lavinia said impulsively. 'I hope I look as good, but I'm beginning to have doubts about me in black.'

'Rubbish,' Isobel said. 'Black is wonderful against that pale hair of yours. We shall have to tell Lucy. She's good with her fingers and we shall need some help with this lot.'

Lucy was unhappy about matters. 'Oh, Miss Isobel, I don't think your grandmother would approve of all this. Those dresses are downright indecent, particularly Miss Lavinia's.'

'They can't possibly be indecent, Lucy. They're beautiful gowns and were probably once worn by my great-grand-mother, who was also a Carradice. Everybody was so sancti-monious and prim and proper under Queen Victoria; I expect that when she died King Edward opened up all the windows to let the fresh air in. That's when the fashions changed. Isn't that so, Jacintha?'

'Yes, I'm sure it is. I hated those silly crinolines and bonnets they wore in the old queen's reign. These are so much prettier,' I said, backing her up.

'Well, we all know King Edward was a wicked old lecher,' Lavinia said. 'He probably liked all that bosom showing.'

'You shouldn't be saying such things, Miss Lavinia, and you certainly shouldn't be wearing that black dress in front of all those strange young men,' Lucy admonished. 'If you want me to do any stitching, I am going to fill in the front bit.'

'You can't,' Lavinia wailed. 'You'll ruin it.'

'Well, we'll see. I shall have to find the housekeeper or she'll wonder where I am. I don't think she'll approve of all this, Miss Isobel.'

'It has nothing to do with her. When my grandmother is not here, I am the mistress. I'll speak to the housekeeper and tell her you're all invited to the concert.'

That night we told the officers what we were about and they were without exception delighted with the idea. Fortunately, one of the young lieutenants was no mean pianist and he set out immediately to prove his ability by organizing rehearsals. For the rest of that night, we decided which of them should be asked to entertain and I was amazed at the talent we un-covered. Tenors and baritones we had in plenty, as well as Major Griffiths with his monologues and Captain Winstanley with his conjuring tricks. Indeed matron came to call lights-out long before we were ready for it.

As Martin and I clung together at the bottom of the stairs, he whispered, 'We'll do something together, darling. Sing a duet or something.'

'Well, everybody who's taking part will have to come to rehearsal, so you'll have to think about what we should sing.'

'I already know.'

'What, then?'

' "If You Were the Only Girl in the World". It's a song from *Floradora*; it was made for us.'

I laughed, deliriously happy with his choice, and quite determined that I would play Isobel's record of that song until it fell to bits in my effort to do it justice.

What fun we had at those rehearsals! Fortunately, our pianist was able to pick up anything after hearing it only once, and he was a great improviser. Teddy, too, worked like a Trojan, arranging chairs and carrying furniture, although he was only at Ravenspoint to recover from a bout of influenza and his return to the town was long overdue.

On the night of the concert, the officers took their seats in the drawing room, to be followed by the servants after they had completed their duties. All the lights were switched off except the ones over the improvised stage. The library next door was used as a dressing room.

For the opening number, we wore our long Edwardian gowns and large hats and were partnered by three young officers who were considered fit enough to dance and accommodate us on their knees for another song, also from the show *Floradora*, called 'Tell Me Pretty Maiden'. After that, the seal was set on the success of the evening. We danced and we sang. My duet with Martin was warmly applauded so we sang an encore, then the whole cast came back on stage to sing whatever was asked for.

Naturally, everybody's favourites were the songs our men were marching to, but the one they called for again and again was that which had been composed by a young Welshman called Ivor Novello, 'Keep the Home Fires Burning'. The melody was so hauntingly beautiful and the sentiments so in keeping with our thoughts at that time that I began to think they would never let us stop, while Isobel, flushed with the success of the evening, waltzed around the room inviting everybody to join in the singing. It was matron who finally put an end to the proceedings, but Isobel promised recklessly that there would be many more such evenings. Later that night, in the schoolroom, happy in her role of impresario, she started to plan what we should do on the night of the next concert.

'We shall have to be quick,' she urged. 'Some of the men who are fit will be going back to the front and we don't know what kind of men will replace them.'

Momentarily, all my joy faded when I wondered if Martin might be one of those going back to the front. I remembered how warm his smile had been and how tightly his hand had clasped mine during our song. Surely he must tell my grandmother soon that he wanted to marry me and, although I knew she would raise every possible objection, she couldn't make us wait for ever. Soon I would be old enough to marry Martin with or without her permission.

Looking back on those days I believe they were the happiest I remember from my girlhood. Every day, whenever we had a moment, those of us who had taken part in the concert rehearsed in the schoolroom. Isobel was in her element conducting operations and, although we were dismayed when two young men were recalled, two others came to replace them who were equally enthusiastic and only wounded superficially. Lieutenant Allinson, our pianist, had shrapnel close to his lungs and would be with us for a long time.

We found new songs to sing, mostly from shows which were cramming the audiences into the London theatres. Isobel's indulgent father had always kept her well supplied with gramophone records and we tried very hard to copy the more professional artists.

We found more clothes in the attics and we sewed and improvised with the help of Lucy, so that by the time the next concert came around we had more costumes and a larger repertoire. The night was an instant success. Martin and I rendered more ambitious love songs, Isobel did a decidedly competent impression of Vesta Tilley, and Lavinia's 'My Old Man Said Follow the Band' brought down the house.

We were halfway through a repetition of 'Tell Me Pretty Maiden' when we became very conscious of an uneasy silence. Chairs were pushed back and one by one the servants quietly left the room. In the doorway stood my grandmother and Ruthie, looks of incredulous amazement on their faces. There we were, the three of us, sitting on the knees of three young officers, Isobel in her nodding apricot feathers, Lavinia in that all-too-revealing black dress and I in my jade-silk gown with its preponderance of pink roses.

Our song faltered to a close and one by one the officers made their excuses, painfully embarrassed and casting sympathetic looks in our direction as they left. It was humiliating standing there in our glad rags, our heavily made-up faces looking harsh now in the light from the chandeliers, which my grand-mother had switched on to illuminate the entire room.

'You will go upstairs and take off those ridiculous costumes,' she said, her words falling like chips of ice in the silence of the room, 'and the paint from your faces, then you will come to my sitting room as quickly as possible.'

I scrubbed my face until it hurt. Then, with trembling fingers, I removed my dress and struggled into a blouse and skirt. By this time, Ruthie had come up to our bedroom and was calmly unpacking her suitcase. I looked at her once or twice for any signs of sympathy or amusement but she never looked my way. There was no emotion whatever on that pretty Dresden-china face but I permitted myself one remark. 'We were not doing anything wrong, Ruthie.'

'Perhaps not, but I don't suppose my grandmother had any idea that you intended to turn the drawing room into a third-rate variety theatre.'

'You obviously know what a third-rate variety theatre looks like,' I retorted and immediately I recognized that those were the first really harsh words I had ever said to Ruthie. As I left the room, I saw Isobel and Lavinia were already halfway down the stairs and I ran to catch up with them, so at least we would present my grandmother with a solid front.

She sat before a fire that had obviously just been lit and had not yet begun to blaze properly; the room still felt cold. She had not bothered to remove her outdoor clothing and the hat with its osprey plumes seemed to make her appear more like a haughty bird of prey than ever. She looked at us in turn without speaking, then addressed herself to Isobel. 'Now, young woman, I want to know what was the meaning of that deplorable exhibition in the drawing room.'

Isobel's face was pink with indignation as she answered boldly, 'We were having a concert. There was no harm in it.'

'A concert! Is that what you called it?' And who was the instigator of that concert?'

'We all were. We thought it would be nice for the officers to have a little music and sing some of the songs everybody is singing. After all, there's absolutely nothing for them to do here.'

'They are not here to *do* anything. They are here to recover from their wounds in an atmosphere of calm and stability. If they require entertainment of that calibre, they should not be here; they should be frequenting the music halls. They are quite obviously wasting the country's time and money and most certainly they should not expect my granddaughters to entertain them.'

'But it wasn't their fault,' I burst in. 'We thought of it. They had nothing to do with it and we haven't done anything wrong.'

She did not look at me as she answered. 'If smothering your faces with paint and wearing clothes that would have done credit to street women is not doing anything wrong, I fear the years under my guardianship have done nothing to prepare you for a life of respectability. I shall write to your parents, Isobel and Lavinia, and none of you will mix with the officers again until you have proved to me that you can be trusted. Now you will go to your rooms and stay there until morning.'

'But grandmother, we can be trusted,' I wailed, but she had turned away and Lavinia was prodding me into silence. Miserably I turned and followed the other two out of the room and up the stairs. A small group of servants stood waiting in the hall, clearly the next people to earn my grandmother's displeasure.

As we reached the landing, Ruthie was leaving the bedroom. In answer to Isobel's defiant look, she gave a little smile and walked quickly down the stairs.

'Smug little beast,' Isobel said. 'I expect she's enjoying all this.'

Teddy was hovering outside his bedroom door. 'I say,' he said, his face red with embarrassment, 'did she give you a rollicking?'

'Your turn will come,' Lavinia snapped at him. 'Don't think

you've got away with it.'

'Did she say anything about me?' he asked.

'No, she didn't, she was too busy chastising us. I'm fed up with living here,' Isobel wailed. 'I hope she does write to my father, I shall write to him too and ask him to come and get me. You could do the same, Lavinia.'

'In the middle of the hunting season! My parents wouldn't want me at home now – you know what they're like.'

We went to our respective bedrooms, and frustrated and unhappy I cried myself to sleep. The thought that I was not going to be allowed to see Martin was paramount on my mind and, when I awoke in the morning to a cold grey dawn, misery flooded over me so I felt I was drowning in desolation.

The next three weeks were the longest I had ever spent. We read, we sewed, Isobel wrote innumerable letters, but most of all we talked – or rather Isobel and Lavinia talked while I listened. We saw little of Ruthie and imagined she was still allowed to help any of the officers who needed it. I realized now that neither Isobel nor Lavinia liked Ruthie and, when she did come into the room where we were, all talk immediately ceased until she went out again.

'It's not Ruthie's fault that we're in disgrace,' I said to them one day, 'so I don't see why we shouldn't speak to her quite normally.'

Isobel scowled darkly at me. 'Ruthie's loving all this, you little silly. You're so blind when you like somebody.'

'I just don't see why nobody's speaking to Ruthie. I know she can be smug and I know she thinks we've been foolish, but she's not responsible for our being kept away from the rest of the household.'

They ignored me, so I decided I would not refer to Ruthie again. Lucy, too, for those first few days went about the house with red-rimmed eyes, avoiding us whenever she could, but that state of affairs was not destined to last long. One day, after lunch, Isobel came across her in the corridor and literally pulled her into the bedroom where we sat on the floor talking in conspiratorial whispers.

'Oh, miss, I shouldn't be here. The mistress threatened me with instant dismissal if I so much as talked to you again.'

'But what have you done?' I asked her.

'I was the one who helped you with those dresses, wasn't I?

97

Please, Miss Isobel, let me go now. There's precious little work around here. I don't want to lose my job; I don't know anything else.'

'I don't know why you stay – there's plenty of work in the towns on munitions and such,' said Lavinia stoutly.

'But I don't know anything except housework, Miss Lavinia. Besides, I don't want to live in a town with all that smoke and all those people. All my folks are here.'

'Oh, Lucy, where's your sense of adventure?' Isobel cried.

'It's all right for you, Miss Isobel. You've got your father at the back of you. Your grandmother'd dismiss me and send me off without a reference, she would. Nobody else'd take me on without a reference.'

'I'll get my father to give you one. He will, if I ask him.'

'It's not the same, miss. I haven't worked for your father.'

'All right, you can go, but first you must tell us what is happening downstairs. Hurry up and then you can go.'

Lucy edged nearer to the door, but she could not evade Isobel's long steely fingers round her arm.

'Some of the officers asked to see your grandmother this morning. Your young man was amongst them, Miss Jacintha.'

'How do you know?' I asked sharply.

'I saw them going in. They came out in about half an hour, all except Captain Vasey, that is.'

'Do you know why they went in?' Isobel asked.

'I think so. They gave Mrs Parry a note to give your grandmother asking her if she would see them. I think they felt so sorry for you they meant to ask her to forgive you.'

'And what did she say?'

'That she'd consider it, miss.'

'But you say Captain Vasey remained behind?' I asked feverishly.

'Yes, miss. I don't know why, but he stayed another half-hour after that.'

My heart was racing. Surely in that half-hour Martin would have told her how much we loved each other; he must have asked her if he could marry me and now I wondered desperately what her answer had been.

'Don't you know anything about why he was in there, Lucy?' I begged.

'No, I don't, miss, and as soon as he came out Miss Ruthie

went in and stayed for the rest of the afternoon. Please, Miss Isobel, honestly I've told you all I know. I must go now before I'm missed.'

I heard nothing more about my grandmother's meeting with Martin and she ignored the officers' pleas for her forgiveness. The days crept by without a chance of meeting Martin.

I was sitting alone struggling with the heel of a sock when the door opened and Lavinia crept in, shutting the door behind her and holding a finger to her lips.

'I've only got a minute so listen carefully. I've just heard that Martin is leaving this afternoon.'

My heart missed several beats and I sprang to my feet, knocking the knitting onto the floor.

'What time is he leaving?' I gasped.

'About four o'clock. There's a car coming for them so there must be more than one leaving. What are you going to do?'

'Lavinia, I've got to see him. He can't go away without seeing me – I won't let him. I've got to know what he said to my grandmother.'

'But you can't go into the rooms downstairs where the officers are. Perhaps he'll write to you after he's gone.'

'I'm going to see him. I don't care whether she punishes me or not; I don't care if she kills me, I've got to see him.'

Before Lavinia could stop me, I was running wildly down the stairs. I flung open the door of the first drawing room I came to and all those in it looked up startled at my frantic appearance. Martin wasn't in that room nor in the next, and I stood hesitantly in the centre of the hall when Major MacGregor came slowly down the stairs, cramming tobacco into his pipe. Impulsively I ran towards him.

'Major MacGregor, have you seen Martin? I've heard he's leaving today?' I asked him breathlessly.

He looked down at me for a moment in pitying silence, then he pulled me into the shadows at the side of the stairs.

'Be careful, lassie, are you sure you're doing the right thing?'

'I don't know what you mean,' I said trembling.

'Well now, is it any time to be wanting to see any young man with your eyes full of tears, particularly when they're such beautiful eyes?'

'Please, Major MacGregor, you can tease me tomorrow, any other time, but I have to see him. He's going back to the war. I'd never forgive myself if I didn't try to see him before he goes. I don't care about my grandmother, I don't care about anybody – I have to see Martin.'

He looked at me sadly out of wise kind eyes, then taking my arm and walking beside me he said, 'Aye well, I suppose the young have to learn about life the hard way and it's your own life, I suppose. I saw your young man go down the garden towards the cliff path; I expect he'll be taking another look at the sea before the car comes for him.'

Without even bothering to thank him, I ran out of the house and towards the cliffs, oblivious of the icy wind and the sharp sting of rain against my face. I reached the cliff top and looked down towards the beach. Martin was standing at the edge of the waves looking out to where the great rollers crashed against the rocks, and my call to him was lost against the wind. Without any thought of danger, I stumbled down the cliff path, slipping and sliding in my haste and cutting my shoes on the cruel corners of the stones. Once safely at the bottom, I ran with flying feet across the wet sand, calling to him as I ran. I was nearly beside him when he turned and saw me, and the next moment I was in his arms, my tears mingling with the salt spray and the rain on my face.

'Martin, would you have gone without trying to see me?' I asked him through my tears. Without waiting for his answer, I cried, 'Where are they sending you? How soon will you be able to write? When shall I ever see you again?'

His face was pale, stricken, and I sobbed in his arms with his chin resting on my hair. Then slowly we started to walk back across the sand. 'You'll catch cold, Jacintha,' he said. 'You should have put a raincoat on.'

What did raincoats matter, I thought wildly, what did anything matter except that Martin was leaving me, that I might never see him again? I wept anew at the thought of those last few weeks which had been a bitter and meaningless waste. As we reached the top of the cliff path, he took his arms away from me and we walked back to the house without speaking until we reached the door. Then he said, 'I'll go into the house by the conservatory door, Jacintha. I don't want to get you into more trouble than you are in already. Do get into something warm and dry, dear girl, before you catch pneumonia.'

I looked up at him piteously. I didn't care about pneumonia. I didn't care that my hair was soaking wet and that icy trickles were running down my face and down the collar of my dress. I didn't care if I died. All I cared about was that Martin was leaving me and there were so many things unsaid and time was running out.

'Martin, I must know, what did you say to my grandmother?'

'We told her you had done nothing to deserve her anger, that you had all behaved perfectly respectably.'

'I don't care about that, but she kept you when the others had gone – what did you say to her then?'

'She knew my family, we talked about them, I can't tell you anything more now, dear.'

'Is that all? Didn't you tell her that you love me, that you want to marry me?'

'The time wasn't right, I can't explain now, Jacintha, but I couldn't talk to her about such matters then.'

'But now you're going away. When will there ever be another time?'

'There will be. Your grandmother is going to visit us, perhaps on my next leave.'

'But you'll write, Martin, you'll write soon?'

'Yes, I promise. Please go in now, darling, you're soaking wet and so am I.'

So I went in by the front door and crossed the hall without looking to either right or left. I was halfway up the first flight of stairs when I became aware that from the landing above me Isobel and Lavinia watched with pale blurred faces. From the open doorway of my grandmother's sitting room I heard her cold clipped voice call, 'Jacintha, come in here. I wish to speak to you.'

I paused for only a moment on the stairs and she called to me again. Then, lifting my head high, I climbed slowly up the rest of the stairs.

6

Isobel was in Yorkshire. We had watched her depart from the upstairs window, waving to us as she got into her father's car. Earlier that morning, she had informed us, 'My mother's to give a Red Cross ball and she thinks I should be there. You could have come too, Lavinia, if your parents had seen fit to come for you.'

Lavinia had been openly scornful. 'Who wants to go to a ball when the place will be crawling with wounded heroes? I can think of nothing worse than having to sit round the ballroom with a crowd of giggling girls waiting for some man on crutches to ask me to dance.'

Not in the least put out, Isobel answered gaily, 'Well at least it's preferable to sitting here waiting for that elusive American to show up. Besides, all the men won't be on crutches. There'll be plenty of young officers on leave and not *all* the young men have gone to the war. There are others with more sense in reserved occupations.'

'Who wants one of those? If it's wartime, I want my man in uniform. In peacetime I'd prefer him with money. A combination of the two would be ideal.'

'You won't know whether your American has got money or not; you'll only know what he tells you.'

'I shall know,' Lavinia persisted. 'He won't get me until I'm sure.'

'How about you, Ruthie?' Isobel asked sweetly. 'Don't you fancy mother's ball or have you already met the man you intend to have?'

Ruthie didn't answer and I looked at Isobel sharply. I knew she didn't like Ruthie but I had not expected her to be deliberately unkind. Personally I didn't think Ruthie's lack of suitors was a subject she should have been unkind about. Her parting words to me were, 'Really, Jacintha, you are getting to look like a scarecrow worrying about Martin Vasey. Why not make

102

up your mind that there are better fish in the sea?'

It was March when we saw her again. We were just finishing our lunch when the door was flung open to admit a radiant Isobel who waltzed round the room flaunting the largest diamond I had ever seen on her engagement finger.

She perched on the corner of the table and allowed us to bombard her with questions. Who was he? Where had she met him? How long had she known him?

'As to the first,' she sparkled, 'he's called Henry Clifton-Webb and I've known him for ages – ever since we were children.'

'When will you be married?' Ruthie wanted to know.

'In just a few weeks. There's no point in waiting, and I want you all to be my bridesmaids.'

'How can you possibly get married in wartime? You'll find nothing decent to wear, and where is the food coming from for the reception?' asked Lavinia.

Isobel tossed her dark head. 'I'm a Carradice and all the Carradices have big weddings and that's what I'm having. My mother has the material for my dress, yards and yards of it – she's been saving for years – and the food and drink will be no problem. The ceremony is to be at the abbey at twelve o'clock and the invitations are going out next week.'

'How can we go from here?' I asked stupidly.

'You won't go from here, silly. You'll have to come and stay with me, and Lavinia and Ruthie will go home. You should be thrilled to get away from this place for a few days.'

'Why isn't he in the army?' Lavinia wanted to know. 'Is he deformed or something?'

'No, he is not,' snapped Isobel. 'I've told you, he's a Clifton-Webb, with as many mills as ours – our biggest competitor, in fact. After the war, he's going into politics and that means a house in London with all the life that goes with it.'

'You are in love with him, Isobel?' I ventured, stunned into silence when she threw back her head and trilled with laughter.

'Really, Jacintha, you are a little ninny. What has love got to do with it? Henry adores me; he'd jump off the cliffs out there if I asked him to. He's over the moon to have captured me.'

'I don't see why, if he's as rich as you say he is,' Lavinia muttered.

'I've never heard you speak of him, Isobel. Now you're suddenly engaged to him. How long have you known him?' Ruthie wanted to know.

'Oh, I don't know, years and years,' Isobel said airily. 'He went to dancing classes when I did – a horrible fat little boy with round steel spectacles who trod on everybody's toes. All those silly simpering girls giggling whenever he went near them. Now they're all itching to have him dance on their toes because he is somebody.'

'Wasn't he somebody then?' Lavinia asked.

'He was little Harry Webb. His father was a grocer and his mother had a roving eye which caught sight of old Mr Clifton and his woollen mills. He was a bachelor and, when her husband died, leaving her with little Harry to bring up, she flung herself at old Clifton. Overnight, it seems, little Harry blossomed into Henry and became Clifton-Webb after the old man adopted him. Now he's come in for the Clifton mills and it would appear his mother's ultimate triumph is for her son to have captured me.'

'He'd have done better to have got somebody without your conceit,' Lavinia snapped.

Isobel's laughter rang out delightedly.

'Oh, I don't know. After all, I am beautiful. All those young men who have told me so can't have been lying. I shall have lots of my father's money and I've been finished in Switzerland. He couldn't have done much better, because he's no great shakes to look at.'

She was deliberately baiting Lavinia, I knew, and even Ruthie was frowning. I had never thought much of Isobel's sense of humour anyway. Suddenly I was unable to stand her flippancy any longer and I cried, 'You're not the least bit in love with him, are you, Isobel?'

Her eyes looked at me mockingly. Then, in her old sarcastic drawl, she said, 'No, darling, but I'm very fond of him and a lot happier than you are, eating your heart out for Martin Vasey. You'll find out, Jacintha . . . it's so much more wonderful to be adored by a man than to do all the adoring. Men are such selfish creatures anyway.'

Ruthie sprang up from the table and left the room, closing the door behind her sharply. Isobel shrugged her graceful shoulders and I said, 'Now see what you've done. Ruthie is as exasperated with you as I am.'

'But for different reasons,' Isobel said softly. She was eyeing me with such a degree of malicious humour that I felt uncomfortable. Then she laughed a little before embarking upon further details about her approaching marriage.

After that, events moved fast and, the week before Easter, I found myself staying at Uncle Robert's house instead of with my grandmother in the gloomy mansion in the centre of Wellsford. Ruthie and Lavinia were with their own parents and I had seen nothing of them since the wedding rehearsal.

I had met Henry on two occasions and he was not at all the sort of man I had thought Isobel would marry – perhaps because I had always visualized her standing at the altar with Adrian. It was doubtful if he was as tall as Isobel, but then he was inclined to portliness and this disguised his actual height. He had a kind face, although by no stretch of imagination could it be called handsome, and he watched Isobel with the eyes of an adoring spaniel. I told Isobel I thought he was nice.

'Oh, Henry's all right. Wait until you meet his mother, though. The woman's a positive fright.'

'If she's so frightful, how are you going to put up with her as a mother-in-law?'

'From a distance, I hope. It's too bad our house won't be ready to move into right away, but I've insisted that we stay here until it is. I couldn't bear to start my married life in that mausoleum Henry lives in, and with the added problem of his mother.'

Dark, leaden skies heralded Isobel's wedding morning. I had been awake since first light and, after tossing and turning in the unfamiliar bed for what seemed like hours, I decided to get up and look out of the window. It was a cold grey morning for early April and a light drizzle of rain was falling. The parkland was shrouded in mist, mingling dismally with the pall of purple smoke which drifted up from the town. It felt cold in the great lofty bedroom with its heavy mahogany furniture and large draughty windows.

After the timeless symmetry of Ravenspoint, I disliked this big stone house surrounded by parkland. I thought its pillared portico and tiled hall ostentatious. It looked as though the builder had borrowed from many styles and different centuries before he was satisfied with the finished result. Ravenspoint had mellowed in wind and rain like the rocks and crags and it was a house, not an apology for a Grecian temple or a Gothic museum. The homes of the Carradices in the city spoke only of financial standing, unconcerned with beauty.

On my first morning in the city, Teddy had taken me on a conducted tour of one of the mills. I had seen the women who tended the looms bob their little curtseys respectfully, but the noise had been deafening and I could hear nothing that was said to me. The stone staircases between the floors were steep, but the men we met on the way touched their caps and stood on one side to allow us to pass. I couldn't help wondering to myself what it must be like to work in such places. Perhaps, if my grandmother hadn't done her duty by me, I too might have been forced to find out, and such thoughts made me wonder if Martin was right and I really did owe her a great deal. The workers seemed to treat Teddy with a great deal of respect, and standing beside him I couldn't help thinking how different he seemed with the working people, obviously doing a job he knew well. I couldn't imagine Adrian in such an environment.

The morning loomed ahead of me uncertainly. I was debating whether to get dressed or return to my bed when there was a knock at the door; next moment, one of the maids entered with a small tray containing a teapot, milk and sugar and one cup and saucer.

She smiled at me brightly. 'Good morning, miss. I'll put the tea on the table by the bed unless you're wanting it somewhere else.'

'That will do nicely, thank you. Is anybody else awake?'

'They've all had their tea, miss, except Miss Isobel. I went to her room but she's riding in the park.'

The surprise must have shown plainly on my face.

'She's been out over an hour, miss, and it's raining hard now. It's a good thing the hairdresser's coming in at nine thirty.'

I ran to the window but the mist had crept in now so it was barely possible to see beyond the formal gardens. I was glad of the hot tea, pulling the eiderdown round my shoulders while I drank it, then disconsolately I decided to wander along to Isobel's room to see if she had returned.

I found her still in her riding clothes, rubbing her hair dry on a towel, a fresh pot of tea by her side.

'Oh, Isobel,' I cried, 'you're absolutely drenched. What a time to go riding – on your wedding morning!'

'You sound like my grandmother,' she laughed. 'I like to ride when there are things on my mind. Here, help me off with this jacket. It's so wet it's sticking to my skin.'

I rubbed her shoulders dry before she slipped into a dressing gown, still wearing her shirt and riding breeches. When I remonstrated with her, I was told not to fuss so much, then she rummaged in her handbag for a box of matches, which she used to light the fire.

'Is there a fire in your bedroom?' she asked.

'No.'

'My father's as mean as hell when it comes to spending money. He objects to fires in the bedrooms after the end of March, regardless of the temperature, but I'm not spending my wedding morning shivering to death. The hairdresser's coming, but I've forgotten what time.'

'Half past nine.'

'Good, then she can do yours as well. You can get dressed in here. I'd like to see how you look in your dress now that it's finished.'

'Are we having breakfast in the dining room?'

'I'm not having breakfast. Really, Jacintha, if you must eat like a horse, you'll have difficulty in getting into the dress.'

She eyed me with a great deal of laughing good humour. 'I know exactly what you're going to be thinking about as you drift down the aisle in my wake today,' she said provocatively.

'I shan't be thinking about anything. I shall be far too nervous.'

'You'll be wishing it was you in a cloud of white lace and Martin Vasey standing at the altar waiting to meet you.'

'What nonsense you talk,' I protested. 'For one thing Martin and I have decided to be married very quietly because it's wartime – probably in a registry office, and I shall not be wearing white.'

Her delighted laughter pealed round the room.

'But you will be thinking about it, won't you, Jacintha?'

'Perhaps,' I admitted at last. 'Oh, Isobel, I do so want us all

107

to fall in love and be happy. Lavinia and Ruthie and Teddy, too.'

'Well, we all know what Lavinia's waiting for, don't we? She's made up her mind it's to be an American or nobody, and the poor lamb will find her sitting here waiting for him like a spider.'

'But she doesn't know any Americans.'

'She will. They'll come into the war before it's over; they'll have to.'

'Well, you can't be so unkind about Ruthie.'

Quite suddenly, the laughter seemed to leave her face and she looked at me strangely.

'You're so single-minded, Jacintha, when you care for somebody. Ruthie, who is always so sweet and docile, always gets what she wants. Lavinia's like me – we're often outrageous and quick-tempered but we are never devious. Ruthie is gentle and clinging but what she has set her heart on she gets. It's always been like that.'

She was so serious it was hard to imagine that a few moments before she had been teasing. The morning was chilled for me by her words and I felt that in some way they conveyed a warning for me. I wanted to ask her to explain them but, just as I opened my mouth to speak, Isobel's mother swept into the room in a flurry of pale-pink chiffon night clothes.

'I'm glad you're up, Isobel. You haven't forgotten the hairdresser is coming? Don't let Jacintha delay you.'

'Don't fuss, mother. I asked Jacintha to stay.'

But she did fuss. About the time and the arrangements, about Isobel's state of undress, about the arrival of the hairdresser a good half-hour before the poor woman was due. In the end, utterly exasperated, Isobel begged her to leave us alone.

The rest of the morning passed so quickly it seemed like a dream sequence as we waited for Isobel in the gloom of the abbey porch. Soft rain fell upon ancient tombstones and daffodils while from inside the church the organ boomed appropriate music, though no bells rang. It felt cold in the great stone porch and our delicate chiffon dresses were no proof against the morning mist, which still lingered on the streets. The large bouquet of irises and lilies-of-the-valley was becoming increasingly heavy in my hands and it was with a feeling of relief that I saw the long black limousine bringing Isobel and her father to the gates.

A gasp of admiration went up from the crowd of well-wishers lining the path leading up to the church door, and Isobel smiled at them serenely, enchanting and virginal in masses of white lace. The spectators were mostly working people from the Carradice and Clifton mills, who had come after hours at their looms to pay homage to a Carradice bride. As I fell into step beside Ruthie, I was aware that I too came in for curious stares and whispered comments. I was Mr Allan's daughter – the one who had married the governess and defied his mother to do so. No doubt they were also thinking how forgiving and gracious my grandmother had been to welcome me to the fold.

The occupants of Carradice pews seemed unduly sombre until I remembered that most of them were in mourning for Roger. Even at Isobel's wedding, they made a show of their grief, and I thought how hypocritical it all was when Roger's wife had not even been invited to be present.

All these thoughts passed through my mind as we made our way along the centre aisle towards the high altar, and it was only when Lavinia stepped forward to take Isobel's bouquet that I gathered my wits. Beside Isobel's willowy slenderness, Henry looked short and stocky. I was busy thinking how wrong they were for each other when I was suddenly shaken by the look I saw on his face as he turned towards her and, unbidden, the hot salty tears rose to my eyes and rolled slowly down my cheeks. I, too, knew that look of love but, try as I might, I could not picture myself standing next to Martin in such a setting. I wondered if it was an omen that our future was not to be together.

Later, at the reception, numerous young men in morning clothes and officer's uniforms tried to be helpful. They flirted with us bridesmaids and admired us. They saw that we were supplied with food and drink and endeavoured to isolate us from the rest of the party. It was all light-hearted and charming but it meant nothing to me, nor it would appear to Lavinia or Ruthie.

My eyes met Henry's across the room and he smiled encouragingly. He and Isobel were circulating and he was talking to his mother, a garrulous woman, resplendent in furs and feathers, thin to the point of emaciation but obviously delighted with the day's events.

Henry made his way over to my side.

'Isobel told me her little cousin was a beauty,' he said with heavy heartiness. 'Are you enjoying yourself?'

'Yes, thank you, Henry. It's been a lovely wedding.'

'It has, hasn't it? Everything of the best and nothing stinted, to say nothing of the beauty of the bride and her bridesmaids. You go right on enjoying yourself and, when we get settled in our new home, you must come to stay with us for a few weeks.'

Quite suddenly I liked him. He was a little pompous, and his acquired wealth had not obliterated the picture of plump little Harry Webb, but he was kind. Isobel sauntered towards us with a glass of champagne in her hand and Henry said, 'I've been telling Jacintha she must come to stay with us, my dear. It will help her to get over young Vasey.'

My eyes opened wide in astonishment and he became confused, helplessly attempting to cover up his words, while Isobel said, 'Don't mind Henry, darling. He's not exactly the soul of diplomacy but his heart's in the right place. Can't we tempt you to any of these handsome young men?'

I smiled weakly, shaking my head.

'Jacintha is turning out to be one of those completely boring creatures, a one-man woman. Can you think of anything more absurd?'

She laughed gaily at her own witticism before she moved away but I could tell by his expression that her words had wounded him.

Next day Lavinia and I returned with our grandmother to Ravenspoint.

I willed the car to go faster along the tortuous twists and bends of the lakeland roads, my eyes fastened hungrily on the lakes we passed and the mountain peaks I had come to know so well in Martin's company. The winter snows had melted on the highest peaks and waterfalls gushed down the mountainsides. Around the margins of the lakes, daffodils bloomed golden beneath the dark evergreens and the maples flamed beside the sombre pines. Soon we would be travelling along the quiet lanes which led to the sea and we were all three silent, busy with our own thoughts.

Every bend in the road, every enchanting vista, brought back memories of Martin, so all I could think of was *this* that I had done with Martin – and this and this – but, if my grandmother was aware of our silence, she said nothing, indeed she seemed unduly preoccupied throughout the journey.

She walked into the house ahead of us and my eyes flew immediately to the silver salver on which the post lay. The officers at Ravenspoint received their post from the hands of their nurses so only the family post lay on that salver. I stood watching my grandmother's long thin fingers leafing through the envelopes until she looked up impatiently.

'Why are you waiting, Jacintha?' she inquired coldly.

I swallowed, helplessly aware of the sudden dryness in my throat. 'I was wondering if there was a letter for me.'

'Were you expecting one?'

'Yes.'

'There is nothing for you, Jacintha. You have time to unpack your case and wash before dinner.'

She went into her sitting room, closing the door with a faint slam behind her, and I climbed the stairs up to my room. Lavinia stood on the first landing waiting for me.

'He hasn't written?' she asked quietly.

'No. Surely they can't possibly have sent him back to France so soon. I'm frightened, Lavinia.'

She shrugged her shoulders indifferently.

'I don't know. I don't know anything about Martin Vasey.' She went into her room, closing the door quietly behind her.

It was the not knowing I hated most. Not knowing if he was alive or dead, whether he still cared or had forgotten my existence in the sterner ways of war. I thought the wretched war would go on for ever and the early days of summer only mocked me with their promise. Now I hated the shafts of bright green along the hedgerows and the pussy willow bursting into gold beside the lake. The gentle summer rain filled the mountain streams as they gurgled and gushed across the fells, but in my private misery I somehow failed to see the look of hope on the eyes of those I met in the country lanes around Ravenspoint. In the end it was Lavinia, animated and happy, who made me see the new squareness in country shoulders and the dawning of relief. At last America was coming into the war and all too soon young American heroes were arriving at Ravenspoint to lick their wounds.

I realized then how tired England was of those years of war; now it seemed as though the windows in every room had suddenly been thrown wide to let in the sunshine. How different they were, these tall carefree young men, brash and impudently abrasive after our own war-weary troops, but I didn't care. They brought the end of the war so much closer and I came to accept their strange humour and stranger English. They addressed my grandmother as 'ma'am' and abbreviated Lavinia's name and mine into diminutive forms which bore little relation to their originals.

Lavinia seemed to blossom overnight. She dieted to get rid of her lingering puppy fat and took more trouble with her fine fair hair, particularly after the arrival of a young lieutenant called Russ Stedman from Boston. He was a tall gangling boy with blond smiling good looks who was flattered by Lavinia's interest. I wanted Lavinia to be happy with her American. I listened to her confidences cheerfully, only wishing I had some of my own to impart to her. Then, one day, she showed me a letter she had received from Russ's mother and a parcel of exquisite underwear, the like of which had not been seen in England for years. I hadn't wanted gifts from Martin's mother, only a letter acknowledging my existence, and after that the old miseries returned and the desire for solitude.

I was much on my own now. In the same disreputable two-seater I had shared with Martin, Lavinia and Russ explored the lakeland countryside until the morning when she came into my bedroom dressed for travel to say she was going with him to London on four days' leave.

'What about grandmother?' I asked, appalled at her unconcern.

'Well, she's not here is she? I'll write to her from London.' I watched her running down the stairs in joyful leaps, straight into the arms of Russ, who waited for her in the hall.

After that, there was little for me to do and few people to talk to, since the Americans had brought their own nurses with them. It was my day for visiting the sewing circle in the village and I was finding little joy in the prospect. Ruthie came so seldom now to Ravenspoint and, although I had written to her several times, she had answered only one of my letters. What surprised me most was that grandmother, who had insisted that we stay in the country, seemed not to object to her absence.

As I walked slowly up the hill on my way back from the village, a long black car pulled up beside me, hooting so loudly I jumped.

'Really, Jacintha, you're going to get run over if you go about like a zombie,' came Isobel's familiar teasing drawl and I looked up in delighted surprise.

'Come on, jump in the car,' she urged me, and I needed no second invitation. She was driving the car herself. A brand new rakish model, and she drove it with obvious aplomb along the narrow twisting lane.

'How long have you been driving?' I asked her.

'Oh, for ages now. You needn't worry, I'm quite good.'

'Is it Henry's car?'

'Of course not, it's mine. I hate that thing he drives, it's like a hearse.'

Inside the house she eyed me critically, and I was suddenly very conscious of my faded cotton dress and shapeless cardigan.

'You do look a mess, Jacintha,' she said with her usual candour. 'You needed to lose some weight but there's no need to go about looking like a fugitive from an orphanage. Have you any decent clothes?'

'Not many, but they wouldn't be much good to me here anyway.'

'Come on upstairs and let me see what you've got.'

I followed her up the stairs, admiring her slender elegance in pale green crêpe de Chine, her legs encased in pure-silk stockings and high-heeled shoes.

Without ceremony, she threw open my wardrobe doors, taking in at a glance my few clothes. She took out my best skirt and a pair of court shoes, the only pair I possessed, then she flung the bridesmaid's dress I had worn for her wedding on the bed.

'I suppose this is the only dress you have that could serve as an evening gown?'

'Yes, but what on earth are you doing? I don't need to wear it here in the evening and it's getting creased on the bed.'

113

By this time, she was rummaging in the dressing-table drawers, going through my underwear.

'How are you for money?' she inquired.

'I have a small allowance, but it's very small. You should know that.'

'Well, come on, put these things in a case. We shall have to get you some more.' She looked at me critically. 'I expect you can get into some of my things now. You're about my size.'

'Isobel, what is all this?' I cried. 'Where are we going?'

'I'm taking you back to Edgemoor with me.'

'To Edgemoor!'

'Yes.'

She had busily crammed my few clothes into a small valise she had found in the wardrobe and now she was bundling my toilet things and hairbrush in with them.

'If you'd like to tell the housekeeper, Jacintha, I'll put these things in the car so that we can get off.'

'But we can't just go like that.'

'Why ever not? Have you something better to do?'

'No.'

'Well, then. Do hurry up, Jacintha, we have a long way to go and I'm not particularly keen on driving along the lakeland roads after dusk. We'll stop and have a meal when we reach civilization.'

The housekeeper showed no surprise. Indeed, I doubted if anything Isobel chose to do would have surprised her and in no time at all we were speeding along the winding lanes along the margin of the lake.

We spoke little. I felt she wanted to concentrate on her driving as the roads twisted and climbed, at times through forests of evergreens, at other times with a sheer drop to the dark waters of a lake or through mountain passes of wild splendour. It was almost dusk when we pulled up outside the imposing entrance of an hotel built like a medieval castle.

'It's not bad here,' Isobel said. 'I've eaten here once or twice in the past so they'll probably recognize me and see that we get a decent meal.'

Considering it was wartime the meal was excellent but we spoke little over it. She answered my questions in monosyllables, so in the end I decided to wait until we reached our destination before asking for explanations.

It was well past midnight when we arrived at Edgemoor. Henry came out of the house to meet us, surrounded by a pack of fawning dogs of all shapes and sizes. They leapt up at Isobel ecstatically, eyeing me with suspicion until Henry put his arms around us both and walked with us into the house.

I remember very little of the rest of that night. They allowed me to go straight to bed, to the cool luxury of smooth linen sheets and a glass of hot milk, 'with something in it to help you to sleep', said Henry.

I awoke to bright sunlight shining in through the open window and the sound of bird song. The curtains had been pulled back by someone who had not disturbed me; my watch had stopped at six o'clock, and I was convinced it must be much later than this. I was debating whether I should get up or not when there was a soft tap on the door and a young maid entered carrying a breakfast tray. She smiled at me shyly as she laid the tray on the bed and I struggled to sit up.

'Mrs Clifton-Webb says there's no hurry to get up, miss, she'll be in to see you when you've eaten breakfast.'

'Is she up already? My watch has stopped and I'm not sure of the time.'

'It's nearly ten o'clock, miss, but the mistress isn't an early riser. She's still in her room.'

She smiled at me briefly and left me to get on with my breakfast. I was on my second cup of coffee when Isobel sailed into the room, beautiful and glamorous in a black lace négligée, her worldly sophistication somehow making my buttoned-up nightdress seem immature and childlike.

'It's terribly late, Isobel,' I said, troubled by my lethargy.

She waved an airy hand. 'I can't cope with guests who get up at the crack of dawn and expect me to do likewise. If you rise any earlier than this, I can promise you you'll be breakfasting with Henry.'

She removed the tray unceremoniously, then perched on the end of my bed.

'What shall we do today?' she asked brightly. 'We could go to the shops and have tea at one of the hotels. It's time you saw a bit of life.'

'I'd like to leave that to you, Isobel. I honestly don't mind where we go. Does my grandmother know I am staying here?'

'No. She's away at the moment anyway so she needn't know.'

'Perhaps we could call and see Ruthie one day; she's such a bad correspondent.'

Isobel jumped to her feet and went to stand at the window, looking out across the park. For a few moments I thought I had made her angry by my mention of Ruthie, but when she returned to my bedside her face was serene, if unsmiling.

'You can't go into town in that skirt you brought with you. We'll have a look in my wardrobe to see if there is anything I can lend you.'

'It's my best skirt. I haven't had it very long.'

'I know – it seems timeless, like all the other things one buys from those country shops. Come to my room when you're ready; it's at the end of the corridor.'

She left me abruptly. I was worried by her behaviour. Her attitude had changed after Ruthie's name was mentioned and I had to find out why.

I bathed quickly and shrugged my arms into my dressing gown before going to Isobel's room. I found her standing in front of her wardrobe with a pile of clothes over her arm. She deposited them on the back of a chair one by one and started to look for more. I had never seen so many coats and gowns in my life before, and they all seemed to be new.

'Have a look at these, Jacintha; there should be something in that lot that will fit you. Take a few afternoon frocks and some evening ones, then we'll look for a coat and a decent evening wrap for you.'

They were elegant clothes and I couldn't help asking, 'Where have you managed to buy these in wartime?'

'You can still get them if you've money to pay for them. I bought some of them years ago – in Switzerland, probably.'

As I made my selection, I asked innocently, 'Isobel, why were you so evasive when I mentioned Ruthie?'

'Was I evasive? I wasn't aware of it.'

'You don't like her, do you?'

'I have no feelings for Ruthie either one way or the other.'

'But she's your cousin.'

'She's your cousin too, but that won't stop her taking what's yours if she feels inclined.'

'What do you mean by that?'

116

'Oh, leave it alone, Jacintha. I don't want to talk about Ruthie. We're wasting this glorious day when we could be out and about.'

She forced me to choose what I would wear: a pale-blue linen dress, beautifully simple and exquisitely cut, and a small flowered hat of the same shade. She stepped back to look at me.

'You're beautiful, Jacintha, do you know that? Nobody would have looked twice at you in those country clothes, but in that dress and that hat you look like a princess.'

I blushed at her unaccustomed praise, back-handed though it was, and I enjoyed the day. We walked through the park in the bright sunshine and watched the children sailing their boats on the shallow pond. We looked in shop windows and took luncheon in the grill room of the town's largest hotel, then promptly at four we returned for the afternoon tea-dance. It was attended by a host of Isobel's friends and a plentiful supply of young officers on leave from the front or convalescing from wounds. Isobel was popular, which did not surprise me at all. She was beautiful, vivacious and often outrageous, and I as her young cousin came in for my share of flattery and light-hearted flirtation.

We were on our way out when a girl's voice hailed us from a corner table and Isobel caught me by the arm saying, 'Oh, drat, it's Iris Devenage; she's the last person I wanted to see.'

It was too late to do anything about it. She bore down upon us with outstretched hands and a smile of welcome on her pretty vapid face.

'Isobel, darling, they said you were with your cousin but I thought it was Ruthie.'

'No, this is my cousin Jacintha.'

'I've been trying to get hold of Ruthie all day. Is she away?'

'I believe so and I'm not sure when she will be back.'

'That's a nuisance. I did so want her to make up a four for a supper party tomorrow night, but I suppose I'll have to look for somebody else.' She fixed me with a bright smile and asked, 'I don't suppose you would like to come instead, Jacintha?'

'Not tomorrow. I'm sorry, Iris, we are having friends in for dinner,' Isobel said easily. 'You don't mind if we rush off, do you, darling? I'm expecting Henry home early tonight.'

As we hurried out of the hotel, I asked if Isobel knew Iris well, adding as an afterthought, 'You don't like her, do you?'

'She's the world's worst busybody. I'm never sure what she's going to say next.'

'Are you really having friends in to dinner tomorrow evening?'

'Of course. Just some old friends and one or two young officers on convalescent leave.'

I was quiet on the way home. I couldn't help wondering how much convalescent leave wounded officers got or how soon before they might be expected to return to their units. Once more I began to experience the fluttering sensation of unease. There was something wrong in Isobel's bringing me here and it was connected with Ruthie's absence from the city.

'Isobel, why did you bring me here? It wasn't because you thought I needed a holiday, was it?'

'Not entirely.'

'I know what it is – something has happened to Martin, he's dead, isn't he? He's dead and my grandmother has gone to see his parents.'

I was shaking by this time, my hands clenched together in my lap. I could tell Isobel was frightened by her face and the way she jumped to her feet shouting, 'Jacintha, stop it, stop it. Of course he isn't dead.'

She came to sit beside me on the couch, taking my trembling hands in hers. Then, in sheer exasperation, she said, 'If you must know, Jacintha, grandmother has gone to see the Vaseys, and Ruthie and her parents have gone with her.'

My eyes opened wide with amazement.

'But why Ruthie?' I gasped. 'Anyway, Martin isn't there, is he?'

'Oh, he's there all right. Listen to me, Jacintha, I tried to warn you on the day of my wedding, but you were so sure then that Ruthie was your one true friend you wouldn't hear anything bad about her. Ruthie's always been like that, sweet and fragile and as strong as steel. Lavinia and I always said what we wanted and didn't always get it, but Ruthie never wanted anything until somebody else wanted it. Then because she was delicate with pretty ways, everything had to be handed to her on a platter.'

'But Ruthie didn't want Martin.'

'Of course she wanted Martin. I thought if I was scathing enough about him you might realize he wasn't for you and fall out of love with him, but you were so besotted you couldn't see any further than your nose.'

'Oh no, no, I don't believe it. I would have suspected if there'd been anything. Martin couldn't have been so loving if he'd wanted Ruthie and not me.'

'He didn't want her, you little ninny. It was you he wanted then, but Ruthie wanted him. That's why she sulked in her room, why she stayed away for whole weeks at a time, why she didn't answer your letters. Don't you see, Jacintha?'

'I only see that she might have wanted Martin. I don't see how she could get him if he loved me.'

Her face was mocking me with its old malice. 'Don't tell me he didn't encourage you to make your peace with grand-mother, to be a good little girl and play it her way. He may have loved you, Jacintha, but he wasn't a fool. You haven't enough money for Martin Vasey and I tried to tell you he's got none of his own and, although cotton's in clover while the war's on, Henry says it's an industry that could totter into trouble quite soon afterwards. Ruthie's a different proposi-tion altogether. She's an only child, her father's a director at Carradice's and, if Martin marries Ruthie, he could conceiv-ably take her father's place on the board at some future time. Why, Jacintha, you haven't even got your mother's diamond ring to call your own.'

'How do you know about that?' I asked sharply.

'You seem to forget Lavinia's fondness for listening at doors.'

I was silent because suddenly there seemed nothing more to say. All the past months seemed to be fitting into place and I was remembering Martin's face, troubled when I talked about the antipathy which flared between my grandmother and me whenever we met and my father's disobedience which had caused it. Isobel was right. Compared to Ruthie, I wasn't a very good proposition for a younger son with no money and no profession. She watched me in silence, seeing the various emotions flit across my face, until in the end there was accep-tance.

'Forget him, Jacintha. Henry and I will give you the time of your life, you'll see. You'll meet lots of young men here only

119

too willing to take you out and give you a whirl.'

'No, thank you,' I said bitterly. 'Young men are the last people I want to be with. I might meet others with Martin Vasey's ideas.'

'What utter rubbish! You don't mean to tell me he's going to be the solitary passion of a lifetime? You are going to wear some pretty clothes and get your hair done properly. I shall ask Henry for some money and we'll go out together and spend it.'

'I can't possibly take money from Henry.'

'*I* can. Besides, I'm always telling him he shouldn't be such an old skinflint. His mother thinks I'm wickedly extravagant and I suppose her ideas rub off on him. He might enjoy spending it on you, though.'

'I don't see why he should.'

'Oh, you know, the motherless waif, the child who came in from the storm. It will make him feel all good and worthy.'

'And you make me sound like a charitable institution.'

I couldn't argue with Isobel, I never could. I couldn't tell her I didn't want a good time on Henry's money, dressed up in clothes I had no right to, and, in the numb misery which came over me, I allowed her to sweep me along in her wake. Henry gave me a generous dress allowance and with it I bought clothes under Isobel's guidance. I had my hair styled and discovered three-inch heels, and I tried desperately hard to enjoy the concerts and the tea-dances in smart hotel rooms, as well as the evening balls in aid of some war effort or other.

I never lacked for partners. I was always surrounded by a crowd of young officers but cynically I suspected they were more interested in Henry's hospitality before and after the balls than they were in me. When I said as much to Isobel, she laughed merrily.

'If you don't watch it, Jacintha, you are in danger of becoming something of a wit, and a wit at your age could be a shrew at thirty. Stop judging all men by your experience with one.'

So I jumped on Isobel's merry-go-round that never stopped and, if our laughter seemed a little too shrill, a shade too hysterical, who could blame us as we strove to forget the tragedies of war in the fleeting joys of the moment? The nights were filled with the wailing of saxophones as we danced until dawn in the arms of young men who laughed and flirted with us but whose eyes were still haunted by the horrors they had seen and might soon see again. They were constantly changing, those young officers of 1917. One night they were there, the next morning they were just another name in a newspaper to be tossed around the breakfast table.

I can see Henry now, calmly drinking his coffee while his eyes scanned the centre pages of the newspaper, then saying casually, 'I see young Fielding's bought it on the Somme.'

'Who?' Isobel asked, leafing through her morning mail and smoking one of her Turkish cigarettes from an incredibly long ivory holder.

'Fielding. Bob Fielding's youngest brother.'

'Do I know him, darling?'

'You should. You spent enough time dancing with him at the Eldridges'. Tall fair boy, nice-looking lad. Yeomanry.'

'Of course. Yes, darling, I do remember him now. You knew him too, didn't you, Jacintha? I rather thought you two were getting on awfully well together. I hope not too well as things have turned out.'

'Yes, I remember him very well. He wrote to me after he left.'

'Did he, darling? How nice. How positively frightful to die so young.'

Then Henry would turn the pages to find the stock-market prices and Isobel would continue to smile or frown over her mail. Once, after such a conversation, I had burst into tears and run from the room, only to be upbraided by Isobel later for being silly and emotional.

'We have to live with this sort of thing, Jacintha,' she told me sternly. 'Look at me after poor Roger was killed. I had to get over it the best way I could. After all, if you go around with a permanently long face and burst into tears at the drop of a hat, nobody, absolutely nobody, wants to know you.'

So I learned to flirt and talk insincerities, and it was only when I heard some tune I had once heard with Martin, or caught sight of a gilded fair head over officer's khaki, that my heart missed a beat and the old misery returned.

I had been with Isobel a month when Ruthie returned to Wellsford. I was alone in the house because Isobel had gone to a fête at the City Hall in aid of the Red Cross and I had stayed home with a headache. It was raining and I sat alone in the drawing room overlooking the tennis courts at the back of the house. I felt restless, the book in my hands failing to capture my interest, and I looked up eagerly at the click from the opening door. Instead of Isobel, however, it was Ruthie who stood there, blinking at me in pink confusion.

We stared at each other stupidly for several moments and I watched the rich red colour flood her cheeks and slender neck, while her hands played nervously with her gloves. We were like two adult cats eyeing each other suspiciously, both wary, wondering which would be the first to pounce, and I was surprised that I could be cruel enough to enjoy her discomfort. I was determined that she should be the first to speak and when she did her voice was breathless and uncontrolled.

'I rang the bell but nobody came,' she stammered. 'The door was off the catch so I came in. . . . I didn't expect to see you here, Jacintha.'

'No.'

'Have you been here long?'

'Almost a month.'

She consulted her watch, frowning a little.

'I really came to see Isobel, but if she isn't at home perhaps I could call again later.'

She was nervous, but as she hovered at the entrance to the door other expressions chased themselves across her face – defiance and the spoilt petulance of a child.

'Why not wait for her? I don't expect she will be long,' I said, indicating that she should take the chair opposite my own.

The silence between us was charged with undercurrents and she was the first to break it.

'When are you going home?' she asked at last.

'To Ravenspoint?'

'Of course. Have you enjoyed it here?'

'Very much. Have you enjoyed your stay with the Vaseys?'

'Isobel told you?'

'Yes.'

'I'm sorry, Jacintha. It was grandmother's idea that we went with her; she didn't want to travel alone.'

'Oh, Ruthie, let us at least be honest with each other. She knew how important it was to you that you went with her.'

She jumped to her feet so suddenly that the cushion on her chair tumbled to the floor. Then she went over to the window and stood for a moment staring out into the garden. I waited as calmly as I could, my hands clenched so fiercely together the nails bit into the palms.

'All right then,' she said at last, 'I did go to the Vaseys and I did see Martin and . . .'

The door opened again and this time it was Isobel who entered the room. Her eyes took in at a glance both the situation and the atmosphere, and from her expression I knew she was prepared to enjoy it.

'So you're back. Grandmother too?' she asked.

I felt sick with resentment watching Isobel perched on the arm of the chair Ruthie had left, her eyes filled with that malicious humour I knew so well, and Ruthie standing near the window, slight and elegant, meeting Isobel's amused eyes with pink defiance.

'And how were the Vaseys, and Martin in particular? Martin was on leave, wasn't he?'

'Yes.'

Isobel turned to me, her face mocking.

'You see, Jacintha, like I told you, Ruthie would have had the opportunity to get to know him very well and it's a fallacy that absence makes the heart grow fonder. It's much more accurate to think that out of sight is out of mind.'

Ruthie came to stand behind the settee, her hands clutching its back.

'Honestly, Jacintha, we didn't mean it to happen, neither of us could help it.'

'If you believe that, my dear, you'll believe anything,' Isobel said drily.

'Oh, shut up, Isobel, you're making it worse than it is,' Ruthie snapped and even in the midst of my misery I was surprised to hear that note of anger in her voice and see the fury in a face I had always thought of as sweet. Now she resembled a spiteful kitten.

'I'm sorry, but do go ahead. Tell Jacintha just how bad it is and leave her to judge for herself.'

'I'm going to marry him, on his next leave if that's possible, quietly, in Lancashire.' Her voice was rushed and breathless, and she spoke with her eyes looking at some corner of the room far over my head. 'When the war is over we'll get a home, either near his family or near mine – it doesn't much matter since my father will find him a job at the mill if he doesn't wish to go back into cotton.'

I had loved Martin and I had lost him, but Ruthie had been my friend and now I had lost her too. It was a strange moment to think of the words old Meg had said to us all those years before. She had promised me bitterness and tears, yet at that particular moment I was too stunned for tears.

Isobel was watching me closely and I did not miss her grudging look of admiration when I raised my head in proud defiance.

'I think I'll go to my room now, Isobel. My headache's come back and I'd rather not come down for dinner tonight if you don't mind.'

'Of course not. I'll have something sent up to you and I'll explain matters to Henry.'

I rewarded her with a tremulous smile, then went upstairs.

For a long time I stood staring out of the window at the grey misery of the day. The sodden garden was in keeping with my mood, the puddles along the garden paths and the steady drip of rain from the leaves of the beeches hanging dejectedly still, the flower heads drooping, heavy with rain, while the birds huddled miserably together on the branches of the trees all found a response in my own sorrow.

I made up my mind that next morning I would tell Isobel that I was going home, but matters were taken out of my hands. Henry had to go to London urgently on business and Isobel had a feverish chill which confined her to bed. It would have been ungrateful for me to have left her at such a time.

I stayed for several weeks because, each time I suggested that it was time I went home, Isobel found a hundred and one reasons why I should stay at Edgemoor.

I was becoming increasingly uneasy. Everywhere we went, at every party, every concert, every meeting with friends, Isobel gravitated towards one particular young officer. He was a Canadian major, Brian Downson, tall, handsome, with bold laughing eyes and an assured way with women.

More and more I found that Henry was becoming my escort and watching his face I was convinced that he was miserably aware of what was going on. There were times at the theatre when I would see Brian's hand reach out for Isobel's under cover of the darkness and I would sit there terrified in case

Henry should see. Henry was no dancer, therefore Isobel danced with Brian. I found myself chatting feverishly with Henry in order to keep him away from the dance floor, but then, when some man asked me to dance, I was painfully aware of Henry standing at the edge of the floor, his eyes searching for Isobel's gay laughing face amongst the dancers. It was even worse when he looked in vain, when I knew she was with Brian in the conservatory.

After such episodes, I dreaded Henry's sarcasm and bouts of depression as much as I dreaded Isobel's tantrums and her angry rejoinders. He adored her and she was openly flirting with disaster. I realized I must return to Ravenspoint as soon as possible.

'Isobel, I have made up my mind to go back to Ravenspoint tomorrow.' When I started to tell her, her face changed and became petulant, like the spoiled child she was.

'Why tomorrow, for heaven's sake? You could at least wait until after the Jeffersons' party at the end of the month.'

'I don't think they'll mind in the least. I shall of course write to Mrs Jefferson, but most people will probably think I've overstayed my welcome anyway.'

'If you think Ruthie's going to be at the Jeffersons', she isn't. She's in Lancashire with the Vaseys.'

'I wasn't thinking of Ruthie.'

'What on earth do you want to go back to Ravenspoint for? A lot of wounded heroes and that dreary foghorn sounding night and day. You really are an ungrateful little brat, Jacintha.'

'I'm not in the least ungrateful. I've loved being here and you and Henry have been more than kind to me, but I can't stand to see you becoming so careless. Pushing me off with Henry isn't going to work forever. He's getting very suspicious, you know, and you and Brian are becoming careless.'

'Has Henry said anything to you?'

'He doesn't have to. He's unhappy and worried, and it's so pointless to jeopardize your marriage for something that can't possibly come to anything.'

'Who wants it to come to anything? Brian is married anyway.'

'Are you in love with him?'

'Really, Jacintha, you seem to be obsessed with the whole

idea of love. I don't know whether I am or not, but I do know that Henry bores me to tears. All he's interested in are his wretched mills and the money he makes.'

'You'd be more bored if he hadn't any. You certainly know how to spend it.'

'Well, you don't think I married him for his charm or his fascinating good looks, do you? Things like that are not all-important when you have as much money as Henry's got.'

When she saw that I was adamant about leaving Edgemoor, she began to cry, stormy, self-indulgent tears which embarrassed me, so I left her alone, glad to escape into the privacy of my own room. Resolutely, I took out the things I had brought with me from Ravenspoint and laid them on my bed. I decided I would travel home in the skirt and blouse I had worn on my arrival, and the rest of the things I had brought with me packed easily into the valise. The clothes I had bought with Henry's money I left in the wardrobe. I knew I would not be able to carry them and I thought I should speak to him about them before I assumed they were mine to take away.

Dinner that night was a silent meal. Isobel had the sulks and Henry too seemed troubled. I was determined, however, that this time nothing was going to deter me from my purpose and over coffee I said, 'Henry, I have decided to go home to Ravenspoint in the morning.'

He looked up surprised, then asked, 'When did you decide to do that?'

'I've been thinking about it for days now. I've been here too long already and I thought if I begged a lift from you to the station in the morning I wouldn't be putting anybody out.'

'But what about your luggage?'

'I have very little. I have left my clothes in the wardrobe, the ones you paid for, I mean. In any case, they won't fit into my small valise.'

'Those clothes are yours, my girl. Never let it be said that Harry Webb gives presents with one hand and takes them back with the other.'

'You see, Jacintha,' Isobel drawled sarcastically, 'how readily my husband reverts to his origins when he needs to boast a little.'

I jumped to my feet, all too aware of Isobel's mood and

Henry's heightened colour. Impulsively, I bent down and kissed his cheek as I passed his chair, excusing myself on the grounds that I still had packing to do.

I did not sleep well and the early morning light found me dressed and ready to leave. It was long before breakfast so I let myself out of the side door and through the greenhouses. From the bottom of the garden I could look out across the city with its domes and steeples and factory chimneys still sleeping under the ever-present pall of purple smoke. In the mills, the night shift would just about be finishing and along the cobbled streets the next shift would be hurrying to start the day's toil. Sauntering back to the house through the gardens, I wondered about those people who toiled like ants in those giant mills, while people like the Carradice women filled their lives with frivolous things, and I resolved that some day soon I would speak to my grandmother about my own future.

After I had eaten breakfast I went upstairs to say goodbye to Isobel and found her sitting up in bed reading her mail. She was still annoyed with me, showing her displeasure much as my grandmother did by allowing me to stand beside her while she continued to read. After several minutes I said, 'I'm sorry, Isobel, but I'm keeping Henry waiting. I just came to say goodbye.'

She looked up then.

'You're really going, then?'

'Yes. Henry says you'll be coming to Ravenspoint before the end of the summer. Perhaps you can bring the rest of my clothes then.'

She shrugged her shoulders indifferently. 'Oh well, if he says so.'

I bent down to kiss her cheek but she turned her head away impatiently.

'You are a fool, Jacintha. You could have had such a good time here. This is a garrison town filled with young officers from all over the place. Who knows, you might even have captured a husband. That would certainly have been one in the eye for Ruthie and Martin Vasey. What are you going to do at Ravenspoint, for heaven's sake?'

'I love it there. I'm not like you Isobel. I love the sea and the lakes and that dreary old house you dislike so much.'

'Well, it's not your house. One of these days the war will be

127

over and Adrian will come back to Ravenspoint. He'll want you out of it and then what will you do?'

'I don't know, but it's a problem I shall have to face when the time comes.'

'Well, here we are offering you an escape from all that and you won't take it.'

'It's not my escape you are thinking about, Isobel, it's yours. And I think too much of Henry to help you deceive him.'

'I wish you wouldn't be so smug. I missed all the good times I was promised because of this stupid war and marriage was the first chance I had of getting away from grandmother and Ravenspoint. I want my good times now before I'm old and creaking with rheumatism. You'll see, after the war I'll settle down with Henry and bring up a brood of little Henrys, but not until I've made up for all the things I've missed. If you'd any sense, you'd be doing the same thing.'

I smiled at her gently and left her, closing the door quietly behind me. I didn't know who was right, but I did know that I wanted to go home to the peace of the long summer evenings and the sound of the breakers crashing on the rocks below the house. I wanted to fill my lungs with the sharp salty tang of the sea and see the dark dismal beauty of the pine forests along the rim of the lake and the clouds resting dreamily on the distant peaks.

Perhaps Isobel was right and there was very little time left for me to enjoy the things I had come to love, but as I stood with Henry on the station platform my heart felt lighter than it had done for days.

He had pushed newspapers and chocolates into my hands saying, 'There aren't any magazines, Jacintha, and the papers won't do much to cheer you up, but you needn't read them if you don't want to.'

I kissed him warmly, then hurried down the platform towards the waiting train. I turned to wave to him before I climbed into the compartment, pleased to see him waiting bareheaded at the barrier.

I shared a carriage with an elderly couple and a young officer travelling north to Scotland and they were glad to share my newspapers. Henry was right – they depressed me with their inner pages filled with the casualties of war and I was far happier to be gazing out at the scenery. The wild moors of Yorkshire were already purple with heather and, on either side of the carriage windows, the rolling fells gave way to the bleak Pennine hills which form the backbone of England. I was a different girl from the one who had driven so light-heartedly with Isobel on that afternoon in the spring. Now there was disillusionment in my heart, where there had once been hope, and cynicism where there had once been love.

It was late afternoon when I finally descended from the little country train onto the village platform. The evening breeze was warm and I decided to walk the distance between the station and the house. Smoke drifted upwards from cottage chimneys and a white mist hung low above the fields. I could smell the sea but my dragon was quiet and my heart leaped at the sight of the house standing lonely and splendid on its rugged point.

I let myself in by the conservatory. The house was quiet and the hall was in darkness except for the light from one crystal chandelier over the staircase. The officers would be in their rooms before the evening meal. I escaped into my room unseen and hurried to unpack my case and change into something more comfortable than my travelling clothes. I wondered if I should go down to the kitchens to announce my arrival and was on the point of opening the door when it was opened for me by a young girl who stood blinking in the light. I had not seen her before, but I thought her to be a girl from the village, little more than fifteen years old.

'I saw the light under the door, miss. I wondered who was in here.'

She spoke shyly with a soft lakeland burr, which I guessed would become more pronounced as she lost her shyness.

'I'm Jacintha Carradice,' I explained. 'I have been away and I haven't seen you before. Are you new here?'

'Yes, miss. I'm Mary, Lucy's niece, I've allus lived int' village.'

'Do you live in now, Mary, or do you go home in the evening?'

'I goes home wi' Lucy, miss. Mi mither's her sister.'

'But Lucy lives in.'

'No, miss, not since Sam were killed ont' Somme. She's stayin wi' us fert' time being.'

I sat down weakly on the side of my bed shaken by her news, remembering how proud Sam had been in his new khaki, and how firm Lucy had been in her conviction that he bore a charmed life and would return to her unscathed.

'Oh, I am so sorry. Poor Lucy, she'll be absolutely grief-stricken.'

The girl nodded her head and I said, 'I'll go down to the kitchen to see her as soon as the evening meal is over. Perhaps you would tell them I'm home?'

She nodded her head again and with a swift awkward little curtsey she let herself out of the room.

What could I say to Lucy to give her comfort, I wondered. So many fine young men had died and so many more would die before this dreadful war was over. We had grown accustomed to living with disaster but that did not diminish personal grief.

I bolstered up my courage and went down the stairs, intending to go down to the kitchen immediately. However, Lucy was just emerging from my grandmother's sitting room carrying an empty coal-scuttle in her hands. She put her finger to her lips to caution me to silence, then she whispered, 'Mrs Carradice is here, miss. I should go in to see her. She's been grumbling to the housekeeper every day that it was time you came back from Miss Isobel's.'

I wished I didn't fear my grandmother so. With Lucy's words, the same old hostility was making my tongue and throat dry with apprehension, making my heart race and my limbs feel that they no longer belonged to me, and when her cold voice bade me enter her room I felt sick with anxiety.

She stared at me in silence and as always I was not invited to sit.

'So you are back, Jacintha. When did you arrive?'

'About an hour ago.'

'You did not see fit to acquaint me of your arrival.'

'I'm sorry, but I didn't know you were here.'

'Nor did you acquaint me of your departure.'

'But you were in Lancashire, grandmother. It was not possible for me to do so.'

Her ivory face coloured slightly and I could feel my courage returning as I recognized for the first time that she was confused.

'I am surprised you stayed so long. It is not usual for a newly married couple to invite long-staying guests so early in their married life.'

I did not think that statement required an answer. I could tell my silence irritated her from the way she twisted the long strand of pearls she wore round her neck.

'I am displeased with Isobel and with you, Jacintha. Isobel's behaviour is on everybody's lips and Henry's mother is so scandalized by it she came personally to see me. You, it appears, have been her aider and abetter. You have disappointed me, Jacintha. Isobel has always been spoiled and wilful but I credited you with more sense.'

I stared at her incredulously, at first not believing what I had just heard – the injustice of the automatic assumption that I was as much to blame for Isobel's vagaries as she was. Then I got angry and I was glad of my anger for with it the fear went as swiftly as it had appeared.

'How dare you accuse me of condoning Isobel's behaviour? I had nothing to do with it; in fact, it was one of my reasons for leaving.'

'That does not alter my opinion. Isobel is spoiled, you should know better.'

'Nobody can accuse you of spoiling me, grandmother.'

'Nor am I here to bandy words with you. You will not go to Isobel's again without my permission, nor anywhere else for that matter.'

'There is nowhere else I wish to go.'

'You have other cousins.'

'I have one who has not been ashamed to steal the man I loved and another who will leave this house as soon as she is able, probably never to return to it.'

'If you are speaking of Lavinia, she knows which side her bread is buttered. Lavinia, like you, will do as she is told.'

'And Ruthie?'

'I have long been acquainted with the Vasey family, and from their point of view and the point of view of the Carradice family Ruthie's marriage to Martin Vasey is a desirable one and one to the benefit of both families. If the man in question had truly cared for you as you have said, Ruthie would never have been able to usurp his affections.'

She had won, again she had won and she knew it. My anger

evaporated and left between us a deep-seated resentment and the spectre of an old hatred. There was no sound in the room apart from the scratching of her pen and the sighing of the night wind outside the house. I waited by her chair until at last she laid down her pen. Fixing me with her penetrating stare, she said, 'You may go to your room now, Jacintha, and I will have a tray sent up to you. I want no whispered conspiracies with Lavinia or talk with Lucy. The girl has suffered a bereavement like so many of our young women. It is one she will have to recover from and hard work is worth more than tearful condolences. Close the door quietly as you leave.'

It was incredible. I was nineteen years of age and I still felt like a child when faced with her implacability, that same child who had been unceremoniously dragged up the stairs years before.

I sat in my room smarting under her unfairness and I had little appetite for the food Mary brought to my room. After she had taken the tray away, I tiptoed along to Lavinia's room but there was no light showing under her door and when I opened it quietly the room was empty. Lavinia's dressing gown was thrown across the bed and her slippers had been kicked off hurriedly so that one lay near the window and the other at the foot of the bed. The room had a lived-in untidiness but, although I waited for over half an hour, Lavinia did not come. I lay awake until long past midnight hoping she would come to see me and I could only assume she had been told to keep away.

During the next few days I saw her seldom. If we met on the stairs, she would smile briefly and hurry away – a state of affairs which went on for several weeks until I was almost at screaming pitch. I did get the opportunity to speak to Lucy and, although her eyes filled with tears, she looked round swiftly to see if we were observed before she thanked me for my sympathy.

At the end of November, Ruthie came with her parents to Ravenspoint. I recognized their voices and heard their laughter and I ached with the hurt inside me. As I passed Lavinia on the stairs, she shrugged her shoulders expressively but no words passed between us.

Needless to say, Ruthie never came near the room we had shared, but late in the afternoon I passed Aunt Ruth on the stairs. She greeted me more effusively than usual and with such heightened colour I could only assume she was embarrassed by our meeting. I in turn was respectful but distant, glad that I was able to excuse myself quickly on the grounds that I was keeping one of the officers waiting for the book in my hands. I have no doubt she was as pleased to see me depart as I was to be doing so. One good thing alone emerged from their visit; when they left Ravenspoint, they took my grandmother with them.

It was barely daylight next morning when I found myself being shaken awake and Lavinia's voice urgently saying, 'Wake up, Jacintha, wake up.'

Rubbing the sleep from my eyes I struggled to sit up. Then I saw Lavinia standing over me in her outdoor clothes.

'What time is it?' I mumbled, fumbling on the bedside table for my watch.

'It's half past six. You can go back to sleep again when I've gone.'

'Gone! Gone where?'

'I'm catching the milk train to Carlisle, then I'm getting the London train from there. I packed all my stuff last night as soon as I knew she'd gone back to the city. Most of it's been packed for days anyway.'

'But why are you going to London? You can't, Lavinia. What will grandmother say?'

'I'm going to stay with friends of Russ's until we can be married. He knows. I wrote to tell him that the first chance I got I would leave here and he gave me an address to go to. They're expecting me.'

I was wide awake now and anxious.

'Lavinia, you don't have to go like this. Surely you can marry Russ openly and honestly? He comes from a good family, he's nice and presentable. What makes you think the family won't approve?'

'You still don't know what being a Carradice is all about, do you, Jacintha? They were all here when you were away. I know, I listened at the sitting-room door. They were going on about you and Isobel, then they started on me because I had been up to London with an American officer whom I was

133

under no circumstances to see again. My grandmother is not concerned that Russ's family is as good as ours. All she wants is to keep us close to her so that she can move us about like pawns on a chessboard. You should get away too, Jacintha, it's the only way.'

'Before she makes me marry somebody I don't want, you mean?'

'I don't think she intends you to marry anybody at all. You're to be her companion when she grows too old to manipulate people.'

'That's nonsense. She wouldn't choose me to be her companion, I'm not malleable enough. Besides, we don't really like each other.'

'All the more reason to keep you near her. It would be your punishment.'

'One day Adrian will come back. Things will be different then.'

'Oh yes, but they won't be any better. He'll marry, probably Leoni de Montforte – his mother would like that – and in the end it will be my grandmother and Aunt Marguerite who will fight over Adrian.'

'This is a terrible family to belong to. Will he bring her here, do you think?'

'Of course. Adrian will want the best of both worlds. He won't let the Carradice mills slip through his fingers. Anyway, there's no time to talk about it now. I've left a note on grandmother's desk, she'll see it when she gets back.' Her voice trilled into laughter. 'Poor you, I wouldn't like to be you when she knows where I am, she'll be vile.'

'But when will you be married?'

'Russ got his commanding officer's approval when we went away for those few days in the spring. We can get a special licence and get married immediately. I haven't told my grandmother where I shall be staying and I'm not telling you, otherwise she'd get it out of you sure as anything.'

'Will you ever come back to Ravenspoint, Lavinia?'

'Not if I can help it. I've taken all the clothes I shall want, if there's anything you need help yourself. The rest you can take down to the village hall; somebody there might be glad of them.'

'Wait,' I cried. 'Let me put some clothes on and I'll come to

134

the station with you.'

'There's no need. I'm taking the pony and trap but I'll leave him outside the station where he can nibble the grass. I'll tie him to the rails. Will you collect him later this morning and bring him home?'

I nodded and for several moments we stared at one another wordlessly, then impulsively she bent forward and hugged me.

I had never thought that Lavinia was emotional but there were tears in her eyes which she hastily brushed away. She laughed a little shakily. 'I can't really believe I'm leaving here for the last time,' she said.

'Will you never come back?'

'No, never, not even when I'm old. What's the use of being nostalgic about the past? I'd be a hypocrite to say I've been happy here; it's wild and lonely and I'm like Isobel – I love life. Russ says the war will be over soon and I'll be off to America. I'm going to be happy, Jacintha, believe me.'

'What about your parents, have you thought of them?'

'Oh, they'll forgive me in time. They always have.'

She went quietly for Lavinia. I strained my ears to hear the sound of wheels and hoofs on the gravel outside my window but I heard nothing, only the sound of the surf upon the shore and the wild mournful cries of the gulls. All the same, Lavinia's departure from Ravenspoint seemed to me like the closing of another chapter of my life.

7

In the autumn of 1918 it was all over, the weeping and the wailing, the prayers of thanksgiving and the victory marches. The men were coming back to the farms. They sat with their families in the little church on Sundays dressed in their ill-fitting suits, shorn of the glamour of their uniforms, but they were not the same men who had marched so blithely to war. Their eyes were still haunted by the horror they had seen, by the envy and the hatred that had brought about such horror, unmindful now of the reserves of latent courage and talent that had emerged from it.

That first Christmas after the war the Carradice family assembled in its entirety at Ravenspoint – apart, that is, from Lavinia and Adrian. My grandmother was bitterly disappointed that Adrian had not come to stay with her for Christmas and remained unmindful of his greater need to see his parents. Lavinia wrote to me under the cover of a letter she had sent to Teddy, and he surreptitiously passed it to me under cover of the dining table on Christmas Eve.

It felt strange to be sitting at the same table as Martin, now that he was married to Ruthie, but the old enchantment was gone and I was glad of it. I could now look at him in the same way I looked at Henry or Teddy, dispassionately, uncaringly, but I was cruel enough to notice that his eyes were afraid to meet mine and that Ruthie too seemed uncomfortable in my presence. I often wondered if she was happy. One never knew with Ruthie; she had that detached lack of substance which I had once taken for gentleness. Now I knew it to be the gentleness of tempered steel.

Grandmother presided over the festivities with her usual autocracy. Teddy jumped whenever she spoke to him, but she seldom spoke to me and, when Isobel's eyes met mine across the table, I was only too aware of the mockery in them. The family deferred to grandmother's wishes, her comfort and her entertainment, but on Christmas night, bored with talk of the manufacture of wool and the comings and goings of a workforce she had little interest in, Isobel suggested that the younger members of the party should go up to the old schoolroom to dance to the gramophone records she had brought with her.

'Gracious, how we've dwindled!' she complained. 'I remember thinking that after the war there would be more of us. Instead, we've lost Adrian and Lavinia, as well as poor Roger. We've collected Martin and Henry, of course, but it's high time Teddy and Jacintha produced somebody.'

At one time, taunts such as this would have embarrassed me into anguished silence, now they had no power to hurt me. Nevertheless I remembered Teddy's rebellion at any talk of dancing and I had no reason to suppose that his accomplishment in that direction would have improved. His feet had never gone the way he wanted them to, and one look at his sulky face proved that I was right. I smiled at him sympathetically since it would most likely be assumed that he should be my partner, and I felt more than a little surprised that Henry went along with his wife's suggestion without protest. He good-humouredly carried the gramophone while Martin and Teddy carried the records. Then we pushed the furniture back against the wall while Isobel searched for her favourite foxtrot.

'I'm no dancer, as you well know,' Teddy said dismally.

'Don't worry, I'll pull you round, but I don't really mind if we sit it out.'

'You know what Isobel's like. We shan't be allowed to sit it out unless she's changed considerably these last few years.'

Teddy's tall, gangling body was not made for dancing, but by marching the length of the room, performing some sort of shuffle in the corner and marching back again in a manner that would have done credit to a guards regiment, we managed to get through the dance without falling over anybody else.

Isobel turned the record over and this time it was Henry who invited me to take the floor.

'You've had lessons,' I accused him, and indeed the improvement was obvious. Like many portly men, he was surprisingly light on his feet and I enjoyed our dance together.

He admitted that Isobel had cajoled and bullied him into doing something about his dancing and had finally confronted him with the ultimatum that if he didn't take her dancing she would find somebody else who would.

I could see her valiantly trying to teach Teddy in one corner of the room a more intricate step than his marching performance with me, and her obvious impatience when he made little progress. Martin and Ruthie danced well together and I remembered the night I had danced with him when his wounded leg was still giving him pain. Over Ruthie's silver-fair head our eyes met, solemn, unsmiling, then the music ended and Isobel rushed to the gramophone to find another favourite.

'You must change partners,' she cried gaily. 'There is to be no clinging to one partner. It's not allowed.'

The music started and across the room I saw Isobel smiling, her face bright and mischievous with laughter. The smooth lilting tenor voice on the record sang 'If you were the only girl in the world' and this time it was Martin who drew me into his arms, his voice barely above a whisper against my ear saying, 'Our song, Jacintha. You do remember it, don't you?'

I didn't answer him – somehow the audacity of his words momentarily robbed me of speech – and he said, 'Please don't be angry, but I shall always think of this as our song.' He drew me closer and I felt my body stiffen in his arms as the smooth seductive voice sang its insincerities.

'Will you ever talk to me as you did in the old days?' he persisted.

'I shall always talk to you, Martin, but perhaps not as I did in the old days.'

'I need to see you alone, Jacintha, but you always avoid me.'

'Not intentionally, but please be discreet, Martin, people are watching us.'

'Promise you'll let me see you alone one day. I know you hate me for what I did but I've got to make you understand.'

'Please Martin, the best thing both of us can do now is forget it.'

'But I don't want you to hate me.'

'I don't hate you. There was a time when I thought I did, but now you see I no longer love you, so how can I hate you? Hate like love is a powerful emotion and what I feel for you now is only friendship.'

The music came to a stop and slowly he released me, more slowly perhaps than convention demanded, so that when I turned to leave him I saw Ruthie watching us, her eyes filled with hostility.

One of the servants brought coffee and drinks in for us and while I poured out the coffee Isobel took the opportunity to whisper, 'I deliberately chose that record to see if the flame of young love still burned.'

'I know you did, and it doesn't.'

'Rubbish! Don't think I didn't see the way he was looking at you.'

I was saved from answering by Ruthie saying, 'I'm bored with dancing. Can't we go downstairs to join in the adult conversation?'

'Pussycat,' Isobel said. 'You know what they'll be talking about – the Carradice wool empire.'

It was left to Teddy and me to replace the furniture and leave the room in some semblance of order and, as we made our way downstairs, Teddy said, 'You won't tell grandmother about Lavinia's letter, will you?'

'Of course not. I'll read it in my room later,' I promised him.

I read it in bed by the light of my bedside lamp, warmed and amused by its affectionate terms. Lavinia was in love with America, with her new home, her new relatives and her way of life. I smiled at some of the expressions she used, thinking that in no time at all Lavinia would have lost her English accent and have become completely Americanized. I was quite sure nothing I could tell her about Ravenspoint would either surprise or amuse her.

My earlier conversation with Martin troubled me long after I had turned the light out. There was a full moon outside on a cold and frosty winter's night and I lay in my bed looking up at the shadows and the pattern on the ceiling cast by the stark branches of the trees. The sea below murmured with a disturbing intensity but the night was a calm one and I knew, if I took the trouble to look through the window, I would see it rolling in gently in silver ripples along the sand.

The family stayed at Ravenspoint until 2 January, when Henry said he needed to return to his business. I thought that in the main they were all relieved to go. I was secretly hoping Aunt Myra would take grandmother back with them, but on

139

the morning they left dark storm clouds hung low over the mountains and the sea crashed and moaned on the rocks. They left in a convoy of cars immediately after breakfast. By this time, it was sleeting and I did not envy them their journey along the twisting lakeland roads and the bleak climb over the Pennine hills.

Isobel and Henry had been the last to leave. I stood with Isobel in the hall waiting for Henry to bring the car to the front door. She was cross with the weather, standing in the open doorway frowning at the threatening sky and the sharp wind blowing in from the sea. Pulling her dark mink coat closer round her body she complained bitterly, 'God, what a place. You'll not see me very often when my grandmother's gone. I can't imagine why she keeps this place on; I can't see Adrian ever wanting to live in it. Do you know why he isn't here?'

'I have no idea, but probably because he wanted to spend the first Christmas after the war with his parents.'

'What was there to stop them from coming too? You know, if Adrian doesn't watch it, he could stop being her favourite. Ruthie keeps very close to her with Martin's encouragement. She could cut Adrian off without a shilling. She might even transfer her affections to you – and her money.'

'I don't think that's very likely.'

'No, perhaps not. Have you thought what you're going to do when he does come back? You'll have to be making your mind up soon, Jacintha, unless you intend to live in Yorkshire with grandmother permanently.'

'That's the last thing I want.'

'Well, as I see it, Adrian will be at the mills and will probably buy a place in Yorkshire, but he'll want to come down here to unwind. Your days at Ravenspoint are numbered, my girl.'

'Yes, I expect they are, but that's a hurdle I'll face when I come to it.'

'Well, don't say I didn't warn you. I don't know why we didn't stand in the hall instead of hanging about on the door-step here. I can't think why Henry's so long with the car.'

'Here he is,' I said thankfully, walking down the steps with her to the car door.

'Think about what we've just been talking about,' was her final shot before she climbed into the big car. I stood in the wind on the drive until the car left the gates but, although Henry turned his head to wave to me, Isobel, huddled in her furs, did not.

Looking back, I still cannot think why that day should have been any different from the others, but this was the day I took stock of my life and found it wanting.

Most of January had been cold and blustery with dark-grey seas crashing along the shore and torrential rain filling the lakes and tarns to the brim. On this day, however, I awoke to pale-golden sunlight and cotton-wool clouds scudding across a bright-blue sky. White horses rode on a deep-blue sea and I had no difficulty in recognizing the high peaks of Scafell and Gable now that the clouds had lifted.

I remember sitting in front of my dressing-table mirror gazing critically at my appearance. The mirror showed me a tall slender girl with dark-blonde hair tied back from a pale face and wide dark-blue eyes. I was too pale and far too thin. There was a wistful curve to my soft red mouth and my teeth were good, otherwise it was just a face like a million others and I decided that if I didn't do something about myself nobody else would.

I rummaged at the back of my wardrobe and found a dark-blue skirt I had worn at Isobel's. It was well cut and gave my figure a flattering roundness, and the pale-blue blouse I hadn't worn for months lit up my face and found sympathetic echo in my eyes. I took off my restraining hair ribbon and brushed my hair until it shone, then I tied the ribbon in a different way, allowing my heavy hair to fall around my face, giving it a more gentle frame. In the mirror I looked like a different person. My face seemed somehow softer and my figure had a new maturity. I snatched a fawn trenchcoat from the wardrobe and a scarf for my hair, determined that, although this was only February – an unpredictable month in the lakeland fells – I would take advantage of the unexpected sunshine and the rise in the temperature.

The horses were inside for the winter but the pony was always ready and waiting for exercise. He greeted me with enthusiasm and my spirits were high as I drove along the narrow country lanes. My last view of them had been from the train window on my way back from Isobel's, and now, instinctively, I made for the lake I had come to think of as my own.

The west wind, straight off the sea, brought in the rain clouds, but they passed swiftly overhead, scudding eastwards towards the mountain range dominated by Helvellyn. I could see the turmoil of clouds that seethed and rolled upwards from the sides of the dark-indigo fells and the columns of mist writhing and turning among the black crags and gullies below. Occasionally a gleam of veiled sunlight lit up the fells but before me now stretched the dark blue-black lake flecked with white-crested waves.

That first shaft of sunlight lit up Middlefell, leaving Gable, Kirkfell and Mosedale in even deeper shade, but hard on its heels came a veritable flood of golden sunlight on bracken and scree, rock face and shingle beach, and now the shreds of grey mist were being torn off the top of Gable and Scafell and above, the sky was a deep and cloudless blue.

On this morning, the water was the deepest blue-green and the screes stood high against the light. Between ledges and slopes of glowing orange bracken the outcrops of granite sparkled in the sun. Across the great pyramid of Yewbarrow the sunlight shone in sharp contrast to the dark-grey screes and the deep-green water into which they seemed to plunge but, although this valley had such a powerful presence and atmosphere, I looked at it with love rather than awe.

There were more beautiful lakes, soft, gentle lakes dotted with lush wooded islands, where stately trees dipped their branches into the water, and stolid lakeland cattle stood dreaming in the shallows. On these lakes in the summer months, pleasure craft of all kinds bobbed upon the water, but on this lake no boats came to ripple the dark surface. Wastwater was different. Its dark sombre beauty found an echo in my lonely innermost heart and I halted the pony so I could sit in rapt contemplation of its silence. It was possessed of a wild primeval beauty, like the first lakes must have been before men came with their boundless energy and their desperate needs. I would have sat there longer, but a lone gull flew screeching across the water and with dismay I saw that the lake was changing from deep green to black and overhead once more the storm clouds were gathering.

It was mid-afternoon by the time I got back to the house. I left the pony in the care of the stableboy and walked towards the front of the house. An unfamiliar low-slung car stood in the drive outside the front door but I gave it only a cursory glance. My uncles were constantly changing their vehicles, although this particular one did seem a little too racy for any of them. It was quiet in the hall but, as I moved towards the stairs, I could hear my grandmother's voice raised louder than usual coming from the sitting room, and the deeper tones of a man's voice. I paid little attention. She often received visitors at Ravenspoint and it was quite possible to believe that neighbours had taken advantage of the change in the weather. I had no intention of intruding and, after I had taken off my outdoor garments, I decided to go to the library to find a book. On my way downstairs I met Lucy, who pulled me into the shadows away from the sitting-room door.

'It's Mr Adrian, miss. I don't know what he's been saying to her but she isn't half in a state. I shouldn't go in there, if I were you.'

I had no intention of going in there, but my heart sank at her news. So at last Adrian was back at Ravenspoint. Now what was to become of me?

'What time did he arrive, Lucy?'

'Just before lunch, miss. They ate in the dining room but she's been going on like that most of the afternoon.'

'Has she asked after me at all?'

'She asked at lunchtime where you were. I told her you'd taken the pony and trap but she hasn't asked since. I don't think she's given you a thought, Miss Jacintha. She's too annoyed with Mr Adrian for that.'

I was cold and hungry but I had to get out of the house. I couldn't bear to think that my future might be decided in the midst of her anger and, because it was Adrian who was in there with her, I could not believe her anger was directed against him.

I set out once more in my old trenchcoat with a scarf thrown over my head and the collar turned up against the wind. This time I took the path down the cliffs. The tide was ebbing and there were shallow shell pools all along the beach. As far as I was able, I kept to the soft sand so as not to get my feet wet, making for the shattered stone wall which had once surrounded Meg's plot of land. It was lonely on the beach, as wild and lonely as the lake had been and a chill wind was blowing in from the sea. On the horizon dark clouds were gathering, and behind me the house stood stark and dismal on the towering cliffs.

What would they do with me, Adrian and my grandmother? What plots were they hatching together for the years immediately ahead of me? I walked along the shore, kicking the soft sand with my shoes until I reached the end of the bay and had to retrace my steps. In my vanity I could only think that it was discussion about my future that accounted for raised voices and my grandmother's anger, and miserably I made my way back across the bay, my eyes on the ground, unaware of the light and colour in the pools left by the sea.

Under the shadow of the cliffs, I looked up to see the solitary figure of a man walking towards me across the sand. He was in uniform, wearing a peaked officer's cap and a white riding mac, but I knew instinctively, even though he walked in the shadows, that it was Adrian. No man I had ever met walked with quite such tall, lithe grace and I could feel myself trembling and the warm blood suffusing my face.

I paused, waiting for him to reach me, and he was smiling. I looked up surprised. I had thought him taller, until I remembered that the last time I had looked up into his face I had been only a schoolgirl. Stupidly, I could only think how handsome he was, but as his eyes smiled down at me there was an amused twitch at the corners of his mouth. I thought there was something different about him, then I realized with a sense of shock that it was the wings of silver hair under his cap, which had not been there on our last meeting.

'Did I not tell you that we would both have changed when next we met, Jacintha?'

'Hallo, Adrian,' was all I could manage.

'I always know where I may find you, don't I? This beach seems to be your special domain.'

'A few hours earlier I should not have been here.'

'Where were you then, I wonder?'

'Driving the pony and trap along the banks of Wastwater.'

'Frightened by its loneliness or impressed by its grandeur?'

'A little of both, I think. Adrian, why was my grandmother so angry? Was it anything to do with me?'

144

'Do you expect it to be something to do with you every time your grandmother is angry? Shall we walk back to the house before it starts to rain?'

I fell into step beside him, aware that I had amused him by my question. As we started the long climb upwards towards the house he placed his hand under my elbow – something he had not done for the schoolgirl I had been on our last meeting. We did not speak again until we reached the summit of the cliff. Then, in a light unconcerned voice, he said, 'You need not worry about your grandmother's anger, Jacintha. It was not directed at you.'

'Who, then?'

'At me, I think.'

As long as I could remember, Adrian had been held up to us all as the shining example we must follow if we wanted to enter grandmother's good books. The astonishment he saw on my face caused him to throw back his head and laugh delightedly.

'It would appear my grandmother's anger isn't troubling you much,' I remarked with some degree of asperity.

'On the contrary, I have not enjoyed causing her either pain or anger but there was no choice. I wonder why you thought it was directed at you.'

'Because it nearly always is.'

'You should be happily relieved then.'

We continued our journey in silence for several minutes before I asked the question which was puzzling me so greatly.

'Adrian, what could you possibly have said to make her so angry?'

'I told her I was not coming back to Ravenspoint.'

I stopped abruptly in the middle of the path, hardly believing what I had just heard.

'Not coming back! Not ever?'

'I'm afraid not.'

'But you must come back. This is to be your house, you are to be the head of the business, everything one day is to be yours.'

He was looking down at me seriously with all the laughter gone from his face and my words faltered.

'I am not going to live in the city where the mills are, I am not going to be master there, and I am not coming back to live in England now or at any other time, Jacintha. That is what I told your grandmother and that is what made her angry.'

I couldn't believe it. All the years of my life which I had spent under the roof of Ravenspoint had been but a marking of time for the day Adrian would live there. The years of the war had merely been a deferment of that time and now here he was telling me he would never come back. No wonder my grandmother was angry. She had hurt me too much and too often to warrant my pity, but I could understand her chagrin and sympathized with it.

'What are you going to do?' I asked him dismayed.

He answered my question with one of his own.

'Tell me about your war, Jacintha. What have you done these last four years to make you realize that life as we knew it was precarious? What did you really know about the war?'

He was looking down at me intensely and suddenly I saw the rolling of bandages and knitting of scarves and gloves as little things. The balls and performances in aid of the war effort, the band concerts in the parks, these all became banal, contributing little and affording the participants but momentary pleasure. I looked up miserably and murmured, 'It was hard to stay at home and wait for news, Adrian. I prayed for the end of the war and I wept for all those poor young men who died.'

He smiled and gently took hold of my hand. 'Don't look so guilty, child. I'm not blaming you for any of the safety you found here. I am glad that it was so but, as I tried to explain to your grandmother, England was incredibly lucky to have been an island. You did not have to suffer the enemy on your soil, in your homes, on your roads. No German soldier ever molested you on your way home from the village, no German officers ransacked your home or lived off your land. I am going back to Fontinelle, Jacintha, to try to salvage whatever is left. My mother needs me desperately and there are other factors to consider.'

'What factors?'

'Too numerous for you to understand.'

'Is Leoni one of them?'

'What do you know of Leoni?'

'Only what Isobel and Lavinia said – that perhaps you would marry her and bring her here.'

'Like my mother, Leoni is afraid. There are four years of hatred and bitterness in their hearts. It may be that they will never recover from them, but I would be worse than the men who caused that bitterness if I deserted them now.'

I couldn't understand myself. Once again I felt that sense of utter desolation because Adrian was going away and I envied Leoni de Montforte who would be able to lean on his strength. How desperately he must love her to be willing to give up so much just to be by her side, and how much I longed to be loved like that! He was watching the expressions on my face closely and I asked quietly, 'Will your father not mind what you are doing?'

'I think my father would only approve of what I am doing, if he was aware of it.'

'Will you see my grandmother again?'

'I have the strongest conviction that she will not wish to see me. She has retired to her room after expressing the wish not to be disturbed again today. It rather looks as though you and I will once more be dining alone together.'

'When will you go away?'

'Early tomorrow morning. As soon as I can hand in my commission I shall return to France.'

'I may never see you again.'

'No, and that is a pity. I believe we could have been friends, you and I.'

I had never been so glad of the clothes Henry's money had paid for. That night I chose a long evening gown in dark-blue velvet the exact colour of my eyes. The last time I had worn it had been on Christmas Day and I had seen admiration raw and painful in Martin's eyes. Now, perhaps perversely, I wore it for Adrian.

He did not refer to my appearance but he put himself out to be charming, deferring to my wishes on the food that was served to us and the wine we should drink with our meal. I in turn was glad that my grandmother had elected to eat alone and, if at times she heard our laughter across the hall, I was glad of that too.

I was surprised how knowledgeable Adrian was about the lakeland fells and the mountains. I mentioned tarns and mountain passes and he knew about them; he talked about the lakes with affection and regret because he was leaving them and he said, 'You have been fortunate to have been able to see so much of the district – not on horseback surely, the distances are too great.'

'No, one of the officers had an old car which he allowed us to use.'

'Us?'

I could feel my face blushing furiously. 'One of the officers who was here, Captain Martin Vasey, do you know him?'

'I don't think so. Should I?'

'His family have cotton mills in Lancashire. Grandmother and the others know the family well.'

'I see. So where is he now, this Captain Martin Vasey? Are you still friends?'

'He is married to Ruthie.'

His eyebrows shot up in surprise and the tone of his voice became suddenly serious.

'I had no idea Ruthie was married but, if he married her so short a time after discovering the lakes with you, why wasn't it Ruthie he saw them with?'

'That is a question I have asked myself many times.'

'You mean they were not even friends then?'

'No.'

'Does it pain you to talk about it?'

'Not any more. I didn't have enough money for Martin Vasey or his family. Ruthie was a better proposition. Her parents, his parents and my grandmother fostered their friendship.'

'I'm sorry, Jacintha. When I saw you wandering along the beach, long before you looked up and saw me, I wondered what they had done to you, the four years of war and the Carradice family. You'll see, there will be somebody more suitable for you, a kinder man, I'm sure.'

My lips were trembling and my eyes smarted with unshed tears. He leaned forward and covered my hand with his own. 'Is he really worth crying about, Jacintha?'

I brushed the tears away angrily with the back of my hand. 'No, no, he isn't and I haven't cried for months. It's only because you are being kind. I really don't want to talk about Martin any more, Adrian.'

'Then we won't. I'm sure I don't want to talk about him. He seems an odious young man to me. Have you nothing else to tell me after all these years?'

'My mother is dead.'

'Oh, my dear, I'm sorry. How did you hear about it? Did you ever make contact with her?'

I shook my head. 'No. A friend of my mother's came here. She brought me a few of her things, just a few pieces of jewellery and her workbasket.' I told him about the ring and how my grandmother took it away. He made no comment and I could not tell from the expression on his face whether he approved or disapproved of her action. For a few minutes we sat in silence, then I asked abruptly, 'Adrian, if you are not coming back to Ravenspoint, what do you think will become of me?'

'Well, I can't think my coming back or not coming back would have had any bearings on your future. I can only think that for you life will go on as it always has. You will stay here or in Wellsford and now that the war is over you will meet new people, perhaps build a whole new life for yourself. Perhaps Lavinia will invite you over to the States and, who knows, that could really be the start of things for you.'

'My grandmother would never let me go.'

'You won't always be nineteen, Jacintha, and your grandmother will not always be here.'

I told him then about my stay with Isobel and the construction my grandmother had placed upon it.

'It does seem a bit harsh on the face of it,' he agreed. 'Isobel was always high-spirited; in fact, there's a lot of my grandmother in Isobel and I very much doubt if Henry Clifton-Webb is capable of curbing either her extravagances or her flirtations. I was always rather fond of Isobel in spite of her witchery.'

I laughed at that because I too was fond of Isobel, of her sense of humour and her airy assumptions that people and life revolved around her for the sole purpose of affording her pleasure, and I laughed too because the word witchery so aptly described her impudent behaviour.

He listened with interest to my tale of Lavinia and her single-minded conviction that the Americans would enter the war and that one of them was destined to be hers. I told him

149

how much she had changed from the rather podgy little girl into a slender faithful copy of Isobel but without her dark hair and outrageous ways.

I even told him about Meg and the strange words she had said to Ruthie and me in her cottage on the beach and he listened to me gravely, instead of being disparaging as so many men would have been.

'I never knew Ruthie very well,' he said. 'I thought she was a pretty, shy little thing, always hanging over the balustrade or running round corners whenever she saw me. I don't think I addressed more than a dozen words to her in all the time I came here, so you see, as far as I am concerned, Ruthie is a nonentity. You are a much more interesting subject, Jacintha. Tell me about you.'

I felt inordinately pleased by his words, but how could I tell him what I didn't know myself? How can you say to a man who looks at you with grave dark eyes in a tanned handsome face that all you have ever really wanted from life was to be loved? Instead, I told him how much Ravenspoint meant to me, how very much I wanted my time there to go on for ever with the sea pounding the rocks and the dark dismal beauty of the fells for company.

'Is your life then to be dictated by the years you are spending here?' he asked. 'It seems to me a pretty bleak future you have set yourself.'

'What else do I know? The others hate it, and even you are turning your back upon it, so how can I expect you to know what I feel about Ravenspoint?'

He leaned over and refilled my wine glass, then he sat back in his chair, his right hand idly toying with the stem of his glass. His thoughts were turned inward and for a moment it seemed as though he had forgotten my existence. I found myself studying his face, lean and brown in the candlelight with the silver at his temples more evident now against the raven black of his hair. I looked for some resemblance to other members of the Carradice family but found none, unless it was to Isobel and that only because they were both dark. He looked up suddenly and I blushed in confusion at the amused cynicism in his smile.

'I wonder what you are thinking now,' he said. 'Are you going to tell me?'

'I was thinking you are not much like any other member of the family. You are very like your mother, Adrian.'

'Yes, that is the popular view.'

'You are not like Uncle Roland at all.'

'And whom are you like, I wonder? Certainly not your respected grandmother. You are like your mother, you have her colouring though you are much taller and you have more spirit.'

'Why do you say that?'

'By the way you have antagonized two or three members of the family whom your mother would have been terrified of. Perhaps there is something of your grandmother in you after all.'

I frowned angrily, whereupon he threw back his head and dissolved into laughter. Then we talked until the hours were flown, and it seemed we could have gone on talking until the morning light came through the long french windows, but Adrian looked at the clock in some surprise and accused me of losing my beauty sleep.

Once more we stood together at the head of the stairs and once more the moonlight silvered his hair, throwing his profile into sharp relief so that I was troubled by the haunting quality of the memories it evoked. As on that other occasion, he bent his head and lightly kissed the top of my head. This time I impulsively threw my arms around his neck and held him close, my cheek against his, so close that I could feel the beating of his heart through the velvet of my dress. I believe that he too was shaken by that moment but I could not see the expression on his face in the shadows.

'Shall I ever see you again?' I asked him in a voice strangled by tears.

For a moment he seemed bemused by my question, then he regained his composure and his smile became impersonal as though he wanted to be gone from a danger he was afraid of. My heart ached with the pain of belonging, whether from the past, the present or a moment belonging to the future, and I felt frustrated because I sensed it so painfully and he apparently did not.

'It is late, Jacintha. If we are not very careful, you will receive a further reprimand from your grandmother for idling on the stairs with one she is displeased with and I shall not be here to take your part, remember.'

He smiled again, a cool impersonal smile, then he left to go to his room.

He was almost at the turn in the corridor when I called to him. 'Adrian, wait, there was something I meant to ask you and I forgot.' Breathlessly, I ran across the landing and along the corridor until I reached his side.

'Adrian, did you ever feel that Ravenspoint was haunted?'

He looked at me incredulously. 'Haunted! Whatever gave you that idea?'

I rushed to tell him of the sunny afternoon and the gossamer shadow of something cold on the stair before the news of Roger's death; then I told him the things Lucy had told me and he listened gravely, a small amused smile hovering about his mouth.

'Are you quite sure Isobel didn't have a hand in all this? Have you forgotten the Carradice dragon?'

'Isobel doesn't know and I didn't tell her. I thought she would be amused like you are now. Please don't laugh, Adrian, I thought it was a warning that you might be killed.'

'You thought it came to warn you about me?'

'Yes, but then, you see, it was Roger. It came for my grand-father and my father. Besides, they talk about it in the village.'

'Well, I haven't seen anything strange, Jacintha, and I have been coming here since before you were born. It was nice of you to be so concerned for my welfare but I hardly think the Carradice ghost would have concerned itself about me.'

'Oh, but it would; you're a Carradice and I was afraid for you.'

Suddenly, as swiftly as it had come, the frown of irritation passed from his face and his eyes softened. For a brief moment, he laid his hand against my cheek.

'I don't know anything about ghosts, my dear,' he said quietly. 'All I do know is that it is long past your bedtime and mine. I shall not be awake to catch my train in the morning if I do not leave you now.'

I nodded mutely, and turning on my heel I walked away from him disconsolately. I turned once before I reached the door of my room; he was standing where I had left him. After a brief smile, he was gone.

*   *   *

152

The days that followed were tortured ones for me. I had been afraid of Adrian's return to Ravenspoint but now that I knew he was never coming back it seemed that a great gaping void had opened up, leaving me more aimless and helpless than before. My grandmother stayed in her room, eaten up with misery, and the rest of the household went about their duties quietly, speaking only in whispers as though there had been a death in the house.

At the weekend, the family came en masse and on Sunday morning they gathered in the library where my grandmother had summoned them. I stayed out of it. I had not been invited and I did not believe their discussions concerned me. I sat on the window seat in the corner of the small drawing room, looking out to sea, my book idle in my hands, and now and again when the library door opened I could hear their voices. When my lunch came, it was served to me on a tray and I realized their deliberations were likely to linger on into the afternoon.

Mist rolled in from the sea and I added logs to the fire, drawing the curtains early to shut out the sound of the fog-horn echoing mournfully from across the bay. Soon after four, the door opened and Isobel came in. She was wearing a skirt and a cashmere twin-set in a soft pink shade but I thought she was thinner. Somehow her mannerisms were more nervous than usual and there was a restlessness about her I had not noticed before.

'How can you bear to sit here listening to that unearthly sound all afternoon?' was her opening gambit.

'The mist has only just come down, that is why I drew the curtains so early.'

'Why didn't you come into the library? You are part of the family.'

'There's enough of you without me, I'm sure.'

'Did you see Adrian when he was here?'

'Yes.'

'To talk to?'

'We had dinner together.'

'Grandmother, too?'

'No, she was angry with him so she didn't join us.'

She knelt on the rug in front of the fire, holding out her long white hands to the blaze.

153

'What on earth possessed Adrian to say he was never coming back? I wouldn't be surprised if she doesn't cut him right out of her will, she's so furious.'

'But that would be monstrous. After all, it's only natural that he should put his parents before his grandmother. It's not as though she isn't already surrounded by her family.'

'What family? My father and Uncle William resent her interference at the mills, Aunt Myra and Teddy are frightened to death of her and she's never been able to stand Uncle Gwillam. Thanks to Henry's money, I don't have to toady to her and she's already lost Lavinia. There's you, Jacintha – she might suddenly decide to leave all her money to you.'

'What rubbish you talk, Isobel! She's got Ruthie and Martin, she helped to engineer their marriage.'

'Well, well, so that still niggles you.'

'No, it doesn't, but I just happen to think it would be sinful to cut Adrian out in favour of the rest of you simply because he got his priorities right.'

'Throwing the Carradice mills in her face was tantamount to sacrilege, my poppet. I don't see why it was necessary for us to come. What Adrian does or doesn't do is no concern of Henry's. How do you think I look?' she asked, changing the subject rapidly, as she always did.

'You've lost too much weight and I thought Henry seemed tired. I suppose it's all those parties you go to.'

'For heaven's sake, don't you start, you sound like Henry's mother. He's thinking of putting up for the city council. Can you imagine it, all those boring meetings and those silly dinners with boring people? I just hope he doesn't expect me to go to them, that's all.'

'I should think Henry would make a very good councillor. He's a successful businessman. If he can handle five mills and a tremendous workforce, he shouldn't have any difficulty in lending some weight to the running of a city.'

'Oh, Henry will be in his element. It's me I'm thinking of. His mother is giving him every encouragement; she says if he does get on the local council his silly frivolous wife will have to conform. Seeing her little Henry emerge as Councillor Clifton-Webb will set the seal on her ambitions for him. Heaven preserve us, he might even make Lord Mayor!'

I had heard it all before. She was trying to shock me,

perhaps even make me angry, but I was equally determined not to be drawn. I couldn't resist asking, 'Has grandmother said she would cut Adrian out of her will?'

'Not in so many words, but something is going on in that head of hers and whatever it is it bodes no good for my respected cousin.'

'Perhaps he won't care. His mother's family are wealthy.'

'They *were*, you mean. We don't know what the Germans did to them, do we?' How did he look, Jacintha, and what on earth did you two find to talk about? I thought you didn't like him.'

'That was a long time ago. Besides, when I said I didn't like him, I didn't really know him.'

'And you do now, don't you? Why are you blushing, Jacintha? Could it be that now you like him too well?'

'No, I don't. You were the one he was going to marry, remember? I hardly knew him.'

She laughed gaily, well pleased with her catechism.

'You know, Jacintha,' she mused, 'I was always a little in love with Adrian, he was so beautiful to look at and so untouchable, if you know what I mean. Perhaps it's a pity you two are cousins; it would certainly have been one in the eye for the rest of the family if you could have landed Adrian.'

I ignored that last remark. I thought that anything I might say would only fan the flames.

Dinner that night was a meal I would like to forget. Grandmother presided over the long dinner table, her dark sunken eyes glittering in her pale haughty face. Her thin clawlike hands over which the brown patchy skin was stretched tight played erratically with the cutlery in front of her and she ate sparingly.

Once, when I looked up from my plate, I found Martin watching me with a strange intensity. My grandmother's eyes were watching us, and I was only too aware of the mockery on Isobel's face. But I could look at Martin dispassionately now, see his fair good-looking face without an inner pang, at last aware of the coldness of his blue eyes and the weakness of his mouth.

After dinner I asked Ruthie, for the purpose of making conversation, if she had heard from Lavinia, but she merely shrugged her shoulders saying, 'No, I don't suppose she will write to me. We were never what you might call good friends.'

I couldn't resist saying, 'She writes to me, and I'm glad to know that she is well and happy.'

'Who's well and happy?' Isobel joined in.

'Lavinia.'

'Well, why shouldn't she be, living in California where the sun shines and with a divine man?'

She was doing it deliberately, I knew. Her mother looked up nervously, cautioning her with a glance and there was a chill ominous silence until my grandmother's voice with a distinct edge to it said, 'When I decide what is to be done about Adrian, I shall know what to do about Lavinia.'

Swiftly, Aunt Myra flew to Lavinia's defence.

'Mother, you surely don't intend to penalize Lavinia for what Adrian has done. Lavinia is happy in America. She is married to a charming boy with a delightful family. What will they think of you, of any of us, if Lavinia does not get her share?'

Grandmother's eyes snapped dangerously, and in her most acid voice she said, 'As I have already said, I shall know what to do about Lavinia when the time comes. I am tired, Myra, please accompany me to my room.'

I longed for the evening to be over. Isobel played endless patience and Ruthie sat chatting to her mother, mostly in whispers, then the men joined us and the talk turned to Adrian.

'You found him well, Jacintha?' Uncle Robert asked.

'Very well indeed,' I replied.

'Relieved that the war was over and anxious to get back to France?'

'I would imagine so, Uncle Robert. He spoke little about the war.'

'Did he say if he was returning to France immediately?' Aunt Celia asked.

'Within the next few days, I believe.'

'So soon.'

'Did he have the presence of mind to invite you to the chateau, Jacintha?' Isobel asked. 'If not, it was very remiss of him.'

This question I decided to ignore and quickly they lost interest in me. They talked about the state of my grandmother's health, the possibility of her changing her will and Adrian's fall from grace, then my eyes met Isobel's across the room and I found her convulsed with laughter.

The visitors were leaving on the following day directly after lunch and I decided that I would be absent from the house during most of the morning. Long before they rose from their beds, I had saddled Isobel's horse and, following the old bridle paths across the fells, I put considerable distance between us.

The morning was fresh and invigorating, and the keen February wind brought a sparkle to my eyes and warm fresh colour into my cheeks. From the summit of the hill I turned to look down upon the house. Smoke curled lazily from several of the chimneys now, while above me the wind stirred mournfully in the cluster of Scots pines. From the stables behind the house, a solitary rider emerged and he too took the path that led upwards, fringing the forest of dark-green spruces. He rode well, handling his horse with consummate skill over the stone walls and the shallow burns. I dared not believe my suspicions. Surely he would not have the nerve to follow me, but as horse and rider grew nearer there was no mistake – it was Martin Vasey who interrupted my morning ride.

He pulled up his horse beside mine and we stared at each other without speaking, until he looked away.

'I knew it was you, Jacintha. How far do you intend to ride?'

'I have no plans.'

'Do you mind if I ride with you?'

I hesitated the merest fraction but in that time he must have been aware of my reluctance.

'If you wish, Martin.'

Our horses fell into step and we rode side by side without speaking. I did not want his company. I did not want to make polite conversation with Martin and I considered his intrusion upon my privacy an imposition. Once we had ridden over these same fells with laughter and warmth between us – now there was nothing to say. Once we had galloped recklessly down the hillside to throw ourselves off our horses and into each others arms, and then the future had stretched out joyous and tender before us. What point was there in taking this morning ride together, sitting astride our horses in grim

157

silence with unspoken resentment like a living thing between us?

Martin was the first to break the silence.

'The view is magnificent from here,' he said. 'I have always loved the Lake District, although I knew little about the Cumberland coast until I came to Ravenspoint.'

When I did not answer him he leaned over and took the reins of my horse, pulling us both to a standstill.

'I had to talk to you, Jacintha,' he said solemnly. 'I tried to see you alone at Christmas but it wasn't possible. I made up my mind then that the next time I came to Ravenspoint nothing would stop me seeing you alone.'

He had my full attention now, but I did not prompt him. I sat quietly on my horse, my eyes searching his face.

'I wrote to you, many times, but the letters were inadequate and I never sent them. I couldn't tell you in a letter. I knew one day I would have to speak to you. Please help me, don't make it any more difficult than it is already.'

'But it's so pointless, Martin. Anything you say to me now can't alter what has happened. Can't we just let it be and try to be friends?'

'I still love you, Jacintha.'

'I'm sorry, Martin, I'm afraid I no longer love you.'

I watched the warm blood colour his face and his pale-blue eyes become bleak, but I could feel nothing. He seemed to pull himself together by a supreme effort. 'I can't blame you for that,' he said. 'I behaved disgracefully. Try to understand, darling, all my life it's been hammered home to me that I must marry money even if I had to love elsewhere. I tried to get you to make your peace with your grandmother but you were too short-sighted and too independent.'

The expression on my face must have been so cynical it brought shame into his, and I hardly recognized my own voice when I said coldly, 'You have achieved the first of your ambitions, Martin; do not look to me for fulfilment of the second. In time, I hope, we can be friends. Be very sure we can never be lovers.'

With my head held high and with a haste born out of anger, I brought down my whip on my horse's flanks and raced away down the hillside, leaving Martin staring after me.

I was still smarting with anger when I reached my room and

my mirror showed me a pale face with two bright spots of colour burning in either cheek. I delayed going down to breakfast until my heart stopped racing and I felt I could face the rest of them with composure.

I need not have worried, only Isobel and Henry were at the breakfast table. Henry was anxious to get back to the city and impatient with Isobel, who was still in her négligée and dawdling idly over her breakfast. Although Henry was polite to me, he slammed out of the breakfast room after informing her that he was going for the car and expected her to be ready on his return.

She lit another cigarette and sat drinking her coffee as though she had not heard him.

'You really are the limit, Isobel. Why do you antagonize him all the time?' I asked.

'I hate to be rushed in the morning. It upsets my entire day. Why can't we set out at a civilized hour like everybody else? He has enough underlings at that office of his, surely they can manage without him for an hour or two. If he doesn't want to wait for me, I shall go later with my parents.'

'It's a long journey for Henry to take alone.'

'Oh, he's used to it. Besides, he's in such a foul mood I wouldn't enjoy the journey anyway. Since you're already dressed, run round to the garage and tell Henry I've decided to travel later, there's a dear.'

'Tell him yourself,' I snapped, but instead of being annoyed she laughed gaily. 'Who's put you in a bad mood this morning? I suppose it was Martin.'

'How do you know?'

'I thought I might ride myself until I saw him saddling Peel. I didn't want to interrupt any assignation you'd planned together.'

'Martin Vasey knows better than to attempt to make any assignation with me. I am not interested in him now and well he knows it.'

'I take it you've told him.'

I was saved from further discussion by the return of Henry, who stood at the door wearing his overcoat and with extreme displeasure written all over his face.

'I'm ready to leave, Isobel,' he said.

'I haven't finished my breakfast and I'm not dressed. I'll

come along later with my parents. You don't mind, do you, darling?'

'Yes, I mind, but I don't suppose that makes any difference. If you don't intend to travel with me, stay as long as you like. I suppose I shall be at home when you decide to return to it.'

I had never seen Henry so angry – nor, I think, had Isobel. She sat staring at the closed door with the mockery entirely gone from her face, then her eyes met mine and she laughed a little.

We finished our breakfast in silence but I knew that she was as troubled as I had ever seen her. I wished fervently that they would all go and leave me to my sand and sea, and I wished they would take my grandmother with them. I was troubled too with the tantalizing belief that something was going to happen soon to change my life at Ravenspoint and, because I had had those moments of knowing before, I waited, wondering.

8

Spring came again to the lakeland fells and on the mountain peaks the snows melted and waterfalls gurgled and gushed down the mountain sides to swell the swiftly flowing rivers and the lakes. Tender shafts of green appeared along the hedgerows and the azaleas and rhododendrons bloomed, showy and glowing between the dark conifers.

Much as I loved the coming of spring, I felt my life to be aimless. What use was I in the world, I asked myself. I had no career, no husband, no lover, and my family cared nothing for me. I talked to the lake and the sea and, because there was nobody else, to the gulls. I let the sun and the sea bleach my hair and my pale skin tanned in the wind that swept inland.

My grandmother usually drank coffee from a tray taken into her sitting room in the middle of the morning. I was, therefore, surprised one morning to receive a summons to her bedroom while I was only halfway through my breakfast. In her night attire, sitting up in the enormous bed against the whiteness of her pillows, she seemed somehow very frail and vulnerable. Her now-white hair, which she normally wore immaculately dressed, was wispy after sleep and she had the appearance of a piece of old ivory. Her eyes, however, were as keen and piercing as always and her voice had lost none of its authority.

'Sit down, Jacintha,' she said, and my surprise must have been evident in my face because I had never in my life been asked to sit on any of the occasions she had summoned me.

'I have sent for you to tell you that I am going to France and I shall expect you to travel with me. You will need a passport and there are other preliminaries. However, I wish to travel no later than the middle of June and I have asked my lawyer to call to see me this afternoon. I am an old woman and I want to know that I have left my house in order before I embark upon this journey.'

I stared at her in stupefied amazement, and irritably she said, 'Well, girl, have you no interest in where we are going or why?'

'I'm sorry, grandmother. You have surprised me, that is all. I would very much like to know more about the journey.'

'We are going to see my son Roland. I am not satisfied with the excuses Adrian gave me for returning to France, particularly for his need to remain there. I shall be the judge of who needs him most.'

'I know little about Adrian's home or even where it is situated.'

'In the valley of the Marne, in a district they call the Ile de France, within easy reach of Paris. Dawson will drive us to the south coast and accompany us on the ferry. I dislike Paris and I have no intention of staying there so we shall continue by car from Dieppe. I prefer the longer sea crossing and Dawson is more conversant with the route. How is your French, Jacintha?'

'Not very good, I'm afraid. I have had no occasion to use it and it was only schoolgirl French anyway.'

'You should have been more diligent in your studies. I remember giving you a French and English dictionary when you were a schoolgirl. Adrian, of course, speaks fluent French.'

'He does have a French mother.'

'And Isobel.'

'She finished her education in the French-speaking part of Switzerland, grandmother. I expect she needed to use it then.'

'Well, I shall expect you to remember what little you know and make use of the dictionary I bought you. There is no reason why you can't make yourself useful on the journey.'

It seemed that overnight my entire life took on a new dimension. I was going to France and I was going to see Adrian. I had thought long and often about Adrian on my lonely rides across the fells and in the house, too, I could not rid myself of my memories of his tall figure at the head of the stairs and his face darkly handsome by the glow of the candles on the dining-room table. I remembered sharply the low musical timbre of his voice, gentle and teasing, and the superb grace with which he sat his horse. I had hugged his memory to my heart as something precious and strangely innocent, but that had been when I did not think I would ever see him again. Now my dreams took on a new substance and I became afraid of the intensity of my feelings for Adrian. I did not want to fall in love with him, I could not risk being hurt a second time and there were too many barriers between Adrian and me, not least the elusive shadow of Leoni de Montforte.

The next few weeks were exciting enough without thoughts of Adrian. My passport came through and I found my old French exercise books and the dictionary. I felt ashamed of the red markings on my old books, written by a frustrated French mistress who had found her pupil sadly wanting, and I prayed that those I came into contact with would speak English so that my stumbling French would not be put to the test.

It was the second week in June before we started our journey and the changing scenery of every English county filled me with delight. It was the sea voyage I looked forward to most. Dawson parted with us at the gangway – with something like relief, I thought. He was to travel in the steerage part of the ship while grandmother and I had sleeping berths in the saloon. My grandmother went immediately to her berth, advising me to do the same. She ordered a pot of tea, with which she took a sleeping pill, informing both the steward and myself that she did not wish to be disturbed until the vessel docked in Dieppe harbour.

I felt like a caged bird which had suddenly been set free. I explored every corner of the ship I had access to and, although the boat rocked a good deal in the storm which blew up suddenly, I was happy to discover that I was a good sailor. Because of the gale, the passage took longer than usual, but eventually we sailed into Dieppe harbour with the morning sun lighting up the old French town and the multitude of fishing boats bobbing about on the water.

At last I was on French soil and I didn't care that my grandmother was complaining about the porters who knew no English or the fact that the car which should have been waiting for us at the quayside had not arrived. When it eventually came, she looked at it in disgust. It was big, black and dusty, of extremely ancient vintage and Dawson, too, regarded it ruefully with distrust.

The Frenchman who had delivered it shrugged his shoulders

indifferently in the face of grandmother's tirade, and Dawson kept a stoically British face as he argued in loud precise English, which had the effect of making the Frenchman even more voluble.

'Where is your French, Jacintha?' my grandmother snapped. 'Explain to this imbecile that we need a decent car, not that monstrosity.'

I looked around helplessly and caught the eyes of a man surrounded by luggage nearby. He smiled, sensing our predicament.

'Can I be of any assistance?' he asked. 'You appear to be having some difficulty.'

I explained the situation as quickly as I could and to my relief he spoke in fluent French to the man from the garage. A lengthy conversation followed with much gesticulation on the part of the Frenchman and passive patience on the part of the Englishman. We looked on helplessly until the Englishman turned to explain the reasons for the argument.

'This man says you ordered a car to meet the boat and this is the only one available. He says there has been a war, new cars have not been made and the better ones were taken by the Germans. I'm sorry, ladies, but it's either this one or none at all, I'm afraid.'

'Thank you,' my grandmother said. 'If that is the case, I suppose we shall have to make the best of it.' She nodded to him and I thanked him cordially for his help.

'Have you far to go?' he asked politely.

'To the other side of Paris,' my grandmother told him. 'It will not be a comfortable journey, but then what can one expect from foreigners?'

I looked at him helplessly after she had climbed into the car and he smiled sympathetically. 'It may be better than it looks,' he whispered. 'I wish you a pleasant journey, anyway.'

The engine purred healthily in spite of the dusty and decrepit air of the interior, and I soon forgot the car in favour of the landscape. The war had barely been over eight months but my imagination ran riot as I looked ahead at the long straight road lined with poplars, at the rolling rich soil of the fields ploughed in long straight furrows and the dusty villages largely in ruins. The old people sat outside their houses staring at the road with sad unseeing eyes, and all along the route there were farm buildings and corn mills standing like great gangling skeletons against the blue sky. I thought about the journey we had taken through English villages, whose life had altered hardly at all in those four long years of war. England had sent her sons to war, but her soil had remained her own. How grateful I was for that strip of water which had separated us from the torment the Continent had suffered.

We took our first meal at an hotel my grandmother had known from previous visits before the war, but she grumbled that it was not up to its usual standard and the service was poor. We had come to France too soon after the end of the war; the French needed time to adjust to peacetime living, time to lick their wounds, but my grandmother saw time as a commodity we could do without.

The villages we passed through depressed me unutterably. I knew that one day corn would wave once more in the dark-brown fields which stretched out on either side of us towards the horizon, that there would be laughter inside the white-washed walls of old farms and cottages, and that children would sleep peacefully beneath red tiled roofs, but not yet. There were so many dead trees in the vast forests of the Ile de France, casualties of gunfire and blundering tanks, but men and women were working in the clearings. I saw the signposts for Paris but I was glad my grandmother did not want to go there. Paris was for lovers. It was not a city to be wept over or ignored and the mere thought of her criticisms of bad food, poor service and tarnished glories filled me with despair. If ever I saw Paris, I wanted it to be with joy and with one who would show me its beauty without reference to its shortcomings.

We talked little on the journey, but every now and again she would ask Dawson if he was on the right route. We came at last to a fork in the road and this she seemed to recognize. Her interest quickened and she sat forward on the edge of her seat to speak to the chauffeur.

'I recognize the place back there, Dawson, the gates to the chateau are only a few miles up the road.'

'I know it too, Mrs Carradice. It doesn't seem to have changed as much round here.'

'Does all the land now belong to the chateau?' I asked curiously.

'For as far as you can see and beyond. We are now on Fontinelle land. On the other side of the river, the land belongs to the de Montfortes.'

My heart lurched painfully. Adrian would indeed be a vast landowner if he married the heiress to such an estate and combined it with his own. It was no wonder he had been able to spurn so lightly the Carradice empire.

In some quite inexplicable way, the countryside was different. Here the dark forests were dense on either side of the road – it almost seemed as though the war had escaped this land. We came at last to a pair of great ornamental wrought-iron gates bearing a coat of arms, and my grandmother leaned forward eagerly as Dawson turned the car in at the gates. The road before us stretched uphill now as far as the eye could see, but still the great forests of trees grew on either side of the drive with its edging of verdant green.

'Drive slowly,' my grandmother commanded, and we drove forward at a crawl. I too was sitting on the edge of my seat, my eyes trained upon the road ahead, my heart beating fiercely. At the top of the hill, my grandmother said, 'Stop the car, I want to get out.'

Dawson came round to open the door so that we could step out onto the gravel of the drive. Below us, the late afternoon sunlight fell upon the pointed turrets and mellow stone of what appeared to me to be a fairytale palace surrounded by beautifully laid formal gardens. The road wound down the hill, crossing the lake by an ornamental bridge until it reached the oval courtyard in front of the great centre door, but one look at my grandmother's face silenced the cries of admiration which sprang to my lips.

Her face looked pinched and dark with anger and she was gripping her ivory-handled walking stick so tightly that the knuckles showed white through the wrinkled skin of her hands.

'He lied to me,' she cried in disbelief, 'how dared he lie to me!'

Adrian had loved Ravenspoint, but in no way could the two houses be compared. Ravenspoint was a part of the rocks and the sea; it was at one with the lonely lakes and the dark dismal beauty of the fells and mountains. The chateau was civilized. It was a part of the history of France, built and lovingly extended by generation after generation of French noblemen. Seeing it now, mellowed and golden in the late afternoon sunlight, I could only think how arrogant my grandmother was to expect Adrian to desert it for anything as mundane as five woollen mills in a Yorkshire city. Adrian had made his choice. If he had told her a lie, it was no doubt to soften the blow. I don't suppose he had ever thought that she would make this journey to France to discover if he had told her the truth. I was already hating my part in it and hating the evening ahead of us, when no doubt he would be made aware of her displeasure.

'Drive faster,' she commanded, so that in no time at all we were crossing the bridge across the lake and now I could see the pink and white water lilies in the shallows and the swans, white and majestic, with their brood of cygnets.

My grandmother disdained my helping hand, as she stomped towards the front door, relying solely upon her walking stick for support. Catching my eye, Dawson shook his head sadly, and we followed and stood behind her while she brought the heavy knocker down upon the door so sharply that the noise echoed hollowly in the rooms beyond. We waited, and again she brought the heavy knocker down so that it seemed to me the house shook with the resonance of that sound. We listened again but there seemed to be no life in the rooms behind that enormous door and my grandmother stamped her foot impatiently.

After what seemed a small eternity, we heard the sound of bolts being drawn back. Whoever opened it was frail and experiencing difficulty with the stoutness of that solid door. An old man stood blinking at us in the sunlight. He was tall and stooped a little; he was so painfully thin that the skin seemed to be stretched tight across the bones of his face. He evidently did not recognize my grandmother and looked from one to the other of us through watery, short-sighted eyes.

My grandmother stared back at the servant for several seconds, then in her usual brisk voice she said, 'I can see you do not recognize me, Jules. I am Mrs Carradice.'

He did not respond but merely stepped back, allowing us to enter the hall. I did not know what I had expected to see on the other side of that massive door but I stared round me with the utmost amazement. We were in a large, beautifully proportioned hall with a domed roof lavishly decorated with exquisite murals showing paintings of fat pink cherubs sitting on woolly clouds, below which the graceful pillars of ancient Greek temples vied with scenes of pastoral beauty. The floor was inlaid with many different woods, once polished to a high gloss but now dulled and neglected. From the centre of the hall a wide marble staircase swept upwards in a long graceful curve, with balustrades on either side in ornate wrought iron, but what made the hall look so vast was the complete absence of any sort of furniture. Marble pedestals stood in alcoves, but the ornaments and busts which had once stood upon them were no longer there and on the white walls were the marks where once a great many paintings had been displayed. My grandmother advanced into the centre of the hall and stood looking around her in astonishment.

From somewhere above, the sharp closing of a door made us all start nervously and we looked up towards the staircase. I had not seen my aunt, Marguerite Carradice, for over ten years, and if we had met in the street I would not have known her. Her once-luxurious black hair was now silver and her face, though still beautiful, was the saddest face I had ever seen.

She was thin, and the dress she wore seemed to hang on her limbs as though it had been made for someone else. Once, it had been fashionable and even now its exquisite cut gave it a strange elegance, but there was no time to notice anything else. In that split second before she came forward to greet us, I knew by her expression of dismay that we were unwelcome at Fontinelle and I hung back miserably behind my grandmother.

She came forward and kissed my grandmother's cheek dutifully, then she stood back unsmiling while the two women looked at each other. My grandmother was the first to break the silence. 'Have you been ill, Marguerite? I would not have known you.'

'I am well now but I have lost a great deal of weight.' She touched her silver hair nervously with her long white hand. 'You should have let us know that you intended to visit us. The welcome would have been more to your liking.'

'What has happened to the chateau? Where are the pictures and the furniture? Are they in store?'

My aunt smiled wryly. 'Alas, no. Some of our friends received more warning than we did and were able to do something about their treasures; we had no warning. The Germans came quickly and just as quickly they took everything of value. Now that the war is over, we are trying to trace our possessions and recover them if possible, but you must see it will take a long time. We had high-ranking German officers here during the war – anything they fancied they took and I do not only mean inanimate objects.'

'You say you are trying to recover the paintings and furniture?' my grandmother asked.

'Yes. Adrian is in Chartres today to look at some pictures that have been recovered. They may be ours, they may have belonged to the de Montfortes – until he has seen them we cannot be sure. At least the chateau is still standing. We are very lucky. The de Montforte chateau lies in ruins; they burned it down for sheer devilry and forced us to watch it burn from the brow of the hill. We were told a similar fate lay in store for Fontinelle if we failed to play our part.'

'And your part was?' my grandmother prompted.

'To house them and feed them, to cook for them and entertain them.'

Marguerite turned to look at me with a half-smile on her lips, and I saw then that, although she had aged a thousand years since the last time I had seen her, she was still a beautiful woman. Neither age nor sorrow could destroy the beauty of her bone structure.

'You must forgive me, my dear, I have forgotten your name,' she said quietly.

'It is Jacintha.'

'Of course. You were just a little girl the last time I saw you and indeed Adrian speaks of you still as though you were a schoolgirl.'

As I bent forward to kiss her cheek, I reminded myself angrily that that was all he did think of me – a schoolgirl, fit only to run along the shore without my shoes and stockings, swinging my satchel above my head.

'I am not sure if you will be comfortable here,' my aunt was saying. 'There is only Jules and his wife Marie and two young girls who come from the village every morning and go home in the evening. Once we had a houseful of servants but the men have not yet drifted back; some of them will never return, and the women are working in the fields. It is too soon, there is too much forgetting and forgiving to do.'

'You say Adrian is in Chartres?' my grandmother asked.

'Yes, he left soon after breakfast. I am expecting him home for dinner.'

'And my son, is he also in Chartres?'

The silence which followed my grandmother's question was pregnant with emotion and my aunt's reply so long forthcoming that the question was asked again.

'I told Adrian he should have told you about Roland, but he thought he had distressed you enough at the time. I am sorry to say that my husband had a stroke during the occupation and I fear he will never fully recover from it.'

'A stroke! That is terrible. I should have been informed at once.'

'Mrs Carradice, we lived like zombies in a world that was not of our making. It was not possible to tell you. You have only to look at me and then think of the woman I once was to learn something of what those four long years did to us.'

'You say he will never fully recover. How is he affected?'

'He is in a wheelchair, he cannot walk and he speaks seldom, although his speech came back after only a few days.'

She gave the information calmly and without emotion. Although I did not love my grandmother, at that moment I admired her indomitable spirit which refused to accept defeat, for the only signs she gave of her anguish at the blow she had received was the tightening of her hand on her stick and the squaring of her thin shoulders.

'When can I see him?' she asked.

'He rests in the afternoon but we shall meet for dinner, and by that time I hope Adrian will have returned. You will need to rest before dinner. Let me show you to your rooms and have some refreshment sent up to you.'

In some way I was relieved that my grandmother's room was some distance from my own, but walking along the corridors of the chateau it was hard to realize that once this great house had been a showplace for travellers to exclaim over, filled with precious and beautiful things. Now it was merely a shell containing the bare necessities for living. The bedroom I was shown into was of princely proportions. The murals on the ceiling were as exquisite as those in the hall, the drapes at the long windows overlooking the moat at the side of the house were of heavy embossed velvet, their pelmets edged with deep fringe, but the only furniture in the room was a large bed, one solitary chair and a bedside table.

My dismay must have been very evident for my aunt said, 'We are fortunate, my dear, that the curtains were left at the windows and the carpet on the floor. The Germans took a great many of our carpets, most of them were oriental and of great value. I will leave you to unpack, then one of the girls will have the bed made up for you. We dine at eight, Jacintha. Until then please treat the house as your own.'

In the dressing room adjoining the bedroom, huge wardrobes ranged across one wall and I was pleased to see that there was one chair upholstered in rose-pink velvet and that there were mirrors for the full extent of another wall. The little maid who arrived with my tray could speak no English and my French was too inadequate for conversation, so I merely smiled at her and murmured a swift 'merci'.

Nothing at Fontinelle was as I had thought it would be. I had been prepared for desolation and the terrible aftermath of war. I had not been prepared for the beauty of a house that was merely a shell and the despairing bitterness that was so apparent in everything I had heard and seen. I stood at the window looking down upon the moat, its water almost hidden by water lilies. On the other side, there was a narrow path, then the grass sloped away towards the lake and the vast dense forest beyond. I was about to turn away when I saw the figure of a girl walking slowly along the path, her eyes on the ground so that I was unable to see her face. She was of average height and very slender and she was wearing a white dress in some soft material which made her seem ethereal. She paused opposite my window to look down into the moat and I watched her fascinated, willing her to look up. Some instinct told her she was being observed because suddenly she raised her eyes to look straight into mine and I caught my breath sharply, startled. Whoever she was she was beautiful, but after she had gone all I could remember was that her eyes had seemed too large and dark in her pale lovely face and that it had been surrounded by a frame of dark cloudy hair.

I was trembling. I was sure that the girl I had just seen was

Leoni de Montforte, yet she was not at all as I had imagined she would be. I had thought she would be a high-spirited, proud beauty much like Isobel, and I was not prepared for the sad wistfulness of the face of the girl I had just seen. All at once I was dreading the evening in front of me, when I would have to watch Adrian effortlessly surrounding Leoni with his charm. He had been kind to me, his little English cousin. How much more tenderness would he show towards the girl he loved? At that moment, I wished with all my heart that I had not set foot in the Chateau Fontinelle.

Once again, I blessed Henry and his generosity as I dressed for dinner. My grandmother had raised her eyebrows at my travelling dress but had refrained from offering any comments. Now, but for Henry I would have had little in the way of a dinner gown and I chose my favourite pink chiffon with considerable pleasure. It was a beautiful thing, exquisitely draped, with a long floating skirt which made me appear somehow fragile. At its waist was a spray of silk roses in a deeper shade of rose with pale-green leaves hanging almost to the hem of the gown. I looked at myself in the mirror, wondering, a little cynically perhaps, if I wouldn't look too much like an English rose in the company of my dark French relatives.

I badly wanted to wander round the chateau but hesitated in case I got lost or wandered into some room where I would not be welcome. From somewhere in the house came the notes of a piano, falling on the night breeze as though they were a part of it, plaintive and beautiful. Whoever played was an expert and Chopin's music could have been made for the stillness and the perfumed beauty of the garden. I got up from my chair and went out of my room in search of the music. Once again, I was struck by the emptiness of the great hall, and I felt surprised that the Germans had left a piano in the house when everything else of value had been stolen. I followed the sound along the corridors until suddenly the music stopped and I heard the quick closing of a door and light footsteps running away from me. I paused helplessly without the sound to guide me, but I knew without any shadow of doubt that it had been Leoni who played Chopin's music so skilfully. I felt suddenly disconsolate when I thought about my own accomplishments, which were either modest or negligible.

I made my way back to the hall and the room which my aunt had pointed out to me as the drawing room where the family assembled before dinner, surprised to find that this was furnished more adequately than the other rooms I had seen. I could see from the state of the walls that one or two paintings were missing and no doubt several ornaments also, but the furniture was elegant, the carpet and curtains rich and tasteful. My aunt was the first to join me. She too had changed into a dinner gown, beautifully cut if not fashionable, and once again I was struck by the timeless beauty of her face as well as its haunting sadness. She came forward to greet me.

'You are early, Jacintha. Have you seen anything of the house?'

'No, it is so big I was afraid of getting lost. I heard the piano and came down to see who was playing but the music stopped before I could find the room.'

'We will go into the music room after dinner. It is fortunate that we still have the piano and the room is not greatly changed. The officers were fond of music, which seems strange, perhaps, in a people so given to atrocities of one kind or another. Every evening after dinner they gathered in the music room to listen.'

'They were talented, too?'

'No, they did not expect to be asked to entertain themselves.'

I looked at her face, sharp and bleak with distasteful memories. She smiled quickly to reassure me. 'Come, Jacintha, the family are in the Chinese drawing room. Unfortunately that room suffered more than any during the occupation, but my husband is fanciful tonight and the rest of us are pandering to his whim. It is a beautiful night and the views from the windows of that room are particularly lovely.'

'Has Adrian returned from Chartres?'

'Yes, and happily he has recovered two of our pictures. They are by Monet and once hung in the library.'

I have little memory of my first sight of the Chinese drawing room, aware only that Adrian came forward to meet me with a smile on his lips as forced and unwelcoming as his mother's had been earlier that day. I was not wanted at Fontinelle, although his words were more generous than his smile.

'Welcome to Fontinelle, Jacintha. I am sorry you find the

173

house in such an unhappy state. I would prefer you to have seen it in happier times.'

'I am very glad to be here, Adrian. I know how beautiful the chateau must have been and still is.'

Suddenly the coldness left his smile and I felt the pressure of his hand on mine. He led me towards the window, where the small upright figure of a woman dressed entirely in black was sitting in a tall, straight-backed chair, her dark hair drawn back from her pale face severely, her long white fingers nervously plucking at the material of her gown.

'This is my Aunt Monique,' Adrian said, 'my mother's cousin, the Comtesse Daubigny.'

The comtesse acknowledged my presence by the merest inclination of her head, nor did her dark sad face show any sign of animation at our meeting.

I returned with Adrian to the couch set before the ornate marble fireplace. Because the night was warm, there was no fire burning but instead flowering plants had been arranged to cover the gaping void of the empty grate and I exclaimed delightedly at their beauty.

'Yes, we are fortunate that the gardens and greenhouses were preserved. The German officers would not destroy the view from the windows they spent so much time looking through.'

His face was cynical, his voice bitter, but he could say no more because at that moment the door opened to admit my grandmother and Jules, the butler, pushing my uncle in his wheelchair.

He was exactly as I remembered him apart from his disability, his silver-fair hair and pale-blue Carradice eyes so like the memory I had of my father. But my father's face had been kind; this man's face was cold, as cold as the east wind which swept down from the lakeland fells.

My aunt went forward to meet him, taking his chair from the butler and pushing it herself towards the centre of the room. My uncle was a large man and the chair seemed almost too heavy for her slender hands. I was surprised that Adrian did not step forward to assist her; instead, he went to my grandmother and briefly kissed her cheek. At that moment I pitied her as she looked up eagerly into his face. She loved him as she had always loved him, but I was saved from further speculation by the arrival of the girl I had seen in the gardens earlier that afternoon.

Adrian took her hand and led her towards my grandmother, saying gently, 'This is Leoni. It is many years since you met so no doubt you will both find each other changed.'

The old woman and the young one looked at each other gravely, then Leoni bent forward and swiftly kissed my grandmother's cheek. The older woman's face relaxed a little and she said graciously, 'It is true I would not have known you. Have you been ill, child?'

Leoni shook her head, then, a little confused, she looked up at Adrian, who led her over to me. She had changed her gown for another, also white, but this one swept the floor, its only relief a bunch of silk violets at the waist. I was struck again by the ethereal beauty of her face and figure, which made me seem more hale and hearty than ever by comparison. Understandably Adrian was protective towards her.

I do not think I shall ever forget my first evening at Fontinelle. Dinner was served in the large family dining room on the first floor overlooking the terrace and the lake. Here again the pictures had gone from the walls but the great long table was polished to perfection. Down its centre, tall, deeply chased silver candelabras vied with heavy bowls filled with roses, and the silver cutlery and tableware decorated with pure gold, all bearing the Fontinelle crest, made me open my eyes wide with delight. Adrian, who was sitting opposite, smiled his slow dark smile and said, 'You are surprised to see these things, Jacintha?'

I nodded, speechlessly.

'These are small things we managed to hide away. The Germans couldn't find them and so after the war all we had to do was bring them out again for our own use. Enjoy them, my dear, you will find little else to exclaim over in the Chateau Fontinelle.'

Considering there were so few servants, the meal was simple but excellent and I for one did it full justice. Once or twice I caught Adrian's eyes upon me and always they were filled with amusement, probably because I was the only member of the dinner party with a healthy appetite. It was a sombre gathering. My uncle barely touched the meal set before him and now and again I was aware of his light eyes upon me, filled with a strange speculation. I tried smiling at him but my smiles were met with a cold uncompromising stare, and he appeared fretful and ill-humoured. I thought my aunt handled him with great patience and gentle forbearance.

I felt that the meal was painful for my grandmother. She looked at my uncle constantly and at Adrian, too, but her conversation was minimal. Leoni and Aunt Monique sat at the table like two wraiths I might have conjured up from the deepest fantasies of my imagination. Once Leoni's eyes met mine, only to be withdrawn quickly while the blood suffused her cheeks.

'You grace our dinner table like the perfect English rose, Jacintha,' Adrian said quietly, and I looked up quickly, anticipating the laughter I should find in his eyes. I was surprised to discover his face so serious that my cheeks imitated Leoni's in their confusion.

The music room was next door to the dining room and it was here I got my first glimpse of the real beauty of Fontinelle. Here the crystal chandeliers still hung from the white and gold ceiling and the great windows stood open to the balmy beauty of the night. Long blue velvet drapes hung at the windows and ornate blue velvet chairs and couches were arranged about the room. The grand piano stood on a dais at the end of the room and as we took our places Adrian took Leoni's hand in his and walked with her to the piano.

She looked up into his face with all the simple trust of a child, asking in a small breathless voice, 'What shall I play?'

'Whatever you like, my dear. Liszt, Chopin, I don't think any of us mind what you play.'

She sat at the piano and lightly ran her fingers over the keys, then, once more, the melodies of Chopin played upon our senses. Adrian went to sit beside his mother and I forgot the sadness of the chateau and my own problems in the rapture of the music. Her slender white fingers rippled over the keyboard in melodies which had defeated my own fingers so dismally under Miss Hanson's less than expert tutelage, then falteringly the music stopped and I looked up, thinking she had forgotten how the nocturne ended. She was staring at the keyboard, her hands idle, then suddenly she brought them down on the keys in one gigantic chord which reverberated round the room, causing her audience to look at each other in

176

startled consternation. The music she played now was different – wild sweeping music, the tragic impassioned third movement of Beethoven's Moonlight Sonata. Adrian leaped to his feet but, before he could reach the piano, Leoni had put her head down upon the keys in a passion of weeping.

I sat in stupefied silence. It was as though I watched actors in a play; Adrian leading the weeping girl from the room, his arm about her shoulders, his mother and her cousin, the comtesse, sitting erect with white faces, and my grandmother taking hold of her son's hand to comfort him in case the scene we had all just witnessed might have added to his pain.

Suddenly I felt stifled. I could no longer stand the atmosphere of tension in that lofty beautiful room and I escaped through the french windows onto the terrace. The night was beautiful, one of those perfect nights that come so rarely. The gardens stretched before me bathed in bright moonlight and it was so still, as though some giant hand had reached down to halt even the light murmuring of the breeze through the branches of the trees. The perfumes of the summer night were all around me, the warm earth and roses, and as I walked the length of the terrace the moonlit garden became blurred by my tears. Somewhere in the house behind me Adrian was comforting the girl he loved with all the tenderness I knew he was capable of, and I longed at that moment to escape into the dark reaches of the forest that climbed the hill on the other side of the lake. I did not hear Adrian until he came to stand beside me and I looked up at him startled. At that moment the moon was hidden behind a silver-edged cloud and he seemed a man of darkness in his sombre evening clothes.

'A summer night can be deceptive, Jacintha,' he said gently. 'My mother is afraid you will catch cold.'

He draped a light chiffon wrap across my shoulders. It was edged with white fox fur, a beautiful thing, and I hugged its delicacy to me, glad of its unexpected warmth.

We stood together quietly looking out across the gardens and I was painfully aware of his dark presence and the aroma of his cigar. Surreptitiously I reached up my hand to wipe away my tears and he turned me towards him smiling a little.

'Tears? And on such a perfect night!'

'Perhaps that is why I am touched, because the night is so

beautiful. There may never be another night as perfect as this one.'

'That is a foolish thing to say at your age. Shall we walk a little or would you prefer to go inside?'

'Oh no, please let us walk.'

We fell into step side by side, but before we stepped down into the garden I paused and he looked at me inquiringly.

'Perhaps we should ask Leoni if she would like to come with us.'

'Leoni has retired for the night. She was upset and Marie has given her a sleeping draught.'

'Why was she suddenly so upset? She was playing so beautifully.'

'She has not been well. But come, we must not speak of tragedies on such a night.'

We walked a little way in silence until I said, 'How still it is except for the crickets.'

'They are not crickets. They are tree frogs. We may be lucky enough to hear the nightingale, I have heard him several times recently singing in the forest.'

'Oh, that would really make everything perfect. Are they really the most beautiful songbirds in the world?'

'Well, they have no competition, have they? If we heard them in the daytime they would have to compete with a thousand others. Where would you like to walk?'

'What is that white building up there at the top of the hill?'

'Only a summerhouse built like a tiny Greek temple by one of my ancestors who had a classical turn of mind. It is quite a long way and those shoes you are wearing might not be equal to the climb.'

'I could always take them off.'

'You are not walking on the beach, my girl, when you walk through the forest. There is quite a good path, however, with steps at the end of it. I can promise you a magnificent view from the top if you care to make the effort.'

We climbed the hill in silence, the scent of the pines in our nostrils, the moss-covered path soft and often slippery under our shoes so that Adrian took my arm lightly until we came at last to the steps. The little summerhouse was charming, its white marble startling in the moonlight, and we skirted the balcony around it until we were standing on a shelf of rock.

Below us, the ground dropped away and I drew in my breath sharply with delight. Below us the river wound its way like a silver ribbon through fields and woodland, with the bright moonlight lighting up homesteads and villages along its banks. Words of delight poured from my lips and I turned to look at Adrian, suddenly silenced by the expression on his face. At that moment, I felt like an interloper into sorrows of which I had no part, and looking at his dark severe profile I shivered in spite of the warmth of the night and our exertions in climbing the hill. I pulled the soft wrap closer around my shoulders and immediately his brow cleared and something of the old Adrian shone through as he turned his head to look down at me.

'If you are cold, Jacintha, we will go back.'

'Oh no, Adrian, no, I am not in the least cold. I don't know why I shivered; it was something I don't understand, and you were looking so unutterably sad you seemed like a stranger.'

With his arm he made a broad sweep around the scene which faced us.

'That is the valley of the Marne, Jacintha. I couldn't begin to tell you how many men fought and died and suffered in those few miles that you can see from here, or expect you to understand the appalling conditions the ordinary people of this valley lived in for four long years while men were slaughtering each other over the same piece of blood-soaked ground.'

'Perhaps it is the atmosphere of this place that made me feel so sad. There are so many things I do not understand, I feel so stupidly young and silly when I think how little I know. I have done nothing with my life.'

'Good gracious, child, your life is still in front of you. Every girl can't expect to be a tragedienne before she is twenty-one.'

'But Leoni is only a little older than I and she has seen so much unhappiness. Tell me about Leoni, Adrian. I want us to be friends; it would help if I knew more about her.'

'What is it you want to know?'

'I want to know why she looks so afraid and sad, and why she suddenly played so differently before she burst into tears, and why everybody looked so bleak and uncomfortable as though they had been half expecting it.'

I thought at first he would not answer any of my questions and I felt miserable in case he thought me presumptuous and far too curious. I moved away from him and went to stand on the extreme edge of the precipice. Almost immediately I felt him take my arm and roughly pull me back.

'Try not to be so touchy, Jacintha. I too can be vulnerable.'

I was instantly contrite. How could I expect him to treat me like an adult, if I didn't behave like one?

'I'm sorry, Adrian, perhaps it was foolish of me to ask you to talk about Leoni after all.'

'Yes, well, perhaps not tonight. You should enjoy your first night at Fontinelle without any discussion on the darker aspects of this sad house.'

He turned to leave the little summerhouse and reluctantly I followed him down the hill to where the great house stood serene amongst its gardens, its domes and turrets gently bathed in silver moonlight. At the bottom of the hill, he surprised me by taking another path, which led us beside the lake and towards the stone ornamental bridge we had passed over earlier that day in the car. The water shimmered and danced in the moonlight and as we climbed the banking to the path above he took my arm, cautioning me to stand still beside him. From the depths of the forest came the hauntingly, piercingly sweet tones of a nightingale, so tender, so isolated, in the stillness that they brought an ache into my throat.

At that moment I longed to rest my head against his breast and feel his arms around me and I stepped back sharply, afraid of the strange unpredictable emotion he and the night aroused in me. In silence we resumed our walk back to the chateau. We did not speak again until we reached the open windows. Then he asked, 'How long does my grandmother intend staying at Fontinelle, do you think?'

'I have no idea. She hasn't said.'

'Oh well, she will probably stay awhile, the journey will have tired her. I have to go into Chateau Thierry tomorrow. Would you like to come with me?'

'Oh yes, please, that would be lovely. Just you and I, do you mean?'

I thought his eyes shone with amusement and for a brief moment he did not answer me. Then he said, quite seriously, 'I doubt if Leoni would find much pleasure in wandering around scenery she has known since childhood.'

'Do you think I should ask my grandmother if I can go with you to Chateau Thierry? She may have other plans.'

'You must do as you think fit, Jacintha, but I hardly think she will wish to accompany us; she will probably be weary after her journey.'

I didn't want her to come with us. I wanted to go with Adrian alone; I scanned his face anxiously but he was not looking at me. He was looking upwards at the full moon riding high in a cloudless sky. Why did his face etched in silver light evoke old memories and trouble my heart with new ones? He turned away and immediately the spell was broken.

9

The next few days opened up for me an enchantment I had never believed possible and, although I was at the mercy of my grandmother's unpredictable nature, on the morning after our arrival at Fontinelle I set out with Adrian to Chateau Thierry. My grandmother had not appeared for breakfast but Aunt Marguerite wished us a happy day and even Aunt Monique managed a parting smile.

Our route followed the river as it wound its stately way through old brown-roofed villages and hillsides covered with new vines. Adrian told me that many of the rooms at Fontinelle had been adorned with paintings by Corot of the same scenery we were seeing now. He had loved the paintings, but now none of them was left, and for a while he sat brooding and silent beside me in the car.

It was market day in Chateau Thierry – a bustling street market beneath the castle walls – and we left the car and climbed towards the ruins. The town was beautifully situated on two banks of the Marne, dominated by the park which surrounded the castle ruins, and Adrian told me that it was famous as the birthplace of Jean de la Fontaine, whose fables had enchanted the children of France for generations.

We ate lunch by the banks of the river at an old inn and, warmed and made mellow by the bottle of wine the innkeeper had produced, we laughed a lot. I felt closer to Adrian than I had ever felt to any other human being.

I was silent in the car on the way back to the chateau, and Adrian teased me gently by saying, 'You are very quiet, Jacintha; you are probably not accustomed to drinking wine with your lunch.'

'I was just thinking how heavenly it would be if this day could go on for ever to the end of my life.'

'Would you not be afraid of too much happiness and the effect it might have on your character?'

We entered the grounds of Fontinelle by a different gate and now vast areas of pastureland lay on either side of the long straight drive and cattle grazed. We came upon a small paddock where a group of horses stood with their heads leaning over the road and Adrian brought the car to a halt saying, 'Perhaps you would like to meet an old friend, Jacintha.'

'A friend, here?'

He held the car door open until I stepped out on the road and mystified I followed him towards the railings which edged the drive. He whistled softly and almost immediately one of the horses left the group and came cantering towards us. He pushed his long silken head against Adrian's shoulder and instantly I recognized him. It was Caliph, and I said, 'How gentle he has become.'

'Yes, but he too has his memories. See, I want to show you something.'

He took hold of Caliph's mane to bring him round so that his flanks faced us and I was horrified to see a long jagged scar showing white and cruel against the black satiny coat.

'But that is terrible, what caused it?'

'Shrapnel.'

The horse winced and shied away as his hand lightly touched the scar. 'I thought at first I would have to have him shot but he recovered. It will always pain him – he will never be able to be ridden again.'

'Will you always keep him?'

'As long as he lives, I owe him too much ever to part with him.'

I had always been afraid of Caliph, now he allowed me to stroke his head and his proud arched neck before we got back into the car.

I awoke next day to grey leaden skies and a steady drip from the trees outside my window. The gardens and parkland were shrouded in a light swirling mist and the day stretched ahead of me obscure and lonely. Adrian decided over breakfast that we should put off our visit to Vincennes until the weather cleared and immediately after breakfast he left the house to visit his tenants in the villages around the estate.

After he had left, I wandered disconsolately into the library, but the great heavy volumes filled me with dismay and I knew my French was not equal to any one of them. I wondered idly what time the rest of the household appeared. Adrian said his mother read her correspondence and replied to it in the morning room, so I did not want to interrupt her; my grandmother never appeared much before eleven, and I could not think that I would find anything to talk about with Aunt Monique. I wished that I could be friends with Leoni, but she, like the rest of them, was elusive.

Making up my mind suddenly, I ran upstairs to my bedroom and put on my old trenchcoat, which I had had the presence of mind to bring with me, and a rain hood for my hair, and I let myself out of the house. I did not mind walking in the rain – after all, I had had plenty of practice in the Lake District – and the light rain felt soft and sweet upon my face. The swans huddled dejectedly in the shallows of the lake and I turned away from the forest and its dripping trees.

I was about to retrace my steps towards the rose gardens when I saw Leoni leave the house by the conservatory door. She was wearing a blue waterproof cape and a blue scarf on her head, and she was running with deliberate purpose towards the shrubbery. Perhaps I had no right to follow her, but I was lonely and in need of company, and to be honest I was curious. The path she took was narrow and twisting as it climbed upwards through the shrubbery; it was also slippery and my feet slithered through puddles and clay until at last I came to a stone wall which bordered the estate. There was no sign of Leoni, but I had seen no other paths except the one I had followed. I stood peering across the wall and then I saw her again, running down the hillside on the other side of it. I realized there must be a door in the wall somewhere close by. She had left it standing open, a stout, newly painted door in the grey stone wall, and I too set off down the hillside in pursuit of her flying figure. In the distance now I could see what looked like a ruin, perhaps of some old castle, and Leoni was running towards it, her blue cape flying back in the chill little wind that had blown up suddenly. There was a path leading to the ruin and, although it was broken up and uneven, it was easier to run on than the slippery grass. As I got nearer to the ruin, I could see that it was the charred and burned-out remnants of a chateau, once no doubt as beautiful and proud as Fontinelle. Now its windows stared out at me sightless and dejected, the roof was gone and the walls looked like skeleton hands reaching upwards, jagged and somehow obscene. The drive was overgrown with moss and weeds and the once-formal gardens were wildernesses of overgrown rose bushes and shrubs. Around the ruin the trees were merely stumps of charred wood which told their pitiful story only too well. This was all that was left of the Chateau de Montforte.

There were no signs of Leoni, so I could only assume that she was not interested in the ruin of her home and had gone on along the path towards the forest. Breathlessly I followed, until at last I came to a little clearing and what looked like a private burial ground. Panting a little, I stood back, afraid to startle the girl who stood in the midst of that clearing with the hood thrown back from her cape and her dark hair hanging lank and saturated with rain around her shoulders.

She was sobbing quietly as she stood before one tomb in particular and I knew then that I could not intrude upon a grief so private and so intense.

I waited under the trees with the rain dripping dismally onto my head, finding its way down the turned-up collar of my coat, my feet cold in the damp grass. I did not go immediately to look at the tombstones in case she came back and found that I had followed her all the way from Fontinelle. The smaller graves were those of servants, old family retainers both recent and dating back many years, but the larger vaults were those of the de Montforte family itself. Many of them were crumbling with age but the large vault seemed as though it would defy time itself. I read the inscriptions on the walls, oblivious now of the driving rain and the wet misery of the morning. The carving was fresh on the large plaque and looked as though it had been carved only recently. Philippe de Montforte, born 18 May 1858, died 12 March 1917; Louise de Montforte, born June 1867, died November 1897: Leoni's parents. There was one other – Armand de Montforte, killed in action on the Somme, 1916, aged twenty-three; her elder brother.

I too was crying now, the hot salty tears falling down my cheeks onto my coat to mingle with the rain. Slowly I went back the way I had come, my throat aching, my mind in a turmoil. There were too many things I did not understand. I had not had a happy life and there had been precious little love in it, but I had been sheltered from the sort of tragedies Leoni had been confronted with, tragedies that endeared her to Adrian, whereas mine must only appear trivial and even contemptible by comparison.

I entered the chateau through the conservatory, hanging up my coat and hood to drip onto the tiled floor. As I let myself into the hall, I encountered my Aunt Marguerite, who eyed me with great surprise.

'Why, Jacintha, your hair is dripping wet. Surely you haven't been out on such a morning?'

'It was only raining in the wind when I left the house; it came on heavily later.'

'But where have you been, child?'

'I followed Leoni through the gate in the wall. I didn't want her to think I was prying, so I stood under the trees to shelter.'

'I see. Where did Leoni go?'

'To the house that was burned, the Chateau de Montforte.'

She looked at me, startled. 'She surely did not attempt to go into the house? It is considered quite unsafe. The sooner it is taken down the better.'

'She wasn't interested in the house. I followed her to a private burial ground, but I didn't speak to her.'

'Yes, you were quite right not to speak to her. Poor Leoni, she suffers so much and, though we all want to help her, it is not easy.'

'Perhaps in time. . . .'

'Ah yes, time. In time perhaps we shall all forget the tragedies of these last few years. I am no longer young and there are times when my thoughts are so bitter that I wonder if I shall ever be able to forget and forgive, but Leoni is young, she should not have such memories.'

'The Chateau de Montforte must have been very beautiful once.'

'Yes, it was very beautiful. I can remember when I was your age – the balls and the garden parties with all the young gallants and the beautiful girls. It seemed we lived a life of enchantment then, which makes it doubly hard to reconcile the present with the past.'

'The house will not be rebuilt?'

'How can it be? They stripped it of everything, leaving only a shell, then they set fire to it. Philippe died before he knew what they did to his home and Armand too was killed during the war. There is only Leoni left; her mother died when she was born.'

'She will be happy with Adrian. How could she not be happy in this beautiful house where everybody is so kind to her?'

My aunt smiled her sweet slow smile, so like Adrian's own, but offered no comment about Leoni's happiness.

'I wish I could make friends with her,' I said impulsively. 'I feel she should have some woman friend of her own age.'

'Yes, that would be good for Leoni. She should relate to people of her own age, but perhaps she is not ready for it yet. She is ashamed and afraid of the past, despite the fact that she was not to blame for anything that happened.'

I waited, hoping she would say more so that I might understand Leoni but, as though she had already told me too much, she said, 'Go upstairs and change into some dry clothing, Jacintha, I should not be talking to you here while you shiver in those damp things. When you come down, help yourself to a glass of cognac; it will warm you.'

By the time I reached my bedroom I was shivering. The room felt chilly. The wet misery of the gardens and the lake beyond had its effect on the strangely bare room and I was glad to rub myself briskly with a towel and change into something warm and dry. Taking Aunt Marguerite at her word, I decided I would like a glass of brandy, so I went into the library, where I knew the tray was kept. I wished immediately, however, that I had not when I found my uncle sitting in his wheelchair beside the fire which crackled and burned in the hearth. I smiled at him tentatively but he merely looked back stonily, his eyes pale and cold behind their steel-rimmed spectacles. At that moment, he reminded me of Teddy as I had first seen him sitting at the old schoolroom table, his short-sighted eyes peering at me from behind his glasses.

'It is beautifully warm in here,' I began in an attempt to make conversation. 'I have been out into the park but it is cold out there and it is raining quite heavily now. My aunt said I should have a glass of brandy. May I pour you one?'

'Thank you, no. I do not drink cognac in the morning.'

I felt rebuffed as I poured a minute quantity of brandy into a glass, promptly drowning it with soda water. I saw him put the newspaper he had been reading down onto the table by his chair rubbing his eyes a little as though they troubled him.

A great wave of compassion swept over me for this man who reminded me so forcibly of my father. He looked so forlorn in his wheelchair, like a sad little boy rubbing the sleep out of his eyes.

'Would you like me to read for you, uncle?' I volunteered hopefully.

'I read perfectly well, Jacintha. I come into the library in the mornings so that I can be alone to read the English newspapers without fear of interruption.'

I felt as though he had quite deliberately slapped my face, and with my head held high I marched out of the room wishing him all the solitude he desired. He was like my grandmother, perhaps the only one of her children to inherit her coldness, but that it should have been Adrian's father who had spoken to me so sharply and unkindly hurt me especially. I found myself wondering if Adrian too possessed those traits of coldness and remoteness, and if he did perhaps I should be relieved that he did not love me.

The long day stretched ahead of me aimlessly and I did not know what I should do to amuse myself. Slowly I walked down the stairs, pausing to look at a Renoir, recently recovered, then I heard the sound of the piano played softly in the music room and I decided to go in there, telling myself that surely it was not possible to be rebuffed twice in one morning by members of the household. Leoni sat at the piano. She had changed into a soft pale-blue wollen dress and her hair curled about her face, completely dry and tied back at the nape of her neck with a velvet bow. The tune she played was a Chopin waltz, haunting and sad, and I went to stand at the piano so that I could watch her fingers coping with the intricacies of the composition.

She smiled at me, and her smile was so natural and normal I responded to it warmly.

'Do you play, Jacintha?'

'Very badly, I'm afraid.'

'Would you care to play now?'

'I would much rather listen to you.'

188

'Isn't there some little thing you play well? This is a beautiful instrument, far more worthy of your efforts than the piano you had at school, if it was anything like the one at my convent.'

'I love music, but I would be reluctant to play for you.'

'Why not try? Some favourite you have not found too difficult.'

She rose from the stool and I hesitantly took her place.

I really did not want to play for Leoni but I did want her friendship and it seemed ungracious to be coy and silly about my small accomplishment. I had no doubt that she would be generous instead of critical.

I played first a simple piece written by an obscure English composer. It was light and tuneful though never destined to take its place in the annals of classical music. Then, a little afraid, my fingers went into the second movement of Beethoven's Pathetique Sonata. I was so engrossed in my attempts to play well that I did not look up until I heard the sounds of Leoni quietly sobbing beside me and immediately I stopped playing in consternation.

The great tears rolled down her cheeks and after murmuring 'Please forgive me,' she spun round and ran towards the door. Just as she reached it, the door was flung open and Adrian stood there with dark anger written all over his face. Without a word, Leoni ran past him and out of the room, but he strode over to the piano where I was sitting in stupefied silence. Firmly closing the piano lid, he looked at me out of dark eyes filled with hostility.

'What in heaven's name possessed you to play Beethoven in this house?' he demanded.

'I don't understand.'

'Have some sense, girl. You saw what happened the first night you were here. It was the music of Beethoven then that caused that hysteria we witnessed.'

I too was hurt and angry with this man who towered over me like a dark and menacing angel. He was not the Adrian I had laughed and chattered with only the day before. This Adrian was a stranger, the sort of man I believed I hated while I was growing up at Ravenspoint.

An angry retort came readily to my lips. 'How could I know Beethoven made her sad? She asked me to play. I would much rather have listened to her.'

'Haven't you any idea what German music means in this house? Have you so little imagination that you can have forgotten how recently such music was played here to entertain German officers?'

I stared back at him with wide hostile eyes and, with my head held high, I said, 'You have forgotten, Adrian, that I know nothing of the happenings in this house except that the Germans were here. I asked you to tell me about Leoni and you refused. How can you expect me to use my imagination about things I do not understand? Besides, Beethoven's music is beautiful. Are you telling me France must never listen to it again because of the war?'

He did not answer me, but there was no forgiveness in his dark angry face and mine too was filled with resentment. I walked out of the room with all the dignity I could muster, then I ran for dear life towards the sanctuary of my bedroom.

Leoni did not appear that night at the dining table and, because Uncle Roland was fretful and peevish, my aunt had little time to notice that Adrian was silent too. The food stuck in my throat and I had a headache, caused no doubt by too much weeping.

One of the servants came to take my plate away and my grandmother noticed that the food had hardly been touched.

'Why have you not eaten your dinner, Jacintha? I hope you are not sickening for something. There is not the staff here to care for an invalid.'

'I have a bad headache, grandmother, and I am not really very hungry.'

'Then perhaps you should go to your room and get into bed.'

'Yes, perhaps that is best. I am sure it will be better in the morning.'

I folded my table napkin and placed it in front of me. Then, without looking at anyone in particular, I rose to my feet and wished them goodnight.

'I will have something hot and a draught to cure your headache sent to your room, Jacintha,' my aunt said. 'I expect it is the sudden change in the weather. No doubt tomorrow we shall have the sun back with us again.'

I thanked her politely but was glad to escape from their presence.

I told myself angrily that I had seen the real Adrian Carradice that afternoon. My early childhood opinion of him had been right after all and I was a fool to be swayed by a dark handsome face and a charming manner, which had no doubt hoodwinked my grandmother too. Quite suddenly I wanted to go home to Ravenspoint. I longed for the peaceful beauty of the lakeland fells and the majestic grandeur of the stone house standing on its rugged cliffs. I had been lulled into an awareness of him by the slow charm of Fontinelle, but I was built for sterner things. Let Adrian have his Leoni, let him pamper and cosset her and protect her from Beethoven and all the other beautiful music the Germans had composed – that was his business and I did not care.

How empty and foolish are assertions of that nature when we are young and hurt and in love. Our quarrel was the first thing on my mind when I awoke next morning, and I lay in my bed staring miserably at the ceiling, dreading the day ahead. If I stayed in my room until mid-morning, I would not have to see him because he would be out in the estate, and I could feign another headache in the evening to keep me from the dinner table. Unfortunately I was hungry.

A breakfast tray was brought to my room – delicious French coffee and warm rolls and fresh country butter. On the tray also was a sealed envelope with 'Jacintha' written on the front in Adrian's flowing handwriting. I waited until the servant had left the room, then eagerly I snatched it up, opening it clumsily with my butter knife. The note was brief, but how could I resist its invitation?

As you will see the sun is shining, I have to go into Vincennes but the errand will not take long. We could go to Fontainebleau. Please, please, come with me. Adrian.

I forgot that I was never going to speak to him again. I relegated his cold angry face into the far reaches of my mind and thought only of his warm kindness on other days, and I dressed to please him, arriving on the terrace rosy and joyful to find him waiting for me.

It was a morning filled with delight. Neither of us referred to the previous afternoon. Adrian set out from the very first moment to entertain me and make me feel wanted. Whilst he kept his business appointment in Vincennes, I looked at the castle – almost hidden amongst the trees on one side, it was a great fortress, remodelled and restored under Napoleon III but still retaining much of its medieval aspect. Then Adrian came to look for me and, after drinking coffee under the awning outside a small cafe beneath the castle walls, we returned to the car for our journey to Fontainebleau.

We drove through the great forest of Fontainebleau and picnicked in one of the clearings. Adrian must have planned this day with care; he brought out of the car a hamper containing a feast, as well as a bottle of champagne to go with the food. It was warm in the morning sunlight. We explored lanes where time seemed to have stood still over the centuries; we found cobbled streets and crumbling walls where hollyhocks cascaded over the garden walls of coquette cottages; and I tried to remember all I had ever read of Dumas and other French writers whom poor Mademoiselle Rousseau had been so anxious to introduce to her uncaring English pupils.

Right from the first moment I loved Fontainebleau. The magnificent chateau was built originally as a hunting lodge in the twelfth century and its great richness in works of art was due to the love of the kings who collected them for what they considered to be their own country house. Adrian told me that almost every king in the history of France had added to its splendour, although it owed most of its beauty to Francois I, who employed famous Italian decorators to remodel it – indeed the Italian influence was very strong.

Later, when we emerged from the chateau into the warm sunlight, we fed the carp, great busy fish who were so tame they would even take food from our fingers. To me, however, Fontainebleau means above all things the forest which reaches down to the Seine and the delightful riverside villages at the edge of the forest which we happily explored together.

As we drove home that evening in the soft scented dusk, I thought quietly about the day which was almost over. I was very aware of him sitting beside me in the car, of his hands firm yet light upon the wheel, and his profile etched against the fading light. For the first time that day, I thought about the scene in the music room the day before and I wondered if we would speak of it. We could not behave as though yesterday had never happened, yet I did not want to be the first one to mention the issue. We drove in silence, but it was a companionable silence, apart from the delicate unspoken question of Leoni. He drove to the back of the chateau and I waited while he put the car away in the long garages behind the house, then we fell into step side by side through the gardens.

'Thank you for today, Adrian,' I said, feeling that I must be the one to say something. 'I have enjoyed myself so much. I can't tell you how much I appreciate your asking me.'

'Thank you for coming, Jacintha. I can't tell you what I should have done if you had refused.'

'Why would I do that?'

'Because you were angry with me, because I was angry with you, and that I had no right to be.'

'Oh, but you had. I obviously did something dreadful to cause Leoni so much distress, but I don't understand what it was. I need to know, Adrian. In my ignorance, I could quite easily do it again.'

'You will never play Beethoven again.'

'No, I shall not do that, but there are other things I might do. If I am to behave like an adult woman, please treat me like one. Why is there all this mystery surrounding Leoni? This wall of protection from you all? Yesterday we were talking so happily together I thought at last we were beginning to be friends. Then, for what seemed like no reason at all, she was rushing out of the room in tears and you were angry with me. If we are friends, Adrian, surely you can tell me why that music made her so unhappy.'

We walked in silence and, when I stole a quick glance at his face, I found it dark and brooding and I wondered if I had made him angry again by asking too many questions.

He surprised me suddenly by taking my hand in his, holding it tightly without saying anything until we reached the terrace. Speaking very softly, he said, 'We will talk in the house, Jacintha. If we linger on the terrace our voices will carry upwards and who can tell who may be listening?'

At the time I thought it a strange thing for him to say. His parents' rooms were immediately above the main terrace but the rest of us were scattered throughout the chateau. My grandmother and Aunt Monique had rooms at the far side overlooking the pastureland and Leoni's rooms were beyond mine at the side of the house. But I followed him without question and waited until he closed the doors and drew the curtains at the windows. I stood in the darkness until he switched on a lamp standing on a small marble table near the fireplace, then he indicated that I should sit down across from him with a long ornate table between us.

'Would you care for a glass of wine?' he asked solicitously. When I shook my head, he poured out a glass for himself and I watched for several minutes while he sat idly twirling the stem of his glass between his fingers, his face brooding, as though the words he wanted to say would not come easily. I became restless, playing with the chain about my neck until that moment when his eyes looked straight into mine, bringing the rich blood into my cheeks. How dark and sombre his eyes were – not the glacial Carradice eyes of his father.

'You know the Germans were here,' he began. 'You know what they did to Fontinelle. What you don't know is what they did to the people who lived here. My mother was expected to wait on them, clean their rooms, care for their laundry, cook their food – my aunt, too, who came to Fontinelle after her husband was killed. The whole place crawled with the enemy and there were only old Jules and Marie. Who else do you think looked after them?'

'I didn't realize, Adrian. How could I?'

'You must remember how different you found Ravenspoint after it became a convalescent home, but at least they were our own soldiers. The men who were here were the enemy, living in this house, eating our food, stealing our treasures, treating my mother little better than they would have treated a kitchen maid. If it was vile for them here, it was much worse for the de Montfortes. Philippe de Montforte, Leoni's father, was a proud man, an aristocrat of the old school. He made life difficult for the Germans in every way he could. He undermined their authority, he ridiculed their goose-stepping arrogance and their love of regimentation; even their attempts to treat him with politeness were rejected. Fortunately, or unfortunately, he had a heart attack and died suddenly in 1917. That night they set fire to the chateau, calling it his funeral pyre, and Leoni and her old nurse were taken to the top of the hill and made to stand there while the house burned. They came to Fontinelle that night, too, and they forced all who lived here to stand on the hillside in the pouring rain at the height of a blustery March gale to watch the flames from the de Montforte chateau leaping into the sky. They threatened my mother that such would be the fate of this place if any member of the household failed to conform. That night my mother began to wonder if courage and fortitude would be enough. Leoni was brought here – she has no other home.'

'I see,' I said, my voice a mere whisper.

'No, my dear, not yet you do not see. Leoni was young and lovely and men away from their womenfolk grow frustrated. They treated Leoni worse than they treated the women they found out on the streets after curfew. They did not seem to care that she came from an old and noble family or that she was a girl who had been sheltered and protected from the harsh realities of life. None of that mattered to the Germans, who took her and used her as it pleased them. Then there were other nights when she was forced to play that goddamned music, German music. Perhaps now you can understand why it is forbidden in this house – not because we are insensitive to its beauty but because Leoni associates it with despair and all that is most bestial and hateful in her life.

I was staring at him, my eyes wide with horror, picturing in my mind Leoni with her dainty fastidiousness, and those stiff-necked German officers. The implications of what I had just heard hit me so cruelly I could find no words of sorrow or comfort and as though he sensed my dilemma he said, 'I wanted to spare you from this, Jacintha. Such stories are not for young girls on the threshhold of life. When I first knew about Leoni, I was so filled with rage I thought I would go mad; yet, strangely, one of the things that kept me sane was the memory of a young English girl, serene and untouched, dancing along the shore on a summer afternoon in the days before the war. I blessed that stretch of water that separated Europe from England, never more so than when I came home after the war and heard what had happened to those I loved. You may think I am over-protective towards Leoni – perhaps I am, but I remember her as a gay beautiful girl before the war. When I see her now, I can feel only revulsion for the men who have caused the change in her.'

I stared at Adrian through a blur of tears. It was a terrible story he had told me and my words were pitifully inadequate. As the great tears rolled down my cheeks, I said tremulously, 'But you will be kind to her, Adrian. When you are married, you will surround her with so much love she will be happy with you.'

His expression changed and became so kind I was unprepared for his next words.

'My dear child,' he said calmly, 'I shall not marry Leoni de Montforte.'

Suddenly my heart gave a wild leap of happiness but he was looking away now, his profile remote, cold almost. The next moment he had risen from his chair and was switching on the main lights in the room.

He would not marry Leoni because he was afraid for her sanity, or perhaps because in some way he felt she had been dishonoured by those others, but that was not to say he did not love her and would continue to love her. I stared at him standing impersonally by the door and wondered what sort of pride could make a man reject a woman even when he loved her desperately. One thing was sure; there was no hope for me in his rejection, and forlornly I asked, 'Does that mean that you will never marry?'

'One day, perhaps,' he answered. 'I do not want to be the last of our family to live at Fontinelle.' Quietly he held the door open for me to pass out of the room in front of him and I took this as a cool indication that our conversation was at an end.

As I ran upstairs to my room, my thoughts were in a turmoil. So, one day he would marry for convenience – as Frenchmen, according to Isobel, often married. Some lady he could respect and who would be able to take over the duties of chatelaine easily and naturally without the added encumbrance of being in love. He would have his heir to Fontinelle and no doubt a life as serene and uncluttered as those swans out on the lake gliding dreamily along without a care in the world. Perhaps Adrian thought the absence of love was a small price to pay for such serenity, but, I wondered savagely, would he ever be able to look at Leoni dispassionately, having once loved her so dearly, or was he like

Martin, anxious for the best of both worlds?

I decided that I didn't really like men very much.

That night I slept badly. The story Adrian had told me troubled me so much that I tossed and turned in my bed until the first light of dawn dispelled the shadows in my room. I understood Leoni's distress now, but I loved Adrian. I loved him desperately and because I loved him I wanted him to be happy in his life, even when it was not with me. Lying sleepless in my bed in the quiet of the enormous room, I asked myself questions to which there seemed to be no answers and I tried to put myself in her place. If I had Leoni's memories, would I be able to be loving and natural with a man, any man who professed to love me? Or would his passion only evoke memories of other passions which had been savage and meant nothing? I wanted more for Adrian than Leoni would be able to give him; wearily, I recognized the selfishness in my reasoning.

I rose late, lethargic and heavy-eyed, and I was glad that Adrian had gone to Chartres without me.

'He thought you might be tired after your busy day yesterday,' his mother said. 'In any case, the weather has changed again and there will probably be rain.'

'How does Leoni occupy her time?' I asked her curiously. 'I hardly ever see her, but I hope she doesn't mind my going off with Adrian.'

'I am sure she does not. It is nice for you to see something of the area whilst you are here.'

'Has my grandmother said anything about returning home?' I asked, fearing her reply.

'Nothing. But then you are welcome to stay here as long as you please and it is nice for Roland to have his mother here.'

'Will there ever be any improvement in his condition?'

'I think not, and unhappily he grows fretful and often difficult.'

How formal it all was. Two women talking as though they sat in a restaurant over the teacups instead of in the morning room of a chateau which was still shaking from the effects of the past.

After breakfast I went into the library to write letters to my cousins in England and to Lavinia. I said exactly the same to all three of them, but how could I talk about hidden tragedies and expect them to understand? I could imagine Isobel opening her mail sitting up in her elegant négligée in her elegant bed saying in her low amused voice, 'Gracious, she's taken the trouble to write and said absolutely nothing. I wonder why she bothered.'

I knew my grandmother always sat in the Chinese drawing room in the mornings so I gave it a wide berth, deciding to walk in the gardens instead. It was much cooler outside than the day before and I was glad of my woollen jacket and the silk scarf round my neck. I walked down towards the lake and found a stone seat, from where I was able to watch the swans with their brood of grey cygnets busy squabbling amongst themselves. I had taken a book with me and became so engrossed in it I did not hear Leoni until she stood beside me. I looked up startled as she bade me good morning, and saw that she carried a sketching pad and watercolours.

I watched as she put up her easel on the grass beside the lake, pleased that she had come to sit by me rather than in some secluded spot where I would not have seen her.

'Do you mind if I watch you?' I asked her.

'Not at all, but please do not expect too much. Do you also paint, Jacintha?'

'It was my favourite subject at school, probably because I wasn't too bad at it, but my grandmother said it wasn't a subject likely to do me much good.'

'Oh, but that is sad. One can find so much pleasure in painting. You should ask Aunt Monique to show you some of her pictures. She is very good. Indeed, before the war, she regularly held exhibitions of her work in Paris and elsewhere.'

How naturally she spoke about the war! I would have expected even the merest mention of it to have brought back distasteful memories.

I watched the picture taking shape – the swans and the lake, the tall irises in the shallows and the wrought-iron lamps at regular intervals across the ornamental stone bridge.

'Is this the first time you have painted this scene?' I asked her curiously.

'No, but today it is clouded and always before I have

198

painted it in sunlight. I wondered what it would be like to paint it in more sombre colours. Once I took my watercolours into the village but the people gathered round me and I did not produce a good picture.'

'No, I should not like that either.'

'Did you enjoy your time with Adrian yesterday?'

'Yes, very much. We went to Fontainebleau and picnicked in the forest. You should have come with us.'

'No, you were right to go with Adrian alone. I have seen Fontainebleau many times and shall no doubt do so many times in the future.'

'Do you ever go with Adrian when he visits the towns in the area?'

'No, he goes on business. I would be left waiting for him and I prefer to remain here. If you could move your chair so that the light is on your face, I will try to paint you. Please don't expect too much, but I have wanted to paint you ever since you arrived.'

'To paint me! But my face is nothing out of the ordinary.'

'Oh, but it is. You have beautiful colouring and your face is warm and alive. I only hope I can do it justice.'

I sat facing the lake with my back against the trunk of a tree, fervently wishing that the morning had been sunny so that I could have worn something more flattering than my washed-out blue-linen dress and the nondescript jacket I had draped round my shoulders. She was completely absorbed in her work and I longed to see what she would make of my portrait. At last she looked up with a smile on her lips.

'It is finished. Come and look.'

Eagerly I jumped to my feet, hobbling a little as my legs were seized by a sudden cramp after having remained still for so long. Looking over her shoulder, I gasped with delight. The picture was charming, all greens and blues – the green grass and the leaves of the beech tree behind me, the blue dress and the pale-blue sky. The colours were muted, but my face was vividly alive, a gay piquant face surrounded by cloudy hair, my eyes, startlingly blue, staring out of the picture as though they asked a question.

'But that is beautiful, Leoni. Do you really see me like that or are you flattering me?'

'Would you rather I had flattered you?'

'No, of course not, but I am flattered nevertheless.'

'I see you like that. Once, long ago, I asked Adrian what you were like, what all his English cousins were like, but he was not good at describing any of you. He said Isobel was gay and beautiful and wayward, and that you were a child of the sea, with hair the colour of wet sand and eyes as blue as the ocean.'

'Did he say anything else about me?' I asked, intrigued by his description.

'Only that you were fiercely independent and kept a pet dragon in a cave underneath the rocks.'

Our eyes met and in that moment I saw that hers were filled with laughter. I thought I knew then why Adrian loved her; she was an enchanting creature and would be again if only she could forget the sorrows of the last few years. Miserably I wondered if it was my fate in life always to love a man who for some reason or other could not love me. I wondered at that moment how long it would be before we could go home to Ravenspoint.

'You look sad,' Leoni was saying, interrupting my dismal thoughts. 'I have often seen you looking sad and it has puzzled me. You are young and beautiful and carefree. Why are you sad, Jacintha?'

'Perhaps I am not quite as carefree as you suppose.'

'I thought you would be like Isobel, but you are not. She came here several times and we all thought her very beautiful but a terrible flirt. Adrian brought her to a ball at the chateau and all the men fell in love with her. None of the girls liked her; they were left sitting round the ballroom like pretty white wallflowers, while all their favourite beaux danced with Isobel.'

'That I can imagine – she has not changed.'

'There we all were fresh out of convent school and there was Isobel in a bright-red dress, far too old for her but so very daring. Adrian was cross because the dress was outrageous and because she flirted and teased, but she only tossed her head and told him not to be so stuffy. I suppose she has married somebody wildly handsome who is tall and charming and desperately in love with her.'

I smiled a little, thinking of Henry. She was waiting for my answer so I described him, not forgetting to add that he was very kind.

'But he adores her.'

'Yes, I'm sure he does, and she doesn't always deserve it.'

'But you will deserve it, Jacintha, a nice man who is kind and who will adore you.'

I smiled a little, not daring to trust my voice. I did not want Leoni to dream up some man for me when the only man I wanted was the one who loved her.

There were days when I did not see Adrian at all. On others we drove together through the countryside or rode our horses in the vast parkland and forests which surrounded Fontinelle. At times there was an air of constraint between us and I found it difficult to talk to him in the old familiar way, then I would find his eyes upon me, strangely puzzled, and I would look airily away, changing the subject lightly in case our talk became too serious.

I told him that Leoni had painted my picture and he said, 'I know. I have it.'

'You have it? But where?'

'In the drawer of my desk.'

'But why did she give it to you?'

'She showed it to me and I thought it was charming. I asked her if I might keep it.'

When he did not appear for dinner, I thought that was the last I would see of him for that day. Invariably in the evenings, after dinner, Leoni and Aunt Monique played a card game together, my aunt worked at her tapestry and I was left largely to look after myself. When Adrian was present, and as though by mutual consent, we avoided the gardens after dusk; but now, in his absence, I decided to walk alone in the Italian gardens below the terrace. I had not been there long, however, when I was surprised and disconcerted to see him come striding towards me along the path.

'My mother said I should find you here, Jacintha. I have a surprise for you tomorrow.'

'What sort of surprise? I love surprises.'

'What would you say to coming to Paris with me in the morning?'

I looked up at him with shining eyes. 'Paris! Oh, Adrian, I

do so want to go to Paris. My grandmother wouldn't entertain the idea when we were coming here, but this is much better.'

'Is it?'

'Of course it is. I would much much rather go with you than with her. Shall we be able to see everything in just one day?'

'You would need a lifetime to see all there is to see in Paris, Jacintha, but in the one day we have I will show you as much as I can. I have a business appointment in the morning but it shouldn't take long. After that, the day is our own.'

He was highly amused by my excitement, but I sobered up sufficiently to ask, 'Do you think that perhaps we should ask Leoni?'

'I doubt if she would come. She is visiting the Duprés tomorrow with my mother and Aunt Monique – a long-standing commitment, I believe.'

I am ashamed of the relief I felt then. I wanted tomorrow. If nothing else happened to me for the rest of my life, I would have tomorrow and, like an excited child, I danced and chattered beside him. I beseiged him with questions and he fell into my mood so that we found a new awareness in our being together and recklessly I welcomed it, no longer caring for the dangers it offered. There was no desire on my part to steal what did not belong to me. I only wanted a memory that would sustain me in years that promised to be empty and dreary.

We stood on the bridge looking down into the lake and we did not speak for so long that he asked at last, 'What are you thinking about, Jacintha?'

'I was thinking how different all this is from Ravenspoint.'

'But you love Ravenspoint. I have heard you say so.'

'Yes, I love it, perhaps because it was the only thing in my childhood that was real and honest.'

'Are you saying that Ravenspoint is the only thing in your life now that has any meaning?'

'Am I? I don't know. I always felt secure there with the sea and the gulls and the wind – these things never change. I suppose they will be there even when the house itself is no more.'

'But the sea and the wind can be treacherous. You say they are always the same, but they are not. Given time, they could destroy Ravenspoint.'

'Then I don't know what I do want', Adrian.'

'People are the only thing that matter, Jacintha. Surely you don't want to be a recluse in your old age like Meg and have nobody to care whether you live or die?'

I didn't answer him and he reached out and turned my shoulders so I faced him. His voice was insistent. 'Is that how you want to live your life, Jacintha?'

Surely he had asked that question of me before, but where or when I could not know and as I looked up into his face again the old strange feeling was there. Perhaps long ago, perhaps two different people in this same garden, but the feeling was frightening, so frightening that blindly I reached out to him and he put his arms around me and held me against him. The feeling was not strange. It was a remembered bliss.

We walked back to the house in silence, his arm around my waist. I did not want to go into the house. I wanted to stay out on the terrace with Adrian until the stars paled in the sky, and every step we took became a condemnation of the yearnings in my innermost heart.

There were no lights burning in the downstairs rooms and the curtains had been drawn back in the rooms the family had used earlier. He stood away from me as we reached the terrace and I felt like a child who has suddenly been forsaken by familiar joys. I did not look where I was going and I caught my heel on the edge of a crumbling step. I would have fallen, if he had not put out his arm to save me. I looked up into his face, startled. Then his arms tightened around me and he was kissing me, murmuring endearments against my hair, and I was kissing him back with all the passion I was capable of.

I was trembling when at last he let me go, surprised when he put me away from him deliberately with a look on his face I could not interpret. He was looking beyond me towards the windows of the Chinese drawing room and fearfully I spun round to see who was there. The windows stared back at me dark and unseeing but in that brief moment Adrian had changed from the passionate lover to the quietly remote man I had come to know.

I looked at him anxiously and he smiled a little. Then, cupping my chin in the palm of his hand, he said, 'You are something of an enchantress, Jacintha. I had not thought my little cousin could display such wiles.'

'But Adrian. . . .'

I was prepared to burst out with expressions of love which fortunately he saved me from, because I am sure he was well aware of what I was about to say.

'I will see you at breakfast, Jacintha. If you do not get some sleep you will be bleary-eyed and unattractive and I shall be ashamed of you beside those exquisite Parisiennes on the Rue de la Paix.'

There was no argument against his smooth assurance and fortunately my pride recognized that the charade was over. On the way to my room, my common sense told me that we had been victims of the night and its beauty – the proximity of man and woman in a setting so romantic neither of us had been able to resist it. In the morning Adrian would be remotely charming as always and he would expect me too to play my part.

From the top of the first flight of stairs I was surprised to see him open the drawing-room door, letting a flood of light sweep across the hall; then, seemingly satisfied, he closed the door firmly behind him. I wondered who he thought had watched us from the darkness of the Chinese room and, long after Adrian left the hall to go to his room, I lingered with my ears straining for every sound. The moonlight came in through the tall windows and fell in slanting shafts across the hall. Then, in answer to my vigil, I heard the soft click of a door being opened and just as stealthily closed. I stood with bated breath, my hands clenched against my breast, until I suddenly realized that I stood where the moonlight fell on the marble staircase and I stepped back hastily into the shadows. I almost screamed as my arm caught the cold marble pillar against which I had pressed. Without waiting to see who came out into the hall, I took to my heels and ran, never pausing until I reached the sanctuary of my own room.

My heart was hammering against my ribs and I thought I must suffocate, but I stood in front of the window looking out into the night. The moon moved fitfully through the dark branches of the trees and a chill breeze had blown up since we stood in the gardens. My ears strained to hear a sound in the great house but it was as quiet as a tomb, although I could not rid myself of the feeling that something or somebody moved along the terrace. I undressed in the darkness but just before I stepped into bed I looked out once more into the garden, wishing the next moment that I had not.

Leoni was running lightly along the terrace and down the steps into the rose garden. She seemed afraid, looking back constantly as though some menace from the house pursued her. Then lights streamed out into the darkness and I saw Adrian running down the steps towards her. With a sob in my throat, I turned back into the room. I had no wish to witness their tender reunion. He was no doubt already explaining in feasible terms what she had seen from the drawing-room window, blaming the moonlight, the magic of the summer night and perhaps even my own flirtatious behaviour, but somehow all my joy in the prospect of going with him to Paris had gone.

I cried myself to sleep and I slept heavily. I have no memory of what awakened me but the night was full of sounds. People shouting, people screaming and a strange crackling noise interspersed with the sound of wheels on gravel. My room was filled with smoke and I sat up in bed coughing, my eyes smarting as they tried to peer through the fog. I snatched my dressing gown from the foot of the bed and ran over to the window. Below me on the terrace stood a group of people pointing upwards, wearing only their dressing gowns over their nightclothes. I could not distinguish their faces.

I ran to the door but outside my room the smoke was so dense I was forced back, my eyes streaming. I was choking with the smoke and by this time terrified. The chateau was on fire and my first thought was that they had forgotten me. I ran back towards the window and looked down again. Below me the terrace stretched out towards the gardens and it was a long way down. The people below were gesticulating towards me but I could not make out what they shouted to me and, with despair in my heart, I wondered whether I should jump and risk killing myself or wait to be burned to death.

At that moment the door was flung open and Adrian stood there carrying a blanket in his arms. He ran over to me and, throwing the blanket over me, he lifted me bodily into his arms. I must have lost consciousness after that because the next thing I knew I was lying on the grass outside in the gardens while above me the flames leaped upwards into the dawn.

10

I awoke in a hospital room, my eyes blinking in the bright sunlight that came in through the windows, smarting from the glare of sunlight on the clinical whiteness of walls and coverlets. I moved my head, painfully aware that my throat felt sore, and lay with my eyes closed wondering why I was there, before the memories of the fire at Fontinelle came back to me. I tried to sit up, but it seemed as though there was a great weight pressing down on my head and weakly I flopped back against the pillows. There was a great bowl of flowers on the cabinet beside my bed and another on a table near the door; apart from that, the room was impersonal. This much I noticed before once again I drifted into oblivion.

When next I awoke the sunlight had gone and I heard a noise I did not at first recognize – rain pattering against the window panes. I felt more wide awake than before and, as I struggled to sit up, the effort was not as great. The door opened to admit a young nun, all in white and wearing a great white coif on her head. She had a sweet beautiful face and she was very young. Smiling brightly, she exclaimed, 'Ah, mademoiselle is awake. Now you will soon get well.'

'Where am I, please? Is this a convent?'

'No. You are in the hospital at Chateau Thierry.'

'But you are a nun.'

'That is right. We work in the hospitals and wherever there is illness.'

'How long have I been here?'

'Four days only and you have slept for all of them. Now you must eat. Nothing but liquids have passed your lips in all that time.'

'But I must go back to the chateau. We were going to Paris. . . .'

'There is plenty of time for Paris when you are well. Later on you will have visitors who can tell you more than I.'

'Have I had visitors during these last few days?'

'But of course. Madame Carradice and her son have been several times. They brought these flowers from Fontinelle but you were not awake. No doubt they will come again this evening, if that is possible.'

'But why am I here? I am not burned. I was rescued.'

'I know, you were in shock. Your visitors will explain.'

'But sister. . . .' My voice trailed away as she opened the door and with a gentle smile said, 'I must go, I have much to do. Please be patient.'

They served me with food but I was too impatient to eat it. The time passed slowly. My watch was found in the locker beside my bed but nobody had bothered to wind it. It had stopped at three o'clock and I wondered if that was the time Adrian had rescued me from the fire. When I thought of Adrian, memories of our passionate involvement in the garden of Fontinelle brought the warm blood rushing into my cheeks.

He came alone, bringing fruit and more flowers, and his face was pale – indeed, there was such an air of dejection about him I became instantly alarmed, my first thoughts being for the chateau.

'Adrian, the chateau?' I asked at once, but immediately his smile reassured me that his dejection stemmed from some other source.

'Fortunately the fire only affected that part of the house where you were sleeping and it can be put right,' he said. 'The sister said you were awake and feeling much better. I am glad.'

'How did the fire start? We saw nothing when we came in from the gardens.'

'Who can say? A spark, however minute, when old timber is dry can start a blaze and this has been an unusually hot summer.'

'But at that time in the morning?'

'It is a mystery that might never be solved.'

'But everybody is safe?'

I was looking anxiously into his eyes and I could see them suddenly cloud over. 'Is Leoni safe?'

'Quite safe. She is staying with the Duprés until things are normal. Aunt Monique is there also.'

'And your mother?'

'My mother is at the chateau.' He was looking at me steadily, as though debating with himself whether he should say more. The sister came in to say I had another visitor, and burning with frustration I knew the moment to speak of other things had gone.

A few moments later my grandmother's chauffeur was brought to my room, self-consciously clutching a bunch of white daisies in his hands, which he placed at the bottom of the bed.

He stared at Adrian in some surprise. 'I'm sorry, sir. I wouldn't have come tonight if I'd thought you'd be here, but I thought Miss Jacintha would be on her own and needing company.'

'That's all right, Dawson, I wasn't intending staying long and now that you are here I will say *au revoir*. I will come again tomorrow, Jacintha.'

'You are going so soon?' I wailed.

'Dawson will tell you that I have much to do.'

He bent down and swiftly kissed my cheek before striding to the door. He did not look at me again and I could have wept from the sheer frustration of loving him and knowing nothing.

Dawson took the chair beside my bed and, no doubt sensing my chagrin, he said, 'Poor Mr Adrian, he must have a lot on his mind just now with the chateau and the funeral and everything.'

'Funeral, what funeral?'

'Why, Mr Carradice's funeral, miss, Mr Adrian's father.'

'But I didn't know. When did he die. Was it sudden?'

'The night of the fire, miss. He was trapped in the corridors and when the firemen got to him he was dead, suffocated with the smoke, they said.'

'But that is dreadful. Could nobody have saved him? Adrian saved me.'

'They didn't know he was up there, miss. Nobody seemed to know where anybody was, least of all his wife.'

'How is my grandmother taking it?'

'Badly, I'm afraid. She was kept heavily sedated the first day after the fire and she's been so upset since she hasn't thought about anything but her son's death.'

'I expect when everything is settled we shall be returning to England.'

It was a question more than a statement and he nodded his head in reply. 'She won't linger on here any longer than is necessary, miss. You can be sure of that.'

'You have no idea when, Dawson?'

'No, she's said nothing, but as soon as the funeral's over it's my guess our days in France are numbered.'

'I wonder why Adrian didn't tell me about his father,' I wailed. 'Oh, Dawson, I wish we had never come to Fontinelle.'

'Well, try not to worry about it, miss. It's not your fault, and if Mr Carradice had stayed in his room he'd probably have been alive now. Mr Adrian went to his parents' rooms to see if they were safe; his mother said she had been next door to rouse her husband and, when he was not there, they both surmised the butler had rescued him.'

Dawson did not stay long and I thought he was glad to go before I asked too many questions.

How long the days seemed. There was nothing to do, only lie there and think. Adrian brought a selection of books written in English from the library at Fontinelle but I had little patience for reading, and my imagination was beginning to terrify me.

Somebody had watched us from the Chinese room on the night Adrian swept me into his arms, and try as I would I could not accept his version that the abnormally hot summer had turned the chateau into a tinder box. The chateau was old; it had seen many hot summers in its long history without bursting into flames, and the more I thought about it the more I became convinced that somebody had deliberately set fire to the chateau because they wished me dead. I tried to imagine which of the people living in the house hated me enough to do that to me, and always my thoughts came back to Leoni. It was Leoni who had run out into the gardens, looking back fearfully over her shoulder – no doubt for the flames to appear through my windows. What bitterness, what hatred, she must have felt towards me to have done such a thing.

One night when Adrian came to see me alone, I voiced my fears and instantly wished that I had not. He immediately became distant, his eyes cold, his manner remote, and I believed it was because he resented my harbouring such thoughts about the people living at the chateau. For two long days he stayed away, leaving me fretful and filled with deep unhappiness.

I was now allowed out of my bed to sit in the gardens or walk along the ordered paths around the hospital. After the evening meal, however, I could only sit in my room listening for a firm tread in the passage outside, unbelievably desolate when it did not come.

Aunt Marguerite came along, slender and graceful in her funereal black, although I was convinced she could not have loved her husband who was so querulous and difficult. She received my shy offers of condolence calmly.

'You are looking well now, Jacintha. Perhaps it is time you came home.'

I did not answer her. Fontinelle was not my home. Ravenspoint was my home and that was where I wanted to go, and quickly.

'My grandmother has not been to see me.'

'No, but you must remember she is very old and has suffered a grievous blow. Roland was her eldest son.'

I felt rebuked, but immediately she leaned forward and covered my hands with her own.

'You will be leaving us quite soon now, Jacintha, but before I leave the hospital I will speak to the sister to see how long yet you are to remain here.'

'Will Adrian come for me when I leave?'

'Yes, I am sure he will. He is in Paris at the moment but we expect him home very soon.'

Paris! I must not think of Paris. Paris was an illusion, when it should have been a remembered joy. There would be no Paris for Adrian and me; it was a city for lovers and Adrian was not my lover, in spite of those moments of shared passion. Adrian was part of a summer's night and the scent of roses, an enchantment without substance, nothing more. Oh no, I must not think of Paris.

She stayed for perhaps another half-hour and we talked of ordinary things. The grapes ripening on the vines, the orchids, exotic and strange in the humidity of the greenhouses, and the early morning mist over the lake and gardens of Fontinelle which heralded the first signs of autumn.

'Will you be glad to go home to Ravenspoint?' she asked curiously.

'I think so, but my future is very uncertain.'

I thought there was compassion in her large sad eyes but next moment she was taking her leave of me, quietly kissing my cheek.

Adrian came for me the following day in the early part of the afternoon and I sat beside him in the car with a fur rug tucked round my knees in spite of the warmth of the day. He was solicitous about my well-being but we spoke little, and then only about impersonal things. He seemed preoccupied, as though his thoughts were on matters other than the young cousin sitting beside him staring out at the scenery, and it was only when we turned in at the gates of the chateau that he spoke to me again.

'My mother has had your things moved to a room on the other side of the house. I'm afraid some of your clothes were spoiled by smoke; it is almost a worse destroyer than flames.'

I didn't speak. I was sorry about my clothes; I would probably never have clothes like them again, but when I returned to Ravenspoint I would have little occasion for wearing such things.

'My mother has had them cleaned in Paris and most of them are now fit to wear. The rest will be replaced, so there is no need to look so sad.'

'I'm not sad about the clothes, Adrian. They are not important.'

'I never thought I would hear a young girl saying clothes were not important.'

'Other things matter more.'

'That is true, but girls of your age do not often recognize it.'

I wished he wouldn't keep referring to my age – after all, Leoni wasn't much older.

We were driving now up the hill and soon we would be able to look down upon the chateau from the place where I had first seen it.

'Will you please stop at the top of the hill, Adrian? I want to see the chateau from there. I can't bear to see it all burned and damaged like the de Montforte place.'

'You needn't worry, my dear. It is only one small part of the house that has been damaged and already there are workmen repairing it. In time no one will know that there was ever a fire. Besides, I have some good news for you. We have recovered a great deal of the furniture and many of the pictures that were taken away by the Germans during the war. You will be able to see them when we get back.'

The house stood mellow and beautiful in the late afternoon sunlight, the waters of the lake sparkled and the great trees cast their shadows across the lawns as they had done for centuries. There was scaffolding around the area of my windows but apart from that nothing had changed.

'You are surprised?' Adrian asked.

'Yes, I was afraid that part of the chateau would have been completely destroyed.'

'Part of the roof has gone, of course, and in the corridors and rooms themselves there is a lot of smoke damage but this can soon be put right. I have had that part of the house blocked off completely until the repairs have been effected.'

He started the car and we continued on our journey, not speaking again until we had crossed the bridge and reached the courtyard.

'Shall I see my grandmother?' I asked quietly.

Was there a hint of amusement on those firmly chiselled lips, I wondered. I couldn't be sure but he answered me just as quietly.

'You will see her. She is anxious to make preparations to return home.'

So it was finally over, and now that our imminent departure had been put into words I was surprised how little I felt. It was not, however, because I no longer cared. Rather, it was a numbness, as though everything that had happened to me since I came here had not happened to me at all, but to some other person standing outside myself like a silent shadow.

My aunt came into the hall to greet me and, as I looked around the beautifully proportioned room with its wide sweeping staircase, I was delighted to see that where once there had been shapes of dust upon the white walls many of the spaces were now filled with valuable oil paintings. She smiled at my obvious delight.

'You must look at them later, Jacintha, they are very fine paintings and of great value. Has Adrian told you that your room is now on the other side of the house? I thought you would prefer to get as far away from your old room as possible and the one I have given you is furnished with many of the things we have recovered only recently.'

I followed her along unfamiliar corridors in a part of the house I had not seen before. The room she showed me into was charming, much smaller than my old room and obviously arranged and newly decorated to receive me. I exclaimed on its beauty and she took me over to the two large windows overlooking pastureland and the paddock where Caliph champed the short green grass in sublime contentment.

'Perhaps you would prefer to rest a little, my dear,' she said solicitously, 'but if not we are all in the drawing room waiting for tea.'

'All? Is Leoni back then?'

'Why, no. She is still with the Duprés, but your grandmother is there and Adrian. Come down and join us when you are ready.'

I wondered if I was still suffering from my recent experience or if it was a reaction to my return to Fontinelle, but I felt completely drained and apathetic. I did not even bother to look at my clothes hanging in the wardrobe and my legs trembled so much on my way down the staircase that I had to catch hold of the balustrade to stop myself from falling. Adrian came up the stairs to take my arm, looking at me anxiously as he did so, and I was grateful for the pressure of his hand on mine.

My aunt presided over the teacups, favouring us with her small swift smile, but my grandmother sat in her straight-backed chair beside the window making little effort to appear gracious.

'So you are back, Jacintha,' was her greeting. 'Are you fully recovered?'

'Yes, thank you, grandmother.'

'Well enough to travel, I hope.'

I didn't immediately answer her. My aunt was completely engrossed by the task of pouring out tea, although her usually pale cheeks were flushed and I did not miss the sudden look that passed between mother and son.

'Well?' my grandmother snapped. 'I asked if you were well enough to travel.'

'She needs more rest,' Adrian said. 'Surely we can all see

213

how pale and delicate she is.'

'Another week then,' my grandmother said. 'There is no longer any reason for us to remain here. I have been away too long already and now that Roland is dead I want to go home.'

I felt my cheeks flaming at her rudeness. Just because her son was dead and Adrian preferred to stay with his mother, she felt she could say what she liked to them, but neither Adrian nor his mother seemed surprised by her rudeness.

We left Fontinelle early in the morning only three days later. As we drove across the ornamental bridge, the morning dew lay heavy on the grass and the mist drifted eerily across the surface of the lake. Our farewells had been brief. Dawson, in his dark chauffeur's uniform, had stood on the drive holding the car door open, his honest, fresh-complexioned face expressionless, the shining epitome of the well-bred servant, but all I remember of our actual leave-taking was the perfume my aunt always wore as she kissed me goodbye, and Adrian's firm handshake and the fleeting touch of his lips against my cheek. They stood on the steps of the terrace until the bend in the drive hid them from our view, then for the first time I sat back against the cushions in the car.

My grandmother sat beside me with a stern face. She had not once looked back and I wondered if she felt as sick at heart as I did but for entirely different reasons. Her eldest son was dead and Adrian had been her favourite grandson; now she had lost them both, but that cold uncompromising face did not invite my sympathy or my pity.

I remember little of the journey home. She was querulous and fretful, eating hardly at all, and I found that I too had little appetite. All I wanted was to get home to Ravenspoint quickly and find some sort of solace in familiar surroundings. Instead, she decided to return to the big old house in the centre of industrial Yorkshire. I had no say in the matter but, as we drove through the busy roads of the city with the Pennine hills gloomy and dark on the horizon and forests of mill chimneys instead of conifers, I saw them through a blur of tears.

The night was dismal with rain and flashes of lightning but there was something in my grandmother's expression which deterred me from asking questions. How long, I wondered, should we be staying in that grim old house with its heavy dark furniture and dusty windows? Even the rhododendron bushes in the garden had a dejected air and the tall elms which lined the road outside the house tossed their branches wildly in the approaching storm.

Occasionally I caught Dawson watching me through the driving mirror, his face wooden, registering no emotion, and I was not surprised by my grandmother's silence. She had spoken little during the entire journey. As we neared the house, I was uncomfortably aware of an increasing heaviness in her body against mine and my arm ached from the pressure. I tried to edge away but her body continued to press against me and I thought she must have fallen asleep. Outside the house Dawson left the car to open the door for us and, as I moved to leave my seat, she suddenly slumped forward and would have fallen to the floor of the car if he hadn't caught her in his arms.

I thought at first that she was sleeping until Dawson said, 'There's something wrong here, Miss Jacintha. Run into the house and ask Huggan to help us. I think the old lady's fainted.'

With a racing heart I did as he had asked, and between them the two men carried her into the house. Her face was waxen pale like old and yellowing ivory and I felt sure that she must be dead. They carried her up to her room and laid her on the bed, then Dawson went out into the night in search of a doctor. My grandmother detested the telephone. She called it a monstrous invader of privacy and constantly refused to have one installed in her house in the city, although Uncle Robert had insisted upon it at Ravenspoint.

The doctor came quickly, and after a brief examination he stated that she had suffered a stroke but how serious he could not at that time say. Before midnight, two nurses were installed and the next morning the doctor appeared again. He offered little comfort. My grandmother was still unconscious and he said the next few days would tell if her speech and limbs had been seriously affected. I did not love her, but I did not want her to suffer. However, I am ashamed to say that my absence from Ravenspoint in those next few weeks caused me more unhappiness than my grandmother's illness.

For three long months she remained more or less helpless.

We could not understand what she was trying to say to us and she was paralysed down her left side. Her deep-set eyes burned with a frightening resentment that she had come to this. Only her indomitable will kept her alive in those first few weeks but gradually as the days and months wore on she began to improve. Her speech came back slowly and she could walk across her bedroom floor with the aid of two sticks. She disdained the wheelchair that was brought for her and refused to be seen in it outside the house, but that steely strength, against which I had pitted my own puny will for so long, once more became a force to be reckoned with.

Throughout her illness one or other of the family came for some part of every day; the uncles heavily patronizing, their wives speculating on how much I was doing for my grandmother so that they might better be able to judge the reward I could expect to receive. I was ashamed of my cynicism until Isobel put my thoughts into words, then I knew that I had not been far wrong. Aunt Myra shed copious tears in spite of the fact that she had been afraid of her mother, but surprisingly Teddy was the most helpful. He changed my library books, brought flowers and fruit to the house and was not even ashamed to carry groceries and such, because by this time the nurses who looked after my grandmother needed almost as much attention as the invalid herself.

Ruthie and Martin came almost every evening, spending hours sitting with the old lady in her room. I was cynical about their visits, too, because most of the time she did not even know they were there. Later I had no doubt she would be quietly informed of their vigil by either Martin's or Ruthie's parents and because I harboured such thoughts I began not to like myself very much. What was the matter with me that made me so waspish, I wondered. I came to dread their visits, irritated by Martin's covert glances in my direction when he thought he was unobserved. He followed me into the kitchen on the excuse that he would help me with the coffee cups and then made plaintive attempts to extract sympathy because he was unhappy with Ruthie. I hated his nearness, the brush of his hand against mine, his breath against my cheek, and I resented the unspoken accusation I read in Ruthie's eyes when we returned to her; so more and more I contrived to be out of the house when they came in the evenings and once I heard Aunt Ruth say to Aunt Myra that I must be a heartless child to be so bent on pleasure when my grandmother could possibly be on her deathbed.

Isobel on the other hand came seldom and when she did honour us by her presence it was usually to arrive like a whirlwind with an armful of flowers and an excuse that she was on her way to one committee or another and had little time to spare.

'There's no need for you to come at all, Isobel,' I pointed out on one occasion. 'When she is able to recognize her visitors, I will have you and Henry informed. I wouldn't like Ruthie and Martin to get all the praise.'

She laughed gaily. 'What an acid drop you are, Jacintha. Fortunately I am in that happy position of not being in need of money from my grandmother or anybody else for that matter. Honestly, Jacintha, I don't mean to be rotten but you've become such a sourpuss these days. Whatever happened at Fontinelle to make such a change in you?'

I didn't answer her but I could feel my face blushing furiously under her scrutiny and, being Isobel, she was sharp enough to pursue the matter.

'You've never said a word about Fontinelle since you got back. I would have thought you'd have been bursting to talk about Adrian and his mother and the rest of them. What an awful thing to have happened to Uncle Roland, though I never liked him. He was a sourpuss if you like. I don't think Adrian ever got along with him.'

'I don't know. Perhaps he wasn't always like that. He had had a stroke, you know.'

'He was like that before he had his stroke. I don't think Aunt Marguerite ever loved him. She probably had a lover or two – the French do, you know. Just wait a year or two, Leoni won't be the only rose in Adrian's garden, I'm sure.'

She said these things to make me angry and I was quite determined not to be drawn. Isobel was outrageous and tantalizing, and I was glad when Henry had to go to America on business and she insisted on going with him. Their trip was destined to last all of two months and I knew she had every intention of visiting Lavinia while they were there – more, I suspected, out of curiosity than any real affection. Indeed I said as much to Henry, and we both laughed when he

217

appeared to recognize the truth of my statement.

My grandmother's recovery was sustained and in due course the nurses moved on to other duties and Mrs Perry came down from Ravenspoint to care for her for several weeks. She too hated the city and wasted no time in trying to persuade my grandmother to return to Cumberland.

'I'm sure she'll go back there when she's ready, Mrs Perry,' I said. 'The doctor will say when she's fit to travel.'

'Well, she's better,' the good woman admitted, 'but she's always in a brown study these days and when she's like that it usually bodes no good for somebody or other.'

I thought I knew exactly who that somebody was likely to be but I kept my thoughts to myself. I was surprised, however, when the family in its entirety was summoned to her presence several days later.

We ate together in the dark dismal dining room but later, when my grandmother had had her afternoon rest, I did not go with them to her room. They did not seem to expect me to be there but I heard the sound of their voices. At times they appeared to be arguing, quarrelling even, and I wondered what particular commands she was laying down that could possibly make them argumentative when she was still more or less an invalid.

I sat on the window seat looking out into the garden. It had been a fine morning with a pale sun doing its best to shine through the murk and grime of the industrial smog; now, although it was only just after three o'clock, the morning had not kept its promise. It was almost dark, with thundery leaden skies, and already the street lamps had been lit for I could see the glow over the city from the window. Those hurrying along the road outside had collars turned up against the wind and the leaves in the garden outside scampered along the paths like busy sparrows. My grandmother's house was almost in the centre of the city. She hated what she called suburbia, and unlike her children she had not yearned for mansions surrounded by parkland, being content to remain in the old gloomy house that she had come to as a bride. It was not a comfortable house; it was dark, dreary and draughty, and I longed for the beauty of the lakeland fells and fresh pine-scented air instead of the shut-in smells of the city.

I heard her door open and close several times, and the

sound of footsteps and voices on the stairs, then the sound of cars fading on the wind. Uncle Robert was the last to leave and he merely opened the door to deliver the message that my grandmother wished to see me at once in her bedroom.

My heart was pounding as I knocked on her door before entering. She sat in her large comfortable chair in front of the fire and once again I was struck by her fragility. She seemed lost in the huge armchair with its deep cushions, her face wrinkled like old parchment, her eyes deep-set and feverish brilliant. I had seen her like this before, always when she had set her heart on something and would have it at all costs.

'You sent for me, grandmother?' I began unnecessarily.

'Yes. Sit down, girl. Don't stand there fidgeting.'

I sat, and we eyed each other warily like two old adversaries, each well aware of the antagonism of the other, although it was I who felt most awkward and defensive.

'Why were you not here with the rest of the family?'

'I have always been excluded, grandmother. I did not think that this occasion was any different from the others.'

'My plan concerns all of you, although my sons have spent most of the afternoon trying to deter me from it.'

I didn't speak. I was determined to betray no curiosity about her plan and she frowned irritably. Always in the past my curiosity had been rebuffed by her, so I did not speak now even though she would have welcomed it. For several minutes there was no sound in the room except the cinders falling on the hearth and the sighing of the trees in the wind outside the room. She stared gloomily into the fire and I waited, my hands clenched together to stop their trembling, my heart hammering painfully against my ribs.

'After my sons are gone, do you know that there will not be a Carradice at the mills?' she asked abruptly.

'There will be Teddy,' I answered her, hot in his defence.

'Teddy is not a Carradice, although I appreciate his value to the firm and he will not suffer by what I am about to do.'

'My uncles are still in the firm,' I ventured.

'They are no longer young and will certainly not produce sons to follow them. I want a Carradice at the mills. I want a Carradice to sit at the head of the boardroom table under the portrait of his great-grandfather, and until I have what I want I shall never rest.'

'But how is it possible? I am the only Carradice left.'

'Not quite, Jacintha.'

'You mean Adrian?'

'No, I do not mean Adrian, and it is time you forgot about Adrian and all that foolishness. It is largely thanks to you and your disgraceful behaviour at Fontinelle that my son lost his life.'

I could only sit staring at her in shocked disbelief.

'Oh yes, you might well stare, my girl. Don't think I didn't notice how you flirted with Adrian, and if I saw it you can rest assured Leoni de Montforte saw it also. Who do you think set fire to the chateau? It was the only protest the girl could make, and that poor demented creature made it in the belief that if she got rid of you Adrian would return to her.'

Had my feelings for Adrian been so apparent that everybody at Fontinelle had been aware of them? If they had, surely Adrian must despise me for being so naively stupid as to think I could steal his affections from Leoni.

'But Adrian was always hers. Surely she never doubted it?'

'My son noticed your infatuation for Adrian. It was he who first drew my attention to it; I'm not sure about Marguerite, she never could see beyond her nose. Anyway, we are not here to speak of such matters now. They are over and done with and my son is dead. It is time, Jacintha, for you to repay some of the debt you owe me for the home I have given you, and in atonement for your stupidity. I am an old sick woman and this stroke has convinced me that I may not have long to live. I have a mission for you.'

I looked at her dully, the resentment in my heart more painful than any curiosity I might have felt, and she went on.

'There is another Carradice, Roger's son. I have his mother's address. I have seen to it that I did not lose sight of her and I want you to go to her with a message from me.'

'What sort of message?' I asked, my voice sounding strange and incredulous even in my own ears.

'I want that boy. I want him to take what should have been his father's place in the mills and I want him brought up at Ravenspoint while I am alive and after that by his grandparents, my son and his wife.'

'But what about his mother? The boy must be three or four years old by now. She will never let him go.'

'She will let him go. I know the sort of woman she is. Your mother let you go because she was sure you would have a better future with your father's family; this boy's mother will let him go for money. You will say as soon as the boy is handed over to you she will receive the sum of twenty thousand pounds provided she makes no attempt to see him or write to him again.'

I sat before her miserable and mutinous. I was young and strong but I had no armour against this sick old woman with her indomitable will. Because she commanded it, I would go to Polly with her offer of money and, even though I would be sick at heart remembering how she took me under similiar circumstances, I did not have the courage to refuse her.

During the next few days I thought about nothing but the task she had set me. Bravely I determined that I would go to Polly. I would tell her to ignore the offer of money with disdain, that she must keep her son, suffer hardship even, to keep him. I would hold myself up as an example of what my grandmother could do to him, but then I was told by her that Dawson would go with me to London and I knew that she had instructed him to watch me carefully to make sure that I played my part.

'Why can't the lawyers do everything that is necessary?' I asked her.

'I do not intend that the lawyers should know until I am sure that the mother will let me have him. After that, the money will be handed over to her and she will be made to sign the agreement.'

'Did my mother sign an agreement?'

'There was no need, I knew she would keep her promise.'

'I am surprised you hated her so much when you had such faith in her integrity.'

'I did not hate her, I simply did not think she was a suitable wife for my son. This child's mother is a dancer, probably in some third-rate revue. She will be glad that she won't have to provide for him, and no doubt she has men friends who will look more kindly upon her without the encumbrance of a child to support. Most men are not too anxious to take on another man's child.'

'You cannot be sure of any of this. I liked Polly, and I happen to think she loved Roger very much. If that was so, she will never part with his son.'

'You are a fool, Jacintha. You talk of love as though it was the beginning and the end of everything. You have been sheltered and protected from the harsh realities of life, but Roger's wife, if we can call her that, has been out in the world since she was little more than a child. She will know the things that are more important than love – ambition, money and freedom. You will see for yourself how much she understands the value of all three and how much love will count when those greedy little hands can get hold of a cheque for twenty thousand pounds.'

I had no argument after that. Nothing I could have said would have convinced her that she was not right. On the morning of my departure, she sent for me again and this time she handed me a note containing Polly's address.

'How did you come by this?' I asked her curiously.

'That is not your concern. I have a great-grandson who bears my name and I want him here. For the first time in your life you will do something I want you to do and you will carry out my instructions to the letter. I don't know by what silly stage name his mother calls herself, but her real name is Polly Jennings, though she may call herself Paula Carradice now. Here are twenty-five pounds – sufficient to pay for your hotel rooms and any meals you and Dawson may require on the journey to London and back.'

I had never in my life been handed twenty-five pounds before and it seemed a great deal of money. Even so, I set out with a heavy heart and Dawson, whom I regarded as my gaoler, sat looking stolidly at the road throughout our journey, so there was little conversation between us. I wondered miserably what his thoughts were and if his sympathies were with my grandmother and his employer, or if they would be with the girl we were going to see. Surely Dawson must remember that day he had lifted me weeping hysterically into the car all those years before and my mother's face, indescribably tragic, staring after us in the crowd.

The address my grandmother had given me was in Hampstead. They were large terraced houses which had no doubt once been well cared for and housed well-to-do families; now they sadly needed a coat of paint and had for the main part been turned into flats. They were tall three-storey houses with small front gardens and the number I had been given was in the centre of a terrace. The hall was dark and dusty and a stale smell of cabbage and the clanking of buckets came from the open door at the end of the corridor. I closed the door behind me with the merest click but almost immediately a woman appeared from the back of the house, a cigarette dangling from her mouth, wearing a none-too-clean overall and with a thin scarf over her curling pins. She watched me climb the stairs, which were covered with only a narrow strip of threadbare carpet down the centre of the treads, and I had almost reached the top when she called to me.

'Are you looking for somebody in particular?'

'Yes, a Mrs Carradice.'

She took several puffs at her cigarette, scratching her head in a thoughtful fashion.

'I thought I knew most of 'em, but there's nobody of that name, I'd know if there was.'

'Mrs Polly Carradice.'

'Nope. Still, they changes their names as often as they changes their fellas. All airs and graces, that's them, and precious little else.'

She dissolved into laughter at her own humour, then retreated to the back of the house, where I heard again the clanking of buckets as she went about her work.

I went on up the stairs and found myself in a narrow corridor, lofty and so dark that it was impossible to read the nameplates on the doors. I switched on the light but the one unshaded solitary bulb was so dim that it had little effect, and I was just about to knock on a door when the door opposite opened and an elderly woman stood peering at me while a half-grown cat sidled out of the room.

I tried smiling at her. 'I am looking for a Mrs Polly Carradice. Perhaps you can help me?' I ventured.

'I don't know any of them, but if it's one of the dancers try the door at the top of the passage,' she said. Before I could thank her, she closed the door firmly and with disapproval – no doubt thinking I was another of them. The cat sat washing his face, ignoring my presence.

From behind the door to which she had directed me there

was laughter and the sound of women's voices. I had to knock twice before the door opened. The girl who stood there was tall with thick red hair and wearing theatrical make-up that was far from fresh. She wore a faded dressing gown, open to her waist, completely unconcerned that she displayed half her nude body to a complete stranger. I suppose her face was pretty in a bold sort of way and she was eyeing me curiously, blocking the doorway so that I could not see into the room.

I asked for Polly but her expression did not change, and when I gave alternative names she called to whoever was in the room behind her, 'Somebody here asking for Polly. You'd better come and have a word with her, Gloria.'

Gloria came – a tall brunette holding a bottle of bright-red nail varnish in one hand while wafting the other to and fro in an effort to dry the varnish.

I repeated my request and she looked at me sullenly, eyeing me from top to toe in what I thought was a most insolent manner.

'Who are you?' she asked finally.

'My name is Jacintha Carradice.'

She raised her eyebrows.

'Polly's husband was my cousin Roger.'

'A bit late, aren't you?'

'I beg your pardon?'

'You're late, by about four or five years, love.'

'You mean she isn't here?'

'I mean for you to have taken the trouble to look for her.'

'Could I speak to her?'

'Not here you can't. She's not lived here for three years.'

Apparently I was going to have to drag every bit of information out of this girl. Her antagonism was against the Carradice family rather than against me, but whether I liked it or not I was their representative and if she had anything to do with it I was going to squirm.

'Could you let me have her present address?'

'I could, but I don't see why I should.'

'What I have to say to her is very important.'

'You mean their consciences are troubling them at last?'

'Whatever I have to say, I would prefer to say it to Polly.'

She laughed, imitating my voice and my accent, and the girl in the room behind her laughed with her. Suddenly she said,

'The address is 27 Mulberry Grove, Finchley.'

Without another word, she closed the door firmly in my face.

My cheeks were burning as I walked down the stairs and the woman with the bucket, who was now mopping the front-door step, asked, 'Did you find her, luv?'

'No, I'm afraid she's moved.'

'Oh well, they come and go in that profession. Like as not, she's found some man to keep her.'

I went back to the car, aware that none of my movements was lost on the woman cleaning the doorstep or on the two girls gazing after me through the window on the first floor. Throughout the journey I had been happy to sit in the front seat with Dawson, now it gave me a ridiculous feeling of pleasure to have him open the door for me while I climbed into the back seat.

I was more impressed by the address in Finchley than I had been by the one in Hampstead. This too was a road of tall terraced houses, but the road was tree-lined, the gardens well tended, the nameplates on the door polished. The floor in the long hall was clean and the stair carpet was good. If Polly had come here from her last address, she had risen a little higher in the world, and I scanned the nameplates eagerly. There was no Polly Carradice and I felt my heart sinking as I envisaged a search from door to door. I was about to turn away when a middle-aged woman carrying a Yorkshire terrier came through the front door, excusing herself as she passed me to climb the stairs.

I looked at her hopefully asking, 'I am sorry to trouble you, but do you happen to know if there is a Mrs Polly Carradice living here?'

She frowned in a puzzled way, then asked, 'Is she a young person or is she elderly?'

'Oh, quite young really. She has a little boy, about three years old.'

'What does she look like?'

I went on to describe what I could remember of Polly's appearance.

'There is a young lady living in the flat at the front of the house with a little boy. She's a nice, friendly girl, always speaks to my little dog here, and she does have a little boy. I've seen a man going into the flat, too, but I don't know if he is her husband.'

I thanked her profusely and followed her up the stairs where she indicated the door I should knock upon. My satisfaction was short-lived, however, because there was no reply to my knocking and gloomily I turned away to go back to Dawson in the waiting car.

He looked at me sympathetically. 'No luck, Miss Jacintha?'

'No, Dawson, there is nobody at home.'

'Well, the young lady probably works and the little boy could be at school.'

'I suppose so. You know about it, don't you, Dawson? Did my grandmother instruct you to see that I carried out her wishes?'

My words were bitter, although I had no call to speak to Dawson in that manner. From the expression on his kind honest face, I felt certain the errand we were embarked upon was repugnant to him, and his words only endorsed my belief. 'I don't hold with it, miss. I well remember the day we took you from your mother. I said to my wife that very night that I never wanted to be part of such an errand again.'

My heart lifted a little and I smiled at him now as a fellow conspirator. 'What shall we do if she doesn't come home?' I asked him.

'We'll wait a little while, miss, and try not to worry. It may be that the young lady will have nothing to do with the mistress's idea.'

'Oh, Dawson, I do hope you're right. You have no idea how joyfully I shall take her refusal back to my grandmother.'

We sat in the car for what seemed hours and the children returning from school stood around the car in wide-eyed admiration until their mothers called them in for tea. 'She must be away,' I said fretfully.

'We'll give her another half-hour. If she hasn't appeared by then we'll just have to come back in the morning.'

I saw her first – a tall slender girl who walked with the free graceful stride of a dancer and with her, skipping beside her and holding her hand, was the small figure of a child. My heart was thudding sickeningly now. How could I approach that gay gallant girl with my grandmother's monstrous suggestion that would take away the little boy who clung to her hand so confidingly? The child saw the car and leaving his mother's

226

side he came to stand on the pavement staring in through the window. His eyes were wide with delight, pale bright-blue eyes under a shock of silver-fair hair, and I could feel the lump in my throat as I gazed at Roger's likeness staring me in the face after all those years. His mother ran towards us, pulling the child away, smiling at us in apology for the curiosity of the child. There was no recognition in the eyes she turned upon me, but then the last time Polly had seen me I had been little more than a schoolgirl wearing hand-me-downs instead of the fashionable clothes purchased with Henry's money.

A man was running down the road waving gaily and the girl and her son turned to meet him. All thoughts of the car were for the moment forgotten as the little boy ran back along the road and we watched as the man picked him up, shrieking with laughter. Then he was greeting Polly and together, his arm about the girl, the child sitting on his shoulder, they went into the house. I had seen the way she looked up into the man's face and I recognized that look. Hadn't I once seen her looking up into Roger's face in exactly the same way, standing on the station platform while they waited for the train that would take him back to war?

Neither Dawson nor I spoke for several minutes. When I had found my voice, I said, 'Dawson, I can't go in there. Suppose the man is her husband.'

'He probably is, miss. You said her name wasn't on the door.'

'How can I go in there with my grandmother's offer if he is there? It was obvious how happy they were together. How can I face them with such a monstrous suggestion?'

'You can't, miss.'

'Then what am I going to do?'

'Leave it to me, Miss Jacintha. The young lady doesn't know me, I only saw her once during those few days she was at Ravenspoint and she had eyes for nobody but Mr Roger. I'll make some inquiries. Don't worry, I know how to be discreet.'

But I did worry. I sat in the car watching the house and wondering where Dawson intended to make his inquiries. The little boy came to stand at the window of the first-floor flat looking down at the car until the man came to take him away, and my eyes filled with tears at the sight of his child's face and those cornflower-blue eyes I knew so well. I didn't have long to wait.

Dawson came back to the car with a smile of self-satisfied smugness on his homely good-natured face. I looked up at him anxiously, but he climbed into the driver's seat and started up the engine.

'We'll talk on the way, miss, in case they're watching from the window.'

'Did you speak to Polly, Dawson?'

'Yes, miss, I said we were looking for a Mr and Mrs Reynolds who lived there at one time. She asked how long ago, said she'd only been there about three years but she'd ask her husband, he might know.'

'So she is married, Dawson?'

'It would appear so. She brought the man to the door and we talked for a few minutes. He seems a nice sort of chap, the little boy was with him and they're quite obviously fond of one another. All we've got to do now, Miss Jacintha, is think about the story we're going to tell your grandmother. I've worked for Mrs Carradice a long time and I admire her, but there's steel there, miss, pure steel, and there's not many that can outfox the old lady.'

'But we shall outfox her, won't we, Dawson? This time she's not going to get her own way.'

It was early evening when we turned in at the short drive which led up to my grandmother's house in Yorkshire. Lights burned in the hall and in her bedroom on the first floor, and I had barely let myself into the house when Mrs Huggan appeared from the rear of the house, addressing me in an agitated manner. 'Oh, Miss Jacintha, thank goodness you're back, she's been asking after you every hour.'

'We came as quickly as we could, Mrs Huggan. How is my grandmother? Is she alone now?'

'Miss Ruthie and her husband called earlier this afternoon but she said she didn't want to seem the today. I'm to ask you to go up right away, though.'

'I'll go in to her as soon as I've taken off my outdoor clothing and combed my hair. We haven't eaten anything since an early lunch, Mrs Huggan. Is it possible to have some sandwiches made? I'm sure Dawson is dying of hunger.'

'I'll see that he has something in the kitchen, miss, and I'll send a tray into the dining room for you. It'll be something cold, if that's all right. I don't know how long the mistress will keep you.'

'Anything at all, Mrs Huggan. I shan't mind what it is.'

I wasn't really very interested in food, but talk of it helped me overcome a little my racing heart and my fears about the interview ahead. I stood up to deliver my story and not for one moment did her sunken, though feverishly glittering, eyes leave my face. Only her thin hands clenching her ivory-handled walking stick betrayed her feelings, but she seemed to shrink into her chair, so thin and childlike she was more like a caricature than a living woman. The fact that I had done this to her gave me no pleasure or sense of satisfaction. Always when I had hated her most I had thought of this moment when words of mine would give her pain, but now that they had been spoken I could only think how much I would like to have loved her.

She dismissed me curtly, asking for Dawson to be sent to her, and I knew then how little trust she had placed in my ability to carry out her mission. Right from the outset it had been distasteful to me and I waited in the hall in order to reassure myself that Dawson had satisfied her about the truth of my story. His nod of reassurance and his quiet smile told me that at least she had appeared to accept it and I sat down to my belated meal with some relief that it was over. Two days later we returned to Ravenspoint.

11

In those first few weeks after our return, I was content to walk along the shore and the country lanes. It was winter again and the first snow had already fallen, so the mountains were white and stark in the distance, and the sea, which rolled inwards like a sheet of grey steel, took its colour from dark and leaden skies.

Nothing at Ravenspoint had changed and I loved it fiercely. Lavinia wrote to me, ecstatically excited, to say she was expecting a baby in the autumn, and I was so overjoyed for her I immediately telephoned Isobel with the news. She sounded cross, and I wondered if she wasn't a little bit envious.

'How foolish to be burdening herself with a family so soon. One would have thought she'd have had a bit of fun first. After all, she is in a new country with new people,' she sneered over the telephone.

'Well, I think it's marvellous.'

'You would, wouldn't you?'

'Why are you so peevish?'

'I'm not peevish; it's just that I can't stand all this sickly sentiment about having babies. Anybody can have a baby.'

The quick retort was on my lips but I restrained myself, saying instead, 'I'll ring you up again when you're in a better frame of mind,' but all I heard from the other end was a sharp click as she hung up the receiver.

All my spare money went on knitting wool – white, because I thought it nicer for a new baby – and I chose patterns far more intricate than my skill, so that Mrs Perry had to help me out with them. I loved working in soft fine wool after the coarse khaki we had been knitting into gloves and balaclavas in the war years.

I was surprised when Isobel and Henry and Ruthie and Martin all came to visit us on the same weekend. They couldn't have known, or I am quite sure they wouldn't have arrived at the same time.

I refrained from mentioning the baby to Isobel after that telephone call and I was surprised when she came into my bedroom one morning while I was dressing. She perched on the edge of my bed with her feet curled under her, watching me brush my hair.

'Your hair could do with shaping, Jacintha. Are you still going to that woman in the village?'

'Yes, she's the only one for miles. Otherwise I look after it myself.'

'It shows. Why don't you come to stay with us again, then you could go to Paul? He's frightfully expensive but you could get Henry to treat you.'

'I'm not sure grandmother would take kindly to my staying with you after the last time.'

'I don't see why not. I'm the epitome of respectability nowadays. I'm quite enjoying being the loyal and devoted Mrs Clifton-Webb. When I flirt, I do it discreetly.'

'Must you flirt at all?'

'Yes, of course I must or I should go mad. You don't know what it's like being married to Henry. He's so wrapped up in his business and his council work he hardly ever talks to me and his mother has her spies on me wherever we go. Have you heard from Lavinia recently?'

I was accustomed to the speed with which she could change the tenor of her conversation.

'Doesn't she write to you?'

'Not often. I think she was a bit piqued when I didn't go into raptures about the baby. When did I ever go into raptures about anything?'

'Well, you might at least have tried to show some enthusiasm. You'll expect plenty from us when you have one.'

'Oh, I don't know, perhaps I won't bother. Babies are a nuisance. They need too much looking after and I want to keep my figure.'

She jumped to her feet and headed for the door, turning when she reached it to say, 'I don't want you to talk about Lavinia's baby when Henry's there. He's touchy on the subject and I'm not broody enough for children yet.'

From the guest room on the other side of mine I heard the voices of Ruthie and Martin voices and they seemed to be arguing. Their raised voices made me hurry with my dressing

231

and I was about to leave the room when Lucy came in to change my bed linen, her face pink with embarrassment.

'I should go in there, Miss Jacintha, but I can't while they're quarrelling like that. What shall I do?'

'Couldn't you come back later?' I suggested.

'There isn't all that much time. It's my morning for doing the bed linen and you know what your grandmother's like if we get out of our routine.'

'Have you tried knocking on the door?'

'That I have and got no answer.' She dropped her voice to a conspiratorial whisper. 'It's every day they're quarrelling. Yesterday it was in the conservatory, last night it was in the dining room before dinner. I told cook it served them right; they don't deserve to be happy when it was you Mr Martin should have married.'

'Oh, Lucy, that was all a long time ago. It isn't important now.'

'Maybe it was, Miss Jacintha, but it's my belief that if you do bad things to people, sooner or later you've got to pay for them.'

I was not enjoying this conversation but by this time Lucy was throwing the bedclothes about in righteous indignation, her cheeks flushed.

'I can tell you this, Miss Jacintha, he slept in Master Teddy's room the night before last. That was the night they arrived. If all had been right between them, he would never have done that, now would he?'

'Are you sure?'

'I make the beds, don't I? You could have knocked me over with a feather when I went into Master Teddy's room to dust the furniture. There was the bed unmade, not even straightened – almost as if he didn't care who knew about him sleeping there or that they'd had a row.'

'Did you never have a row with your young man?'

She looked at me dolefully, and next moment her anger evaporated and tears filled her eyes. Instantly I wished I'd had more tact and rushing to her side I put my arm around her shoulders. 'Oh, Lucy, I'm sorry, I shouldn't have said that. Of course you didn't quarrel with Sam.'

'Oh, but I did, miss, that's what made me cry. I wish now I'd been nicer to him. All those times when I sulked and it was always Sam who said he was sorry, never me. Do you think he ever forgave me?'

'Of course he did, that's what I've just been telling you. It's human nature to quarrel. I don't believe those people who say they've never had a cross word. Can you think of anything more boring?'

We looked at each other in silence for several moments, then her face broke into a smile. 'I do go on a bit, don't I, Miss Jacintha. It's just that I've never thought the same about Miss Ruthie since she got married. You might have forgiven her but I haven't. What shall I do about their room?'

'Well, can you hear them now? I can't.'

We listened for several minutes but all was quiet, so, thankfully, Lucy departed to carry on the rest of her chores.

The next hint of Ruthie's matrimonial problems came from Isobel.

'I don't understand my grandmother at all,' she exclaimed, as I sat with her in the dining room after lunch, dawdling over our coffee while Henry struggled with his crossword. 'Whenever I snap at Henry she shows her displeasure in no uncertain terms, but Ruthie and Martin can have a stand-up row and she doesn't turn a hair.'

'Are they very unhappy together, do you think?'

'Well, of course they're not happy, and aren't you just a little bit pleased about it?'

'No, I am not. I would be perhaps, if I still cared for Martin. That would be human nature, wouldn't it? But who's to blame, do you suppose? Ruthie wanted him and she got him and he's probably a lot better off than he would have been had he stayed in cotton.'

'Perhaps it's the way Ruthie got him that worries him. It's true Martin's done very well for himself but he's not exactly an asset to the Carradice empire. My father says he's too big for his shoes, doesn't like to be told anything, won't ask, and makes endless mistakes as a consequence. Teddy covers up for him – you know Teddy, anything for a quiet life – but it's causing endless antagonism between my father and Uncle William.

'Does my grandmother know?'

'Of course she knows but, as I said before, she doesn't say a word. I expect it's because she had a lot to do with getting Martin for Ruthie.'

233

'Because she hates me.'

'She doesn't hate you. She just punishes you.'

'Perhaps in time they'll come to their senses, and Martin really hasn't been in the business very long – he'll improve.'

'He's a bit of a spendthrift, you know. Henry had a new car a little while back and soon after Martin got one like it, only twice as powerful and three times as expensive. It's almost as though he's got to show the Carradices that he's as good as, if not better than any of them. Don't you think that, Henry?'

Henry didn't answer, so Isobel repeated her question. 'Really, Henry, I've heard you going on yourself about Martin, particularly when he bought the car,' she ended.

'I'm not being brought in, Isobel. You know my views on the fella so let's give it a rest, shall we?'

'Can't we go home tomorrow? We've paid our duty visit and there's absolutely no reason why we should stay any longer.'

'After lunch, how would that suit you?'

'After breakfast would suit me better,' she snapped, then she jumped to her feet and after a quick glance in the mirror and a pat at her immaculate hair she swept from the room.

Their leaving meant that I sat down to lunch next day in the company of Martin and Ruthie, since my grandmother said she was not hungry and would have a pot of tea in her sitting room. Lunch was eaten in silence and the atmosphere at the table was such that the food tasted of nothing and my few comments about the weather passed with only terse replies from Martin. I excused myself on the grounds of having to go down to the village and was just leaving the room when my grandmother called to me from her sitting room. 'I have letters to write, Jacintha. I shall require you to take them to the postbox about four o'clock.'

I stood for a long time looking out at the grey dismalness of the day. It was drizzling with rain and the sea in the distance looked dark and lonely under leaden skies. I had said I was going out, so out I would have to go – but then anything was preferable to making desultory conversation with two people who were obviously out of tune with each other.

While I was putting on my raincoat, I heard them come into the adjoining room, slamming the door with unnecessary violence. Then for several minutes there was complete silence. It was Ruthie's voice I heard first, plaintively saying, 'I don't see why we couldn't have left after breakfast when the other two left. It only makes my father angry when he is at his desk and you are not.'

There was no reply and after a while Ruthie peevishly began again. 'You never consider my parents, Martin. All you care about are the few extra hours you can spend in Jacintha's company. You could have married Jacintha but you wanted more than she could give you. Instead, you wanted to marry me to get a foot in the Carradice mills.'

'Did I want to marry you, Ruthie? Did I?'

I couldn't bear to hear any more. With my cheeks flaming and my heart beating wildly, I threw a scarf over my hair and fled down the stairs, never stopping until I had put the saturated gardens between me and their bitter quarrel.

I pulled up sharply as I reached the path down to the shore. I was panting breathlessly but I could see that the path was too slippery to venture down and reluctantly I was forced to retrace my steps towards the house. I looked up for only a moment at the upstairs windows, my face flaming with colour as I saw Martin watching me. Our eyes met for a brief second only, before I looked away. It was bitterly cold so I walked briskly, oblivious of the rain in the wind and the thunderous sound of the sea against the point. I was wet and miserable but I could not return to the house until I was sure they had left it. It was almost dusk before I turned in at the gates, more than relieved to see that Martin's new expensive car had gone.

I let myself quietly into the house, and Lucy, who had been hovering on the stairs making a pretence of dusting the balustrades, came running towards me.

'Where on earth have you been, Miss Jacintha? You promised to take your grandmother's mail.'

I looked at her askance and she hurried to say, 'I looked for you in the garden and I couldn't see you on the shore. She wasn't half in a state and in the end Miss Ruthie took the letters; she said she would post them on their way back.'

'Oh, Lucy, I never gave the letters a thought. I suppose I'd better go and apologize.'

'You'll get one of her scoldings and no mistake.'

I was accustomed to her scoldings but I no longer feared them as I had done in the old days. She was reading a magazine when I entered her sitting room and without looking up she said, 'So you've decided to come back, Jacintha.'

'I'm sorry, grandmother, that I forgot your mail. I have been walking.'

'So I see. I don't ask much from you, Jacintha, but even this small thing you choose to forget. What made you go walking on such an afternoon. Isn't the house comfortable enough for you?'

'Well, if you must know, I didn't know where else I could go to get away from their quarrelling voices.'

'Who was quarrelling?'

'Ruthie and Martin, they have been quarrelling since they arrived.'

For once her deep-set eyes refused to meet mine and she looked away quickly, picking up her magazine as though the conversation was at an end as far as she was concerned. Then because I still stood there with the moisture from my raincoat dripping onto her carpet, she said, 'All husbands and wives quarrel, Jacintha. It is their prerogative and entirely their own business. Now I suggest you go to your room and take off that wet raincoat, and find something useful to do before dinner.'

They were the last words she ever spoke to me. Later that night she suffered another stroke, which robbed her of her speech, and all I was conscious of when I visited her room were her dark glittering eyes which spoke of her chagrin at the helplessness of her body.

It was left to me to telephone the family, who came down in full strength the following weekend.

'Have you let Adrian know?' Isobel asked, when I met her on the stairs.

'Yes, I sent him a telegram. He sends his regrets but it is quite impossible for him to be here just now.'

'Is he completely out of his senses? You know what's going to happen, don't you? I'll probably get nothing, neither will you, and the lion's share will go to Ruthie and Martin. Has her solicitor been here recently?'

'He came several times after we came back here but I don't know anything about his visits. She got better the last time; she could do so again.'

'She won't. My father asked the doctor. He says she'll probably have another and that will be the end.'

Isobel was right. Two weeks later my grandmother suffered a third stroke. My two uncles arrived at the house soon after noon, knowing that her death was imminent, and went immediately to her room.

It was dark soon after four that afternoon and it was then I became afraid, of the whispers as the servants went about their duties, of doors opening quietly and as quietly closing, of the shadows that seemed to linger in the corners where the lights in the hall could not reach, and of the eerie stillness of approaching death. Even the sea seemed dull and glassy from my window seat overlooking that part of the garden where Adrian had first made me face my dragon. As darkness came down, I drew the heavy drapes across the windows and built up the fire. The clock hands moved slowly and the food they brought me was sent back untouched. A sullen silence seemed to enshroud the house but I dared not leave the comfort of the drawing room to climb the stairs to my bedroom. I feared the gossamer touch of that sinister shadow I believed I had last seen on a summer's day years before. How much more awesome would I find it on a bleak winter's night when the mist swirled around the headland and the foghorn moaned dismally on the wind?

The fire had burned low in the grate when I awoke, feeling cramped and chilled. Then I heard the click of my grandmother's door and footsteps descending the stairs into the hall. I waited breathlessly, but whoever came down the stairs went into the library and I stayed where I was, afraid to venture out into the hall. Again I dozed, and next time it was Lucy who awakened me in the first cold light of dawn when she came in to make up the fire.

'Bless you, miss, you've never been in here all night,' she said startled.

I nodded wordlessly, then almost afraid to ask, 'My grandmother . . .'

'She's gone, miss, about half an hour ago. Your uncles are in the library. Why ever didn't you go to your room? There was nothing you could do down here.'

'I was afraid, Lucy. I was afraid of the dark and the shadows on the stairs.'

She stared at me stupidly for several seconds, then briskly she went about her duties. 'Eh, love, there was never no need to be frightened of that. It's more than likely we imagined it and in any case it wouldn't have come for your grandmother.'

'Why not? You thought you saw something before my grandfather died and again when my father died.'

'What if I did? Your grandmother wasn't a Carradice, not by birth at least. So, like I said, it wouldn't have been interested in her.'

I stared at her incredulously. Then suddenly, in spite of the weird stillness of death which lay like a grim shadow over the house, I felt a moment of elation. For the first time I realized that the woman who had ruled my life, all our lives, to suit her colossal pride and her steely will, had not been thought important enough to conjure the shadows of death from whatever limbo they inhabited. Now she was dead, and I would never need to fear her or obey her again.

My grandmother was buried in the large family vault in the old churchyard of St Mary's, where she had been married and where all her children had been christened. The churchyard, as well as the church, was crowded because in the city she had been an institution. I was surprised how many committees she had sat upon, and if she had not been loved she had at least been respected. They came from all walks of life and from near and far, and after the funeral we all returned to the house for what I can only describe as a banquet.

I made myself ill with worry, wondering where I would be expected to live, who would be responsible for telling me what plans had been made for my future, and if I would ever see Ravenspoint again. I suspected that the house would be sold – possibly to a syndicate who had already made tentative inquiries about turning it into a lakeland hotel. I had heard my uncles talking in the drawing room after dinner, wondering if the offer was high enough, anticipating others, and their wives too, particularly Aunt Celia, persistently urging my two uncles to dispose of Ravenspoint to the highest bidder. It seemed incredible to me that they were discussing my home in such mercenary terms.

My grandmother's lawyer had lunched with us on the day her will was to be read, and Uncle Robert now interrupted him in the task of taking papers from his briefcase.

'Shall you require my niece to be present in the library, Mr Foster?' he asked.

The lawyer looked up absently. Then, gathering his thoughts, he said, 'I shall require all the family present, Mr Carradice, and perhaps we could start quite soon now so that those of us who have other appointments can leave directly the will has been read.'

A huge log fire burned in the library grate and chairs had been set in rows before the heavy mahogany desk upon which the lawyer spread his papers. I sat at the back, hoping that I would be allowed to remain as unobtrusive as possible, but then Isobel came to sit beside me. I thought she looked particularly beautiful in her funereal black, as dark as her raven-black hair, which complemented her delicate pink and white skin and blue eyes, her gown dramatic with its edging of black mink against the creamy whiteness of her throat.

She was bored, showing little interest in the list of charities names in the will or in the legacies left to the servants both at Ravenspoint and here in the city. It was only when the family's turn came that she smiled at me wickedly, saying in a whisper, 'Now, Jacintha, you will know whether you are to be the rich Jacintha Carradice or whether the rest of us are to support you.'

I turned my head away sharply, and her light laughter was immediately silenced by a warning look from her mother.

My grandmother's interest in the Carradice wool empire was to be divided equally between her two sons Robert and William and her grandson Edward. This caused a small stir of consternation on the part of the uncles and embarrassment on Teddy's part. His usually pale face was flushed, his eyes blinking behind his spectacles, but his mother was obviously delighted and I was too. He worked hard; he had none of the glamour of top management, but he understood the workings of the mills and was closer, I thought, to the working people than either of the uncles, who were boardroom men – figureheads, little more.

Large sums of money had been willed to each of her children. Both Ruthie and Teddy were to receive a sum of ten thousand pounds but there was nothing for Lavinia or Isobel. Isobel's face wore an amused expression which spoke volumes. She had not expected to be left any money and she did not care. I on the other hand had not expected to receive anything but it did not prevent me from feeling hurt that I had been ignored so completely.

The lawyer had now come to her personal possessions, jewellery and paintings, ivories and valuable porcelain – my grandfather had been an ardent collector of beautiful things, largely oriental. Many of these she had left to museums in different parts of the country and others to churches in which she had taken an interest, but her jewellery was left entirely to the family. To Isobel she left her diamond and sapphire brooch, her three strands of pearls and her emerald ring. Ruthie was to receive her ruby and diamond ring, her single strand of pearls and her silver toilet brushes. Lavinia was not forgotten and could expect to receive my grandmother's gold and platinum bracelet. It was then I was shaken out of my torpor by the lawyer's dry voice saying, ' . . . and to my granddaughter Jacintha Carradice I leave the solitaire diamond ring which was to have been her father's on the occasion of his marriage.'

I looked down at my hands clenched in my lap, hoping that the proceedings were now at an end, but still the solicitor fidgeted with his papers, holding up his hand to indicate that he had not finished.

'Whatever next?' Isobel murmured beside me.

'I leave my house known as Moorside in the city of Wellsford to my grandson Edward to be lived in by him or sold at his direction . . . and to my grandaughter Jacintha I leave the house known as Ravenspoint in the County of Cumberland and the sum of ten thousand pounds per year for its upkeep, on the understanding that, should she marry and be known as anything other than Carradice, she will forfeit all right to this property and the sum of money allocated for its upkeep. In the event of such a marriage, it is my wish that the house should revert to my estate, where it will be used to provide a convalescent home for those workers in the Carradice mills who are sick and in need of care.'

I sat without speaking, dumbfounded by what I had just heard, stunned that Ravenspoint was mine and with it all the furnishings and beautiful things I had known since childhood. Isobel was the first to speak.

'Well, well, what does it feel like to be the rich Miss Carradice of Ravenspoint?'

'I can see what mother was thinking about,' Aunt Myra said. 'Where else could the girl go?'

'I'm jolly glad she didn't leave it to me,' Isobel said with an exaggerated shudder. 'It would have gone on the market first thing in the morning.'

'You can't live in that great house alone, Jacintha,' Aunt Celia said, 'it is quite out of the question, and stupid of your mother, Robert, to leave it to a young girl who knows nothing about employing servants or caring for a place of that size.'

'Oh, come on, mother,' Isobel said, 'Jacintha's the only one who's ever cared anything about Ravenspoint. She's more right to it than any of us.'

Her mother smiled incredulously. 'The offer your father had from that syndicate was very generous; it would have made an admirable hotel for tourists in that part of the Lake District. I'm sure Jacintha would be a lot happier living in something smaller and more modern.'

'Oh, but I do want it, Aunt Celia,' I said, thinking it was about time somebody listened to me. 'I love Ravenspoint. I never want to leave it.'

'But what if you wish to marry?' she asked.

'There is nobody I want to marry. If ever there is, I'll face the problem then.'

'It's an unnatural bequest,' she continued. 'You could be torn between your love for that place and affection for any man you happen to meet. Your grandmother had no right to make you face such a choice. It's unnatural.'

'I can assure you, Mrs Carradice, that the old lady was quite sane and sensible when she made her will,' the lawyer said drily. 'She obviously felt she had to provide for her youngest granddaughter and she knew how fond Miss Carradice was of this house. I consider she has been more than generous.'

My eyes met Isobel's and I looked away quickly. Like me, Isobel knew it was not generosity that had prompted my grandmother to leave Ravenspoint to me; it was her final insidious torture, her last revenge on the son who had disobeyed her.

I was glad to leave the dark solid house in the city for the fresh open air and large gracious rooms of Ravenspoint. The

241

servants greeted me warmly, *my* servants now, and, as I stood in my bedroom looking out towards the sea, for the first time in months I felt an inner contentment. I had a home, a house I loved as dear as life, and I had been touched by the welcoming smiles of the villagers we had passed along the lane. Dawson had driven slowly, for the lanes were narrow and the car far too large for them, so those we passed were compelled to stand back against the hedgerows. They recognized the car instantly, the men touching their caps respectfully, the women smiling, sometimes bobbing quaint country curtsies, for tradition dies hard in the Lake District and I was after all a Carradice.

Teddy had given me driving lessons in the city and Dawson helped me to choose a small reliable car for my own use, since he was leaving Ravenspoint soon to live in Wellsford where he was to be employed by the family as company chauffeur. I knew he wasn't happy with the prospect of moving any more than his wife was, but there was now no work for him at Ravenspoint and he had to think about his livelihood. I decided not to part with the pony and trap, however, and I became a familiar figure driving along the country lanes near the house, or at other times venturing further afield in my little car.

Somehow I didn't mind the loneliness. It was summer and the lakeland fells were busy with walkers, the lakes alive with pleasure craft of all descriptions, but, when autumn came with its burst of glorious colour, I felt immeasureably sad. Around the lakes the trees vied with each other in colours of crimson and flame, and once more the heather bloomed purple on the hillsides. Everywhere there was the scent of woodsmoke and at night the moon hung low, surrounded by a halo of mist above lamplit cottage windows, and the days grew shorter and colder. I watched the swallows flying out in search of a warmer climate, and soon the birds of winter took their place, whilst at night the fires were stoked higher, the curtains drawn tightly to shut out the winds which swept in from the sea, splattering the windows with spray. It was on such an evening that I wondered if this was to be the pattern of my future life. Then I remembered the message I had read in Isobel's eyes on the afternoon the will had been read. My grandmother would never come back to Ravenspoint to torment me and hurt me, but she still ordered my life from the other side of the grave.

Isobel often telephoned me – long conversations that always ended in the same way, both amusing me and causing me extreme irritation. She couldn't understand why Adrian had not been named in my grandmother's will and she believed I knew more than I was telling about exactly what had gone on at Fontinelle during our visit. Always I pleaded ignorance, until in the end I made excuses to put down the telephone and there were times when I did not even answer it. Her talk of Adrian was not helping me to forget him, although I could lie more naturally on the telephone than when faced with her mocking blue eyes.

Christmas lay ahead of me, a time when families were close, when there was laughter and feasting, and young and old were happy together. I had no idea how I would spend my Christmas. Always, since I first came to Ravenspoint, the family had gathered there at Christmastime, but this was because my grandmother was alive and it had been her wish that the festivities should revolve around her. Now I was the owner of Ravenspoint and I wondered if the rest of the family would expect the family gathering to remain unchanged. I wrote to them, telling them how happy it would make me if they came as always, but the replies were anything but encouraging.

Uncle Robert and Aunt Celia said they intended to spend Christmas quietly at home, Uncle William and Aunt Ruth had already made arrangements to spend it in Eastbourne, and Ruthie and Martin were going to Martin's family in Lancashire. Isobel telephoned to say she and Henry were going to the Continent; she didn't know exactly where. 'We shall just drive, darling, until we feel the urge to stop – anywhere to get out of this ghastly climate for a few weeks.' In the end only Teddy came to stay with me and then only for a few days.

He arrived on Christmas Eve bearing gifts from other members of the family. We ate alone in the big dining room, sitting formally at each end of the long table. Teddy wore his dinner jacket for the occasion and I chose a simple black gown, which I regarded as the correct attire for the first Christmas after my grandmother's death. I removed a large bowl of scarlet-berried holly from the centre of the table so that we could see each other better, and I felt inordinately pleased that the room looked particularly festive, with a log fire blazing halfway up the chimney and the glow from clusters of tall slender red candles in silver candelabra burnishing the silver and polished glass.

After we had eaten, we retired to the small drawing room, where we drank champagne, laughing inordinately over the card games we had played as children. I couldn't help wondering idly if this was to be the pattern for all Christmases since it seemed pretty conclusive that we were to be the solitary ones.

I was grateful to him for coming, and more and more I warmed to his nice pink and white face, his short-sighted eyes blinking at me through his spectacles as I remembered them doing when we were children. He was the only one who had cared anything about me. The others had gone away without giving me a second thought and Adrian, who occupied my thoughts both waking and sleeping, had not even bothered to reply to my invitation.

As I stood in the bleak wind on the front-door step on the morning of New Year's Eve bidding Teddy goodbye, he held my hands shyly in his. 'I say, Jacintha, I wish I hadn't promised to go to those friends of mine. I don't particularly want to go. I could cry off if you don't want to be alone.'

'Nonsense, Teddy, you'll do no such thing. They'll be expecting you. Off you go. Enjoy yourself and don't give me another thought.'

I waited until the sound of his car had died away before I turned disconsolately to go into the house. It promised to be a long miserable day with little to do except sit watching the waves dashing up against the rocks. A grey mist covered the sea and the foghorn sounded mournfully throughout the house. I tried reading but the noise interfered with my concentration, and the fact that it was New Year's Eve didn't help. Later that day in every house and cottage in the area the curtains would be drawn against the wet misery of the night, and there would be laughter and festivity around hearths rosy with firelight. My own New Year's Eve promised to be like every other night.

Promptly at four o'clock Lucy arrived in the drawing room with my afternoon tea. She seemed to take an inordinately long time arranging the crockery on the small table beside my chair and I looked up inquiringly as she hovered hesitantly near the door.

'It's New Year's Eve, miss,' she volunteered.

'Yes, I know it is, Lucy.'

'Well, miss, are you going out? Or doing anything special?'

'I don't think so. I have not been invited and I have nothing planned.'

'But everybody celebrates on New Year's Eve, Miss Jacintha, particularly now the war's over.'

'Well, as far as I'm concerned, I shall probably have a bath, read a book and retire early.'

I smiled at her as she still hovered. 'Don't worry about me, Lucy, I shall be quite happy.'

'I'm sorry, miss, but it's just that we've all been invited to the party at the village hall; it won't be much but most of the villagers will be there. There's a band and there'll be dancing. Obviously we can't all go with you here on your own, but I'll be obliged if you'll say which of us can go so that I can tell the others.'

'Gracious, Lucy, you can all go. I don't need any of you to stay here with me. I'm not the nervous type.'

'Would you like to come with us, miss. Like I said, it won't be anything like what you're used to, but it's better than staying in the house on your own.'

'It's nice of you to invite me, Lucy, but I would really be much happier here. Now run along and tell the others they may all go, and a very happy New Year to you all.'

For the rest of the evening I was aware of talk and giggles from the direction of the kitchen and I complimented Lucy and her niece on their pretty hairstyles and the new dresses they were wearing under their aprons as they served my evening meal. In the drawing room they had turned the lamps on and the fire blazed invitingly in the hearth. Next to my chair a small table had been set out with fruit and chocolates as well as glasses and a bottle of sherry, and I settled down in the corner of my chair with a book on my lap. Now and again I was aware of rain spattering against the windows and the crashing of the sea. Listening to the wind howling and the branches of the trees tapping against the panes, I told myself that I wouldn't have turned a dog out on such a night, but as I heard them pass my windows laughing and chattering in a happy group on their way to the village the tears welled into my eyes.

How potent with menacing things an empty house can be. The book in my hands was not powerful enough to keep my imagination at bay and slowly but surely I found myself listening for sounds other than those made by the wind and the sea. I listened for the creaks which accompanied the old house, for the distant banging from some open shutter, and I came to fear the knocking of those skeleton branches against the windows. Now my eyes constantly strayed towards the door, as though they expected the door handle to turn, and the shadows behind me teemed with hostile eyes boring into the back of my head. I was afraid to leave that room of dancing firelight for the lofty hall and its floating shadows. Soon every crashing wave upon the rocks below tortured my frayed nerves, every staccato beat of icy rain upon the windows sounded like the hands of some demented soul clamouring for entry.

I tried to think of other things, of calm silver-crested waves rolling inwards along the sand and foxgloves under hedgerows, but not for long did these thoughts sustain me. I was alone in a house peopled with the memories of old anger and half-forgotten resentments, and I was afraid that those tormenting emotions would destroy me now. Resolutely I forced myself to lay my book down calmly on the table, then I went to the window and pulled back the curtains. It was bright moonlight with clouds scudding across a stormy sky. I put out the lamps so that I could see out into the night. I was not afraid of the elements; rather, they seemed to give me the courage I lacked and I revelled in the crashing waves and the tossing branches of the trees locked together as though in some primeval dance. The moon rode high through silver-tipped clouds and below me the sea surged and crashed, sending mountains of spray and spume upwards, so that it lay like snow on the clumps of thrift clustered on the rocks beneath the window.

I turned to cross the room lit by moonlight but my fingers trembled as I opened the door into the vast hall beyond. The moonlight poured in through the tall windows at the head of the stairs and without trying to find the light switch I forced myself to climb the stairs, telling myself all the time that if I gave way to my fears now I would be forever lost.

Upwards I climbed, looking neither to left nor right, and it was only when I reached the first landing, where I had once stood with Adrian with the moonlight silvering his hair, that I paused. Momentarily the wind seemed to have ceased and I turned to look back along the stairs and down the corridor which led to the other wing of the house. Did I see those shadows gathering into the form of a human shape, or did my imagination play obscene tricks in that empty house? I shall never know. Next moment it was as though a hypnotist had snapped his fingers before my eyes and I heard again the moaning of the wind and the rain lashing against the windows. With a sob in my throat, I took to my heels and ran, never stopping until I reached the shelter of my bedroom, my hands searching frantically for the light switch on the wall behind the door.

Instantly the room flooded with light and thankfully I sank to my knees beside my bed, sobbing with fright. I have no knowledge of how long I knelt there but it must have been for some considerable time because it was the sound of the servants returning to the house that finally brought me to my feet, shivering with cold, my muscles cramped and aching. They came with much laughter and singing and, reassured, I undressed and crept between the sheets, only to lie wakeful until the first grey light of dawn encouraged me to leave my bed and put out the light.

The day stretched before me obscure and uneventful. I read a little and played endless games of patience. I even ventured as far as the stables but the ground was treacherous under its coating of ice. From the kitchens came the sounds of laughing voices, while I ate my meals in solitary state in the dining room, wishing fervently that I was one of them instead of being Elaina Carradice's granddaughter and the mistress of Ravenspoint. I thought of Isobel and Henry driving south towards sunshine, and Ruthie enjoying the company of Martin's formidable family. I thought about Lavinia, too, waiting for the birth of her baby, and the tears rolled down my cheeks as I visualized it already in her arms. Deliberately I did not think of Adrian – I must forget Adrian with his handsome face and his devilish charm. He belonged to that unreal summer's night when the nightingale had shed his magic upon the perfumed garden. That night had been as intangible and unreal as the shadows upon the stairs.

Inevitably it was night again, a cold clear frosty night with bright stars in a midnight-blue sky and the wind had died. I amused myself at the piano for a time, then, disenchanted with my accomplishments, I reopened my book. I thought at first it was the sighing of the branches outside my room until I realized that what I was hearing was the sound of a car's engine in the drive. I went out into the hall to see for myself, not bothering to wait for the knocker on the front door to reverberate in the hall or for the servants to attend to it. The bolts were thick and heavy on the door and I bruised my fingers pulling them back, but I could see the car now, the powerful headlights sweeping up the drive until it came to a halt outside the door. Shielding my eyes, I tried to recognize it, but the lights were too bright and it was only when the lights were turned off that I saw it was Teddy emerging from the driver's seat. He came up the steps slowly, wearily, and I saw then in the light from the open door that his face was pale, his hair dishevelled, his eyes dark with fatigue as though he had driven a long way.

'Why, Teddy, what happened? Why have you come back?' I asked him in astonishment.

I turned to enter the house and he followed without saying a word. Inside the hall I repeated my question.

'I had to come, Jacintha. It's Vinie. I knew you wouldn't have heard.'

'Heard! Heard what?'

He stared at me wordlessly, then his pale-blue eyes filled with tears and he took off his spectacles to wipe them. By this time the housekeeper had appeared in the hall, so I took Teddy's hand in mine and pulled him into the drawing room.

'It's all right,' I told her, 'I heard the car on the drive. I'll ring if I need you.'

Inside the drawing room he flopped into a chair, sitting with his head in his hands, his shoulders shaking with emotion. I had never seen a man cry. To me it had always seemed unmanly for a man to cry, but now, listening to Teddy's harsh searing anguish, I was glad that I was a woman to whom tears came naturally.

I poured out a stiff brandy and stood with it in my hands until he recovered his composure, then I watched him drink it in one quick gulp. Even then it was several minutes before he could speak.

'It's Vinie, Jacintha. Nanny Parsons telephoned me last night at Gerald's house. She couldn't get hold of my parents and the others were away. It's Vinie, Jacintha.'

'Yes, Teddy, what has happened to her?'

'She's dead, Jacintha, she's dead. Vinie's dead.'

I sank to the floor beside his chair, taking his hands in mine, my eyes staring into his, unwilling to comprehend the terrible truth that he was telling me. Somehow his use of his childhood name for her seemed only to make it more awful.

'Can you tell me what happened?' I asked him.

'They were driving down to the country for the holiday. Lavinia was driving and the car skidded off the road. I don't know anything else. Only that Vinie is dead, she died the same day in hospital.'

In that first blinding moment I felt angry – it was just like Lavinia to be driving in her condition on icy roads – then Teddy and I wept together as memories engulfed us both. I remembered her on that last morning saying vehemently that she would never come back to Ravenspoint, and she had looked so lovely on that morning with her eyes shining as she went out to meet the man who loved her.

'But you're going home to your parents, of course.'

'Yes, I must.' He spoke so doubtfully that I instantly asked, 'Do you want me to come with you?'

He reached for that like a drowning man reaches for a rope. 'Yes. Oh yes, please, Jacintha. Goodness knows what sort of a state my mother will be in. I don't think I could face it alone.'

'Now you must try to eat something, then we'll both have an early night and get off at first light. We can do nothing until morning.'

He went into the sitting room to telephone them and I sat in the drawing room listening to the sound of his voice. It took a long time and when he came back his face was grey, his eyes hollow with fatigue. In reply to the question in my eyes, he said, 'My mother's hysterical, they want me to go home to-night. I shall have to go.'

'But you can't, Teddy, there's a storm blowing up and you've driven too far already. Surely a few hours won't make any difference.'

'I could hear my mother sobbing in the room where I spoke to my father on the telephone. Don't worry, Jacintha, I'll be quite safe.'

'Then I'll pack a bag and come with you. You can't possibly drive all that way on your own. I'll drive.'

It was a singularly foolhardy promise. The car was strange to me, it was far larger and more powerful than my modest little tourer and as we turned into the lane the first impact of the storm hit us forcibly. Outside the warmth of the car, the wind howled dismally and the powerful headlights found the full fervour of the driving rain. At first I drove slowly, as much afraid of the unfamiliar car as I was of the storm, but gradually my courage returned and I drove like an automaton. Occasionally the sky was lit by flashes of lightning and somewhere above us I heard the crashing of boulders falling down the mountain side. The wind had whipped the waters of the lake into swirling fury, and now the mist was down on the road so that I said a silent prayer that we would not encounter some other motorist foolish enough to be out on such a night. Teddy, unutterably weary, dozed fitfully beside me. I could never have believed it would be possible for me to drive like a zombie without thoughts for anything outside the interior of the car – neither the storm nor the reasons for that mad drive – but I did know a blessed relief when I saw the lights of the city shining through the gloom. I gave Teddy a little shake so that he came to his senses, dully, at first unaware of where he was, until memory came flooding back to him and we stared at each other in dumb misery.

'We're almost there, Teddy, will you take over now? I'm not sure of the way.'

In silence he got out of the car and came to my side whilst I moved over into the passenger seat. Without speaking he put the car into gear and we moved off down the road. It was almost dawn. The streets of the town were deserted; it was too early for the first trams and it looked strangely impersonal without the crowds of people hurrying to and fro.

The sound of the car's engine must have been heard from inside the house because as we neared the front door it was flung open and the lights from the hall streamed out into the wet night. Teddy's father stood blinking in the light from the headlamps, then he came forward to meet us.

Although Aunt Myra was my grandmother's daughter, the first incongruous thought that struck me when I entered that sad house was that she was not like my grandmother. In the face of disaster my grandmother had never resorted to tears. Anger perhaps, cold and implacable as on the day Adrian had told her he was never coming back to Ravenspoint – tight-lipped despair was more potent than tears. Aunt Myra lay on the couch drawn up before the fire, moaning inconsolably, her eyes swollen and red from too much weeping. I stood behind Teddy, thinking that grief should be a private thing, not this noisy luxurious abandonment to grief, while Teddy's father tried to comfort her.

'She's been like this ever since she heard the news,' he said. 'I feel so helpless, I don't know what I can do.'

'Perhaps we should send for a doctor,' I volunteered. 'He would keep her under sedation until she's able to face up to things.'

Nobody answered so, after a few minutes, I went into the hall and telephoned my grandmother's doctor, more than relieved when he promised to come immediately. As I had predicted he gave her a sedative and I helped her to undress and get into bed. Then I went downstairs and made tea for the rest of us.

Two days later Aunt Myra surfaced sufficiently to hear the news that Russ had escaped with only slight injury and that the doctors had saved Lavinia's baby even when they could not save her. It was then that I saw that she was perhaps after all her mother's daughter.

'The baby will be brought here, of course,' she stated. 'How on earth we can be expected to cope at this time of the year I can't imagine, but it's clearly our duty to have the child.'

'Why particularly at this time of the year?' Teddy asked innocently.

'I know you've never been interested in horses, Teddy, but surely even you can't have forgotten that we are in the middle of the hunting season and that your father is the Master. We are wholly committed for the rest of the season, I shall just have to get Nanny Parsons back. You could help, Jacintha. I can't think what you find to do with your time all alone in that great house with enough servants to supply the needs of a family.'

I looked at her askance, wondering if she spoke like that because she was distraught or because she was completely oblivious, as my grandmother had often been, to the feelings of others. Aware of my expression, she snapped. 'It is becoming increasingly difficult to get good servants here in the city. At one time they were glad enough to come and work in the large houses, but now that they have had a taste of the sort of money industry pays, service isn't good enough for them any more. It's different in the country; they are glad of the chance to go into service when it's either that or working on the land.'

She was sitting bolt upright on the couch, her eyes feverishly bright. Neither her husband nor her son spoke. I remarked that the baby had a father and grandparents in America, 'and,' I ended, 'I shouldn't think Russ would allow his child to leave the country.'

She ignored me but speaking to the room at large she said, 'None of this would have happened if she'd been content to marry a decent English boy the family approved of. Always hankering after a life in America, never satisfied with her life in this country. Like my mother said, she was an ungrateful girl.'

'She wanted to get away to lead her own life,' I said, 'I can understand why Lavinia wanted to do that.'

She fixed me with cold baleful eyes and I realized then how familiar they were and I shuddered. It was as though my grandmother looked at me out of Aunt Myra's face.

'I dare say you do understand, Jacintha. My mother always said you were never in the least grateful for all she did for you and no doubt you were a bad influence on Lavinia. I know all about your carryings on with Isobel during the war, dancing until dawn with all those young officers and Isobel married into the bargain. At least nobody can say Lavinia was involved in those goings on. She was never disobedient until you came to Ravenspoint.'

She started to cry and deliberately I bit my tongue. I noisily stacked the teacups onto the tray and carried it into the kitchen, where Teddy found me five minutes later savagely piling them into the sink.

'She can't help it, Jacintha,' he said apologetically. 'Try not

252

to mind. It's the shock that is making her speak like that.'

I looked at him angrily for several seconds, then in the face of his woeful expression, I relented. 'It doesn't matter, Teddy. I should be accustomed to tirades of that nature and your mother is after all my grandmother's daughter.'

He waited while I dried my hands on a towel.

'Do we know what they are going to call the baby?' I asked him.

'Joanna, she's a little girl. They had chosen the name some time ago, I don't suppose my mother will like it. She's to be called after Russ's younger brother who was killed in the war.'

'Well, thank goodness they didn't decide to call her Elaina; I don't think the family could have survived that.'

He smiled a little tremulously. 'I want you to know how grateful I am to you for coming here, Jacintha. I expect my parents will be too when they've got over the shock.'

'Nevertheless, I think I shall go home tomorrow. I don't want you to drive me, if you will take me to the station I'll get the train. I know the time of the connection.'

'But it's a dismal train journey in the winter. You can't possibly make it alone.'

'I shall telephone the house for one of the men to meet the train. Honestly, Teddy, don't look so woebegone. There's nothing more I can do here. Vinie's gone and nothing your mother can say or do will persuade Russ to send his daughter to England. I need to go home, Teddy, and you should go home too or you might find you will be expected to stay here for the rest of your life.'

'Do you know, Jacintha, you are sounding an awful lot like Isobel these days,' he said, smiling for the first time in days.

'Yes, well, according to your mother, I took that downward path during the war. Come on, let's put something warm on and take a walk outside. It's cold and windy but it might help to blow the cobwebs away.'

12

Few people boarded the train that was to take me back to Ravenspoint and Teddy saw me safely seated in an empty compartment with newspapers and magazines to occupy my mind. It was bitingly cold in the fresh wind which whipped along the platform, carrying in its wake all the abandoned rubbish left by other travellers, and I was glad of the warm atmosphere of the train. From the deserted platform, I fully expected to have the compartment to myself for the entire journey.

Teddy took both my hands in his as I leaned out of the train window. 'Thanks again for coming, Jacintha; it's been pretty awful for you, I know, but I hope one day to make it up to you.'

I smiled at him gently, grateful for his tall boyish figure and his fresh English face out of which the blue Carradice eyes blinked at me owlishly from behind his spectacles. A swift rush of affection overwhelmed me for his sweet familiarity in a world that was changing. I leaned over and kissed his cheek.

'Keep in touch,' I called to him as the train pulled slowly out of the station and I continued to look out of the window until I could see him no more.

The Pennine hills, always sombre, were shrouded in mist. The snow was already falling as we crossed the grey moorland and on either side of us I could dimly see the white lakeland mountains. The roads could already be treacherous with snow and I prayed silently that it would not be so thick as to prevent one of the servants from meeting my train.

My connection was late and by this time the snow was coming down in great white flakes. Shortly after three o'clock it was completely dark. It seemed to me that the train crawled painfully into the little local station and, as I was the only person to alight from it, it did not linger long, leaving me in almost total darkness – the flickering gaslamps on the station platform did little to dispel the gloom. The booking hall was devoid of human habitation and I walked gingerly, hardly daring to look outside in case there was no car or friendly face to greet me. My heart sank at the sight of an unfamiliar car standing at the kerb outside the station and I was about to turn back into the booking hall when a man stepped forward out of the shadows. He was tall and wearing a white trenchcoat, and at first I did not recognize him, but when he came towards me the street light fell upon his face. I swayed suddenly in the bitter wind before he came forward swiftly to take me into his arms.

We stood for several minutes with his chin resting on my hair, then slowly he released me, pulling me gently towards the car. 'We must go, the snow is getting thicker. It is not a night for waiting about, unless you feel like spending it in the car,' he said.

I didn't care if we spent the night on top of Scafell. I had longed for Adrian, dreamed about Adrian, but, now that he was here beside me in the dark shelter of the car, I could only think that I was dreaming still and that soon I must wake up to find that the nightmare of the past few days had not happened at all, that Lavinia was not dead and that this was not Adrian who had come towards me out of the snow.

How naturally I had gone into his arms, like a lost child going home. Under cover of the darkness I stole a look at his profile. He was frowning slightly with the absorption of trying to keep the big car on the road, but for a brief moment he turned his head to smile at me and my heart ached with the remembered sweetness of his smile.

I had no thoughts for the danger on that icy road. I was with Adrian and that was all that mattered. I did not want the journey to end. I wanted it to go on and on, just the two of us in a whirling wonderland of white snow, but at last the iron gates were before us and the curving drive. Like one in a dream, I stepped out of the car into the snow and it was only when we were in the hall, shaking the snow from our shoulders, that I came face to face with reality and the knowledge that this was no dream.

'You could have chosen a better day for travelling, my dear,' he said, smiling a little.

'Oh, Adrian,' I cried, 'Lavinia's dead, it's been so terrible.' I blurted out to him all the suffering of the last few days and the

255

sympathy in his face brought the hot stinging tears to my eyes. Those tears were a luxury I had not permitted myself before, and after a few moments Adrian took my arm and led me into the drawing room.

'I'll ask for some tea,' he said, 'or would you prefer a brandy? You look as though you could do with something.'

'Tea, please, Adrian. I'm so sorry to be such a cry baby. Perhaps it's the shock of seeing you as well as poor Lavinia's death. How long have you been here?'

'Since last night. I thought I would surprise you.'

'Are they all well at the chateau?'

'Quite well, my mother is with Aunt Monique in Provence.' Was it amusement I saw then in his dark eyes? I couldn't tell, and next moment he was poking the fire into a bright blaze and I could not see the expression on his face.

'You didn't answer my letter at Christmas,' I said accusingly.

'No, I'm sorry. I was in the South of France and didn't receive it until I got back to the chateau. By that time, it was much to late to do anything about your invitation for Christmas, so here I am in the New Year.'

'You are here on business?'

'Amongst other things.'

'How long will you stay?'

'That depends on how long the mistress of the house will allow me to stay. Now that Ravenspoint is yours, are you happy, Jacintha?'

'I don't know. I'm not sure.'

'Or at least contented?' he persisted. 'I remember how fiercely you loved it. I wonder if it has answered all your longings.'

'I can't forget that it should have been your home, Adrian, and that even now I have no real right to it. Sometimes I wonder if I am meant to be happy here, if I am not an interloper still.'

He smiled but he did not answer.

That night we dined together once more and it felt like remembered joy from some other time and place. We spoke little over our meal and now and again I was aware of his eyes upon me and I was grateful to the candlelight which helped to disguise my confusion.

After we had eaten, we drank our coffee in the small drawing room whose corner window jutted out over the rocky point and he smiled a little. 'Do you remember your dragon, Jacintha? I never enter this room without thinking of that terrified child whose tears turned to anger when she discovered who I was.'

For a time we were silent, each staring into the fire. I longed to ask him the real reason for his visit but shyness kept me tongue-tied.

'You know, Jacintha,' he said, 'there were a great many things left unsaid at the chateau.'

I looked at him questioningly and in answer to my level gaze he said, 'I told you I was not going to marry Leoni de Montforte and you thought it was because she was sick, mentally sick, and that perhaps if she recovered things might be different. I allowed you to think that because I was unsure about a great many things, including you. You were so young, and you had been so recently in love that I wondered if in your heart you had merely turned to me to help you to forget that other unhappy experience. Besides, although you were not aware of it, there were many harsh and bitter things said while we were out exploring the countryside and I could see no end at that time to the conflicts which were not of our making but which in the end concerned us.'

'Are you going to tell me about those conflicts now?'

'I think perhaps you should be aware of them, although I am not sure where to begin. Perhaps a long time ago when my mother was young and beautiful and desperately in love with Philippe de Montforte.'

'With Leoni's father!'

'Yes. The Fontinelles' and the de Montfortes' lands adjoined, as you know, and the young lovers were able to meet constantly. Unfortunately their families were not on friendly terms. Their fathers quarrelled over their lands, their servants and their women, so the blossoming romance between my mother and Philippe was doomed from the start. There was a bitter quarrel and Philippe left the family home to join the army and went immediately to the Military Academy in Paris. My mother's parents, too, were against the match and to salvage my mother's broken heart they took her away to Nice for the rest of that summer. It was there she met a young Englishman by the name of Roland Carradice and he fell in love with her. Before the end of the summer they were married.

'I know now that my mother never loved Roland Carradice

and that never for a single moment was their marriage happy. He was cold, humourless and indolent. He had not been cut out to be a woollen manufacturer, he lacked the capacity for hard work or the willingness to get along with people he considered inferior to himself, but he liked to play the role of a French aristocrat on an estate where the hard work was done by men and women whose families had lived in the shadow of the chateau for centuries and who had known no other masters.

'Philippe de Montforte eventually came back to the chateau when his father was taken ill, but my mother never saw him. He had returned eaten up with bitterness at what he considered her betrayal. Then, one afternoon, he met my mother while they were out riding in the forest. It was the start of an old enchantment and they met often in the forest after that to talk and to make love. When I was born nobody doubted that I was Roland Carradice's son, but Philippe de Montforte was my father.'

'How long have you known?' I asked him quietly.

'I knew after the war when I returned to Fontinelle.'

'You mean all those years when you were a boy growing up in England you believed you were a Carradice, that one day you would really live in England and be one of them?'

'Yes. My mother encouraged me to spend my young days in England, she even encouraged me to spend my school holidays here rather than in France, but I know now it was because she was desperately afraid of her husband seeing Philippe and me together. We were so alike, you see, and by this time he too was married and had children. Too many people were destined to be hurt.'

'Did he know that you were his son?'

'Yes, he knew, and Roland Carradice guessed. He used to watch me, and although I believed he was my father we were never close. I think he must have known for a long time, but the war came and I could not go home until it was over. In the meantime Philippe de Montforte had died, Roland Carradice had suffered a stroke and you know the rest. The enemy had lived on our land, in our chateau and my mother had suffered more than most. She had suffered her husband's spite, the endless years of complaint and coldness, and she had suffered it without a murmur of disloyalty because of the wrong she had done him.'

For what seemed like an age there was silence in the room except for the crackling of the logs in the grate and the steady tick-tock of the clock. Outside the snow carpeted the earth and even the sea was only a murmur on the rocks below the house. Quite suddenly my heart lifted like a soaring bird as I understood at last what Adrian was trying to tell me, the only part of his story that mattered.

'Then Leoni is . . .'

'My half-sister.'

'Oh, Adrian, why didn't you tell me? I thought you were in love with her, even when you said you would never marry her. Would you have told me if my grandmother had been dead, or was it just that you didn't think it important enough at the time?'

'I don't know. I felt that my father – and there are times when I still feel it – watched us together with so much malice I was afraid for you. I knew that before long my grandmother was aware that I was not after all a Carradice. Whether things would ever be right I couldn't tell.'

'But why did Leoni set fire to the chateau? Was it because she too had seen us together?'

'Leoni did not set fire to the chateau. Roland set fire to it. I saw him in the Chinese room that night when we stood on the terrace, that was why I went back to the drawing room to put on the light. The other door leading into the far corridor was still slightly ajar and I heard the wheels of his chair going towards the hall. Leoni had come down to the library for a book and he was there in the shadows staring after her with the most terrible expression on his face. She was afraid and ran out into the garden, where I followed her. Perhaps it was as well, otherwise I should have returned to my room in the other wing and the fire might have gone undetected until it was too late.'

'But why, why should he wish me dead? I had never done anything to harm him.'

'Perhaps it was because he hated me. He had seen us together; it was hard perhaps for a lonely and embittered man to see happiness in others without doing something to destroy it.'

'But it was he who died in the fire.'

'Yes, he was overcome by smoke. Perhaps he didn't know what he was doing, perhaps he didn't really care any more.'

'Why are you telling me all this now, Adrian?'

'Because I love you. When I brought you in here that afternoon years ago I did not then expect to love you, perhaps not even when I saw you dancing along the shore on your last day of school, but I knew at Fontinelle when you stood on the edge of the cliff and I had to grasp you in my arms to stop you from falling. There was always something about you which disturbed me, something intangible that I couldn't entirely escape from.'

'Oh, Adrian, I felt it too and I could never understand it. I used to think I was going mad when I was so aware of other moments, other places, other ages perhaps, when I knew your face and emotions which drew us together. I could not understand why I should feel such things when you apparently did not.'

'And now I have to ask you a question.'

'Will I marry you? But you know the answer to that already.'

'What will you be willing to give up to marry me?'

'I don't understand.'

'Ravenspoint could stand between us. Have you forgotten that to keep it you must remain unmarried, or at least remain a Carradice?'

'But I shall still be a Carradice if I marry you, Adrian.'

We looked at each other without speaking, but I knew in that moment that neither of us would take advantage of a name to cheat my grandmother in death. Adrian rose to his feet pulling me up to stand beside him, then with his arms around me he said, 'I cheated her so long without knowing it, and I shall bear her name for the rest of my life, but we both know the truth. Do you think we could live the rest of our lives on a lie?'

I knew I could not. I loved Adrian, I would follow him to the ends of the earth, I would live with him in an alien land where people spoke an alien tongue and I would leave this house, still loving it, at times yearning for it.

I thought about the chateau, gracious and elegant, standing in the midst of its vast forest and its pretty, ornamental gardens, and I knew that, even surrounded by so much beauty, there would be times when I would hunger desperately for the sound of the ocean on the cruel rocks and the dark dismal beauty of the lakeland fells, but I knew too that Ravenspoint was not enough. I wanted this man's love, his strong arms around me in the night, his compassion when I felt sad, his warmth and his laughter and all the joys and sorrows of sharing whatever fate might do to us in the years ahead.

I knew now with quiet certainty that at last I was free of the chains my grandmother had sought to put around me in payment of a wrong she believed my parents had done to her before I was born. With almost her last breath she had willed Ravenspoint to me, believing that in doing so those chains would stay around me for the rest of my life. Now, in whatever tormented limbo her bitter soul inhabited, I hoped she would know that the prison gates were open wide so that her caged bird could fly free.